M000166137

WHAT
I
KNOW

BOOKS BY MIRANDA SMITH

Some Days Are Dark

WHAT I KNOW

I

KNOW

MIRANDA SMITH

Bookouture

Published by Bookouture in 2020

An imprint of Storyfire Ltd.
Carmelite House
50 Victoria Embankment
London EC4Y 0DZ

www.bookouture.com

Copyright © Miranda Smith, 2020

Miranda Smith has asserted her right to be identified
as the author of this work.

All rights reserved. No part of this publication may be reproduced,
stored in any retrieval system, or transmitted, in any form or by
any means, electronic, mechanical, photocopying, recording or
otherwise, without the prior written permission of the publishers.

ISBN: 978-1-83888-265-5
eBook ISBN: 978-1-83888-264-8

This book is a work of fiction. Names, characters, businesses,
organizations, places and events other than those clearly in the
public domain, are either the product of the author's imagination
or are used fictitiously. Any resemblance to actual persons, living or
dead, events or locales is entirely coincidental.

To Chris. You were right. I love you.

CHAPTER 1

Winter 2000

My brother was thirteen the first time he tried to kill me. Before that, there was only violence in an explainable sense. A smack when I stole a fry. A kick when I took away his ball. I never thought much of it, nor did my parents. He wasn't trying to harm me, I thought. Only retaliate.

He'd broken one of Dad's guitar strings, and even though he threatened me with his stern, squeaky voice not to tell, I did. Mom and Dad unplugged his Nintendo 64 and sent him to bed.

Hours later, I woke up to a strange smell. Between the darkness and my vision impairment, I couldn't decipher anything but lights and blurs. When I put my glasses on and focused, I saw the flames climbing the floor-length curtains of my bedroom window. I sat motionless, too scared to move, breathing in the smoke.

Mom and Dad ran into my room seconds later. Mom scooped me up as Dad got a bowl of water and effortlessly extinguished the flames. Perhaps it was scarier to me than it was to them, but I still remember the staccato thumping of Mom's heart as she held me close.

"No more candles, Della," Dad howled, out of breath from his speedy rush with the water bowl.

"We've told you to blow them out before bed," Mom said, slightly less angry. Her fingers slid under my frames and wiped the tears off my cheeks.

Perhaps allowing an eleven-year-old to burn candles wasn't the best parenting decision Mom and Dad made, but it would also prove to be far from their worst.

"I blew them out," I said. I took a deep breath and clutched the ragged edge of my blanket. "I always blow them out."

"Obviously you didn't," Dad said, shaking the charred fabric.

"I did," I cried. I knew, knew, knew I did, and even if I didn't, the three candles I'd bought with my allowance on our last family vacation sat on my dresser, nowhere near the window. One had been moved, away from its mates and near the scorched remains of my curtains.

"You're lucky Brian came and got us," Mom said, pressing her cool palms against my cheeks.

And that's when I saw him, standing in the doorway. His eyes looked through me and everyone else, as always. The sides of his lips flicked upward. My ninety seconds of horror would provide him entertainment for the next month.

"He did this!" I lifted my arm. My fingers, still clutching the blanket, shook the entire cloth as I pointed. "I know he did."

"Oh, ridiculous," Mom said.

"He did this because you took his stupid Nintendo," I cried.

My parents always told Brian to stay away from Dad's instruments. He never listened. I'd felt a flicker of pride when I discovered one of the strings was broken. Younger siblings are constantly searching for the upper hand, even though I felt guilty when he yelled at Mom and slammed his bedroom door. I knew he'd find a way to get even, but I didn't expect *this*.

"I had to potty and smelled something weird," Brian said. I hadn't heard him use *potty* in forever. Usually it was *pee* or *piss*, and when he felt particularly dangerous, *shit*.

"He's lying," I screamed, my fear twisting into anger. I attempted to wriggle out of Mom's lap, but she held tight.

"Enough," Mom said.

Dad said nothing. Not that night and not the following morning.

Brian went back to his room. Mom and Dad did, too. I cradled myself in bed, unable to sleep. The smell of smoke lingered. I knew what Brian had done and dreaded what he was capable of, perhaps, doing again. No one believed me then, or in the years that followed. No one believed me until it was too late.

CHAPTER 2

Now

Five weeks until summer break. Students think they're the only ones counting down the days until school is out. Even at the high school level, they don't recognize their teachers as actual people. They're lost in the throes of solipsism; I think half the student body believes we teachers only exist within the boundaries of block scheduling.

"Someone's looking tan," Marge says as she stands behind me in the employee lounge. When I turn, I see she's added chunky caramel streaks to her dark, shoulder-length hair since I last saw her. The highlights make her look hip and different, two descriptions Marge is always trying to fit.

"Thanks," I say, moving so Marge can pour coffee. "Danny and I spent spring break in Hilton Head."

"Fancy," she says, pulling back the tab of a miniature creamer and adding the contents to her cup.

"Not really," I say, flipping hair off my shoulder. I'm constantly finding the balance between telling my co-workers what's going on in my life and not sounding like a braggart. "We went last minute and only stayed four days."

That's the beauty of being working professionals without kids. Danny and I have both the time and money to afford nice things. But instead of buying luxuries, we travel. We crave new places like most people do caffeine.

Marge teaches A.P. Chemistry. She's single and doesn't have children either. She might make digs about *fancy* last-minute trips

(I'm married to a doctor, after all), but she enjoys wandering as much as I do. She'll probably leave Tennessee at the end of May and not return until August.

"How was your break?" I ask. I can tell Marge has spent time shopping, too. Her purple blouse and dark pants look new, although paired with a familiar, dusty pair of shoes.

"I took a train to D.C. for a few days," she says. She stirs her coffee and tilts her head to the side.

"Nice," I say, unable to remember the last time I went. "I love it there."

"Me too. I never get to enjoy it when I chaperone trips, but I sure do miss the mountain air."

Marge, like most of my other co-workers, has never lived outside of Tennessee. She has an attachment to home I've never felt. I could change locations tomorrow, and my outlook on life wouldn't change.

"I'd chat longer, but I've got copies to make," I say, gathering my papers and balancing the coffee mug in my hand. "I didn't do near enough prep before break."

She nods. "This close to summer, the admins ought to be thankful we even show up."

"It's not like the students do," I say, walking out the door.

After making copies in the workroom, I enter my classroom and begin setting out the day's materials. This is my fifth year at Victory Hills, which means I'm finally eligible for tenure. I teach American literature to 11th graders. We read Poe and Steinbeck and Hemingway until my students are blue in the face, and yet it never gets old to me. I expect a sliver of optimism from my classes this week, knowing we've all enjoyed a needed break. I know the closer we get to summer, the further away they'll get from me, their minds already fixed on sunny days by the pool and later curfews.

The morning bell rings. A whoosh of voices and feet transform the quiet hallways into a mob. I'm at my desk before the first student arrives. They drip in, one by one, each consumed by their own distracted daze. Some are sunburnt, others are not fully awake.

"Welcome back," I say after the last bell rings. "Let the countdown to summer begin."

Darcy, who always sits in the back, lets out a *woo* and everyone laughs. Adam, her boyfriend, leans in and squeezes her shoulder. So, they *are* alive.

Melanie on the front row raises her hand. "Are we starting *The Crucible* this week?" she asks. She's memorized the syllabus and knows that's the final text we'll study this semester.

"No, we'll start that next week," I say.

"What are we doing?" asks Ben, probably still blazed from his pre-school joint. He's a smart kid, one of the ones that doesn't really want to show it because he thinks it will cramp his style. But he always nods along and hardly needs any revision after a second draft.

"We have some short stories to read," I say. "Grab the blue books in the back and turn to page three hundred and sixty."

They groan, but reluctantly obey. We read Faulkner's "A Rose for Emily". I wait patiently for that chilling last paragraph to thoroughly disgust and entertain them. It's one of the simple pleasures of being a teacher, watching each year as new minds devour the twisted stories that shaped our world.

When we finish, I give them a few minutes to vent and ask questions. I'm standing at my podium in the center of the room when I hear a knock. I walk to the front and open the door, which always remains locked.

"Good morning, Della." It's Principal Bowles, a name I've always considered unfortunate for a disciplinarian. The only hair on his head or face rests about four inches wide above his top lip. He's standing beside a girl I've never seen. "We've got a new student for you. This is Zoey Peterson and she's in your first block."

"All right," I say, masking the annoyance that I'll have to redeliver all my introductory class materials with so little time left in the semester. Not the kid's fault. I smile. "Zoey, I'm Mrs. Mayfair."

"Nice to meet you." Zoey stares at me, taking me in. She's short and slim. Her dark hair falls halfway down her back, her bangs partially covering her wide-set eyes. She's wearing skinny jeans and a pastel cardigan, which screams *not from around here*. Her hand extends to shake mine. Another clue she's not necessarily the type of student I'm used to encountering at Victory Hills. Usually I get a shrug until I've really proven myself.

"Class is about halfway over. Go ahead and grab a seat," I tell her.

Zoey walks into the classroom and sits down confidently. She puts her notebook and pen on the shelf under her chair and straightens her posture. Half of my current students stopped bringing writing tools back in February.

I step into the hallway to make sure the other students can't hear.

"Military?" I ask Principal Bowles. There're only two reasons why a kid shows up this late in the year. A traveling military family is one of them.

"Nope," he says, shaking his head. "Just trouble." He walks away.

Families rooted in stability wouldn't dream of transferring their child this late into the year. Just about anything can wait five weeks. Getting a new student now means her folks either don't care at all or there's a reason she left where she was.

"Oh, boy," I say, before walking back in the classroom.

The students' voices have turned from murmurs to yelps. Each cluster is carrying on a different conversation. Any brief distraction beckons them to socialize.

"Let's get back to the story," I say, after pausing until the room is silent. "Part of the reason the ending is so gripping is because of the story's disjointed structure. Faulkner creates ambiguity by steering away from a linear timeline."

The students, except for Melanie, barely listen. Ben nods. Devon, in the third row, is obviously doing something with her phone under her desk. Darcy and Adam, first block's designated lovebirds, angle their bodies toward one another. I walk behind their desks and clear my throat, prompting them to sit properly and listen.

"I want you to get in your learning groups and create a timeline. I'll give you specific events from the story, and you will place them in chronological order," I say.

"So, like, beginning to end?" asks Devon, chomping a wad of gum.

"Yes, that's what I mean," I say.

"Mrs. Mayfair," says Zoey, raising her hand. "Is there a particular group you want me to join?"

"I'm sorry, Zoey." I'd forgotten there was a new student, even though we'd only met minutes ago. My mind is still back at the beach with Danny. "Grab a book and get caught up on the story. It's called 'A Rose for Emily'. Page three hundred and sixty."

"I figured that out from what you said earlier," she says, bending to the side and retrieving her notebook from under her desk. "I've read it before."

"Great. I'll place you with a group in a minute," I say, looking at the student roster on my clipboard. I don't know anything about Zoey's academic performance, but her familiarity with the story is a good sign.

"It's bizarre, don't you think?" Zoey asks, interrupting my focus. "Reading a story about necrophilia in a high school English class."

The other students snap their heads and stare. People don't typically speak in that tone here. We're a placid school, with even the unruly students understanding they should take advantage of the knowledge being preached so they'll be prepared for college. I notice some students tapping their phones, I'm sure googling what *necrophilia* means. I pray to God they don't click on images.

I clear my throat. "The story is not about that, Zoey."

"Sure it is," she says. "The lady held onto her fiancé's corpse for, like, thirty years. She slept with the body."

"It could be interpreted that way, sure. But there is nothing in the story which explicitly states she was intimate with the corpse."

Most students in my class are seventeen. Some of the stories in our state-mandated curriculum cover intense themes, but we usually try to glide over the sex and violence stuff. It's there, and students can see it if they look closely enough. Most never take the time. Zoey, clearly, has.

"Most great literature relies on inference," she says. She straightens her posture and leans back, waiting for my response. This entire confrontation feels familiar. The way Zoey is trying to challenge my authority. The way she's dissecting the story and extracting the goriest parts. And the way she seems to enjoy causing a scene. It's reminds me of something Brian would do. For a moment, it's like he's sitting in the back of the classroom watching me squirm.

I can tell from the blank stares of the other students that their thoughts are swirling. They're trying to keep up with what Zoey is saying while simultaneously attempting to understand her intentions. Her vocabulary is clearly advanced, but her tone is harsh.

"That's right, Zoey. A lot can be inferred from this story," I say, giving her credit where it's due. "The dead body creates a good twist, but that's not necessarily what the story is about."

"No one reads this story and recalls Miss Emily's objectification by the town, or the subtle racism shown via the character Tobe," Zoey says. If I were grading essays, I'd assume she pulled that line straight from SparkNotes. But there isn't a phone in her hands, and she hasn't been in the room long enough to conduct research. She pushes a fallen strand away from her face. "People remember the dead fucking body."

The curse word drops like a bomb followed by utter silence. If I flicked a rubber band at Melanie on the front row, I think she'd crack. I wait a beat before speaking.

"Go ahead and get in your learning groups," I repeat to the class. The students move immediately, grateful for instruction on how to act. They're a laidback bunch, first period. It's too early for power plays in the morning. Zoey remains seated as I skate toward her desk.

"Zoey, I really appreciate your interest in this story. And, as you'll see, a lot of learning in my classroom is discussion based," I begin. "But you cannot use that language. It's offensive and distracting."

It might be her first day, but it's not mine. Classroom management is a duel of wills. I ignore the majority of inappropriate language I hear throughout the day; they *are* teenagers. But when someone blurts out something so blatant in front of the class, it's a test on both ends.

"This is a warning," I continue.

Zoey stares back, her expression unchanging. It's the same stare she gave me when we met, the same stare Brian gave me half of my childhood. Like she's trying to figure me out. Decide if I'm what she expected. She knows it's her turn to draw a weapon, and she's choosing which one it should be. Then, finally, "I'm sorry, Mrs. Mayfair. I'll watch what I say in your class."

"Thank you," I say. She's clearly smart, albeit a brat. Those are the students who secretly search for common ground. They want to connect but don't know how. I smile. "So, where are you from? Tell me about your last school."

"I'm from Florida," she says.

Saliva stalls in my throat. There's not a big gap between Florida and Tennessee, but Victory Hills is so small, I don't encounter people from the area often. And when I do, I always experience the familiar pang of anxiety. Like Brian is closer than I think.

She continues, "But I've been all over. Most recently, Virginia."

"You move around a lot?" I ask, wanting to know more.

"My mom isn't really one to stay in one place, you know?"

"I see," I say, hesitantly. "That can be exciting, I guess. I'm sure you've been exposed to a lot of different cultures."

"Trust me, my mom's not moving around for my benefit. But I did luck out this time around. My last school was really shitty." She stops, holds up her hands. My eyes take in her chipped purple polish. "Excuse me, crummy. My last school was really crummy. I'll work on the language, Mrs. Mayfair."

She waits for my reaction. She has dark, blank eyes and a subtle smile. I wonder how to address her second slur within five minutes. None of the other students heard, so I let it slide.

"Clearly you're well read," I say. "Your last school couldn't have been that bad."

"Oh, I didn't read 'A Rose for Emily' at my last school," she says, strumming her fingers over her notebook. "I read it for fun."

"I see." It's hard to picture this teenager with her tight jeans and potty-mouth reading Faulkner for pleasure in between moves. "Go ahead and join the group in the back."

She stands and picks a seat next to Ben. She shakes his hand. She nods at Adam and Darcy, her other group members, like she already knows them. Within minutes, she blends in. But I still find her peculiar.

CHAPTER 3

Now

I usually get home by four o'clock. Danny's clinic stays open later, so it's closer to six before he arrives. By the time he walks in the door, dinner is nearly ready. Tonight's menu consists of steak and asparagus covered in a Parmesan cream sauce. I enjoy cooking and get extra practice during the summer months.

He walks in the kitchen, takes off his coat and hugs me from behind while I tend the stove.

"Smells great," he says, digging his chin into my neck. I pull back, and stare at him. Even though he's worked over twelve hours, his gray eyes are still kind. His dark hair is combed neatly to the side, and you'd never guess by looking at his starched clothes he's spent the day poking and prodding all types of sick people. We kiss.

"Thank you," I say, turning my attention back to the stove. "How was work?"

"Busy. People are starting to travel and picking up all sorts of nasty viruses." He sits on a barstool and slumps forward, the first sign that he's tired.

"Yuck." Between his job and my constant exposure to germy teenagers, it's a wonder we're not forever sick. Danny is a general practitioner at a family practice. Womb to tomb, they say. He sees patients of all ages for a variety of causes. Occasionally, he rotates on-call hours at the local hospital.

Everyone looks at Danny and thinks he's a catch because he's a doctor, and he is. But that's not what I love about him. Danny and I grew up together. He knew me before, and he knew me after, and he knew Brian in between. We reconnected when Danny was in medical school. There was an immediate comfort in knowing I wouldn't have to explain what happened. He already knew.

We discuss our individual days over dinner. Nothing heavy, just enjoyable conversation. We share a bottle of wine, which leads to him carrying me upstairs. We slowly and predictably ease into sex. He strips my blouse and slacks, lays me gently on the bed. He glides into me, methodically pushing into my core. When he finishes, we kiss a bit more, until the wine in our blood makes us giggle.

"Do you know what weeks you'll have off for summer?" I ask, mentally Pinteresting all the activities I'd like to accomplish.

"I should by the end of the month," he says, rubbing his finger across my thigh.

"I want to go somewhere big this year," I tell him, hoping he'll agree.

"Europe, big?"

"Why not?"

We toured Italy and France for our honeymoon. Since then, we've mostly stayed stateside, making a commitment to put more money toward his medical school loans than stamping our passports.

"Well, you are receiving tenure this year. This can be our way to celebrate. Start planning," he says. "When I have dates, we'll book."

Danny knows me so well. Strategizing an itinerary is half the fun of traveling. He also knows I need to keep moving. I need to keep experiencing. I need to replace the bad memories with good ones.

"Knock, knock," I say, leaning my head inside the doorway of the guidance wing.

Pam spins around in her chair and flaps her hand for me to come inside.

"Hey, Dell," she says. Her navy suit is professional, but she's already kicked off her shoes for the day. Her bare feet dangle above the ground. "I've not seen you since before break."

"Is this a good time?" I ask.

She smiles, her fuchsia lips popping in contrast to her dark skin. Her braids are neatly pinned to the top of her head. "Fourth block is always a good time."

I love having fourth block planning. I'm able to teach my classes with limited interruption. By 2 p.m., I'm done for the day. I use that time to grade papers so by the time I exit the school building, I don't have to think about this place.

"I do love having afternoon planning. It would be nice to keep it in the fall," I say, smiling. Pam has many tasks at school, and one of them includes creating the schedule.

"I'll see what I can do," she says, twirling a pen in her hand. "But I'm sure that's not why you stopped by."

"No," I say, filling one of the empty seats that line the far wall in her office. "I wanted to ask you about a new student."

"Zoey Peterson?"

"Have others talked to you about her?"

"No, but she's the only enrollee we've had since February. Is she giving you trouble?"

"Not really. She's only been in class two days." There's no use in revisiting the exchange I had with Zoey yesterday. It was annoying, but not concerning. Today, she arrived on time and spent most of the period talking with her classmates. I was surprised by how quickly she seemed to be making friends. "I was just wondering what her story is given how late in the year it is for a transfer."

"Gotcha." She spins to her right and starts clacking her computer keyboard. "Let's see. Her last school was in Virginia. She'd been there since the beginning of her junior year."

"Where was she before that?" I ask, surprised.

"She was enrolled at a Kentucky high school as a freshman and sophomore. Looking at her transcript, there's a lot of moving going around."

"Yeah, that's what she said," I say, trying to conjure an image of what her home situation might be like. "Did you meet the parents?"

"Yes," Pam says, tensing her lips into a straight line. "Only the mother is in the picture. She looks a little bit rough."

It's impossible to not make assumptions about people, even in our profession. Victory Hills High School is a public school, although our prominent location makes it feel private. Most of our parents are the wealthy, PTA type. They want to be involved and want everyone to notice their involvement. Few students have troubled home lives. Of course, I know more than most that looks can be deceiving. My parents had nice jobs and lived in an upscale neighborhood, but they still raised a psychopath.

"Well, Zoey is very smart," I say. I don't want to appear as though I'm bashing the girl already.

"Her test scores are high. She could have been in an Honors group, but she insisted on being in a standard English class." She turns away from the computer and tilts her head. "Maybe she likes being the smartest kid in the room?"

"I definitely sense that," I say, rolling my eyes. As a guidance counselor, Pam deals with all sorts of situations. She has a better understanding of the student body than I do. She knows the attitudes students can display, especially on their first day after an inconvenient move.

"It's a shame she moves around so much," she says. "Imagine what a mind like that could do with stability."

"How old was she when the family left Florida?"

"Florida." She turns back to her computer and strokes the mouse. "I'm seeing Kentucky and Virginia. Florida isn't on the list."

"Maybe I misunderstood," I say. But I know I didn't. When someone mentions Florida, it stings. Her comment seemed intentional, like she wanted to upset me. "I thought she said she was from there."

Pam shrugs and shakes her head. "It's sad, really, what some of these kids go through. No sense of a normal childhood."

We chat a bit longer, but certain words from the conversation stick out in my mind. *Normal* and *childhood* and *Florida*. Pam, like everyone else I've met in my five years of working here, cannot possibly understand how normal means absolutely nothing. The most abnormal person could be living under their noses and they'd never know it.

CHAPTER 4

Now

I placed some stew in the slow cooker before I left for school this morning. It's ready by the time I arrive home, so I toast bread in the oven and the meal is set.

"Everything all right with you?" Danny asks.

"Yeah. Why?" I'm sitting at the table, swirling my meal with a spoon.

"You've barely talked since I got home."

"Sorry." I straighten my posture, trying to literally shake off whatever icky feeling is bothering me.

"Have you started planning the trip?"

"Trip?"

"Europe," he reminds me. "We talked about it last night."

"Of course. Yeah. I've been looking around." That's a lie. I spent my planning period talking to Pam about Zoey. I didn't even google potential destinations. "Where do you think we should go?" I ask. "You know I've been dying to return to Paris."

"Let's look into Spain, too," Danny says. "This guy I knew in med school went last summer and he posted all these amazing pictures."

"Spain." I nod without looking at him. "Yep, sounds nice."

"Dell, tell me what's going on," he says, standing. He walks toward me and kisses my cheek. "I can tell something is on your mind, and if it's not Europe, it must be big."

"It's nothing big," I say, taking the napkin from my lap and hitting him with it. "I got this new student. She got under my skin yesterday." Although it's more than that. I've been thinking about Zoey ever since I realized she lied about Florida. I can't figure out why she'd say that, unless she knew it would bother me.

"What did she do?" he asks with a laugh, returning to his seat to finish his meal. I never let students get under my skin, and even when they dance on my nerves, I don't tell Danny about it. My problems at Victory Hills never leave campus.

"Well, first she went off about this Faulkner story in front of the class." I stop talking because I know Danny is already lost. He's easily one of the smartest people I know, but our intellectual interests occupy opposite sectors of our brains. He cares about Southern Gothic literature about as much as I do about trending probiotics. "She used the word *fuck* in class."

Danny laughs, and I reluctantly join in. Disrespectful behavior takes on a different context outside of the classroom.

"She's a kid," he says. "You don't usually let that kind of thing bother you."

"There was something about the way she acted, though." I could tell Danny wasn't convinced, so I continued. "She said she was from Florida."

"Okay," he says, shifting in his seat. He immediately recognizes my discomfort. "You can't fault the kid for that."

Victory Hills is a good nine hours away from our former hometown. I wish we could have settled somewhere outside of the south entirely; it would have put my past further behind me. But Danny was hired to work in Victory Hills, so that's where we ended up.

"I rarely run into people from there, and when I do, they don't creep me out the way she does." I swallow a spoonful of stew. "So, during my planning period today, I talked to Pam. Turns out the girl isn't from Florida at all."

"So what's the big deal?"

"She lied to me," I say, more troubled by Zoey's fib than if she'd actually been from there. "It's like she said that to annoy me."

"Okay, wait a minute." He pinches the bridge of his nose while he thinks. "There's no way she could know about your brother—"

"I know that," I interrupt. I'm not trying to make my exchange with Zoey about Brian, and yet Brian has this way of hovering over events in my life. As far as I know, no one in Victory Hills knows about my past. Detectives were helpful in keeping my name out of the media, and I've since taken Danny's surname. Thankfully, Brian's crimes happened before social media took over, otherwise I'd have no chance of hiding. And yet I can't help wondering if Zoey knows something and that's why she behaved the way she did. "But still. It's weird, isn't it? She acts out on the first day, brings up my trigger state and then it turns out she's not even from there?"

"I agree." He rests his chin on his hand, staring ahead. Danny has as many memories as I do, and *Florida* has no doubt resurrected them. He clears his throat before re-entering the conversation. "It sounds to me like a kid messing with her teacher on the first day. She had no way of knowing you had a connection to Florida."

"You're right," I say, feeling foolish that I let the interaction bother me as much as it has.

"When do you see Dr. Walters again?"

Dr. Walters is the only other Victory Hills resident who knows about my childhood. Ever since Brian did what he did, I knew therapy would be a lifelong commitment. I used to visit counselors more frequently. Now I visit Dr. Walters twice a month, as a precautionary measure.

"I go tomorrow."

"Maybe you can talk with her about it." He tenses his jaw, immediately regretting his wording. Danny knows I don't want to feel like there's something wrong with me just because there was something wrong with Brian. At the same time, we all left the situation with scars. Danny has a therapist, too.

"Yeah, I will," I say, forcing a smile. I have no intention of mentioning Zoey to Dr. Walters, but I want Danny to know he didn't offend me by suggesting it. "I'm just ready for the semester to be over. I'm not bouncing back from break like I normally do."

"You teachers are so spoiled. You only work nine months out of the year, and yet you're always counting the days until your next vacation."

"Yeah, well." I stand and walk toward him at the other end of the table. "At least you'll be enjoying this one with me." I lean forward, and we kiss.

CHAPTER 5

Now

Normally, I'm an exceptional planner, but occasionally I make mistakes. I had to cancel my appointment with Dr. Walters, realizing I had previously signed up for gate duty on the same afternoon. She didn't mind, agreeing to meet next Tuesday.

Our staff isn't very big. There are about sixty teachers, but a long list of scheduled sports events. We divvy them up, taking turns selling tickets at the gate. Tonight, I'm selling admission to the track and field meet.

The first twenty minutes is always immensely boring. After that, parents start trudging in more consistently. Some are strangers, some I've met before because I've had their children in class. Our locker rooms are indoors, so it's several minutes before the team takes the field, their coach behind them.

"Afternoon, Della," says Coach Gabe, walking toward my table. He hands over paperwork for me to give the referees when they arrive.

"Good luck," I say.

"We're probably going to need it," he says, under his breath. "This isn't a big rivalry, but they've got some good athletes. Our kids will enjoy the practice, if nothing else."

"I'll watch what I can," I say, not sure what else to offer. I don't know much about sports. Track, especially, has always struck me as odd. It's a team sport, with each event racking up a certain set of points, but most achievements are individual. There must be a level of ego involved. Be the fastest. Be the best. Win the race.

"After about an hour, you can head out," Gabe says. "Everyone who is coming should be here by then."

On the field, I recognize several current and former students. They're wearing the same royal blue tops, with gold stripes on the sides. Darcy is in the grass sinking into a lunge position. Because the team is co-ed, Adam is nearby, leaning against the gate and gripping his toes. Zoey approaches him, her raven hair dancing in the subtle breeze.

"Is that Zoey Peterson on the field?"

"Yeah," Gabe says, lifting his chin. "I wasn't keen on adding another member to the team this late in the year, but Principal Bowles asked me to make an exception. I'm glad I did. She practiced with us the week of spring break. The girl is fast as hell."

That explains why Zoey has adjusted seamlessly in the past three days. While she's new to me, Coach Gabe and her teammates have known Zoey over a week. If she is good at sports, it won't be difficult for her to make friends at Victory Hills.

"It must be nice to get a good addition this late in the season," I say. It's no secret the track team loses more meets than they win. Most athletes only sign up to stay in shape while their primary sports are in off-season.

"Some of my existing members are giving her a hard time about taking their spots. Light hazing." He rolls his eyes and readjusts his cap. "They'll sing a different tune if she helps us land a win." Without saying goodbye, he toots his whistle and jogs toward the track.

I'm a dedicated teacher, but I slack when it comes to supporting school events. Some of my co-workers are different, like Marge. She's constantly chaperoning trips and sponsoring lock-ins. She's the type of teacher our students will remember ten years from now. My students will remember the stories we read, maybe a few lively discussions, but my face will blur into unrecognizability by the time they graduate college. And I'm fine with that. I actively try to be forgettable.

An hour later, my assumptions about the team dynamics are confirmed when I see the visiting team has won most events. That tiny voice of professional guilt tells me I should stay, watch the end of the meet and support my students. Maybe I would, if I had any hope we'd win. But it's already pushing seven o'clock. I'd told Danny I'd pick up takeout on the way home, our usual routine for nights I work late. By the time I retrieve Mexican food and arrive home, I'm drained.

The exhaustion stalks me into the next morning, when I find myself more irritable than usual about my abbreviated evening with Danny. We'd eaten tacos and started a Netflix movie, but we both fell asleep before ten without having much time to talk.

"You need a double dose this morning?" Marge asks. I'm standing at the coffee machine idly deciding what I should add to my drink. If only adrenaline came in little packets.

"I had game duty last night," I say. "I'm wiped."

"So, you got to see the big comeback, huh?" she asks, playfully bumping me out of her way so she can fill her cup.

"I didn't stay," I say, guiltily. Marge lives for school events and, although she's not vocal about it, she doesn't understand why the rest of the staff isn't more involved. "When I left, a comeback didn't seem possible."

"It was all over social media last night," she said. She flipped her hand in the air. "Sorry, I forget you don't do that."

I've never had an online account. Social media was just starting to get popular around the time Brian did what he did. In those days, all I wanted to do was disappear. I didn't want to be found, by anyone. More than a decade later, I feel the same way.

"We can't all be hip like you, Marge," I joke. She laughs, because she more than makes up for my lack of interaction. She's always posting and retweeting, then sharing the good parts with me in person.

"Well, it was a big deal," she says, taking a seat in the nearby chair and emphasizing her words with hand gestures. "I couldn't make it because I was hosting an Honors Club function, but my feed was blowing up with videos."

"That's exciting," I say, partially wishing I'd stuck around to watch. I love a good comeback. "What turned things around?"

"Coach Gabe let the new girl participate. She helped the team win several categories. She even beat Darcy Moore's season record."

"Zoey Peterson?" I ask, even though I've already been told she's the only new student on file.

"Yeah. You have her in class?" she asks. I nod. "I have Zoey in fourth block. She's a colorful character. Of course, I had no idea she was such an athlete. An absolute star."

"Huh," I say, stirring my coffee. "That's got to be a great welcome for your first week of school."

"Seriously. She's bright, too. She outscored everyone on yesterday's chemistry test."

"She's only been in class three days," I say, as though Marge is forgetting.

"I know. I'm telling you; this girl is special." She sips her coffee and smiles. Marge's tests are notoriously hard. I'll catch students stealing the last ten minutes of my class to quiz each other before one of her exams. I can't believe Zoey has already outperformed her peers.

"What about her behavior?" I ask. I've had a strange feeling about Zoey since she arrived, but evidently Coach Gabe and now Marge haven't picked up on it. "Don't you think she's a little smug?"

"I'm not sure smug is the right word," Marge starts, but is interrupted by the first bell. She throws up her hands and rolls her eyes. "I guess there's work to be done."

Given Zoey's newfound celebrity, I'm surprised she doesn't arrive to first block. Of course, given how much her family moves around, it wouldn't be surprising if poor attendance becomes habitual.

I log into my school account to post the day's attendance electronically. Normally, if a student is absent for a medical or school-related incident, the system alerts me. I plug in the missing students for the day and notice three letters by Zoey's name: OSS. Out of School Suspension.

Uh oh, I think, almost feeling sorry for the kid. She went from a moody first day, to a team hero, and now she's being punished. For what? OSS is usually reserved for serious offences. I keep my ears open during class. There's plenty of chatter, but nothing pertaining to Zoey or someone being punished. Instead, everyone's buzzing about the Spring Fling dance scheduled for Saturday night. Darcy and Devon share pictures of their desired hairstyles. The students in my other classes act similarly. They're focused on Spring Fling and not much else. I wait until fourth block and visit Pam in her office. If something has happened at school, she'll know about it.

"Are you chaperoning the dance this weekend?" Pam asks when I walk through her office door.

"I am," I say, taking a seat.

"I'll see you there. Any other plans this weekend?" She smiles. It's hard to imagine a more perfect job for her. She immediately makes a person want to share their feelings. Students love her, too. They're so comfortable with her they address her by her first name.

"We have a few tasks around the house we've been meaning to complete. We're redoing our guest bedroom."

When we bought the house two years ago, it needed updating. Since then, we've been tackling the place one room at a time. Soon, the guest room, and the whole house, will be complete.

"You live a charmed life, you know," Pam says. She looks to her left, at a picture of her twin second graders. "We are going to the mall and buying new equipment for baseball season. I know I should be used to it by now, but it really sucks having to get two of everything."

I can't imagine how chaotic life with twins must be. I can't even swallow having one. Any desire to have children vanished after surviving my childhood with Brian.

"I've come to gossip," I say, lowering my voice. "I noticed Zoey Peterson has OSS today. Any idea what happened?"

The friendly sheen in her eyes disappears. She stands and closes her office door.

"Didn't Bowles come talk to you?"

"No," I say, my curiosity heightened.

"Not surprising." She leans against the door, tilting her head upward to the ceiling. "He said he wanted all of Zoey's classroom teachers to be aware, but besides that he's keeping quiet. There was an issue on the school bus this morning."

"What happened?"

She looks at me, crosses her arms and shifts her weight to one side of her body. "The bus driver caught Zoey with a knife."

My mouth drops. This was not what I was expecting to hear. We never have students—let alone female students—being reprimanded for carrying weapons. A series of potential blades flash in my mind, and my pulse picks up pace. "A knife? She brought it to school?"

"Well, not technically." Pam raises her hands in an attempt to calm me. She walks back to her desk and takes a seat.

"She brought it on the bus, which is good enough," I say. "What was she doing with it?"

"She didn't even have it out—"

"Then how did the driver see it?" I suck in a breath and slowly exhale. In my mind, I start counting to de-escalate my worry. *One... two... three.* It's a trick Dr. Walters taught me in one of our early sessions. Any weapon would be concerning, but I'm particularly bothered by knives. I hate knives.

"It was a little pocketknife. She was getting off the bus when her bag fell. That's when the driver saw it."

"Well, what did he do?"

"It's not like he could ignore it. He radioed the SRO and got an administrator to meet Zoey at the bus. Bowles handled it from there."

"Bringing a knife to school is zero tolerance. It should be an immediate expulsion," I say. That's our policy, although in my time at Victory Hills we've never had to enforce it.

"Well, they aren't looking at the situation like that."

"What do you mean?" I remember what brought me to Pam's office to begin with, the OSS flag on the attendance website. "They aren't just giving her OSS, are they?"

"For today and tomorrow. Bowles talked to Zoey. He asked her why she had the knife, and she explained she didn't realize it was in her bag. It was a pocketknife. Not like an actual weapon."

"Yes, it is," I argue. I imagine all the damage a person can do with a *little* knife. The damage that had already been done. The tragedy that could have been prevented, if only I'd acted sooner.

"*A pencil can be a weapon, too.*" Pam's tone mimics that of an obnoxious child. "That's Bowles' theory, anyway."

I sigh at the ridiculous comparison. "Yeah, maybe if James Bond is using it. It's 2020. Every student knows you can't bring a knife to school."

"Look, I hear everything you're saying. I even agree with you, but Zoey claimed to have brought it by accident. They are giving her the benefit of the doubt."

"OSS is a slap on the wrist and we both know it. It's school-approved vacation."

I suddenly feel I am in the position of a student, being counseled from the other side of the desk. *Four… five… six.* I can't help but think Bowles is giving Zoey a pass because she's female. He must not consider her a threat, and maybe she's not. I wonder if I'm hoping Zoey will be punished because of her attitude on her first day. Sometimes it's harder for me to shake a grudge than I'd like.

"Bowles is handling the situation quietly. That's why he wants to speak with all of Zoey's teachers. Make sure they're hyper-aware of her behavior. I mean, why would this kid bring a weapon to her first week of school on purpose? Maybe she did just forget." Pam sighs and looks down at her desk calendar, which is covered in colorful scribbles and doodles. Her efforts to de-escalate the situation aren't convincing, even to herself. "I think Bowles is giving the kid a chance."

There's an edge in Pam's words, like maybe we should do the same. I don't like the feeling. I'm not a ballbuster, but I think this is a pretty big offense to let slide. Even if it is her first week.

I uncross my arms. "This wouldn't have anything to do with Zoey's performance at the track meet, would it?"

She arches her eyebrows and curves her lips. "She *will* return before next week's meet. Interesting timing, huh?"

I shake my head, hoping I am wrong, and our school isn't bending the rules solely for sports.

Pam continues, "We'll keep an eye on Zoey. Maybe this is the environment she needs in her life."

It is an optimistic idea, that a certain place or person can make a difference. We all want to feel that way, like we're doing our part to better the world. Sometimes it works. Sometimes it doesn't.

CHAPTER 6

Summer 2002

"Della," Dad shouted from downstairs. I was still in bed, my lavender comforter pulled tight over my head to muffle the sounds of him and everyone else.

"Della," he said again, this time his voice quieter and closer.

I pulled the comforter down, disrupting a few strands of hair in the process. Dad stood in the doorway. He held a cup of coffee and smiled.

"It's Saturday," I reminded him, as though he'd broken some rule.

"Correct," he said. "But it's also nine."

"On a Sat-UR-day," I said, dissecting each syllable in that way teenagers do when they're trying to make a point.

"Your mom has already called looking for you."

"Why?" I rolled to the side and stretched my legs.

"She's been at the clubhouse for hours," Dad said. "She's decorating for the party and needs your help."

"Have Brian help her," I said, rolling to my left.

"He's been down there over an hour." Dad walked into the room and sat on the bed. He put down his coffee and shook me.

"Why do I have to help?" I whined. "This is her job."

Mom was the Wilsonville community planner. In my short life, I'd never met anyone more perfect for the position. She was responsible for organizing social gatherings and seasonal functions.

Fairs and charity events and block parties. Mom was paid well to do what she loved.

"Ever heard the phrase, *It takes a village*?" Dad always introduced new sayings, many of which I didn't appreciate until later in life. "I've let you sleep in late enough, kiddo."

He gave me another hearty shake. I sighed, slung my legs to the side and placed my feet on the floor.

"Let me get dressed," I said, my eyes squinted against the room's brightness. I grabbed my contacts container on the nightstand and popped the clear discs into my eyes. Now everything was in focus. Dad's face, with his thin beard and thick glasses. His smile.

"That's my girl," Dad said, rustling my hair with his hand before standing.

It didn't take me long to get ready in those days. I hadn't been bitten by the beauty bug that infected my peers. I was thirteen but could have passed for younger. I opened my top drawer and selected a yellow one-piece bathing suit. I pulled it on and layered it with one of Dad's oversized shirts. I braided my hair and brushed my teeth. Ta-da, I was ready for the day.

I slumped downstairs and found Dad sitting in the kitchen, his focus on the morning newspaper.

"You ready, Dell?" he asked when, after several seconds, he noticed I'd arrived.

"I guess."

He stood and grabbed the car keys from the center fruit bowl.

"Why don't we just walk?" I asked. "It's like five minutes away."

"Mom might have something we need to load or pick up." He finished his coffee in one swig and placed it on the counter. "Say, why don't you ever want to help with your mom's events?"

"She's just so…" I scanned the kitchen, as though written on the refrigerator or microwave would be a snarky word that would best describe my mother. "Intense."

Dad laughed. "She can definitely be that." He put his arm over my shoulder, and we walked toward the front door. "But she's intense in the best kind of way."

I rolled my eyes. Minutes later and only a few meters away, we pulled into an empty parking space. The pool area was already decorated. Each gatepost had a red, white or blue balloon attached. Through the metal slats, I could see Mom and Brian scurrying around the pool's edge. When she heard the car door close, Mom jerked her head and looked.

"Thank God," she said. "Honey, I need you to pick up food platters from the deli. Della, come on in here and help me."

"Told you I needed the car," Dad whispered, shrinking back into the vehicle. "Do what your mother says."

"About time," Brian said when he heard the pool gate slam.

"Shut it," I said, walking toward Mom.

"What did you say to me?" Brian put down the roll of streamers he had in his hands and took a step closer.

"That's enough," Mom said, standing between us and using both hands to point. "People will be here within the hour. We don't have time for bickering."

"He started it," I whined.

"Not now, Della." Her voice was firm. "Besides, it *is* about time. What were you thinking sleeping in so late?"

"Mom, I—"

"Enough," she said, stomping her foot on the concrete. "The tables are already set up. I just need you to add tablecloths."

"Fine," I said, biting my bottom lip and storming off.

Brian returned to manhandling the streamers, an aggravating smile on his face.

By noon, the entire pool area was packed. Everyone gravitated toward their usual neighborhood crowd. For Dad, that meant he stood alone by the barbecue hoping to go unnoticed. Mom floated from one cluster to the next, ensuring everyone was jovial and well fed. Brian was talking to his best friend in the neighborhood, Danny.

"The place looks great," said Amber as she walked up. Her blonde hair was piled on top of her head and she wore a striped cover-up. "Did you help?"

"Yeah," I said, thumbing my braid. "It takes a village."

Amber was the only girl in my grade who lived in the neighborhood, which made her my best friend. She lived five houses down on Danny's side of the street. Their row of houses was the most expensive on the cul-de-sac. *That's why they're only children*, Mom would say in a bitter tone. She said Amber's parents couldn't handle more than one, and she referred to Danny as an *Oops baby*, since his mother was nearing forty when she had him.

"I can't believe this is the last week of summer," Amber said.

For Floridians, that wasn't necessarily true. While Wilsonville certainly had cold spells, entertainment was always nearby. An hour's drive in one direction took us to the beach. An hour's drive in another direction landed us near all the major theme parks. Even the community pool stayed open year-round. The days would be unbearably hot for at least another two months.

"I think the party is more about returning to school than saying goodbye to summer."

"Just think, we'll be in high school next year." Amber scanned the area, her eyes landing on the huddle of neighborhood boys. "Should we say hello to our future classmates?"

"Amber, no," I said, sinking my weight into a flimsy patio chair. Amber was my best friend, but utterly exhausting. She loved pestering boys. Brian always seemed part of that group, and I tried to avoid him even more in public than I did at home. "Let's just go for a swim."

"I'm not getting my hair wet." She unwrapped her cover-up and slung it next to my chair. Her fuchsia bikini certainly made her look older than thirteen, which was always her goal.

"Why'd you wear a bathing suit if you're not swimming?"

"Really, Della?" She yanked on my arm until I stood. Suddenly, we were standing next to Brian and his friends.

"Hey, guys," Amber said, poking out her bony hip.

"How's it going, girls?" asked Danny. He looked at me and smiled. Even then, he was the only boy in Brian's clique who didn't seem annoyed by my presence. Everyone else followed Brian's orders.

"Hey," Brian said. He spoke to Amber but looked at me.

Amber started talking with some of the other guys. I think they were more interested in the bikini than anything she said.

Brian yanked my elbow and pulled me a few steps back. "Can't you just leave us alone?"

"I'm trying," I said. "Amber wants to mingle."

"You're so fucking annoying," he said. This time he was louder. Danny darted his eyes away, like he hadn't heard.

"Brian!" I hated when he used those words.

"Not now," Mom whisper-scolded. She appeared out of nowhere, standing behind us in that way mothers do. As usual, she arrived in time to witness my rebuttal without hearing Brian's inciting remarks. "Time for games."

She pushed us forward and made louder, cheerier announcements to the other kids at the pool. I didn't much like being labeled a kid, and Brian liked it even less. Danny and some of the other neighborhood boys joined us, but Amber stayed back. Mom didn't pressure her to participate.

Mom roped the younger children into a relay race. Then, she threw various items into the pool and offered a prize to whoever collected the most from the bottom. When it was time for our age category, we had another race. My team won, although it wasn't because of me.

"Our last activity will be the Watermelon Wrestle," Mom announced to the crowd.

Dad sat at a nearby picnic table slathering the fruit with petroleum jelly.

"Mom," I said under my breath. "I don't want to do this one."

"Come on, Della," she said. "Be a good sport."

The Watermelon Wrestle was when a group of swimmers fought to get the slippery fruit out of the pool. Whoever successfully pulled the watermelon away from the other contestants won the prize. Year after year, people got too rough, and everyone left the competition winded.

I looked around the crowded pool. All the adults stood around, drinks in hand, watching. All the younger swimmers were pulled from the water for safety purposes. To everyone else, this was an entertaining tradition. I worried maybe I was being a whiny teenager about the whole thing, so I reluctantly entered the water.

I waded waist-deep in the pool. It wasn't fair that Amber and other middle schoolers could stand on the sidelines and watch. As I looked up at them, I envied them. Amber's face pitied me. It was humiliating to participate in something so juvenile.

Dad carried the watermelon to the edge of the pool. Mom stood beside him, lifting a whistle to her lips. "One, two, three... Go," she shouted, tooting the whistle. Dad threw it into the water and the older boys pounced.

I waited, allowing them to fight for it. One person would get a hold on it, then their palms would slip, and the fruit would plop back into the water, signaling it was someone else's turn to try.

"Come on, guys," Mom cheered. "Come on, Della."

I moved closer to the rumble, never actively trying to get involved. Water splashed at my chest and hair due to the boys' chaos nearby. Danny and Brian locked arms, each with an equal grasp on the watermelon. They pulled back and forth, neither person giving up their hold. Between their conflicting pulls and the water beneath, something gave, and the watermelon leapt into the sky and splash-landed in front of me.

"Grab it, Della. Grab it," Mom shouted. "Get it to the side."

All the boys were still huddled around each other, unaware of where the fruit had landed. My fingers slid across the greasy shell. It was too heavy and slick to maneuver with one hand. I put both arms around it, hugged it to my body like I was carrying a load of warm laundry, and tiptoed toward the edge of the pool.

Within seconds, the boys were back. They jumped after me, Brian leading the pack. He pounced, landing directly on top of the watermelon and pushing me under the water. I was in no mood to fight. If he wanted the stupid fruit, he could have it. I let go, allowing it to pierce the surface of the water yet again.

"Calm down," I said.

"Fucking loser," Brian said, his volume so low only I could hear.

I splashed him, then lunged forward to grab the fruit again. I was more than happy to let him have the stupid watermelon, but if he wanted to make a big challenge about it, I would fight. He effortlessly pulled it from my arms, pushing me down in the process. I went under again, swallowing a gulp of chlorinated water.

By this point, the other boys in the pool had joined our struggle. I could feel their bony shins bump against my body as I flailed underwater. My head left the water, and I took an interrupted breath before I was pushed under again. I was such a scrawny thing; the boys didn't even realize I was beneath them. They were after the fruit. After the prize. I could only get my arm above water, and it was lost in the thicket of adolescent limbs. Suddenly, I felt fingers graze my scalp. At least, it felt like fingers. Someone pulling me out? Instead, the fingers pushed. They pushed and held still, forcing my body deeper.

My heart pumped harder and I squirmed maddeningly. No one seemed to notice. I tried to fight against the strength of the hand, but there was still a barrier of bodies blocking me. The more I struggled, the weaker I became.

At last, the bodies moved away, no doubt chasing the watermelon. I heard the familiar sound of a splash underwater. Dad lifted me out of the pool as though I weighed nothing and dropped me on the cement. The hit made me cough, and a large gush of water came out of my mouth.

"My God, Della," Dad said, his breath hurried. "Are you all right?"

"I think so," I said. There was a storm of people around staring, but their happy smiles were gone. Even though all I wanted to do was cry, I was in middle school now. I would very much rather drown in a pool than cry in front of my neighbors.

"Poor thing," Mom said, running behind me and blanketing me with a towel. "She's so scrawny they couldn't even see her under there."

"You sure you're okay?" Dad asked again. He whispered, as though he understood my reluctant dishonesty.

"I'm fine, Dad."

He still looked worried. Even Mom did. I think everyone was worried a little, except for Brian. He stood under the pavilion. He'd grabbed a knife and was slicing open the fruit he'd won.

CHAPTER 7

Now

I'm not involved with sports as much as I should be, but I do enjoy chaperoning other events. We have three major dances throughout the year: Winter Waltz, Spring Fling and Prom. Someone like Marge will attend all three. I am required to choose one, and this year it's the Spring Fling. It's not as formal as the other two dances. Instead of gowns, girls wear cocktail dresses. Still, most students have spent weeks coordinating their ensembles and deciding how to style their hair.

The Spirit Club decorated the auditorium, making the usually outdated gymnasium look like a floral hideaway. Flowers made from tissue or cardstock are tacked to the walls and dangle from the ceiling. The aesthetic is impressive; I don't think anyone would guess the room is a place where you typically run laps.

"Love the decorations," I tell Marge. She's the Spirit Club sponsor. Her navy dress clings to her hips and waist, and a sparkly overlay dangles over her shoulders. It looks like she's even curled her hair with a wand. "You should dress up more often."

"Thank you," she says, pretending to curtsy. She looks me up and down, taking in my Hepburn-esque updo and black knee-length shift. "As usual, you're a beauty."

"Thanks," I say, making sure my pearl earrings are securely fastened. I'm even wearing magenta lipstick; Danny says it brings out the green in my eyes.

Marge bites a strip of tape and dances on her tippy toes as she reattaches a tissue hibiscus to the wall. "Each year I think hosting will get easier," she says. "But that's never the case."

"Let me help you," I say.

"Are you being polite, or really offering?" she asks. She dons the familiar look we all get when we've bitten off more than we can chew.

"I'm actually offering." I grab a roll of tape from a table in front of her. "Just tell me what to do."

"Thanks, Dell," she says, instructing me to reattach the flowers that are dangling too low against the far wall.

By the time I've finished, the place looks perfect. Just in time for the hordes of students arriving, as though they timed their entrance accordingly. The guys aren't wearing formal suits like they would for Prom, but jackets in a variety of pastel shades: mint and salmon and daisy.

The girls' dresses are equally colorful, making the entire lot look like a scene from *Seven Brides for Seven Brothers*. It's always nice to see them on nights like this. I'm used to students, especially my female ones, being bogged down in insecurity. Even on the days they arrive to class with highlighter across their cheeks and an intentional wave in their hair. Tonight, they've left the house feeling beautiful. Feeling confident.

The colorful outfits aren't the only reason I enjoy chaperoning Spring Fling; it's also a more laidback event compared to other school functions. We don't crown kings or queens. We don't dole out awards. Students just have fun. There's no competition.

"Where's that handsome husband of yours?" Pam asks. She walks up behind me balancing a plate of food in her hand. She's wearing a red maxi dress, and her hair hangs down her back. It's always up at school.

"Relaxing for a change." I sip my punch. "This isn't really his cup of tea."

"I understand," she says, raising her voice over the blaring music. "My ex never came to stuff like this."

Pam and her husband divorced last year after he got slapped with a DUI. She hardly mentions him at school; I think she feels odd offering advice to people when she knows her own personal life is chaotic. I think it makes her more relatable, knowing she's gone through heartache and made it to the other side. It gives her words weight.

"What time will the dance end?" I ask. I can't remember from last year.

"Nine o'clock, I think," she says. "Gives us plenty of time to clean up before going home."

Another throng of students enters from the outside. This time I recognize several: Melanie and Ben. And Zoey. Her dress is white with sheer sleeves stopping at her elbows.

"What's Zoey Peterson doing here?" I ask Pam.

She tilts her head to get a better listen as I repeat the question. Having heard me, she nods. "I know. Bowles said he wasn't going to make her miss the dance."

"But she's suspended until Monday. That should cover school functions."

"I guess Bowles wanted to give her a pass." Pam shrugs and pops a miniature hot dog in her mouth.

I shake my head. Bowles, who has skipped tonight's event, sending another administrator in his place, has a wobbly backbone. Five years ago, when I first started, he at least followed through with discipline. I didn't think we should send the message that carrying a knife to school was a minor fault.

"Oh dear," Pam says, staring at her phone. "The babysitter is calling already. Pray for me."

She walks away, leaving me alone. I watch the students as they transition from confident to insecure again, working up the courage to ask someone to dance. If it's a friend, it's easy. Those are the ones who walk up to a person, laugh and start dancing. The hesitant ones, those are the students with real feelings involved. Melanie wraps her arms around the neck of a boy I've never met. They sway from one foot to the next in that awkward way teenagers do. Watching them makes me smile.

I wouldn't go back to high school for anything, even if the Brian stuff hadn't happened. I resented my teachers and the overall uncertainty I had within myself. The one thing I do miss, with intensity at times, is the newness of life. The electricity of a new person's hand dancing at your back. That thumping of your heart before a first kiss. The excitement in your gut. The flutter.

When you're older, the newness is gone forever. I love Danny, and he loves me. Our relationship is mature and stable and passionate. But the one thing it is not, and never will be again, is new. Every moment is tried, every sensation is familiar. I'd rather experience a predictable life with him than the thrill of a stranger, which is why we're married. But sometimes I think of that flutter, acknowledge it would be nice to feel it again.

"Want to help me replenish the snack table?" Marge asks when she walks past.

"Sure," I say, following her across the room. We exit the gymnasium and enter the quiet hallway. The roaring party clashes against the quiet halls. The change is almost eerie.

"I've stored the food in Mr. Walsh's room," she says, taking the lanyard off her neck and picking the appropriate key.

As she's about to press the latch, we hear a clatter from the other end of the hall. The empty corridors make the sound echo. Teenage giggling follows. We stop, startled, and look in the direction from where the sound came. Because the door around the corner is locked, the hallway leads to a dead end.

"Come on out," Marge yells. "We know someone is back there."

Darcy and Adam step around the corner. Darcy puts her hands behind her back, and even from several feet away I can tell she's smiling. She's wearing a slinky purple dress with a slit that stops mid-thigh.

"What are you two doing in the halls?" Marge shouts, her voice thundering down the hollow corridor.

"We were just visiting my locker," Adam yells. His tall frame hovers over Darcy. He's more cautious than she is; he wouldn't want any misbehavior to interfere with athletics.

"Yeah, Ms. Helton," Darcy adds. She sounds noticeably less concerned. "We weren't doing anything wrong."

The way she says it makes me think they were precisely doing something wrong. Darcy moves her hands forward, showing she's not holding anything. Adam's hands are also bare. Maybe they're just roaming the halls because they know they're not supposed to.

"All right," Marge shouts. "This is your warning. Get back in the gym and do not leave."

They shuffle back into the crowded gymnasium, Darcy's giggle trailing.

Marge unlocks Mr. Walsh's classroom door and looks back at me. Her stern look drops, and she laughs. "Kids, huh? No telling what they were doing back there."

"Who knows," I say, eyeing the platters of croissants and pinwheels. My stomach rumbles, and I decide I might need a second serving once we return to the dance. "Let's get the food in there and keep a better eye on the doors."

"Yeah," Marge says. "I'll radio one of the security guys and tell them to patrol the halls, make sure no one else has slipped away."

When we re-enter the dance, the music is louder, and the air stuffier. I check my watch. Students won't stay much longer. They'll be off to whatever after-party has been orchestrated, because no teenager is going to call it a night at 9 p.m., especially when they're wearing an expensive dress and makeup.

Across the room, I see Melanie is still gooey-eyeing the tall boy from earlier. She looks weak in the knees going on head over heels. Even when it comes to romance, Melanie is an overachiever. Maybe a fling would help her not be so highly strung about academics.

That's how I felt when Danny re-entered my life, like the load I'd been carrying was suddenly lifted. Before him, every person in my path was someone I had to keep at a distance; Danny already knew my darkest secrets and biggest regrets. I could finally breathe again.

I lightened Danny's load, too. When we reconnected, he was halfway through medical school. His parents were starting to develop health problems of their own. He needed an excuse to be happy as much as I did. We no longer carried the hardships of life alone. Thanks to Brian, we'd both already experienced our share.

At the food table, I see Ben covering his plate with the replenished appetizers. Beside him stands Zoey, holding a plastic cup. Her white dress catches my eye in the sea of colors. A third student, Darcy, is standing with them. Her mouth is moving fast, and her hand is swooshing in the air. Zoey's arms are crossed, and she's listening intently to whatever Darcy has to say. I wonder what they're talking about and why, although it's hard to be certain from across a crowded room, Zoey looks so irritated.

Another minute passes, and Darcy's on the dance floor. Adam stands in front of her, wrapping his arms around her neck. Ben remains by the food table, stuffing his face. Zoey, standing beside him, keeps staring in Darcy's direction. Her eyes leave Darcy and land on me. When she sees I'm watching her, she smiles and waves. As though someone slid a finger down the back of her dress and pushed a button. Brian used to do that; he could change his demeanor in a split second. I see parts of him in her, and it's startling. I wave back.

As I exit the crowded parking lot, I'm thankful for how far I've come. For years, I didn't know if I'd ever find normalcy. Brian had taken that from me. Time brought ordinary back, something you don't even know to miss until it's gone. Danny helped, too. Tonight, I feel more thankful for him than usual as I pull into the driveway. When I walk inside, I see he's taken the opportunity to cook dinner: alfredo noodles with garlic bread and wine. The effort he's put in almost brings me to tears.

"I thought I'd cook since you're working late for a change," he says, lighting the long candle at the table's center. He smiles, then a shadow of uncertainty covers his face. "It's probably too late to eat."

I wrap my arms around his neck and balance on my toes to kiss his lips. "This is perfect."

CHAPTER 8

Now

Monday comes too fast. When I arrive at school, I can tell within minutes something is off. An identifiable sense that something has happened, even though I've yet to speak with a soul. It's the way students murmur as they pass, buzzing from one cluster of people to the next, their voices low. The way colleagues, standing in their familiar positions, stare forward without speaking, their predictable morning chatter gone.

I unlock my classroom and deposit my belongings, hoping I have time to stop by the employee lounge before the first bell rings. I know Marge will be in there, and if something is going on, she'll have all the details.

As suspected, she's just finished pouring her morning coffee when I walk into the room. Thankfully, we're the only two.

"How was your weekend?" I ask. She looks at me like she still wants to be alone. She's shaken, her usual positivity quenched. Something has definitely happened. And it's bad.

"You didn't hear about what happened after Spring Fling, did you?" she asks.

I shake my head, not wanting to waste time by responding. I stare at her and wait to be filled in.

"Gah, Della. You're going to have to get on social media if you want to stay in the loop," she says, putting down her coffee cup. I can tell she's partially joking with me, as she often does in the morning, but her tone is serious. "Darcy Moore was attacked."

"Attacked?" The syllables linger between us. I lower my voice in case someone opens the door. "Attacked how?"

"We don't have all the details," she says, eyeing the door, equally wary someone might walk in. "I'm not sure what happened, but I know her leg was sliced open."

I gasp audibly, and cover my chest with my hand, as if my sorrow will better the situation. My stomach drops, as my mind conjures up past scenarios and images I'd rather not consider. *One... two... three*. Darcy Moore from first block. Darcy Moore, who I'd seen frolicking around the school on Saturday night. She'd been attacked hours later. *Four... five... six*. It doesn't seem possible.

"What do we know?" I ask.

"My feed was full of #PrayforDarcy posts and whatnot, but obviously students didn't mention anything about the attack." She moves closer, further lowering her voice. "I know Pam has been with the Moores since yesterday. And I heard Bowles is planning a meeting with all of Darcy's current teachers. You have her, right?"

"Yeah," I stutter. "First block."

"I have her third," Marge says, taking a sip of coffee. "I guess we'll find out more then. Keep your ears open."

On cue, the first bell rings and another co-worker opens the lounge door. We both leave, separating at the end of the hall to head in the direction of our respective classrooms.

I already know how to act during a situation like this. We all do, if you've been teaching long enough. Everyone at school has their confidants. Mine are Marge and Pam. When you gossip at school, you must do so strategically. Otherwise, you might as well deliver whatever news you have over the intercom for the entire staff and student body to hear. Asking students what happened is another big no-no. No one wants to be accused of harassing students. Besides, you're more likely to hear the truth via eavesdropping.

Much to my surprise, first block is even quieter than I am. They don't say a word upon entering the classroom: not about their weekend, not about the assignment I've given them, not about Spring Fling. And nothing about Darcy Moore. Everyone is present today expect for Darcy and Adam; I suppose your girlfriend being attacked is a good enough reason to skip class.

"Grab your textbooks," I say after several silent minutes. The room obeys without so much as a grunt. I clear my throat before continuing. "We're starting *The Crucible* this week. Go ahead and read Act One to yourselves."

Normally, I assign parts and we read plays aloud. But that feels too much to ask on a day like this. Even if no one mentions Darcy, they must be thinking about her. I'd rather not sit in silence with my thoughts, but I also don't want to push my students too far out of their comfort zones. I lean back in my chair and watch as my students flip pages and stuff earbuds in their ears.

Ninety minutes is a long time to sit in silence, though. By the end of class, students are restless. I invite them to share their responses to today's reading. Most students make random comments about characters or setting, but some of the smarter ones, like Melanie, approach theme.

"It's like everyone is afraid of something," she says, twirling her pen.

Now standing, I lean against my podium. "Can you explain what you mean by that?"

"It's, like, every character so far is either afraid of God or the devil or each other. I think that's why they start accusing people."

"Fear is a huge motivator for future events in the play." I clear my throat. "That's something you should think about as you continue reading. What are the dangers of allowing fear to influence our decisions?"

"It pushes others to make accusations without evidence," Ben says, quietly.

"Good," I say. "Any other ideas you'd like to discuss?"

"Behaviors repeat themselves," Zoey says. Her words are sharp and quick. I don't know if I'd have caught them had her classmates been speaking at their normal volume.

"I don't know if I heard you exactly," I say, straightening. "Can you elaborate?"

"Well, these events took place hundreds of years ago, but people act the same way today."

"You're right," I say, moving away from the podium. "I think that's what's great about this play. It shows that even though almost every aspect of day-to-day life has changed, our behaviors are constant."

I close my book, a silent permission for my students to do the same. They get up from their seats and start walking to the back bookshelf. This is the loudest they've been all morning, as some students start talking and laughing with one another.

"Girls were clearly as desperate for attention then as they are now," I hear someone say, but I'm not sure who said it. Most of the class is up and out of their seats. The clarity and volume of their conversations wave like a staticky radio station. I look at Zoey's desk. She's still seated, staring straight ahead. Staring at me.

"Did you say something, Zoey?"

"I just said…" She stops, looks down and shakes her head. "Nothing. I said nothing."

She stands and walks to the back of the room. Did I hear her correctly? Was she actually taking today's text and connecting it to what happened to Darcy? *Desperate for attention*? Like Darcy is making up this alleged attack?

I'm still standing at her desk when she returns from the bookshelf.

"You okay, Mrs. Mayfair?" Zoey asks, sliding past me to sit back in her chair.

"I, um," I stumble, looking away. "Could you repeat what you said? Before I walked over here?"

"It was nothing," Zoey says, securing a black strand of hair behind her ear. "Probably something really juvenile. I think I need to continue reading in order to get a better understanding."

She smiles, and the bell rings. I stand still, waiting as Zoey and all my other students depart their daily dose of literature. I'm thinking about what Zoey said. Did I hear her correctly? If I did, it's a remarkably insensitive comment to make after a student—a girl who only sits a few chairs away from her—was attacked. She's pulling the wrong message from the text, just as she did with "A Rose for Emily" last week.

By the time second block begins, I'm back behind my desk. I hand down the same assignment, and the room fills again with silence as students read. I think about their stifled reactions today compared to Zoey's callous one. I remember seeing her at the dance. She was talking with Darcy, and their exchange looked problematic. Still, why would she belittle Darcy's situation now? Is this what other students thought, too? That Darcy was grasping for attention?

Zoey had been punished for carrying a knife last week. I know I can't assume everyone who owns a pocketknife will turn out like Brian, but it's awful coincidental another student was attacked days later. And now Zoey feels the need to minimize that situation. There's much about Darcy's attack that remains a mystery, but I wonder if Zoey understands more than she claims.

CHAPTER 9

Now

By lunch, I receive an email announcing a meeting in Principal Bowles' office after school. The email was only sent to four other employees, Marge and Pam included, so he must have made the decision to forgo addressing this weekend's events with the entire staff.

My stomach has been in knots all day, partly because I know what happened, partly because there is still much I don't know. As expected, memories of Brian arise making everything worse. I try to keep my memories dormant, locked away inside, unless I'm searching for cathartic release with my therapist. But various triggers unlock those memories, and what happened to Darcy is an obvious one.

I've spent more time than anyone should imagining what girls who've been attacked must go through. The fear they must feel. The hopelessness. I picture their faces, all those pretty girls Brian hurt. Those pretty girls I failed to protect. The only difference between Darcy and them is they never had the opportunity to explain what happened to them. People weren't organizing staff meetings to strategize and help; they were conducting press conferences, offering up salacious details.

Principal Bowles' office is spacious compared to a typical administrator's workspace, but it feels small when six adults are cramped inside. There's Bowles, Pam, Marge and myself. We're also joined by Mr. Hathaway, the art teacher, and Mrs. Lakes, who teaches American history. I can tell by the looks on their faces they're dreading what we're about to hear but eager for an understanding of what happened. I'm not confident Bowles is going to give any useful information. He's more about damage control.

Once we've all taken our seats, Bowles stands up from his desk and closes the door. "Knowing we have a small academic community, I'm sure you've all heard there was an incident this weekend concerning one of our students, Darcy Moore," he says, punctuating the sentence with a heavy sigh. He returns to his seat and presses his hands together. "The Moores called me this morning. I don't want to exaggerate the issue by addressing this matter schoolwide, but I wanted to speak with you four directly because you have Darcy this semester. Pam is here to help mediate."

Pam nods. She's partially seated on a table in the room and her arms are crossed. Her face looks tired. We rarely have dangerous incidents at Victory Hills. In fact, I can't think of one other tragedy, other than my second year when a student's house caught fire and he lost all his belongings. The entire school banded together collecting donations; I hope administration will come up with the right response for Darcy, too.

"Can you tell us what happened?" asks Mrs. Lakes. She's sitting across from Principal Bowles, her long blonde braid falling over the back of the chair.

"I want to be very careful about how we address this issue," Bowles says, raising one hand. "What we know is this: none of us were with Darcy after Spring Fling. All events took place off campus. Officers responded to her house for a noise complaint. There was some type of party going on. They found her in… an unfortunate state. Darcy is receiving treatment to some wounds on her leg. It's important we remain aware. If you witness alarming behavior, address your concerns with Pam."

"Is Darcy okay?" asks Mr. Hathaway, lifting a foot covered by a paint-smattered Birkenstock as he crosses his legs.

"I know she's getting the help she needs," he responds. "Her parents are adamant they want her to finish the semester. She'll be returning to class next week. As a school, we need to try and eliminate chatter by then."

"I think we should speak with some of our female students—" Marge begins, but she's interrupted by Bowles.

"We're not drawing attention to the matter," he says, raising his hand to stop Marge from speaking. It'll take more than a hand to silence her, though.

"I'm not suggesting that," she says, slowing her pace and staring directly at Bowles. "But if you want chatter to quiet down before she returns, I think we should at least address the incident. We could speak to students about safety measures and how to prevent future assaults."

"No one is using the word *assault*," Bowles says, this time with a sterner voice. "Darcy hasn't even used that word. We don't need to start throwing terms around." Clearly Bowles doesn't want to explore the various implications of the word *assault*.

"Do we know who is responsible for the attack?" I ask.

"No," Bowles says, looking down. "We aren't even certain there was an attack. Now Darcy claims she hurt her leg in a fall. Police are looking into what happened. If you ask me, it sounds like a party that got out of hand. No one seems to remember much of anything. Including Darcy."

Seconds later, we're dismissed. Marge stays behind, I'm sure to argue further with Bowles about what should or shouldn't be said to students. She can do that sort of thing. She already has tenure. I'm not sure how I feel about her suggestion, honestly. On one hand, hosting an assembly might bring more attention to the topic, attention Darcy will surely resent. On the other hand, students are bound to be afraid. Bowles is antsy because he doesn't want to expose students to the world. He doesn't realize it's about preparing them for the world. A world that can be cruel and unforgiving, sometimes evil.

I follow Pam to the guidance wing and walk into her office. She shuts the door and sits. She puts her elbows on the desk and places a palm against her forehead. It's no secret among the staff that Bowles and Pam occasionally bump heads, and the heavier the issue, the harder the collision. Pam is a free spirit, wanting to encourage students to think for themselves. Bowles is as conservative as it gets, wanting students to fall in line and keep their heads down until they walk across the stage with a diploma.

"Are you okay?" I ask Pam, allowing her a few seconds to think.

"This situation is a nightmare," she admits, looking at me with tired eyes. "I can't even imagine what Darcy is going through."

"Can you tell me what really happened?"

"Okay, here's what I know," she says, her voice a whisper. I'm happy she has more information than Bowles is willing to give. The meeting raised more questions than it answered. "Darcy hosted a party at her house after Spring Fling. No parents. Lots of alcohol. Police think some local college kids might have brought the booze and drugs. Darcy thinks someone slipped something in her drink. She doesn't remember much after a certain point in the night."

"She was roofied?" As I say it, I realize I've never used this word before. It's something thrown around on cable crime dramas, never used in connection to one of my students.

"She was knocked out with something. Her friends just thought she was wasted. Didn't even bother to check on her before leaving. Word must have gotten out police were headed that way. By the time officers arrived, there weren't many students left. They found Darcy in her backyard. Her dress was torn, and she had three deep cuts on her thigh."

"Oh my gosh," I say, covering my mouth.

I imagine Darcy outside and alone, her friends too concerned with their own situations to find her. I consider her parents, their reaction to receiving the news their daughter had been attacked at their home. The Moores are a well-known family in Victory Hills. Their son graduated two years ago. Although I didn't have him in class, he was the type of student everyone knew. He played football and earned a sports scholarship to some school in the northeast. Not that he needed it. The Moores are wealthy and involved in the community, less involved when it comes to parenting.

"Do they think she was raped?" I ask Pam. Clearly this is the word Bowles is trying to keep from being thrown around. It's the word that comes to most people's minds when they hear a teenage girl has been drugged and attacked.

Pam looks down, her expression a mix of concern and sickness. "Darcy doesn't remember a lot, but she says she wasn't."

"Do you believe her?"

Pam's nostrils flare as she exhales. "I don't know what to believe at this point. Like Bowles said, Darcy's now saying she hurt her leg in a fall. I'm not sure if she's protecting someone, or if she just wants the whole mess to blow over."

"Did she go the doctor?" I ask. "They should be able to tell if her injury was accidental."

"The doctor pretty much refuted Darcy's claim about the fall. The wounds were too precise. Darcy and her parents were just ready to leave by that point." She seems, for the first time, judgmental. Toward the parents. "What Bowles didn't mention, and what makes everything much worse, is that there were pictures of her taken the night of the party. Very unflattering pictures taken when she was drunk. They were sent to half the school before the party even ended."

As if the situation wasn't bad enough, Darcy has the added humiliation of pictures. A forever memorial to a horrific night.

"Do the pictures provide any insight?"

"Not in terms of *who* might have hurt her," she says. "Although they clearly show she wasn't in her right mind. I question the moral fiber of anyone who would take pictures of someone in that state and pass it around for entertainment."

"You're right," I say, leaning forward against her desk. "How did you get involved?"

"Her mother called me Sunday morning and wanted me to visit with them once they returned from the hospital. She thought talking to someone other than her parents or doctors might help."

"What are the police saying?"

"There's not much they can do if Darcy can't explain what happened. And our only witnesses are a bunch of drunk teenagers who are afraid of getting grounded for being at a party to begin with."

"I can't imagine how scary it all must have been for her." I close my eyes tight, trying hard not to imagine. I've done this before. Imagined another person's pain. Imagined another person's fear.

"Darcy needs time to process everything. Plus, her leg needs to heal." Pam bends her leg around the side of the desk and shows me where the cut was. "There are three eight-inch gashes on her left thigh. If they'd been any deeper, she might have bled out."

What if the police hadn't arrived in time? I'm not sure anyone, even Darcy, appreciates the danger she faced that night. "This isn't some party gone wrong. The girl was deliberately attacked."

"Problem is Darcy can't or won't remember anything." She looks down. "I don't know if we'll ever know what really happened."

I can't relate to what Darcy has been through, but I understand her reaction. Darcy wants to blink it away. When bad things happen, it's easier to pretend they didn't. Acknowledging the bad things gives them power, extends their shelf life. I'm still ignoring the bad things I went through. When I think of Darcy and what she's endured, I'm infuriated. She deserves more than this. It's like her struggle is bringing my own past back to life.

CHAPTER 10

Winter 2003

I sat in the back of the gymnasium flipping through the color-coded sections of my notebook. Now that I was in high school, this was my routine while Brian attended basketball practice. I plugged in my iPod and worked diligently at trying to grasp my freshman year curriculum. I wasn't like Brian. He barely studied and still managed to pull A's in all his Honors classes. If he wasn't reminding me of this, Mom was; it made my 3.0 in standard classes seem like a disappointment.

Of course, Brian didn't only excel academically. He'd made a name for himself on the basketball team, too. His popularity helped me adjust during the first semester of high school. To all the upperclassmen and teachers, I was Brian's kid sister. Amber, my permanent sidekick, benefited from the celebrity, too, and enjoyed it more than I did. Because while everyone at Wilsonville High thought Brian was great, I still saw his unlikeable characteristics.

It was five o'clock when practice ended. I stood by the bleachers, waiting for Brian's teammates to swagger past me.

"Hey, Baby B." It was Coach Lawson, a tall, husky forty-something whose hair was beginning to thin atop his head. He was Brian's head coach and my history teacher. I hated my nickname, even though I knew Lawson only created them for his favorite students. As almost everyone else did in Wilsonville, he liked me because of my connection to Brian, his great athlete.

"Afternoon, Coach," I said.

Brian approached, bumping Lawson's shoulder.

"Good work today," Lawson said to Brian. "Between you and some of the fresh meat, I think we might have a shot at regionals this year."

"You know it, Coach."

We made our way to the student parking lot. I walked a few steps behind as Brian chatted with his teammates. When we entered the car and the door shut, he slammed his fists against the steering wheel.

"What a crock," he said. He often spewed anger, almost like I wasn't even there.

"What's wrong?" There always seemed to be something wrong, despite the fact Brian had life rather easy.

"You were there," he said, stabbing the key into the ignition. "That little punk wouldn't stop blocking my shot."

"What little punk?"

"You come to my practice every day, Della. You expect me to believe you don't watch what happens?"

I came to his practices because I had no other choice. Mom wasn't going to interrupt her schedule to pick me up, and Dad didn't leave the office until after five.

"I was doing homework."

"Yeah." He laughed as he put the car into drive. "You need all the help you can get with that."

"Brian!" It didn't matter that someone else had gotten under his skin. He always directed his insults toward me.

"Well, if you'd been paying attention, you'd see that little punk Logan Hunt blocking me at every turn." He pressed harder on the gas. "It's like he forgets we're on the same team."

I didn't know why this was so offensive, but Brian was aggravated. I knew Logan Hunt, too. We had freshman English together.

"Isn't that the point of practice?" I asked. "Trying out new plays? Preparing for games?"

"Yeah, but he gets carried away with it. Kid's a *freshman*. He's trying to make a name for himself by stopping a top player. Not going to happen."

It wasn't like Brian was in jeopardy of losing his position. He'd been in the starting five since his sophomore year. In fact, he'd been the Logan Hunt of his freshman year, picking off the upperclassmen and taking their spots.

He turned into our neighborhood screeching tires, forcing me to lurch forward.

"Slow down, Brian. We're on our road now."

He revved up the engine, then slammed the brakes as he pulled up to our garage.

"I don't need driving advice from a little bitch like you," he said.

He exited the car and slammed the door, causing the entire vehicle to shake. I sat there for a few minutes, taking in a deep breath. This was every day with Brian. He didn't let on that anything was wrong when he was around his friends, and he'd be all smiles and compliments again by the time Mom and Dad arrived home. He saved all his pent-up anger for me, and it was draining. I couldn't get my license soon enough.

Brian and I were born two years and one week apart. This prompted Mom to plan joint birthday celebrations every year; it benefited the schedule and the budget for us to celebrate together.

The following weekend, Mom held the party in our sunroom because the weekend forecast predicted rain. Most of our guests came from the neighborhood or school. Brian's basketball buddies were there.

"Having fun, Dell?" Dad asked. He entered the sunroom from the outside, where he'd been grilling hotdogs and hamburgers under our shallow awning.

"Yes," I said. It was true. I enjoyed having friends over, even if it meant sharing the spotlight with Brian.

"Your Mom loves a good party," Dad said. His eyes danced across the room. Mom was holding a pitcher, topping off refreshments.

As the party was winding down, Mom requested everyone's attention. "Give me one minute," she shouted.

We could never simply have a party. There always had to be some entertainment. An event. Something that would elevate the gathering to a shindig. I appreciated it, and in some ways, it made me proud she cared so much. But I was at that age where you can never be fully proud of your parents without also being embarrassed. With Mom, especially.

"Maybe she's fishing out a new training bra," Brian whispered. I gave him an angry stare. Normally, I would have elbowed him, but there were people around. And Dad was still holding the video camera.

Moments later, the door leading into the backyard re-opened and a white puppy came running. Our guests released a unified *Aww*, and some of my friends squealed.

I bent to my knees and held out my arms. The puppy came closer, giving my fingers a few preliminary licks before moving to my neck.

"Is he mine?" I asked. Mom had returned to the sunroom. Her cheeks were flushed, and I noticed tears in her eyes. She'd succeeded in creating a heartfelt birthday memory.

"Actually, it's a she," she corrected. "And, yes. She's all yours. And Brian's."

I looked to my left, but Brian was no longer by my side. He walked up to Mom who was leaning against the empty gift table. "You know I hate dogs," he said.

"Not now, Brian," she said, raising a hand.

My friends moved closer, patiently waiting for a turn to pet the puppy. Brian grabbed one of his new gifts and walked away with a huddle of friends. Dad put down the camera and walked toward Mom. I saw them speaking but couldn't hear what they were saying due to the crowd of friends in front of me.

"What will you name her?" asked Amber, rubbing the dog's fur.

"I don't know," I said, looking around the room. The tile floor was covered with wrapping paper, streamers and hollow pixie stick tubes. "How about Pixie?"

"I like it," Mom said. She walked up behind me and put her hand on my head. "I hope you're happy."

"I am." I'd wanted a pet for years. Even if I had to share my party with Brian, Mom had found a way to make me feel special. "Thanks, you guys." I looked for Dad. He was still standing by the food table with a sour look on his face.

That night, I sat in the living room watching an episode of *The O.C.* while Pixie snuggled in my lap. I'm sure the adolescent swarm from earlier rattled her nerves. She hadn't moved from my side since the guests left.

Brian had been upset ever since the party ended. He wanted Danny to stay over, but even Mom had had enough of playing hostess. She was ready to relax. Tomorrow she'd be busy making the house immaculate again. Tonight, she drank wine in the kitchen with Dad. They sounded all giggly. I turned up the volume, wanting to drown out their gross adult merriment.

At the next commercial, I stood to go to the bathroom. Pixie sat up, alarmed.

"Stay here, girl," I said, not knowing if the dog would know what that meant. I'd only had her a few hours. Regardless, it worked. Pixie nuzzled back into the softness of the sofa cushions.

I walked to the half bath by the kitchen. Mom and Dad were still in there, but they were less giggly now. They were talking.

"I wish you'd told me," Dad whispered.

"Why? So you could say no?" Mom countered. "Her fur is hypoallergenic. I was very specific when choosing—"

"You know that's not my main concern," Dad said.

I didn't know what that last comment meant. My whole childhood, that was all I'd heard. We couldn't have a dog because Dad had allergies.

"She deserves this," Mom said. "The thing with the squirrel happened years ago. I don't even think he was old enough to know what he did. He won't do anything to Della's dog."

I heard the pitter patter of Pixie's feet following my trail. I snuck into the bathroom before my parents spotted me, allowing Pixie to follow me inside. I shut the door.

"Bad girl," I said. She looked up and rubbed her furry neck against my ankle.

I didn't know what Mom meant about the squirrel, but I had an idea. Was Dad worried about having Brian around Pixie? Around animals in general? Brian had always acted cruelly to me, but I didn't think he was capable of hurting anyone else. A few weeks later, we learned I wasn't Brian's only target. And this time Mom and Dad couldn't ignore it.

Earlier that day, the three of us—Mom, Dad and I—trekked to the team's regional tournament in Orlando. Wilsonville won by twenty points, Brian being responsible for many of the goals. We all cheered. I couldn't help but feel proud when I saw him on the court. For those brief moments, he wasn't my antagonist. The team had already booked a room for the night and would be returning by bus the following day. It was after midnight when we arrived home, exhausted and craving sleep.

At 5 a.m., the phone rang. It was Coach Lawson, with news that an incident had occurred in one of the hotel rooms. He wouldn't give Dad many specifics—didn't have many concrete details himself—but said Dad needed to return to Orlando to retrieve Brian. Apparently Dad was one of multiple parents to receive a phone call that night.

By the time Dad and Brian returned, we had at least some idea of what had happened. Some of the upperclassmen on the team, Brian included, had snuck alcohol into the hotel room.

They encouraged the younger members of the team to drink in excess. Logan Hunt drank so much he passed out. He ended up in the hospital with alcohol poisoning. That was why everyone got caught, and that was why Dad and the other parents received phone calls.

"What the hell were you thinking?" Dad shouted. He displayed the kind of anger that attracts anyone within hearing distance to come closer.

"We were just having fun," Brian said. He sat on the living room recliner with his arms crossed over his chest.

I sat on the staircase, so he couldn't see me. I had a full view of Dad's angered pacing and Mom's hysterical crying.

"They want to suspend you for the rest of the season," Mom said, choking on her words. "You should have known better than to do something like this on a school trip."

"He should have known better, period," Dad said, jerking his head in Mom's direction. He clenched his jaw and cleared his throat before looking back at Brian. "You're lucky the police aren't involved. That boy could have been seriously hurt."

"It's not my fault he can't handle alcohol," Brian said in a melodic tone.

"That's not the point," Mom said, looking at Dad for help.

"According to your coach, you hadn't even been drinking," Dad said. "You and another boy simply supplied the alcohol."

"That's why I don't understand why you're even mad at me," Brian said, throwing a pillow on the ground. "I didn't even do anything wrong."

"You are supposed to be a team leader. You snuck alcohol into that room and let a boy drink until he was hospitalized," Dad said.

"So dramatic." Brian leaned back in the recliner and started rocking.

"Where did you even get the alcohol?" Mom asked.

"It's not like we're talking about weapons of mass destruction," Brian said. "It was a bunch of teenagers getting loaded in a hotel room. Everyone is overreacting. Whatever happened to team bonding?"

"If it was about bonding, then why weren't you drinking?" Dad didn't pace anymore. He stood still, staring at Brian and waiting for an answer. He'd picked up on something. Brian wasn't getting wasted like a typical teenager. He was orchestrating the chaos and watching madness unfold. Something far more disturbing.

"Dunno," Brian said, shrugging his shoulders.

Dad kept staring at him, while Mom moved closer. "Don't you see what you've done to the school? You should have been celebrating your victory, and now you won't be able to play the rest of the season. You've let your whole team down."

"Our team won regionals, but we're not good enough to advance. This was our big game and we all know it. We *were* celebrating—"

"Don't do that," Dad shouted, interrupting Brian. "Don't patronize your mother."

Brian sighed. "It's not my fault they won't let me play. They're only punishing us because Hunt went to the hospital. They're trying to make an example out of us."

"As they should," Dad said.

"I need some air." Mom walked through the kitchen and out the backdoor. She was humiliated by the whole experience. She'd spent years bragging about Brian's athletic accomplishments; she wasn't looking forward to telling those same people her son was no longer allowed to play.

"Don't you see that what you did is wrong?" Dad asked. His voice was sincere. "You should have been looking out for your teammates, not pressuring them to do things that could get them in trouble. Now you're paying the price."

"I'm not paying anything," Brian said. He stood up. "My ACT scores are high enough I'll get into college with or without sports. No one's got the best of me."

I understood Brian in a different way that night. I think Dad did, too. Or maybe this was the part of Brian he'd always feared. There was no guilt about what happened. Brian knew he didn't have to hurt to inflict pain. Logan Hunt proved that. Brian punished that boy for being weak, as though Logan were no different from a squirrel or a dog.

Brian was right. His popularity wasn't hurt. Logan Hunt—who received an unflattering nickname following the incident—paid the price, alongside his other teammates who'd been punished, the ones with a less than stellar academic record.

By Monday, everyone at school knew what Brian and the others had done. They talked about it with pride, like sneaking alcohol into a hotel room was as worthy of praise as winning the game.

I still had to attend Coach Lawson's history class that day. We avoided each other most of the period. It was awkward, and we both felt it. He finally addressed me at the end of class.

"Hey, Baby B." He stood in front of the door, stopping me from entering the hall. "I don't want you to be angry with me, you know, over Brian. I was only doing what I had to do."

Of course I wouldn't be angry with him. What Brian and his friends had done was illegal, immoral and put the entire team at risk, not to mention Logan Hunt.

"I understand," I said.

"Brian's one of the best players we've had in years. I understand he and his friends were just having fun. I'm still hoping he'll play with us again next year."

Just having fun. Another player ended up in the hospital. They'd pressured him, taunted him. Brian deserved to be punished. "What about Logan?"

"He's young. Probably embarrassed everything came back on him."

What he said didn't sit right, but it was true. Everyone at school treated Logan like he was the screw-up for getting sick, not Brian and his friends for causing it.

"You know, I don't think what happened was an accident," I said, glancing into the hallway through the narrow window on the door. "I think some of the boys might have targeted Logan."

"Targeted? Baby B, what are you talking about?"

"I know Brian had it out for Logan. He said Logan kept messing with him at practice and stuff."

"They're a team. Any frustrations stay on the court. Other than that, they have each other's backs." Lawson shook his head and crossed his arms. "I know it might not make sense to someone who isn't used to sports."

Sure, I was a girl and no expert on athletics, but I was an expert when it came to Brian. I knew what he did had nothing to do with *fun* and *team*. He was looking out for himself. He was getting even.

"I don't think so, Coach. You don't know Brian the way I do. This is what he does when he feels threatened. He lashes out at people. I hate that these other boys were punished all because Brian had it out for Logan."

Coach Lawson looked at the ceiling and whistled. "Geez, Della. Paranoid much? I know he's your brother, but I've had Brian as a student and a player. He's a good kid. What happened this weekend was just boys messing around. Hell, you should have seen the stuff I got into with my friends back in the day." He looked as though he was hoping I'd ask, all too happy to share the details of his misspent youth.

"Brian doesn't mess around. He hurt Logan on purpose. I'm telling you—" I stopped talking when I saw the look on Lawson's face. A mix of annoyance and shock. He didn't believe me, thought there was something wrong with me that I'd even suggest it.

"Look, I know it's not easy growing up in someone's shadow," he said in the most professional tone I'd ever heard him use. "That's no reason to kick your brother when he's down."

I nodded, leaving the room without saying anything else. I looked back to see that disbelieving look still on Lawson's face. It was the same look he gave me the rest of the semester.

CHAPTER 11

On Tuesday, my thoughts revolve around Darcy. How she's healing. What she's feeling. I wonder if she's remembered anything else about the attack but is not willing to come forward. High school is a brutal time. So much shame is brewed between these walls. I think of the pictures passed around at the party. If Darcy already thinks she's a joke, I understand why she wouldn't want to throw the label of victim into the mix.

After school, I have a therapy session with Dr. Walters. I arrive at her office, which happens to be one of the downstairs rooms of her massive house. It's a beautiful place, and I can't help but think the surroundings contributed to my liking her more than any of the other therapists I visited.

Dr. Walters opens the front door. Her auburn curls fall over her shoulders, and she's always wearing glasses with different colored rims. Today's are teal.

"Welcome, Della," she says, stepping back to let me in.

"Sorry again about last week," I say. "It's not like me to double-book."

"Perfectly fine," she says in her calming voice. "I'm happy to see you again."

One hour every two weeks is our standard amount of time together. It's helpful having a person, other than Danny, I can speak with about whatever's going on in my life. Keeping my emotions bottled up increases my volatility. In the years following Brian's arrest, I found it hard to trust people. Neighbors. Classmates. In my fragile, adolescent mind, they were all threats. Committing to ongoing therapy is one way to keep those negative feelings at bay. We don't always discuss Brian. In fact, we rarely do. I'm not in therapy for him; I'm in it for me.

We spend the first half hour discussing our normal lineup: always a few introductory comments about the weather, work, my stress levels. Danny. I tell her about the guest room we're completing, and she breaks role long enough to tell me about a great antiquing spot in the area.

"Anything else on your mind you'd like to discuss?" she asks, sliding her glasses back to the top of her nose.

"Not really," I say, laughing nervously. "I'm sorry you have such a boring patient."

"Never boring. I look forward to our time together," she says, smiling. "You seem more anxious today than you have in previous sessions."

I notice my tapping foot. I've also bitten my fingernails down to nubs. "Sorry," I say, shaking my head.

"Don't apologize," she says, sitting back. She stares at me, inviting me to share what's going on in my head. She knows I'm holding back. I'm so rarely bothered by anything anymore, that when I am, it shows.

"There's this student," I start, not knowing how much of the story I plan on revealing. "Something happened to her."

Dr. Walters locks into her listening position, that's what I call it anyways. When her legs are crossed, and she's got one arm propped under her chin. That's how she sits for long intervals when she wants me to continue speaking.

"I chaperoned the Spring Fling dance on Saturday," I say. "After the dance, one of my students hosted a party. And she was attacked. She's not saying exactly what happened, but it appears her leg was cut." I look away.

"My goodness," Dr. Walters says, covering her heart. I'm certain she's heard worse stories, but they usually aren't delivered by me. "That poor girl."

"I've not seen her yet," I say. "She hasn't been at school. But I can't stop thinking about what happened to her. Victory Hills is such a pampered place, for teachers and students. I've never dealt with this before in a professional arena."

"But you have dealt with this in your personal life," she says. "Do you think that's why it's bothering you so much?"

"I don't know," I answer, honestly. It's impossible not to think about how things unfolded with Brian, and how I made everything worse. "Maybe. I know *I've* never been victimized like that. I can't really understand what she's experienced. But obviously I see the connections to my past."

"What does Danny think?"

"I haven't told him."

"Huh." The sound comes out like a question. She transitions into thinking position, which is a lot like listening position, except she tilts her head a little more to the side.

"It's not come up," I say, picking at my fingers. "Besides, I usually leave work stuff at school."

"But you've not been able to leave this event at school, have you?"

I had trouble sleeping last night. I kept thinking about Darcy, how happy and carefree she looked in the hallway at Spring Fling. A little mischievous, sure. But being a mischievous teenager shouldn't be a punishable offense. I imagined her in the gymnasium, flitting about with confidence, controlling the room. All attributes which had been taken from her that same night.

"It's bothered me, yes," I say.

"Do you think it's because her attack is so similar to the crimes Brian committed?"

I see Brian's face. Not the dominant, controlling one I witnessed throughout my childhood. I revisit the happy smirk he showed the world. The smirk that likely got him in contact with those girls. How many of them had been like Darcy? Were they beautiful and full of promise before Brian got his hands on them?

"I don't think I want to connect the two," I say, grinding my teeth. "But yes, there are similarities."

"I'm surprised you didn't tell me about this incident at the beginning of our session," Dr. Walters says. "And I think it's odd you've not discussed the matter with Danny. This must have been a huge trigger for you. Usually you're good at identifying such situations and dealing with them."

"I am dealing with this," I say, trying not to sound as offended as I am. "I'm just dealing with it myself. I don't want Danny to think there's something wrong with me."

"I understand no one at your school knows about your past."

"They don't," I say, firmly. Even though I am friends with Marge and Pam, I want them to interact with the woman I am today, not be influenced by my history.

"I understand why you don't want to disclose certain details, but I hope you will use your personal experience to help this student moving forward. You have a very different understanding of her situation compared to your other colleagues. You could provide some great insight. Be an excellent sounding board. When she's ready, of course."

"Thank you," I say, feeling silly for not having mentioned my feelings about Darcy earlier. I'm not sure how I thought Dr. Walters would react. Part of me worries I'll somehow turn people against me, even Dr. Walters and Danny. I don't want anyone to look at me like I'm pitiful again. The exact stigma Darcy wants to avoid.

"Does anyone know who might have attacked this girl?" Dr. Walters asks, returning to listening position.

"No," I say. "She's very hesitant about admitting what happened."

"Makes sense," she says, looking down, no doubt thinking about past patients and their stories. "You would be useful in that area, too."

"Excuse me?"

"You could help her come to terms with her attacker. Realize she did nothing wrong, that the person who did this was likely wired that way."

"I see," I say, looking away. I'm not really sure how to take this. Being Brian's sister doesn't make it easier to empathize with people like him. I don't think I'll ever be able to understand them.

"Not to overload you with tasks," she says, then laughs. "I just think it's beneficial whenever you can take your past and use it to bring positivity to the world."

Dr. Walters' words dance in my mind, even after I leave her office. What she says is uplifting. But the reason I don't buy into the notion that my experience could "serve a purpose" is because that means surrendering to another idea. The idea that what those girls went through happened for a reason. I don't want to think that way, that somehow their pain and suffering contributed to a greater good. A better world—in which they no longer existed. I don't want to think Darcy, who'd been found alone and bleeding, was forced into that state simply to spare another girl the experience.

At night, as I struggle to find sleep with Danny's arm slumped over my hips, I look at Dr. Walters' suggestion from a different perspective. Perhaps my purpose wasn't to inject positivity in the world. Even my story, with whatever helpful nuggets it may hold, can only be shared after another person's tragedy takes place. I can't help victims make sense of their pain when I can't understand it myself. I can't relate to victims, but I can relate to attackers because I grew up alongside one. And I saw Brian before anyone else did.

In all the discussions I'd had about Darcy's predicament, with Principal Bowles and Pam and Dr. Walters, their primary concern had been the victim. As it should be. But their ignorance over whom to blame helps mask the culprit. I know what happens when people fail to interpret warning signs. Lives are lost, and I'm already haunted by the reminder I didn't act fast enough last time. Someone hurt Darcy Moore, and as unbelievable as it seems, someone at our school was likely involved. As I sink into sleep, I picture all their faces. Darcy in the purple dress and Adam with his arms around her. Melanie with her curly updo. I think of Principal Bowles, clenching his fists behind his desk. And I think of Zoey and her smug smile.

CHAPTER 12

Now

On Wednesday, Adam returns to class. He takes his familiar seat in the back. The seat next to him—Darcy's seat—remains ominously empty. I'm dreading her return to school, but Adam's presence gives me and the rest of the class an idea of what to expect. No one openly stares at him, but every so often a head turns in his direction.

I redirect their curious minds to our work. "We're going to continue reading *The Crucible* today," I say. "Would you rather read independently again, or work in small groups?"

"Groups," a zoo of voices echoes back.

"All right." I open my book and tell them where to turn. They move to their seats, and I take their willingness to work together as a sign we're moving forward. We'll have to, especially when Darcy returns to class.

The only one who doesn't move is Adam. He remains seated, the textbook in front of him closed. Without attracting the attention of the other students, I walk back to his desk.

"Would you rather read alone?" I ask him, my voice low. Truthfully, I don't care if he reads today; I know he has more serious topics on his mind. But Adam also must realize he can't dwell on what's happened. Sometimes the most insignificant events can take a person back to a neutral place, even completing his or her first block reading assignment.

"Yes, I would." He clears his throat and opens his book. It's almost like he was in some type of trance and my comment ended it. Adam's phone buzzes against the desk, grabbing both of our attentions. Without reading the message, he takes the phone and places it in his pocket. He looks across the room at Zoey, and I do the same.

Zoey has her phone out, her fingers tapping quickly across the screen. Is she messaging Adam? All of his other classmates are actively avoiding him. Zoey barely knows Adam. She turns, her eyes beady, and catches us both staring at her.

"Phones away," I say. I address the entire class, although the announcement has a clear target. By the time I walk by her desk, her phone is out of sight.

The next day, Adam is more angry than unengaged. He sits in the back of the room, resembling a volcano on the verge of erupting. He's got all the characteristics: tight mouth, clenched fists, tremoring leg. Every few seconds, he takes a deep breath and stares at the floor. I'm not sure who is setting him off, but I notice his eyes consistently flit toward Zoey. Was she messaging him yesterday, after all?

"Is everything all right?" I hiss when I pass Adam's desk. Half of my other students are plugged into their earbuds, silently reading Act Four while their music blares. Adam's ears are bare. When I speak, his head turns, although he doesn't look at me.

"I'm fine," he responds through gritted teeth.

As he says the words, his eyes dart, again, in Zoey's direction. Like the others, Zoey now has two strings hanging from her ears, her fingers tapping on the book as she reads. I wonder whether she's listening to music at all. Maybe she hears me checking on Adam. I'm not sure why I think that, but I do.

Adam opens his book and starts flipping pages. I can tell something is bothering him, something more than just Darcy. Something specific. Perhaps, someone.

*

When the lunch bell rings, I open my miniature refrigerator and find it's empty. My mind has been so scattered lately, I forgot to pack lunch. I open my wallet, which thankfully has cash in it. I suppose I'll be scoring a tray from the cafeteria today. I'm usually good about packing lunch, and I always try to cook double of whatever Danny and I eat for dinner so that I can have leftovers. However, I haven't been cooking as often as I did before break. I've been so exhausted by the time I return home.

I enter the crowded cafeteria and bypass the student line. I'm about to drop a slimy mound of green beans on my tray when I hear a shout. Toward the doors, I see Adam, Zoey and a posse of other students. They're standing in that territorial circle which only forms when something bad is about to happen. I rush to the doors, throwing my tray in the trash as I go. As I approach the group, I see Adam take a step closer to Zoey. His clamped jaw and narrowed eyes worry me.

"That's enough," I say, standing in between Zoey and Adam. "Everyone, sit down."

"Yeah, take a seat, Adam," Zoey says, but she's not reinforcing my commands. She's taunting him. Ever since Darcy's attack, Zoey seems to be at the center of drama. Devon, standing beside her, laughs.

"Adam." I pull him out of the cafeteria and into the hallway. I see the huddle of students standing by the door and turn my attention toward them. "Go eat lunch," I shout. "Now."

When the cafeteria door shuts, the lunchroom noise instantly eases. Now I'm staring at this six-foot-two athlete leaning defeatedly against a row of lockers, caving into himself.

"Adam," I begin again. "What is going on?"

He huffs for a few seconds, regaining the composure he'd lost. As earlier, I suspect he is going to respond with *Nothing*. But that would be pointless, and we both know it. Starting the conversation with a student is usually the hardest part. Once they start talking, they want to say more and more. Completely get their feelings off their chests. A catharsis.

"You know about what happened to Darcy," he says. When he looks up at me, I see tears in his eyes. The volcano from earlier has finally erupted: anger, followed by tears. This tall, agile boy shows emotion shamelessly. "Well, some people at school think I'm the one who hurt her. That new girl keeps making comments about it."

That new girl. Zoey. I know I must tread lightly for multiple reasons. Not only am I dealing with a highly sensitive student, he's just admitted that, at least in the minds of some people, he could have been involved with Darcy's attack.

"Why would people say that?" I ask. Specifically, why would Zoey, a girl no one here really knows, say that?

"Zoey is always trying to stir up problems. She even talks about her teachers. She said she researched a bunch of them before she moved here. Ms. Helton. Principal Bowles. Coach Gabe. She thinks it makes her look cool to know stuff about people. I think it's not right."

Students don't typically take such an interest in their teachers. They don't collect their secrets. Zoey likely wants to learn about people so she can use the information against them. Not right, indeed.

"Now she's talking about me. People think I hurt Darcy because she is my girlfriend. *Was* my girlfriend." He pauses. "She broke up with me after what happened. But we were together the night of the dance."

"Darcy might need space now," I say, feeling the need to defend her.

"I know that," he says, still looking down. "I don't blame Darcy for ending things. She knows I would never hurt her, but people around here are so simple-minded. They think I attacked her because we got into a fight at the party." He stops talking, clenches his fists and looks away. "I wish I knew who hurt her. Because if I did, I'd go after him. I'd hurt him like he hurt her."

"Don't say that, Adam." I understand his desire to get even. Who wouldn't want to hurt the person responsible for injuring the person they loved?

"I didn't hurt Darcy," he continues, as though he didn't hear anything I said. "But I blame myself. She made me mad and I left the party. If I'd stayed, she would have never been attacked."

"Don't think that way. Whatever happened to Darcy… you didn't cause it."

"Well, everyone thinks I did. And they won't leave me alone about it. They're leaving stupid letters in my locker, sending me messages, whispering stuff under their breath in class—"

"You should talk to Ms. Pam. She's the best at dealing with school issues like this."

"It's not just at school," he says, slamming his fist against a locker. He realizes he's startled me and takes a calming breath. He moves closer and whispers, "I think someone killed my cat."

I pause, lean back to get a better look at the frazzled teenager in front of me. His eyes are wild, and his skin is red from crying, but he looks wholly convinced—even scared—by what he just said.

"Why do you think that?"

"Well, the cat's dead, for starters. I found her by the road in front of my house. But it doesn't make sense. Tabs—that was her name—never walked to the road. She hardly ever left the porch. Besides, I live in the country. We rarely have cars pass the house, and when they do, they're not going so fast they can't see a cat."

"Are you sure it's not a coincidence?" I hate that I'm even asking the question. I'm now treating Adam the same way I've been treated in the past. Like I'm trying too hard to make events seem connected.

"I knew when I found Tabs it wasn't an accident. The next morning, I found a rock behind my car. And there was a… slur written on it."

"What did it say?"

He looks away from me, then at the ground, ashamed of what he says next. "It said… well, it's a word for a cat but can also be used to describes a girl's—"

"I get it," I say, raising my hands to stop him.

The red in his cheeks deepen. "Interesting choice of words considering my cat just died, huh? People are messing with me because they think I hurt Darcy."

I no longer feel right in telling Adam he is wrong. That he is being paranoid or emotional. Based on what he said, I believe him.

"You need to tell Ms. Pam about this," I say. "All of it."

"Thank you, Mrs. Mayfair," he says, smoothing his forehead. "I'm sorry for causing a scene in there."

"Go eat lunch," I say. "Stay away from trouble."

He nods, opens the door and leaves the hallway. I walk back to my classroom, my appetite gone. I can't tell Adam I believe he really did leave the party that night, unaware of the dangerous predicament Darcy was left in. I can't tell him I think he's right about his cat, that someone really would be cruel enough to harm his pet in hopes of teaching him a lesson. And I can't tell him I think I know who that person might be.

I'm worried for him. I'm also worried about what Zoey may have unearthed. If she's digging up dirt on her teachers, what might she have found about me?

CHAPTER 13

Now

This isn't the first time I've been concerned Zoey might know about my past. It started when she mentioned Florida. If what Adam says is true—that Zoey is looking into the lives of her teachers—then she must know about Brian. The average person may not identify me as Brian's sister, but anyone digging could find out.

I'm staring at the computer screen, seeing nothing. My mind has been pulled in a dozen directions this week. The tiniest occurrence gets me thinking about Darcy, which gets me thinking about Brian. Once I go down that path, my brain might as well be stuck in 2006. Now I'm bothered by what Zoey might know, too. A shift of light pulls my attention to the left, and I see Melanie is standing by my computer.

"What?" I ask, harsher than I should.

"I asked, where do you want me to put this?" She must have been standing there a second. All while her loopy English teacher stares blankly ahead. Now she has my attention, and she's still looking at me, waiting for an answer.

"I'm sorry, Melanie," I say, clearing my throat. "I'm zoning out for some reason."

"That's fine, Mrs. Mayfair," she says, raising the paper in her hand. "It's just, I finished my rough draft last night."

Of course, you did, Melanie, I think. "If you're happy with it, go ahead and place it in the basket by the door."

"Thank you, Mrs. Mayfair," she says, returning to her computer and pulling up what looks like an incomplete PowerPoint.

Because it's Friday, I've arranged for students to work in the computer lab. They're starting their final research essay relating to *The Crucible*. I'm already dreading grading them. Classic literature doesn't get old to me but reading my students' varied analyses eventually does. I've had my fill of reading essays about the Salem Witch *Trails*. Who knew the Puritans were such avid hikers?

I stroll around the room. All around me, students type on their keyboards. Adam didn't come to school today. I suppose two days was all he could handle this week. I worry about him grieving Darcy while simultaneously defending himself against the whole school.

"How long does this have to be?" asks Ben.

"As long as it needs to be," I say, wishing my students would focus more on content than word count. But I know, in their impatient minds, they need parameters for when the job is done. "Think around fifteen hundred words."

"All right," Zoey says, typing away. "When is it due?"

"You should finish the rough draft today. I'll read them over the weekend. Depending on our schedule, we might look into revising them sometime next week."

I realize, after I've shared the timeline, that Darcy will be back by then. This already seems like the longest week ever. I'll have to come up with an alternate assignment for her. I can't have her writing about women who weren't believed—or in some cases, women who were believed for the wrong reasons. I hope other teachers will make accommodations and acknowledge all the triggers she'll be hitting throughout the day.

When I return to my seat, I see Zoey is still watching me. She senses something is wrong. I'm sure all my students have picked up on my attitude, but Zoey is lingering around it. Poking it. Trying to figure me out. I hold her gaze until she returns to typing.

When class dismisses, only half the group has complete drafts. The other half whine about wanting more time. It's always the students that waste the first twenty minutes of class who demand an extension.

"The bell is about to ring," I announce. "Place your essays in the basket by the door."

The sound of groaning doesn't leave me very optimistic about what I'm about to grade.

"Have a good one," Ben says on his way out, tipping his head as though he's wearing an invisible hat. Devon's staring at her phone, shuffling her feet.

"Happy reading," says Zoey. I smile instinctively, the grin dropping as soon as she's gone. I don't trust this girl. I'm fearful of what she might know.

My second and third blocks complete the same assignment and turn in their papers. By the time my planning begins, my ass is sore from sitting in the tight computer chair all day. I gather my belongings, around sixty essays and my coffee tumbler to make the trek back to my classroom for my planning period. I'm not ready to start grading, though. Instead, I log into my classroom computer and start googling potential locations for our summer vacation; it's been over a week since I told Danny I'd create an itinerary, and all that I have produced is a paper labeled: *France and Spain.*

Normally, I look forward to organizing vacations. I put more time into planning our honeymoon than I did our wedding. The ceremony was small, with less than twenty guests in attendance. We married in a chapel near Danny's medical school campus. It seemed like the perfect excuse for avoiding a hometown affair. Danny was already so busy with his studies, and I'd recently graduated and moved there to be with him.

Most girls dream of their wedding day, and maybe I used to be one of those girls, too. But once the day came, I no longer cared about some fancy social gathering. More than anything, I wanted the day to be over. I think I would have avoided a wedding entirely, but Danny's parents wanted a reason to celebrate. It wasn't fair for me to rob them of the experience simply because I wanted to avoid attachments to Wilsonville. One of my sorority sisters, a girl I've not spoken to in over five years, served as my Maid of Honor. Mom was my only family member in attendance. The entire day was a bubble of anxiety waiting to burst.

But the honeymoon, that was my opportunity to truly celebrate. Of course, we had to schedule it months after the wedding, when Danny's school schedule allowed him a two-week absence. Then we took off. We flew to Paris for a few days. We took all the typical pictures at the Eiffel Tower and strolled the historic streets of Montmartre. Then we flew to Rome, which had been Danny's favorite. After we'd had our fill of museums and history tours, we spent our remaining week exploring everything from Tuscan vineyards to Venetian shorelines.

Remembering the trip still produces a smile. I think that was when I felt I'd truly made it as an adult. Made it as a wife. Made it as a person other than Brian's sister. And every vacation since then, whether it's spring break in Hilton Head or a long weekend trapped away in some Virginian lodge, has reinforced the person I've become.

After several minutes of lazy daydreaming, I pull out the essays and decide to grade them. I'm still not inspired to make any concrete decisions about the trip. And frankly, fantasizing about such glamorous possibilities seems unfair given the climate of the past week.

I figure, if I start a rapid reading session now, I might be able to get through at least half of the essays before the weekend officially begins. The sixth essay I pull is Zoey's, and I realize, given her newness, this is her first writing sample I've assessed. She's displayed intelligence during classroom discussions, and her learning group assignments are always orderly and complete. After the first few paragraphs, I can tell she is a strong writer, too. There are minor grammar mistakes, but her comprehension and syntax are on level, if not advanced.

The clock says there's only a half hour left before the dismissal bell rings. I pick through the pile of essays, selecting students whose writing I believe I'll be able to grade the fastest. The next one I pull looks as though it has largely been lifted from the internet. I sigh and shake my head, marking the paper as a reminder to search for plagiarized portions online later.

I pull another piece of paper and immediately sigh in frustration. It's only one sheet, and there's not even writing on the back. We've devoted an entire day to these essays, and one of my students has only managed to produce a few lousy paragraphs. My frustrations build further when I realize there's no name on the paper, either. I understand we're nearing the end of the semester, but is it too much to ask for minimal effort?

I start reading, almost nervous to see what poor topic this student must have chosen:

We go outside. She stumbles, no longer fit to run.

I sit back and shake my head. What the hell is this? Why is it shuffled in between stacks of research essays?

People see her beauty. People see her wealth. I see her meanness. Behind the pretty purple, there's nothing but weak.

Purple. Darcy flashes before my mind. Her satin gown with that bronzed leg poking out, the same leg that was slashed hours later. Is someone writing about her?

I'll make her feel her ugly. The world will see her meanness.

I throw down the paper, tears falling from my face. This is the attack. All the details the school is unsure about, all the details Darcy can't remember, are written on this paper. This is someone's confession. But they're not trying to clear their conscience. They're trying to disturb mine.

I refuse to continue reading. I don't want to know the details; it's too painful. High school students can be ugly to each other, and, on occasion, their teachers. But I can't imagine any of my students making fun of Darcy's situation, especially considering the dim light the school has shed on the matter. Their cruelty would typically be saved for their peers, a crude joke when they think no adult is watching.

No, whoever wrote this essay is *trying* to bother me. They're dangling their confession in front of my face, hoping I won't be able to figure out who wrote it. I recall my rosters. I've had most of these students in class for weeks; I can't imagine any of them would write something like this. Adam, the person everyone believes attacked Darcy, was noticeably absent today.

In the past five years, there has been only one student whom I consider cruel enough to write such a letter. Only one student has ever reminded me of Brian. Zoey. It must be. She'd only been at Victory Hills for a week when Darcy was attacked. She's managed to get her classmates and other teachers to like her, but the charade doesn't fool everyone. It doesn't fool me. When people heard Darcy Moore was assaulted at a party, their minds—even mine—went to a male perpetrator; unfortunately, the story is far too common. Based on the circumstances of the attack, a female could just have easily stabbed Darcy.

My mind goes back to first block dismissal and Zoey's smug threat as she left the room. *Happy reading*, she'd said, that glib smile covering her face. Knowing at some point, whether this afternoon or later this weekend within the comfort of my own home, I'd find her confession and freeze. I slam my elbows against the desk and drop my head into my hands. My gut tells me not to trust Bowles with it; he's already adamant about ignoring Darcy's ordeal. Pam would see the seriousness, but I remember she's not here today; she's with Darcy. Telling the police crosses my mind, but I decide to wait. I should see what Pam has to say first.

Guilt rages, again, when I realize Zoey intended this letter for me. There's a reason she isn't messing with Marge or Coach Gabe. I recall my conversation with Zoey earlier in the week when I overheard her make a wry comment about girls not being believed.

I revealed my buttons and now she's pushing. Zoey wants me to be bothered. If she knows about Brian, she knows I won't confront her from fear she'll out my past.

As much as I want to never read the letter again, I realize there might be some clue tangled up with the other sickening words. I take a deep breath and lift the paper. It's only a few paragraphs, but the contents disturb me. Much like reading all those articles over a decade ago. I read as the disgusting writer—already in my mind it's Zoey—describes violating Darcy, slicing her leg. The essay stops abruptly, as I'm imagining the event did in real time. Maybe this was when the police arrived? Perhaps Zoey was interrupted?

By now, I can hardly read because I'm crying so hard. My contacts are blurry. Because, again, I'm not only imagining these events happening to Darcy, but to all those girls back at Sterling Cove University, too. Except this time, Brian isn't the only abuser who enters my mind. Zoey's there, too. Hurting and slicing, smiling at the pain she's caused.

The dismissal bell rings, and I can hear the thunder of feet as students stampede the halls. I'll have to wait several minutes to leave, now. Otherwise my co-workers and students will see my splotchy face and know something is wrong.

I close my eyes, as Dr. Walters has instructed me to do in times of deep stress, and count. *One... two... three.* Within another two minutes, I've regained composure. I've stored the evil contents of the letter away in my mind, with all the other bad memories. I won't read it again, but I will share it with Pam once I have the opportunity. Maybe this letter will confirm what happened during Darcy's attack and urge the authorities to look more closely at who might be responsible.

I immediately backtrack on my thoughts. Not my commitment to speak with Pam, rather my promise not to read the letter again. There's one sentence dancing around in my mind, and I need to read it once more to make sure it's there. That I haven't just made it up in an attempt for the essay to serve a purpose.

I don't focus on the entire thing. I scan the words until I find that one sentence. It reads:

She struggled to get away…

I stop reading. That's the only detail I need. The image of Darcy wriggling beneath her attacker. It's horrifying, but it proves something. It means Darcy wasn't passed out during her attack.

She was awake.

CHAPTER 14

Summer 2004

I'd been nervous around the pool ever since I nearly drowned. I no longer enjoyed swimming. The cool water reminded me of my struggle to breathe.

Still, it was summer in the suburbs and relaxing at the community pool was the best way to pass the time. Amber spent each day tanning, and she made frequent phone calls begging me to join her. I put on a metallic teal bikini and slathered on sunscreen. Dad had bored me enough with the dangers of UV rays.

"Nice outfit," Brian said, leaning against my bedroom doorframe. "You look like a skank."

I was used to this. His frequent name-calling. In the past, I'd say something snarky back or tell Mom. Telling Dad worked better, but even that didn't stop Brian's cruelty.

"Let's go, Pixie," I said. The little dog jumped off my bed and ran around my feet. I nudged Brian's shoulder as I walked past. He lifted his foot and lightly kicked Pixie's back legs.

"Don't do that," I snapped. I could ignore his callousness toward me, but not my dog.

"It was just a little kick."

"Leave her alone," I said.

"She belongs to both of us, you know." He followed me down the stairs, making it impossible for me to have a carefree escape.

"Then why don't you ever help take care of her?"

"Because I don't like dogs." He opened the refrigerator and pulled out a soda. "They're annoying and they stink."

"Pixie doesn't stink. I take good care of her."

"Don't you think it's gross to take a dog to a public pool?"

"She doesn't get in the water." Even though I knew the entire conversation was a ploy to get under my skin, I still felt the need to defend my actions. "Besides, all the little kids love her."

"Wow, Della. You've finally won a popularity contest among preschoolers."

Mom stampeded past both of us. "Anyone seen my keys?" she asked.

"Check the fruit bowl," Brian said.

"Ah hah." She lifted the keys and gave them a hearty jangle. "Della, you look adorable." I think Mom was relieved I finally put more effort into my appearance.

"You think so?" I asked. "Brian seems to disagree."

"She's my little sister," he said, pointing at me. "I don't want people looking at her like that."

Mom walked over to Brian and squeezed his cheeks. "Such a protective older brother."

As usual, Brian had switched his demeanor in enough time to look like a hero instead of an ass. The tattletale inside me wanted Mom to know what he'd really said. "He's not being protective—"

"Enough. I'm late," Mom said, raising her hand. "Wait and see, Della. One day you'll be thankful to have an older brother. No one will think of messing with you."

I huffed and turned. I followed Mom out the door before Brian had a chance to bother me.

I always thought I looked womanly until I saw Amber in a swimsuit. The breasts she'd had since middle school were getting bigger, and her daily tanning ritual made her appear slimmer. Like Mom said, I was adorable. Cute. Amber was hot.

"There she is," she said when I arrived. Pixie scampered to her lounge chair and nipped at her fingers. "Hi, Pixie."

"How long have you been here?" I asked.

"Since eight."

"You'll be a strip of bacon before summer is over."

"I'll be fine," she said, raising a hand to block the sun. "I want to look my best when we return to school. We'll be driving soon, you know."

"You don't turn sixteen until May."

"Yeah, well. A girl can dream. Speaking of dreaming…" she said, nodding toward the pavilion. Sitting at a table was Jeremy Gus. "Look who I've been staring at all morning."

Jeremy Gus was a college freshman. He'd moved to the neighborhood only a few months ago. We'd seen him jogging around the neighborhood, although we wouldn't dare speak to him. Not only was he older, he was too cute. He was tall and muscular with tight blond curls. Dreamboat status, even I had to admit.

"Got the nerve to talk to him yet?" I asked, already knowing the answer. Even Amber wasn't that ballsy.

"Please," she said, leaning back and closing her eyes. "I wouldn't even know what to say to a man like that."

As much as Amber talked about boys, she was still a virgin. We both were. I'd never even kissed a boy. I'd be lucky if my first kiss could be with a boy like that. I leaned back and started slathering my body with tanning oil. I was soon as slimy as Amber's skin—or like the watermelon's shell that day.

I listened as Pixie barked at a trio of toddlers in the baby pool. They giggled and squealed, and their moms seemed to approve. Once the group started packing away their belongings to leave, Pixie circled the parameter of the pool. I shut my eyes again, the sun's rays burning orange against my closed lids. Moments later, I sensed a shadow and the prickling sense that someone was standing nearby.

I opened my eyes and saw Jeremy Gus. I jumped.

"Sorry," he said, flattening his hands. "It's just me."

Amber heard the voice and flinched when she saw who was hovering over us.

"I'm Jeremy," he said, reaching out a hand.

"We know," I said, before my mind could catch up to my thoughts. Jeremy laughed, while Amber shot me a disgusted look. "I'm Della."

"And I'm Amber," she said, lifting her hand to shake his. I'd left my own hand literally hanging.

"Is this your dog?" he asked. Pixie leapt around his ankles. I felt an immediate surge of embarrassment.

"She's mine," I said. "Is she bothering you?"

"No," he said. He sat down on the chair next to mine and lifted Pixie. "She's a cutie. What's her name?"

"Pixie," I said. I smiled so wide my cheeks hurt. I couldn't believe my dog had established the introductions we were too afraid to make. And he liked her. As if Jeremy could get any dreamier.

"I miss my dog," Jeremy said.

"What happened?" Amber said, popping up on her forearm. She was as excited as I was and didn't want to be left out of the conversation.

"Nothing bad. She's just back with my parents."

"Your parents don't live here?" I asked. I couldn't even imagine such an adult world where one could be living on their own without parents.

"No. I live with my aunt. I go to the community college nearby and she's nice enough to let me crash." He thumbed the fur behind Pixie's ear, making her swoon as much as we were.

"What do you study?" Amber asked.

"Photography." He stood and walked back to his chair to retrieve a camera. It was a big professional type with a long lens and strap. "Want to see a picture of my dog?"

"Yes," we said in unison, failing to keep our cool.

He hit buttons until he found the right picture and handed us the camera. It was a Great Dane.

"So sweet," I said.

"I miss her. Seeing this little gal reminded me of her," he said, cuddling Pixie again.

"What other pictures do you take?" asked Amber.

"Anything, really. Pretty landscapes. Cute animals. Now that I'm taking classes, I've even helped with some fashion shoots."

"That's awesome. I'd like to be a model one day," Amber said proudly, although I'd never heard her say that before.

"Well, you're pretty enough," he told her. Then he looked at me. "You both are."

I felt a wave of heat pass through my body, mixed with a twinge of nausea. I wasn't used to boys being this forward. But again, Jeremy wasn't a boy. He was in college. He was a man.

"Thanks," I said.

"You really think so?" Amber asked, needing reassurance.

"Definitely," he said, rubbing Pixie's fur. "I could take your picture. Show you some of the stuff I've learned."

"Really?" Amber sat upright. "That would be amazing."

"I could take some pictures right now, if you want." He put Pixie down and stood, holding his camera.

"Okay," she said. "What should I do?"

"Move over here," he said, pointing to a chair in the corner. "There's better lighting."

Amber did. I stood in the background and watched, half amused, half jealous.

"Now, just stand naturally," he said. Amber obeyed, projecting her hip. "Perfect." He lifted his camera and snapped a few clicks.

"How do I look?"

"Great. Fluff your hair a little bit," he said.

She bent her head over and gave her locks a healthy shake. When she stood upright again, she had renewed confidence.

"Beautiful," he said, snapping more shots. Then he looked at me, "Would you like me to take your picture?"

I was nervous and didn't want to follow Amber. "I'm all right," I said, crossing my arms over my body.

"Come on," he said. "See how easy it is."

Amber looked at me like I was the biggest idiot for not wanting to play along. Especially after Jeremy was kind enough to show us attention on a lazy summer day.

"Okay," I said, standing in the same area where Amber had stood. The place with the good lighting.

"Great," he said, raising the camera to cover his face. "Now just pose naturally. Put some bend in the knees—"

"What the hell are you doing?" Brian shouted. He appeared out of nowhere, standing by the entry gate. His arms were at his sides with clenched fists.

We all jumped. Jeremy lowered the camera and turned around. "Hey, man. Do I know you?" His casual tone was laced with fear.

Brian walked closer, until he stood a few steps in front of Jeremy. "I asked, what the hell are you doing?"

"Brian," I said. "He's just taking pictures."

Brian's body language didn't react to hearing me, although he obviously did. "Is that all you're doing, *man*?" He took another step toward Jeremy. His head inched forward, like an animal about to bite. "Taking pictures?"

"I take photography classes—"

Brian didn't have to say anything for Jeremy to know it was wise to stop talking. He simply raised his hands, and Jeremy backed away.

"Go home," Brian said. "Now."

Jeremy looked down. Without making eye contact, he walked by us and retrieved his remaining belongings from the patio table.

He slung the camera strap around his shoulder and left. Brian's eyes followed him, even after the iron gate rattled shut.

"He's a photographer," Amber said, breaking the silence. "He was only taking our pictures."

"The guy's a fucking freak," Brian said, snapping his head in our direction.

My cheeks burned with embarrassment. "He was only being nice, Brian."

"You girls leave, too." He walked a few steps to where we'd been sitting. He picked up my towel and threw it at me. Amber walked over and grabbed her pool bag. Pixie, who'd been lounging in the shaded grass area during this entire exchange, followed her.

"That was humiliating." My voice was nasal and on the verge of being overcome with tears. I stomped past Brian, who remained standing by our chairs. Amber followed me.

Before closing the gate, I turned to look at Brian. "What are you doing?" I asked.

"Going for a swim," he said. He pulled off his shirt and dove into the water.

Brian frequently took over situations without me fully understanding why. As though he'd felt a surge of insecurity and needed to re-establish his control. He did it with everyone, even Mom and Dad. But he pulled his power card with me more than anyone. I was the younger sister, weaker and less inclined to retaliate. In my mind, I tried to fight back. I'd name-call or tattle or even shove him, at times. But these were useless weapons against Brian's arsenal.

Brian always won, so eventually I just let him. Didn't even ask him why he said the things he said or did the things he did. He did them because he was Brian and because he could. I was probably the only teenager in Wilsonville who wanted school to start back. I'd had enough of long, summer days with Brian. He always behaved worse when he had too much time on his hands.

The night before school started, Mom prepared spaghetti. It wasn't a fabulous dinner, but they seldom were, unless guests were present. It was only the four of us, with Pixie nipping at my feet from under the table.

We usually weren't allowed to watch television during dinner, but Dad had made a request to watch the news. I was half-listening, half-fantasizing about my first day back, when I heard something familiar.

"Turn that up," I said.

Mom put down her fork and attempted to reason with me. "Honey, don't focus on the television—"

"Please, turn it up," I said. "I think I heard something important."

Dad grabbed the remote by his side and increased the volume. We all turned to better hear the program.

"… Wilsonville resident Jeremy Gus was arrested for the solicitation of a minor and possession and distribution of child pornography," the reporter said. Jeremy's portrait filled the screen.

"Is that the boy from the neighborhood?" Mom asked, now wholly invested in the program.

"From our neighborhood?" Dad asked, confused.

"Yeah. I think he lives with the Hendersons a few doors down," she said. "I've seen him jogging around the neighborhood."

"That's him," I said. My stomach twisted. He was the first person I'd known to ever be arrested for a crime.

"Do you know him, sweetie?" Mom asked, her tone sharp.

"Not really," I said. "I talked to him once at the pool."

"What did you talk about?" Dad asked, his voice calm, but I could tell he was afraid of what I might say.

"He… he said he was a photographer," I stammered, feeling an instant urge to cry. "He asked to take our pictures."

Mom leaned back and placed both palms against her temples. "Oh my God! Oh, honey. Oh, no."

Dad reached his hand across the table and held mine. "Honey, tell us exactly what happened. Did he take your picture?"

"No," I said. "I mean, he almost did. But Brian stopped him."

Brian sat between Mom and me. He didn't say anything, raised his fork and put a lump of twirled noodles in his mouth.

"Oh, thank God," Mom said, leaning over and shaking Brian's shoulder. "I can't believe this. A predator living down the street. Preying on our children."

"You said *our* pictures," Dad continued, ignoring Mom. "Was someone else there?"

"Amber," I said. "He took some pictures of her modeling by the pool."

Without saying another word, Mom left the table. She grabbed the portable phone off the wall charger and started dialing.

I didn't want to cause trouble for anyone, especially a friend. "Mom, don't—"

"I'm a mother. I have to let Karen know about this." She disappeared into the hallway, filled with pride over her call to action.

"I'm afraid I agree with her," Dad said. "Her mother needs to know."

"Nothing happened," I said.

"But something terrible could have. We'll talk about this later." Dad sounded like he was choking. He stood and carried his plate into the kitchen. He didn't look at either one of us, too busy processing everything he'd heard. Before he left the kitchen, he said to Brian, "Good looking out."

Tears filled my eyes. I blinked, and one fell onto my forearm. I looked at Brian and his almost finished plate. It was the first time I realized how dangerous the world could be. Somehow, Brian already knew. He could tell there was something off about Jeremy Gus. That Jeremy's friendly demeanor was masking a darker intent. Brian sensed a similar predator and did us a favor in scaring him off.

"How'd you know?" I asked, wondering why in all the time Amber and I had spent staring at our neighbor we'd never seen the monster he was.

"I told you," Brian said. He smirked. "The guy's a fucking freak."

CHAPTER 15

Now

I pick up pizza on my way home, having decided I'm in no mood to cook. Maybe on Saturday, once I've had the opportunity to sleep in and clear my thoughts, I'll feel better.

The pizza is cold when Danny arrives, and I'm already full after eating three slices. I'm sitting on the sofa, nestled under a blanket. I want to fool Danny into thinking there's nothing wrong with me. One of the best and worst things about Danny is he's perceptive. He's seen me go through enough emotional stages that a simple shrug of the shoulders and avoided eye contact won't keep him quiet. Besides, he's sensed my mood has been off for the past week, and he's been kind enough to let it slide. Tonight, he offers no such grace.

"Are you sure there isn't something on your mind?" he asks, sitting beside me on the sofa holding a plate of reheated pizza. Instead of taking a bite, which I'm sure his stomach is grumbling to do, he looks at me. Wanting a response.

"There's been stuff going on at school," I answer, reluctantly. I sit up straighter, gearing up for a discussion.

"What stuff?" he asks, taking a bite of pizza. He seems pleased I'm not brushing him off.

"Remember when I chaperoned Spring Fling last week?" I ask. "After the dance, one of our students was attacked."

"Oh my gosh," he says, melty cheese still poking out of his mouth. He uses a hand to cover the lower half of his face. "Attacked how?"

"She threw a party at her house. When she passed out, someone cut her leg." This was the short version, but I needed him to understand why the event bothered me as much as it did. "I'm afraid one of our other students might have been involved."

Danny's eyes bulge as he wipes the corners of his mouth. He places his plate beside him, and I feel guilty for having ruined his appetite. "Are the police investigating?"

"The police found her. Someone must have called in a noise complaint about the party. If they hadn't arrived, the outcome could have been far worse." My mind revisits the grim details in the essay. "The girl is now *claiming* she wasn't attacked. She says she hurt her leg in a fall."

"Claiming?"

I sigh. "I think she remembers more than she's saying." I know I haven't talked to Darcy myself, but what I read provided insight into what might have happened. "She's just not ready to come forward."

"I see," he says, looking down. I know he's thinking about someone else now. I'm thinking about her, too. "Is she getting help from someone? Is Pam working with her?"

Danny has always had a soft spot for Pam. They've been around one another a few times at different school functions, and once at our house. Their interests of medicine and mental health overlap, although Danny wouldn't know anything about comforting a teenage girl and Pam would gag if she encountered the number of bodily fluids Danny does throughout the day.

"Pam's been involved since the beginning. The parents contacted her after it happened, and she's been counseling the student. Pam was with her today, actually."

"Good. She needs guidance right now more than anything," he says, returning to the pizza. "Everything makes sense now."

"What makes sense?"

"Your attitude this week. It's understandable why an incident like that would rile you up."

"That's what Dr. Walters said, too," I say, sinking lower into the sofa cushion.

"Well, at least you told *her*," Danny says, his tone hurt.

"What does that mean?"

"You said this happened a week ago, right? I'm surprised it's taken you this long to tell me. Usually you're more upfront about things."

Now he sounds exactly like Dr. Walters, as though I've done something wrong in not sharing this with him sooner.

"Well, I'm telling you about it now," I say, feeling the pressure to regain Danny's approval. "And I think I know who might have attacked her."

He stops eating again and stares at me. "Who?"

"Do you remember that new student I told you about last week?"

"The one who said *fuck* in class?" Danny asks, laughing. "Yeah, I remember."

"I told you she rubbed me wrong from day one. She's done more stuff since then."

"Like what?"

"Well, her in-class behavior is as crass as ever. Then she was caught with a knife on the school bus. Bowles, of course, barely punished her," I say. "And she's made insensitive comments about the attack."

"The knife incident is troubling." He crumples his napkin, places it on the plate. "Wait, you think *a girl* attacked this student?"

I clench my jaw and close my eyes. I know it sounds unbelievable. Untraditional. There isn't enough linking Zoey to the attack yet. "I think this girl—Zoey is her name—is disturbed."

"I'm not saying you're wrong..." Danny pauses, forming his words precisely. "I didn't think girls typically did that sort of thing. You know, with the violence."

"That's why I'm afraid to tell people my theory. No one will take it seriously. Half the school seems convinced the girl's ex-boyfriend attacked her, but I don't believe he has it in him."

"You say this girl—Zoey—is troubled. But why would she go out of her way to hurt another student? There has to be a reason." Danny isn't fully convinced. He's using his pragmatic brain to make sense of everything. "Do you know if Zoey was even at the party?"

"I don't know," I say. "I mean, I've not heard her say."

"That's what you need to find out."

"You're right." I'm frustrated that I'm missing this most basic piece of the puzzle. "But it's all of it together. Zoey is sneaky and smart and able to change her behavior at the drop of a hat. Doesn't that remind you of someone?"

A look washes over his face like I've not seen in years. "Like, your brother? You think Zoey might have attacked one of her classmates because she reminds you of your brother?"

"She reminds me of him in lots of ways. Wouldn't you be nervous if you encountered someone like him?"

"There's been a lot of people who reminded me of him over the years," he says, catching himself. "If you remember, everyone liked him. He was an average guy. No one picked up on the dark stuff."

"And Zoey is exactly like that. The whole school is mesmerized with her because she can sprint and jump hurdles, or whatever. She made the highest grade on Marge's stupid chemistry test. But that's all just a deception."

That remains, still, the scariest part of Brian. That there was a thin line separating him from the rest of society. But that division was important and deliberate. That division helped him mask his monster. And I think Zoey might be following in his footsteps.

"Don't hate me for saying this," Danny begins, cracking his knuckles. "Do you think you just don't like this girl? Maybe your personalities clash."

"I've had several students I didn't particularly care for over the years. But I've never accused them of attacking their classmates. In fact, we didn't have an incident like this at Victory Hills until Zoey showed up."

"I just think throwing a person's name out there can be dangerous. I wish there was a way you could prove this girl was involved."

I walk into the kitchen. Danny remains on the couch, no doubt trying to make sense of everything I've said. I find my school bag and retrieve the anonymous essay. I hand the paper to Danny.

"This is my proof."

He slowly takes the paper from my hands. "What is this?"

"Read it," I say, nodding. "This is what a student turned in today. A student from Zoey's class."

He looks at the paper. He sighs heavily, and after a few seconds starts shaking his head. "Dell, what am I even reading?"

"The girl in the purple dress? That's Darcy. It's describing the attack."

"I don't want to read this," he says, pushing the paper away. "Why would you let me?"

"You're sitting here acting like I'm crazy for thinking Zoey is involved. Look at what I got today. Someone wants to mess with me, and it's more than likely her."

"I never said you were crazy." His voice is lighter, and he stares at me honestly. *Crazy* is a curse word in our house. I spent my whole childhood feeling crazy, like I was the only one who could put together all the disturbing pieces of Brian to see the full picture. "How do you know Zoey wrote the letter?"

"I told you someone shuffled it in with the other essays."

"And there was no name on it?"

"No."

"Don't hate me for this, Dell. But how do you know Zoey wrote it?"

I stare at him, feeling the sudden urge to cry. Earlier, when I thought of Darcy and the pain she experienced that night, I cried from sadness. Now, my tears are arising from a place of anger. I'm livid because I'm confident Zoey did this, and there's no way to prove I'm right. *One... two... three.*

"I have a feeling," I say, finally.

That's enough for Danny. He's a practical person, but he trusts my instincts. "Keep an eye on Zoey. You could very well be right," he says. "I only want to make sure you're handling this the right way."

He rubs the skin from my shoulders down to my elbows. After a few strokes, he pulls me in for a hug. He's trying to mend whatever strings he tore during our debate. He can't validate my suspicions, or erase Darcy's pain; a hug is the best he can give.

CHAPTER 16

Now

I arrive at school early on Monday and wait in the parking lot until I see Pam's dark blue minivan. She often arrives at school early, juggling a slew of different responsibilities. On any given day, I'm performing the same tasks. I'm interacting with students, typing lessons and grading papers. Pam's schedule differs from one week to the next. One day she could be signing students up for classes, the next day she's administering the ACT and she might end the week by making a phone call to Child Protective Services about abuse claims.

I'm sure the last thing she wants is to be bombarded before first block begins. She's probably dreading the arrival of Darcy, which is supposed to be today, even more than I am. At the same time, Pam would want to see this.

Pam gets out of her car, an empty Styrofoam cup falling to the ground as she does. I exit my vehicle, walking straight for her. "You have a second?" I ask.

She's bent over retrieving the cup. She raises her head, sees me and smiles. "Morning, Della. I wish I could talk, but—"

"It's really important," I say, stopping her. I know her morning is busy due to Darcy's return, but I've been holding onto the letter since Friday. I can't stand one more minute of keeping it to myself.

When we enter the building, I don't even bother going to my classroom. Instead, I follow Pam to her office. She fiddles with the lock, and I push the door open for her as she puts the items in her hands on the desk.

"So, Della," she says, staring down at her calendar. "What do you want to talk about?"

"I've been wanting to speak with you since Friday," I say. "I didn't want to bother you over the weekend."

"It's no bother, Della," she says, looking up.

I grab the essay from my bag and pass it over. "You need to read this."

She takes the paper, flips it over to inspect the empty back. "What is it?" she asks, looking at me.

"A student turned this in on Friday. They included it in a pile of research essays."

She takes a seat and begins reading. After a few seconds, she covers her mouth, her eyes still studying the page. "You think this is about Darcy?" she asks finally, looking back at me.

"It has to be," I say. "I mean, look at the details. Her dress. The emphasis on her leg. And what are the odds of receiving something like this a week after the attack?"

"And someone just typed this, printed it off and turned it in with the other essays?"

"Well, you know how it is in the computer lab. Students do their own thing and print their own materials," I say, regretting I hadn't been more aware of what students were doing that day. "Whoever wrote this must have printed it off in addition to their essay and slid it in the stack for me to find."

"Why would someone do this?"

"I don't know. Maybe to brag," I say, shrugging. "Maybe to mess with me."

"Do you have any idea who might have written this?" she asks, looking at me with an intense stare.

"I think so," I say, my pulse quickening as I prepare to drop the name. "Zoey Peterson."

"Why her?" she asks. "Has she said something about Darcy? Did you see her messing with the essays?"

"I think she might have been the one who hurt Darcy."

"You think she attacked Darcy?" She acts like she misunderstands. "What makes you think that?"

"There are several reasons I find her suspicious," I say, knowing I won't be able to explain all my doubts in such a short amount of time. "Could I speak with you during your planning?"

"Sure," she says, lifting the paper still in her hand. "May I make a copy of this?"

"Of course."

"I need to prepare for Darcy's return. She should be coming to my office any minute, which means she'll be in your classroom shortly after."

"Thank you, Pam," I say, standing to leave. "How is Darcy doing?"

"Better. She thinks coming back to school will be easy. I hope she's right," she says, holding her office door open as I leave. "Unfortunately, I'm not as hopeful as she is."

I hurry to my classroom and unlock the door. I've been dreading seeing Darcy since I heard about the attack. I know the looks she'll be receiving all day. That victim look. People can't help it, of course. Most people, like me, are truly heartbroken by what she's been through. That's why they look at her, their eyes wide and glossy. Their mouths strained.

That's the way everyone looked at me after Brian did what he did. Like I was a poor victim. Of course, that's better than the angry reaction. People staring at me with contempt, even going so far as to blame my family for what he'd done. Only one death was really my fault. I'm sure Darcy will get loads of those looks, too. The darting eyes and arched brows. Like she brought this on herself.

*

Darcy is the third student to enter the classroom. She's wearing jeans, a black shirt and a sweater tied around her waist despite the warm temperatures outside. Her hair is in a ponytail. I give her a smile and nod before looking elsewhere. She doesn't smile back, instead taking her seat and pulling out her phone.

Adam is only a few steps behind her. He picks the seat closest to her and skids the chair across the floor. Normally, I would tell him to leave the chairs alone. But today, I'm willing to let protocol slide. She doesn't stop him from moving closer, but she doesn't acknowledge his presence, either.

Darcy attempts to look normal, like nothing happened and this is an average Monday at Victory Hills. Even though everyone on campus is aware something did happen to her. I imagine what her scar must look like under the tight denim fabric around her legs. I wonder how deep it is, if it's covered by a bandage and if it's already starting to heal.

"Good morning," I say to the class once the final bell rings. As they retrieve their textbooks per my instructions, I realize Zoey is absent. I'd been so focused on Darcy, I'd forgotten about her. That seems to be the stance the entire school has taken. Forgetting there is someone out there to blame for Darcy's hurt.

We're not in class ten minutes before there's a knock at the door. I look through the tiny pane of fiberglass and see Zoey standing there, peering into the room. I open the door to let her in.

"Zoey." I study her reaction. If she wrote the essay, she must know I've read it by now. Perhaps that's why she's late today, so she can have me, briefly, all to herself.

"Here's your note," she says, holding eye contact.

"Excuse me?" I say, my mind immediately returning to the anonymous paper. I look down and see the miniature pink slip she's holding between two fingers.

"My tardy slip," she says, holding it out further. She offers a smug smile, but that's no different from a typical day.

I take the slip, looking away as she walks past. She sits three rows in front of Darcy. I expect the two to ignore each other; instead, Darcy raises her head and nods. Zoey returns the gesture. The only other person who seems to notice the exchange is Adam, and he doesn't seem happy. He clenches a fist and stares at his desk.

All weekend, I've been considering how Darcy might act in front of Zoey. If she knew her attacker, the pain of being in the same room must be unbearable. Darcy, however, seems unbothered. She's got both hands back on her phone, tapping away.

"Have you graded the essays?" asks Ben, snapping me out of my trance. My eyes instinctively go to Zoey, who is already staring at me, the smile on her face still there.

"Um," I start, but my voice sounds not fully awake. "Yes, Ben. Most of them. I'll have them all done by tomorrow."

There are a few grumbles, my students disappointed by their teacher's sudden struggle to keep a deadline. But none of them know about the distractions I've faced this weekend. Well, one of them does.

"Will we get a chance to revise them?" asks Melanie.

"As usual," I answer. "You'll have an opportunity to read my feedback before submitting a final draft."

"Will we be going back to the computer lab for that?" Zoey asks.

Is she thinking of typing another note, I wonder? Sharing more details of the grisly account only she can remember. I can't completely hide my irritation toward her. "Do you think that's necessary?"

"I don't have access to a computer at home," she says. Suddenly, I'm the teacher picking on the poorest kid in class.

"Yes, Zoey," I say, adopting a more professional tone. "We'll be returning to the lab soon."

Given Darcy's return, this isn't the best day for group work. I give them an individual assignment, hoping some quiet and introspection will help Darcy ease back into routine. Adam takes the assignment and immediately starts working, as though through him, Darcy would see how to adjust. How to be normal again. Zoey starts working, too. Occasionally, she looks toward the back of the classroom. Everyone is writing or reading, except for one person.

Darcy unwraps the sweater from around her waist and bundles it on her desk. She places her head on the makeshift pillow and closes her eyes.

I'm waiting outside of Pam's office before the fourth block bell even rings. I've been dying to hear her take on the letter.

She walks down the hallway, carrying a takeout food box. Pam's able to leave school grounds during the day and pick up her lunch, on occasion. She's still talking with another teacher but acknowledges me at her door by offering a simple wave.

"Can you talk now?" I ask when she approaches.

"Yes, just give me a minute," she says, opening her door and allowing me inside.

I wait as she deposits her leftovers into her miniature fridge. She flattens out her pants before sitting, twisting in her chair to face me.

"How was Darcy in class today?" she asks, folding her hands together on the desk.

"A bit testy," I say, thinking of how much she reminded me of someone else. "I was dreading seeing her, really. I thought she might be despondent, defiant. She didn't do any of her assignments."

Of course, it didn't bother me she didn't do her work. She has more on her mind than completing worksheets. However, I think her refusal to participate says a lot about where she is mentally.

"That's a normal reaction for girls in her situation. They've lost control in a horrendous way, so they're trying to take it back any way they can. It wouldn't surprise me if her attitude gets worse in coming weeks."

"I understand," I say. "Have you talked to her today?"

"I have," Pam says, looking down. "I think today has been tougher than she expected. I wish the parents weren't so insistent about her completing the semester."

"What do you think about the essay?" I ask, having waited long enough to hear Pam's response.

"I find it very concerning," she says. She reaches into a folder on her desk and retrieves the paper. "I can't figure out why a student would write this considering what happened. I think all our students are too mature to view something like this as a joke. I'm wondering if it's not more a cry for attention."

"If someone wanted attention, I think they would have put their name on the paper."

"You're right," she says, scanning the page again. "Maybe it's a way for a student to work through their grief."

"Look at the POV, Pam. It's written from the perspective of the attacker. It's like someone is reliving the moment, and they left it in the stack of essays because they wanted someone to read it. They wanted *me* to read it."

"I understand," she says, putting down the paper. "You mentioned you think Zoey Peterson might have been involved. Can you tell me why you think that?"

"Well, she was in the computer lab. And she's rubbed me the wrong way since she got here—"

"Rubbed you the wrong way, how?" Pam interrupts.

"Just little things. Saying inappropriate stuff in class. When we were reading *The Crucible*, she made a remark about girls crying out for attention. And that was after Darcy's attack."

"Huh," Pam looks away, then back at me. "It's odd to hear you say that. All of her other teachers have said nothing but positive things about her."

"Yeah, I know all about Marge and the chemistry test," I say, frustratedly. "She's a smart kid, obviously. But there's just something off about her."

"It's hard to be the new kid at school, especially a school like this where everyone is so cliquey. She seems to have got along fine with everyone."

"Well, there was the knife incident," I remind her.

"I think that was, perhaps, blown out of proportion. I don't think we can necessarily hold it against her."

I'm not sure what's changed about Pam since this morning, but something has. Then, she seemed willing to hear what I had to say. Now it's like I'm playing defense. *One... two... three.*

"There's not a glaring incident which makes her look bad, I see that," I say. "But there's a bunch of tiny details which, when put together, form a red flag."

"What else?" she asks. Despite her skepticism, Pam wants to know more. I sense she wants to believe me, but it's not like I can tell her why I'm so convinced. No one at Victory Hills knows about Brian, and, at this point, I'm not sure if the connection would help or hurt my cause.

"I saw her with Darcy Moore at the dance," I say. "It looked like the two of them were arguing."

"When at the dance?"

"I don't know. Just at the dance."

"Marge Helton said Darcy was with Adam most of the night."

"Yeah, I saw her with Adam, too," I say. "But you know Darcy, she hops around from one person to the next." I stop myself, realizing I sound like I'm shaming her, and that's not my intention. "You know what I mean, right? It was a dance. There were a lot of people interacting with one another."

"Yes, I understand. Which is why I'm wondering what makes you so convinced Zoey Peterson is the one who hurt Darcy. You said yourself she talked to several people."

"Because of everything else. Her behavior and the knife and the fact she's new to the school. It looked like there was something going on between them at the dance. What if Zoey got upset about something and then sought revenge at the party?"

"It's a possibility, although we've never had an incident like this involving two girls," she says, staring at her desk. "Here's the thing. I discussed the essay with Principal Bowles. He's not convinced it proves anything."

Pam's skepticism makes sense now. She's already addressed the matter with Bowles, and he shot me down. She's trying to break the news gently. I've experienced this before, people thinking I'm wrong. Believing I'm crazy or irrational. Refusing to see the evidence right in front of them.

"That shouldn't surprise either one of us, Pam," I say, trying to sound calm. "You know how Bowles is. He's not going to willingly admit there is an attacker roaming the halls."

"I agree," she says. "I don't think Bowles has handled Darcy's situation properly, but I felt obligated to tell him."

"What was his theory?"

"He thinks it's a crude joke. Someone trying to fan the flames of hysteria. He pulled up the camera footage to see if anyone outside of your classes entered the computer lab that day, but no one did. He assumes it's someone who got bored, typed it up and wanted to cause a big fuss out of nothing."

"If the cameras confirm my students were the only ones in the computer lab, it becomes more likely the letter came from Zoey." Bowles' disinterest aside, the footage only strengthens my theory. But Pam remains silent. "What do you think?"

"Zoey might have written the letter," she begins. "But, honestly, I'm unconvinced she attacked Darcy. I don't know enough about Zoey. Yet. I'd like to talk with her myself."

Pam's reaction wasn't what I expected. She's promising to look into the matter because she's my friend and she's good at her job, but I recognize her doubt. She doesn't believe me.

CHAPTER 17

Now

The week moves slowly. Usually the days fly this time of the semester, but Darcy's attack has shaken the familiar routine. Now each day feels like a long act in a play. I can't focus on summer and touring Europe with Danny. Not when I stare at Darcy Moore each morning.

I've mastered the art of observing student dynamics without being noticed. Darcy, for example, hasn't even opened her book all week. She's either fiddling with her phone or putting her head on the desk. Pam says this is normal, and I agree. I'll have to address her lack of effort at some point, but it's still too soon for her to be taking orders from anyone, even me.

Darcy's disconnected from everything, including Adam. On Monday, he appeared concerned and attentive. On Tuesday, less so. He still stared at Darcy, even whispered to her at times, but he didn't move his desk to be near her. By Wednesday morning, he looked depressed again. He didn't acknowledge anyone, not even Darcy. I wonder what's going on between them behind the scenes, in the other twenty-two hours and thirty minutes of their lives outside of my class.

Thursday is probably the first time this entire semester I haven't seen Adam and Darcy interact. It's like they are strangers sitting four feet apart. When students break into their learning groups, Adam approaches my desk.

"Mrs. Mayfair, can I join Melanie's group today?" he asks. Typically, people only volunteer to work with Melanie because of their expectation she'll do all the work. It's sad, really. Today, I sense Adam simply wants to avoid Darcy. Or maybe it's Zoey he wants to avoid.

"Sure," I say, making my way to the back of the room to hand out papers.

As I walk along the rows of desks, I notice Darcy look in Adam's direction for the first time. She rolls her eyes when she sees him take a seat next to Melanie.

"Everything good over here?" I ask.

"Fine," Darcy says, reaching out her hand to grab the worksheet. I realize this is the first word I've heard her speak all week.

Zoey walks by me and takes the seat next to Darcy. This provokes a reaction from Adam. He doesn't say anything, but he resembles the angry volcano I witnessed last week.

I sigh. Teenagers often carry their personal lives into the classroom; this isn't the first time I've witnessed the aftermath of a bad breakup or a dirty rumor. But everything feels so much darker this time. Dangerous. You can't send a student to the office for rolling their eyes. So I wait and monitor, hoping nothing escalates.

We make it until the last two minutes of class before there's an eruption. As students are returning to their desks, Zoey brushes against Adam. Adam reacts by slamming a textbook on his desk.

"Adam!" I cry. The sound of the book thudding against the tabletop startles everyone in the room.

"She bumped into me on purpose!" Adam shouts, looking at me as a toddler would during a tantrum. Like I have all the answers, which I don't.

"Are you always this angry around women?" Zoey asks. Her voice is calm, and she smirks like this is the funniest thing she's seen all day. She's both baiting him and perpetuating the theory he hurt

Darcy. Thankfully, Adam doesn't bite. He grabs his backpack and slings it over one shoulder. He walks toward the door.

"Adam, you can't react like that." I keep my voice low and my face neutral. I know the entire classroom is looking at me.

"She keeps trying to mess—"

I cut Adam off before he starts shouting again. "Go to second block. I'll have to report this to Ms. Pam." I can't condone his yelling at another student in front of my entire class. Even if he's yelling at Zoey.

Adam pushes open the door, which causes another loud slam as it hits the wall. Moments later, the bell rings and my other students make their exit. Most keep their eyes low while some, like Devon, chuckle. Darcy looks mortified, and I wonder what exactly is going on between these three students. Clearly something.

Zoey walks toward the door.

"Not so fast." I block her from entering the hallway.

Darcy looks back before leaving, closing the door behind her. She mouths the words *Thank you* to Zoey, which feels like a punch to the gut.

"I'm in trouble, too?" Zoey asks once we're alone, although she's nowhere near as angry as Adam. She's bored. "I told you I brushed against him by accident."

I narrow my eyes and search her face. It's not a small classroom. I find it hard to believe she accidently managed to bump against the one person she'd had words with just last week.

"What's going on, Zoey?" I ask, folding my arms across my body. I'm uncomfortable talking with her, but I don't want her to see.

"What do you think is going on, Mrs. Mayfair?" She copies my body language, crossing her arms but adding an extra layer of cool by leaning against the wall. "Why are you keeping me in here?"

I finally have Zoey alone. Now is the time to ask if she knows about Brian, but I'm afraid of her answer. She's been testing me with her comments and the letter because she assumes I'm weak. If

I ask her about Brian, she'll know she's winning. And if she doesn't know about him, I'll open a whole other can of problems.

"You're provoking arguments with another student in class." I stare at her, wishing I could say more. Wishing I could accuse her of more than causing a scene. But I can't. Not yet. "Do you want to tell me what's going on?"

"If you must know," she starts, darting her eyes at the door, "I'm trying to defend another classmate."

I shake my head, not believing her story. "Defend another classmate how?"

"Darcy. Adam won't leave her alone. He's smothering her like some creep. The whole school knows he's the one who hurt her."

I'm not convinced Adam is the one smothering Darcy. For whatever reason, Zoey has taken Darcy under her wing. They're becoming friends. Maybe she's trying to protect herself from future suspicion, although that seems unlikely; I seem to be the only person who has concerns about Zoey. Perhaps she likes watching the aftermath up close. I know Brian did.

"Why are you getting involved with Adam and Darcy?" I ask, trying to keep on topic.

"I don't know," she says, uncrossing her arms. "I thought that's what we were encouraged to do when we see bullying. If you see something, say something."

As usual, Zoey is taking a positive concept and spinning it to fit her needs. Brian used to do the same thing. "Zoey, that's not the complete meaning of that phrase. If you see something, yes, you should say something. But not to a student in the middle of a crowded cafeteria or by bumping someone in class. All that does is create a spectacle. If you think someone is being bothered, tell a teacher."

"Well, I'm telling you now, aren't I?" She tilts her head to the side, and a strand of ebony hair falls by her nose. She grabs it, starts twirling. "The way he treats Darcy is bullshit."

"Zoey—" I start but she interrupts.

"Sorry, Mrs. Mayfair. Sorry. I just think Darcy has been through enough, don't you? It's not in my nature to sit back and let someone hurt women."

There it is again. That knowing tone. Like she's trying to dig into my wounds and open them. She looks at me, studying my reaction as closely as I'm studying hers. She wants to rattle me by hinting at Brian, so I throw her off with a question of my own.

"Were you at the party?" I ask, locking my eyes with hers. I've been instructed to avoid the topic with students, but I can't keep my professional mask on around Zoey. I think she's lying. I think she's playing me, and I'm going to play back.

Her pupils enlarge, and she sucks in a quick breath. She's smart enough to know I shouldn't have asked her the question, and yet I broke protocol anyway. "No," she says. "And I don't know why it would matter if I was."

She crosses her arms again, trying, a little too hard, to appear at ease. I know I should let the incident go, tell Zoey to head to her next class. My second block students are standing in the hallway, waiting for me to open the door. But I can't dismiss Zoey yet. I've had to bury my concerns for more than two weeks. I have Zoey alone, and I'm not going to waste the opportunity to figure out, for myself, what might have happened that night.

"The other day in the computer lab," I start, whispering even though we are the only two in the room, "someone turned in an essay. Do you know anything about that?"

She shifts her weight. She looks confused, but I can't tell if she is. "Mrs. Mayfair, I turned in my essay. I'm not sure what you're talking about."

"You didn't type anything else that day?" I ask, taking a step closer to her. "You didn't write anything about the party?"

Her eyes grow large and she steps back. "I don't know what you're talking about," she says, raising her hands. "I turned in my essay. The essay I wrote for your class. That's it."

"And you're sure you weren't at the party?" I finally have the chance to question her, and it's making me high, feeling for once like I'm the one in control. Inside, I'm all flutters.

"I already told you. No!"

"I don't know why you're being so defensive, Zoey."

"I'm not," she says, brushing the hair off her shoulder. "I just don't know why you're asking me all these questions. It's like you're interrogating me."

The word *interrogating* snaps me out of my trance, and I suddenly look at this situation in a different light. I'm a teacher questioning a student about a non-school incident without cause. It doesn't matter if I think I'm in the right when it comes to Zoey, anyone else walking into this conversation would say I'm out of line. I clear my throat, taking the opportunity to back away. *One... two... three.*

When I speak again, my professional tone is back. "I was only asking about your involvement, given you are defending Darcy."

"It's not easy being new this late in the year," Zoey says, looking at the floor. "Everyone already has friends and connections. I'm just trying to fit in, you know? Darcy seems like she needs a friend as much as I do."

Zoey suddenly seems younger. Gone is the student who excels in every avenue. Now she looks as insecure and desperate as her fellow classmates. This is typical with teenagers. Under all the cool and tough is a thick layer of uncertainty.

"I understand you want to help. But if you think someone is being unfairly targeted, speak to Ms. Pam in guidance. Her job is to mend situations like this one."

"All right," she says, lifting her backpack off the floor. "Can I go to second block now?"

"Yes," I say, walking to my desk. "Let me write you a note."

She swings the bag over her shoulder and follows me to the desk. I hand her an orange Post-it with my signature. The paper sticks to her finger. She walks toward the door, then stops and turns.

"Mrs. Mayfair," she starts, slowly. "Do you like me?"

"Excuse me?"

"Maybe I'm just being paranoid," she says, turning away from the door to face me fully. "I get the impression you don't like me very much."

"I like you fine, Zoey," I say, wishing I wasn't such a shitty liar. "You're a very bright student."

"It hasn't been easy, you know," she says, sounding more immature than I've ever heard her sound before. "I've been the new kid a lot, but it's especially hard coming to a place like this."

"I know what you mean," I say, and I do. I was also once new in Victory Hills. And while the town looks like it was designed by Norman Rockwell, that cliquey exterior can be hard to crack. I still feel like an outsider, and Danny does, too. "But it does seem like you've made friends quickly."

"Why? Because I can run a straight line?" She sounds defeated. Even though she's winning popularity contests, she feels like a loser. That's another teenage thing. Constantly feeling like you're never enough.

"That's not the only reason," I encourage her. "But I'm sure it helps. I've heard nothing but wonderful things about your performance on the track."

"You know my own mom won't even come watch me?" she asks, a new sadness in her voice. "It's bad enough we move all the time because of her. I come to a new place and I'm actually good at something, and she's too self-involved to care."

A pang of sorrow enters my gut and I try to swallow it down. I've not considered Zoey's predicament. Her role as the new kid. Coming from a chaotic home life. Maybe I'm only seeing what I want to see, ignoring the full picture.

"I'm sorry, Zoey." It's all I can say. My feelings about her are still conflicted. "You better get to class."

She nods, opens the door and leaves. My second block students fill the classroom, annoyed my impromptu meeting with Zoey disrupted their routine.

CHAPTER 18

Now

Rarely do I feel I abuse my position as an authority figure, which is why I find it difficult to stop thinking about Zoey and our conversation yesterday. I've spent so much time viewing her as a threat, I didn't consider her unsettling behavior might have reasonable explanations. I suppose that's what Pam was insisting all along. In the past, I'd projected my own fears about Brian onto others. Is that what I'd done with Zoey? Was this my way of bringing a dose of excitement into my life? Bringing back the flutter of the new?

"I'm ready for the weekend," Marge says, walking up behind me in the employee lounge. I'm shakily pouring a cup of coffee, still not feeling fully awake. "Any plans?"

"Yes, actually. Danny rented a cabin in the mountains," I say, smiling. "We leave tomorrow morning."

"A cabin in the mountains," Marge says, arching her eyebrows. "Sounds romantic."

"I need to get away," I say, although Marge has no idea how much my mind has been longing for an escape.

"You going to the track meet tonight?" she asks, as if I'm no different from one of the students. Because that's how Marge is, forever winning the award for Most School Spirit.

"I don't think so," I say, failing to come up with a speedy excuse as to why.

"Well, that's where I'll be," she says, pushing open the employee room door with her backside. "That Zoey Peterson is one helluva runner."

Zoey Peterson. Oh, this kid won't stay out of my head. She displayed a different side of herself yesterday. I remember that gleam of desperation in her eyes when she admitted, through shame, that her mom wouldn't even come to her meets. It's bad enough she's made Zoey change zip codes three times in the past year. I can't imagine having a child, but if I did, I'd support their activities.

When Zoey walks into my classroom, I feel the dynamic between us has changed. Her posture is straighter, and she seems attentive during my lecture.

"Good luck at the meet today," I tell her, at the end of the block.

She flips her ponytail to the opposite shoulder. "Thank you, Mrs. Mayfair."

Darcy, who barely spoke today, follows her out. And Adam follows Darcy. I feel sorry for my students. Still, they trudge through their days with summer on the horizon. I suppose you can put up with anything for a few weeks.

My planning period is interrupted by the buzz of my room intercom.

"Della?" asks the secretary's voice from overhead.

"Yes?" I respond to the ceiling.

"Pam would like to see you in her office."

"Thanks." I pause the Europe itinerary that I've (finally) taken the time to plan. I'm six days in, having us fly into Paris and then take a train further south. Once I finalize our course and book hotels, I can put more detail into the daily excursions. The museums and parks and tours. Danny did give me a budget, but it's so large it's almost insulting to call it that. At least now when he asks how planning is going, I won't be completely lying.

"You rang?" I ask, standing in the doorway of Pam's office.

"Sorry to make you walk down here," she says, waving for me to come inside.

"No problem," I say, taking a seat. "I wasn't very busy."

"Good," she says, clearing a stack of papers and placing both forearms on her desk. "I was out yesterday, this time because Daniel broke his arm."

"Oh goodness," I say, a rowdy image of her twin boys entering my mind. "Is he all right?"

"Yes," she says, sighing. "They were roughing around outside with the neighbors and Daniel fell off the trampoline. We always tell them one at time, but what can you do?" She raises her hands and shakes her head. I'm not even sure Pam was aware, all those years ago when she conceived, how chaotic her life would become.

"Don't you have one of those safety nets?" I ask, immediately regretting the question. I don't want to come off as one of those childless people who thinks they know everything about raising children.

"Yes, well, we did. They broke it some weeks back, and my ex never came over to fix it." She shakes her head again. "Oh well, enough about my problems. Otherwise, we'll be here all afternoon. I wanted to let you know I *did* speak with Zoey Peterson about the paper you received."

"Oh good," I say, straightening my posture.

"Of course I didn't let her see it. I only told her you had received a disturbing writing sample in the computer lab and that I was questioning multiple students about it. I was pretty stern with her," she says, clenching her jaw. "She claimed she had no idea what I was talking about. You know, I hear lies all the time in here. I think I'm pretty good at figuring out who is telling the truth. I must say, I believed her."

Pam's right. Students do tell her lies. They also tell her legitimate information, claims that should be taken seriously. They trust her, which is why she was the first person on staff Darcy's parents called after the incident.

"Did she say anything else?" I ask. "Did she have any idea who might have written it?"

"No," she says, looking down. "She said she was so busy finishing her own essay she didn't have time to pay attention, let alone write a second one."

I remember grading Zoey's essay. It was well written, which wasn't surprising considering how intelligent she is. In fact, it was one of the best in the group. And none of her paragraphs were pulled from the internet, unlike some of the others.

"All right," I say. "Maybe I jumped to conclusions." My conversation with Zoey yesterday changed my perspective. Before I'd seen her as a monster. An extension of Brian, in some ways. I'd forgotten she was a teenage girl struggling with her own problems, searching for a way to adjust.

"She actually seemed bothered. She wanted to know what it said and why it had disturbed you. I didn't tell her it was about Darcy."

"Either way, thanks for asking," I say, standing to leave.

"It's what I'm here for," she says, smiling. "I meant to tell you yesterday, but the unfortunate trampoline incident impeded my plans."

"No worries," I say, opening the door. Then, I pause. "You weren't here yesterday. When did you talk to Zoey?"

"On Wednesday afternoon. I actually went by your room after school, but you'd already left."

"You're sure it was Wednesday?"

"Positive."

I return to my seat. "I spoke with Zoey yesterday. Briefly. I brought up the letter. She acted like she didn't know what I was talking about."

"Really?" She leans back in her chair and rocks.

"Yes, I specifically asked her if she'd written anything off topic in the computer lab. She looked at me like I was crazy. Like she had no idea what I was talking about. You'd think she'd mention you already questioned her." I pause, re-examining my conversation with Zoey and trying to remember her exact reaction. "Are you sure you told her the letter was in my class?"

"Yes. I told her all the specifics without revealing the contents."

"Then she knew exactly what I was getting at during our conversation. She played dumb. Didn't let on she'd already talked with you about it." I look down and grit my teeth. "Even gave me some sob story about her mom afterwards, like she was trying to gain my sympathy."

Pam, still rocking in her chair, stares at me and thumbs her chin. "And you spoke with her yesterday?"

"Yes," I say, a bit too loudly. "Don't you think it's manipulative of her to act like she has no idea what I'm talking about?"

"Look," she said. "I do think it's odd, but sometimes high schoolers do odd things."

Yeah, I think. *Like assault their classmates and write about it.*

"I'm telling you," I say, standing again. "This kid is up to something weird."

"I'm not sure why she would play dumb, but maybe she really was clueless. Maybe she didn't connect the two essays."

"I don't buy that," I say, picturing those puppy dog eyes she displayed when discussing her mom. "I think she's playing you and she's playing me. I'm convinced she wrote that paper now."

"Stay calm, Dell. Getting worked up won't help anything."

What I can't get her or anyone else to realize is staying calm won't help matters either.

I'm furious Zoey lied to me. She's had fun dropping hints about Brian and she wanted to further rattle me by writing that essay. When I asked her if she attended the party, her attitude changed. She knows I see past the shiny hair and good grades and speedy running time. And everything I'm seeing, down to her manipulative actions, looks all too familiar.

I'm no longer in my teacher mindset; instead, I'm contemplating ways I can confront her again. By now, it's after three o'clock, and the dismissal bell has turned the hallways quiet and empty. Zoey is at the field, preparing for her afternoon meet. I consider taking Marge up on her offer to join her in the stands. Maybe my presence will make Zoey uneasy.

But then, who might see me? Who might question why I'm targeting a student? I've already been told to let the subject of the essay rest. I can't. Not when I know it's the closest thing to a witness of Darcy's struggle.

Then I consider a different option. Perhaps I don't have to go to the game. Perhaps I don't have to interact with Zoey at all to get a better understanding of her.

I return to my computer and log in to the information system that hosts the personal details of every student in the building. Their medical conditions, their semester schedules and their home addresses. Despite her recent arrival, all of Zoey's information is up to date. Her file tells me she lives in a house down the road from the local library; depending on how far, it could very well be in the middle of nowhere. She only has one family contact on file. Mother: Tricia Peterson, age 37.

I print the information.

CHAPTER 19

Now

Twenty minutes later, I'm driving past the library, edging closer to nothingness. The buildings grow shorter and farther apart as I move toward blue sky and grassy fields. Less than a minute before I'm supposed to reach my destination, I see a lone house surrounded by trees. I think this can't be the right location, but it's the only one within sight. As I pass the mailbox, my phone dings to let me know I've arrived.

I drive down the gravel driveway and watch as the white farmhouse grows before my eyes. This can't be the place where poor Zoey lives. With her unstable mother who is constantly moving her from one school to the next. This seems like the type of home people would aspire to have. It might be a bit outdated, but the bones are good. Even Danny and I talked about one day renovating an old farmhouse like this.

I park my car beside the only other one in the driveway, a rusty minivan. I turn off the engine, pull out the keys and freeze. I realize I have no idea what I'm doing here. This is the type of thing Marge would do, inserting herself into the lives of her students in hopes of making a change. Or even Pam, abandoning her weekend for a student in need. But I've never done this type of thing, and what would I even say? *Hi, Ms. Peterson. I've known your daughter for three weeks and think she attacked her classmate.* What was I thinking coming here without a plan?

I push the keys back into the ignition, hoping I can pull back onto the main road without being seen. But I'm too late. When I look up, there's a woman standing on the front porch, staring at me.

I smile at her and sigh at myself. I'm in over my head and I know it, but I can at least speak with the woman. Ask her about her daughter without necessarily sharing my concerns.

I step out of the car, press away the wrinkles on my skirt and walk toward the porch. "Hello," I say as I approach. "Are you Ms. Peterson?"

She has a slim torso and straight dark hair, like Zoey. As I move closer, I see her beauty is corroding. Wrinkles branch out from her mouth and eyes, which are rimmed with dark circles. *Easy, Dell,* I tell myself. *She's thirty-seven. This is you in six years.* And yet, I don't think that's true. She appears to have lived hard.

"Yeah," the woman says, one hand on her hip, the other on the railing. "Who are you?"

"I'm Della Mayfair. I'm Zoey's English teacher," I say, offering a smile.

The stern look Ms. Peterson wears doesn't completely drop, but she seems more at ease. As though she was expecting someone worse than myself. "What are you doing here?"

I'm asking myself the same thing, as I mount a rickety porch step.

"I was hoping to speak with you about Zoey," I say, clutching my purse like a badge. "I apologize for not calling first."

She looks down and gently taps the railing with her feet. "Phone's messed up right now. Wouldn't matter if you had."

"Okay," I say, standing awkwardly on the porch. Still smiling.

"Would you like a drink or something?" she asks. "I just brewed sweet tea."

"That would be lovely."

She walks across the long porch and scoots a chair toward me, the legs scraping against the wood. "Wait here," she says. "I'll be back in a minute."

I take a seat as Ms. Peterson walks inside. I scan my surroundings, immediately taken aback by how quiet it is. I've lived all my life surrounded by neighbors. First, the Wilsonville suburbs. Then cheap apartments and college dorms. Even now, Danny and I could throw a rock and hit homes on either side. Here, there is nothing. If I squint, I can see a small house in the distance, which could be a mansion up close for all I know.

An afternoon gust whooshes, grabbing the tall patches of grass in the yard and shaking them. There aren't many flowers around, and I imagine if I lived in a place like this, landscaping would become my newest hobby. I'd do something about that gravel driveway, too. I imagine how beautiful the place could be with a little bit of work.

Ms. Peterson comes out carrying a round serving tray. There's a pitcher and two tall glasses on it, along with a miniature bowl of cut lemons.

"You want lemon with your tea?"

"Please," I say, straightening and placing my bag on the porch.

The ice cubes tinkle against the glass as she pours.

"You said your name is Mrs. Mayfair?"

"Yes," I say. "Zoey is in my first block."

"I think she told me about you. Are you the one reading about witches?"

"Yes, that's my class," I say, taking a sip of the tea. I'm surprised Zoey would tell her about me, or any of her other teachers. Brian never talked about school, unless he was ranting about how intellectually superior he was to everyone there. Perhaps that's how my name came up in conversation.

"Yeah, she's mentioned you," she says, taking a sip and looking over her empty yard. "She's a smart one, isn't she?"

"Yes, Zoey is extremely smart. I know she's doing well in other classes, too. You must be very proud."

Ms. Peterson doesn't say anything. She keeps staring at the fields.

"I was wondering," I say after several seconds of silence, "if you could tell me a little bit about her educational background."

"We've moved around a lot," she says, at last. She holds her glass with two hands and looks down in her lap. "When my parents died, I figured it was time to finally move back home. Give this place a try."

"You're from Victory Hills?"

"Born and raised. I left when I met Zoey's father, but that didn't last. When she was a baby, I moved us around hoping to find a better place. Didn't want to be the stereotype who ends up where they started, you know?"

It explains why they would have such a nice piece of land. They inherited it.

"What do you do, Ms. Peterson?"

"Oh, I've done a lot of things. I work from home mostly," she says, taking another sip of her drink. "You know those people who call you asking about health insurance? Well, I'm one of them now."

"It must be nice being able to stay at home. You've got a beautiful property."

"A roof is a roof, even if it's the same roof you've lived under most of your life, I guess. I'd like to fix the place up. Maybe I will after Zoey leaves," she says, raising a single finger into the air. "One more year."

I understand the relief most parents feel when their life is finally their own again, but I've also heard of empty nesters. I find it odd that Ms. Peterson, who seems very much alone, is anticipating the departure of her only child.

"Does Zoey talk about college?"

"Since we've moved here, she thinks she might have a chance at an athletic scholarship. Between that and her grades, she should get most of it paid for. As long as she doesn't set her sights too high."

I'm trying to figure Ms. Peterson out. *Disengaged* would be an appropriate word. She's friendly enough, but I question what type of mother would rather sit at home alone than watch her daughter excel in a sport.

"Well, I'm sure Zoey will find a way to do whatever she wants," I say, wondering, still, what I hoped to figure out by coming here.

My mother never believed Brian was dangerous. I'm not sure why I'd thought Ms. Peterson would be any different.

Ms. Peterson looks at me for the first time since she sat down. "Is she in some sort of trouble?"

"No. Not really," I say, stumbling over my words. I have to give her some reason for why I'm here besides sipping tea on her front porch. "I do worry about her socialization. It's hard for students when they enroll in a new school late in the year."

"Well, it's not like we had much choice," she says, taking another gulp. "Not sure how she makes it sound, but all the leaving isn't because of me."

"I'm not trying to pry—"

"Yes, you are," she says. Her eyes aren't accusatory, but honest. "You're trying to figure out Zoey. And I'm trying to figure out why. Has she done something?"

I consider telling her about the essay and Darcy, but that would be a complete breach of ethics, and I'm already straddling the line. Instead, I try to fish for more information. "Does Zoey seem bothered by something?"

"She said some of her teammates gave her a hard time at first. Things are better now. They can't hate on her too much if she's helping them win. She told me your school's track team is lousy, no offense."

"Well, that's true," I say, forcing a laugh, but Ms. Peterson seems as dry as ever.

"Track has helped her make friends faster than she has before." She stares at the landscape past the porch. "She made a big deal about going to the dance and that party. It's not like I really wanted her to go, but what can you do?"

My throat feels dry and I take another sip, wide-eyed. Zoey *did* go to the party.

"Has Zoey had problems making friends at other schools?" I ask.

"Zoey eventually has problems everywhere she goes."

"I see."

"I'll ask you again," she says, hardening her stare. "Has she done something I should know about? I've had teachers from other schools visit, and it's never to tell me how smart and popular she is. Zoey knows we need to stay here this time around, now that we have the house and all. There's got to be a reason you'd spend your Friday afternoon sitting on the porch with me."

I want to tell her, but I don't know how. I'll sound like a lunatic if I tell her Zoey might have attacked Darcy. I can't prove it. I could barely tell my own mom about Brian, even when I had evidence to back up my suspicions.

"I think we bump heads sometimes," I say. "I don't think she interacts with the other teachers that way. It makes me wonder if it's just me."

"It might be just you this time, honey," she says, reaching into her pocket and pulling out a pack of cigarettes. She lights one, releasing a gray plume into the air. "But you aren't the only one she's rubbed wrong."

"Has Zoey been in trouble before?"

"Well, I'm not going to tell you something if you aren't telling me," she says, hitting the cigarette hard.

"I can't say she's done something specific," I say, hesitantly. Our conversation is becoming more contentious, and the last thing I want is to upset this woman.

"It's just a feeling, isn't it?" she asks, looking at me again with those honest eyes. I realize she knows exactly what I cannot say. There's something wrong with Zoey, but neither one of us can define it. "When it comes to Zoey, she runs hot and cold. People either love her or they hate her. And she either hates you back, or she doesn't. I'll tell you this, if you're skating on her bad side now, it'd be best to back off. Once you're on her list, there's no getting off."

I look back at her, mouth open. I've never heard someone describe their own child so harshly. They say mothers know their children best, but after Mom and Brian, I didn't believe that was true. Staring at Ms. Peterson, I see the opposite. She's a mother who sees there's a darkness residing in her daughter, but like me, she knows there is nothing to be done about it.

"If I were you," she continues, taking another hit of the cigarette, "I'd keep my distance. It's what I try to do."

"Is that why you don't go to her track meets?" I ask, the question leaving my mouth so suddenly I overlook how rude it sounds.

She puts out the cigarette, takes a lengthy swig of her drink before pouring more in the glass. "People will judge me, sure. Zoey figured out a long time ago that the Bad Mom card was her ticket out of trouble. And it works. Most of the time. I'd love to cheer on my daughter. But Zoey's not that daughter. She tells me not to go. Says her *drunk, skank Mom* has no business being seen at school." She reaches back into her pocket, takes out another cigarette and lights it.

"That's a horrible way for her to speak to you."

"Yeah, well. You should hear what she says when she's mad."

She stands and stumbles back to her chair. Instinctively, I try to help her.

"I got it," she says. I'm close enough to smell the alcohol on her breath now.

"Ms. Peterson, maybe you can talk with someone. Maybe you and Zoey would benefit from family counseling."

"Like I told you, I've got one more year." She slides her flat palms through the air. "Then I'm done."

I want to tell her how dangerous that position is. That her inability to do something now could hurt Zoey, and others, in the future. But it's not my place. Maybe I should try, because of Brian, but she already seems rattled. I remember what it's like living under the same roof as someone so hostile. I see what it's done to Ms. Peterson. Zapped her of her former beauty, forced her to work from home, drink heavily and smoke.

"I tell you what," she says, standing again. This time her stance is solid. "You seem like a nice teacher, and you've got to be smarter than most if you're able to pick up on the real Zoey. But it would be best if you don't get involved. I appreciate you trying to help. I really do. But you should just get in your car and go. The track meets always seem to end early on Fridays."

She's asking me to leave in the nicest way possible because she feels threatened, for herself and for me. I pick up my purse and walk down the steps. She remains standing, watching me leave.

As I open my car door, I turn again. "You should ask Zoey about the party after the dance."

Before she can respond with another question, I get in my car and go.

CHAPTER 20

Now

"You aren't sleeping?" Danny asks, breaking my concentration. He's seated to my left, driving our sedan down the interstate. This hour on a Saturday there's little traffic. We loaded the car and left Victory Hills before seven, which is too early for me to be awake on a weekend. For Danny, it's more like sleeping in.

I didn't tell him I threw up this morning. I brushed my teeth and hopped in the shower, not wanting to spoil our weekend ahead. This Zoey nonsense has a hold over me, and visiting Ms. Peterson yesterday seems to have strengthened the grip.

"You know what it's like once you're awake. Sometimes it's hard to go back down," I say. Usually, when we have an hour or more drive, I'm passed out. I can't tell him I'm awake thinking about Zoey and Ms. Peterson. My most logical option, as Pam suggested, is to leave the matter alone. Deep inside, something refuses to let me do that. Maybe it's my guilt.

"Just making sure you're okay." Danny senses something is on my mind. He knows me too well, and that is rather annoying right now.

"I'm fine," I assure him, our hands now connected in between our two seats.

"I can visit her with you," he says, and I wonder how many minutes he's been contemplating whether to make the suggestion. "She's my mother-in-law, after all."

"No," I say. "That will make the visit that much longer. I'm only stopping because it's Mother's Day weekend."

That's not entirely true because whenever we drive this direction, we make a pit stop to visit my mother; she now lives two hours from Victory Hills along the highway. We must, otherwise my daughterly guilt screams so loud I lose concentration.

"I just don't want you getting upset."

"Do I seem upset to you?" I ask, kicking my foot onto the dash.

"Not yet," he says, shyly. *Yet*. Twice in the past five years I've had a meltdown, and now he expects it every time.

"I'm the only family she has left, Danny. She deserves some one-on-one time with me."

"I know. And I think you're an excellent daughter. You visit her a lot more than I do my folks, and they still have their wits about them." He stops, knowing his words came out differently than he meant. Mom has dementia. It's not like she wouldn't have her wits if the choice was hers to make. "You know what I meant."

"I do," I say. "But she's also the only family I have left."

Now it's his turn to feel guilty, even though I wasn't intending to hurt his feelings. Of course Danny is my family. As we get older, we have the luxury of choosing who we want in our lives. Your childhood family is different from your adult family for this reason. I didn't get to choose what happened to Dad or Mom; and none of us chose what happened with Brian.

Mom never made me promise not to put her in *a place like this*, so perhaps that's why I feel only partially culpable when I visit. Besides, it's good she's surrounded by peers; Mom has always loved a sense of community. Out of the three facilities I toured, it was undoubtedly the best option, and the closest to Victory Hills. The visiting area looks more like a family living room, only with more tables and chairs. Each bedroom has a fireplace, although it doesn't work. It's all about the look. Make a space look like home, and it won't serve as a constant reminder that it's anything but.

Mom's dementia showed up early; like, scarily early. She was in her early sixties when she started displaying signs. Danny was the one who officially figured it out, and at first, I thought his assumption stemmed from his role as a medical student: when you think every person you know, including yourself, is suffering whatever illness you're studying that week.

I thought Mom was being her normal, flighty self. And when symptoms occurred that I couldn't brush off as just Mom, I thought maybe she was faking. Being Brian's mother, after all, was far worse than being Brian's sister. I think Mom handled it worse than most mothers would, considering she was always so image conscious. I thought her early episodes were nothing more than an excuse to trick everyone, including herself, that she wasn't fazed by the evil crimes her son committed.

Five years ago, not long after Danny and I moved to Victory Hills, she almost burnt down her apartment complex by leaving the stove on. A neighbor called the fire department. When they arrived, she claimed my father was at fault, then blamed Brian. Neither man had lived with her for over a decade at that point. Thankfully, if there's any thanks to be found, the incident took place during summer vacation. I stayed with her for two weeks, which presented event after event highlighting Mom's weakened state of mind. I couldn't bear the thought of leaving her alone again; that's when we decided to move her into Melody Springs Living Facility. It didn't even bother her she was moving, although I did receive several calls from the nurses in those beginning weeks. Apparently, Mom demanded Brian pick her up and take her home.

Now, I'm sitting in her bedroom. The walls are lavender with white molding, and the barren fireplace is in the center. This could easily pass as a suite in some fancy hotel, and it never has that dank smell so many other facilities have.

Mom and Violet, her nurse, walk into the room.

"There's my baby girl," Mom says, coming in for a hug.

I stand and embrace her. I'm always comforted by how little she's changed. Her mind might be going, but she still has the same friendly eyes and wildly curly hair.

"Hey, Mom," I say, breathing into her neck. When she pulls away, I look at the nurse. "Nice to see you, Violet."

"That's funny," Mom says. "Violet standing in a violet room." She kicks back her head and laughs. She makes the same joke every time, but it's not some side effect of the disease. She always found something funny and said it over and over again. If I were to visit and she didn't say it, then I would be worried.

Violet laughs. "I'll let you two visit. Call me if you need me," she says, exiting the room.

Mom waits for Violet to be out the door before she speaks again. "Call if we need her." She rolls her eyes. "It's not like I'm some deranged citizen."

"She knows that, Mom. Violet is just being helpful." Violet started working at the facility a few months after Mom arrived. They hit it off, and I think they both benefited in making the other feel comfortable, but typical Mom means if she really likes you, it's only a matter of time before she also finds reasons to not like you.

"Where's Danny Boy?" she asks, leaning back and propping her feet on a tiny stool.

"He's golfing," I say, twirling my wedding band with my fingers. "You know he loves the courses around here."

"Yes, he does," she says, with a disbelieving tone. Again, Mom's not that out of it. He'll be here around Christmas; any other time, I keep him away. "How's school?" she asks, graciously changing the subject.

"Only two weeks left."

"I guess it is May, isn't it?" she says. "You and Danny going anywhere this summer?"

"I think Europe," I say, and I ramble off the list of possible destinations I've still not taken the time to plan, let alone book.

The conversation bounces back and forth. She tells me this story about when she and Dad first started dating and went to France. They missed their train and ended up spending a bulk of their vacation in the countryside as opposed to Paris, as they'd planned.

She smiles as she speaks, and there's a renewed life to her face. She always gets that look when she talks about Dad, and I can't imagine the pain she must feel knowing he's gone. I feel it too, but it's different. I imagine Dad strumming his guitar strings in some flower field while Mom got drunk off a bottle of wine. These are the best visits, when we can talk back and forth about material things; it's what our relationship has always been about.

"Who needs the Louvre?" she asks, still laughing about the missed train all those years ago.

"Well, let's hope we don't have any traveling snafus."

"Let's hope you do," she says. "Those make the best memories."

"They do," I say, trying to discreetly look at my wristwatch. I've been with her for almost an hour, which is what I promised Danny I'd do. He's not actually golfing, instead he's going to the store and buying a few groceries for the weekend.

I feel guilty, wishing away my time with her so I can go relax with my wonderful husband at a secluded cabin. Talking to her about my summer vacation, knowing she'll never have a trip so wonderful again. Or a man as wonderful as Dad or Danny. But then I remind myself we probably wouldn't even be this close if it weren't for the dementia. Our bond was strained growing up, and her diagnosis gave me the incentive to strengthen it.

"You feel all right, darling?" she asks.

"Yeah, I'm fine," I say, pushing my hair behind my ears. "Just tired."

"Your color is off," she says, squinting.

"We've barely eaten," I tell her. "I think we're going to grab lunch soon."

"You need to eat. Are you eating well during the week?"

"Yes, Mom."

"Grab dinner with friends. That's what I used to do," she says, smiling. "You still have friends up there?"

"Yes, Mom," I say, remembering how important her social engagements with other couples were to her. "Loads of them."

"Good," she says, patting my hand as it rests in my lap. "What about Brian?"

"What?" I ask, stuttering the word as it comes out.

"What about Brian? How's he doing?" she asks, staring at me with the same direct demeanor she's displayed throughout our conversation.

"Mom, I don't talk with Brian."

"Well, why the hell not?" she asks, her tone sharpening. "Your dad and I gave you a brother, and you don't even talk to him."

"It's not like that, Mom," I say, trying to avoid why we no longer speak. "Brian is—"

"Oh, here we go again." She throws back her head and gives her curls a hearty shake. "Brian this and Brian that. You know you were always so jealous of him."

I open my mouth, but words fail to come. I lean forward so my hair covers my face. I take a deep breath. Mom literally doesn't know what she's saying, and I don't even have the heart to correct her. But she'll never know, right mind or not, how hurtful these words are to hear. Like somewhere, in the same place where she's locked away those happy memories of Dad in France, there's the memory of me being jealous of Brian.

"You're right, Mom," I say. "I'm sorry."

"It'll really be better for you," she says, unaware of how much she's destroyed me with a few simple words. "Maybe if you act a little more like him, you'll feel better about yourself."

"I'll try, Mom," I say, pushing the silent button which notifies Violet to return to the room. *One... two... three.*

"When is he going to come visit?" she asks. "He's yet to see the place since we painted."

"I know," I say, my heart beating faster as I wait for someone to interrupt us. *Four… five… six.* I don't want Mom to see me cry. I stand, trying to turn my face.

"He's just so busy at school, you know," she says, twirling a ringlet of hair. "I bet Amber is still kicking herself for letting him go."

Suddenly, the room is spinning and I'm falling against the carpet, closing my eyes as the sound of Mom's voice fades away.

CHAPTER 21

Fall 2004

"Finish putting up the clothes," Mom said. She sat at the breakfast counter typing away on her laptop. She'd recently attended some planning convention where they taught her how to use PowerPoint. Since then, every spare moment seemed devoted to some adorable flyer or brochure.

"I put up mine," I said. I was in the living room, a fortress of folded towels and linens surrounding me. Pixie slept peacefully on my lap.

"Take Brian's clothes to his room," she said, still typing.

I rolled my eyes and lifted Pixie's tiny body off my legs. I loaded Brian's clothes into a basket and made the trek upstairs. Surprisingly, the door was open. I was used to knocking at least twice before he'd respond. He was gone.

I pulled out drawers and deposited the folded clothes. Looking around, I realized how long it had been since I'd been inside his room. It smelled raunchy. I spied three varieties of crumpled potato chip bags in different corners of the room. Dirty shorts and socks were wadded on the floor. An assortment of metal rods hung over his bed. I moved closer, knowing I'd never seen them before. Upon closer inspection, I grasped the rods were various knives, their pointy tips covered. I looked each one over. All were different lengths, some short like daggers, others longer like bayonets.

"What are you doing in here?" Brian asked. He threw his car keys onto his dresser.

"Putting away laundry," I said, returning my stare to the knives above his bed. "Why do you have knives on your wall?"

"Because they interest me." He brushed past me and sat on the bed, looking up at his possessions. "Each one has a different story. Would you like to hear them?"

"Different stories? I—"

Before I finished speaking, he pulled a small knife off the wall and held it. "This one is a Civil War bowie knife. Every Confederate had one. Neat, huh?"

"Where did you get it?" I asked.

"I get them online." He extended his arm. "Would you like to hold one?"

He had a blank expression as he offered over the weapon. I took it. My fingers rubbed the grainy imperfections along the hilt.

"How do you know it's real?" I asked.

"I vet the sellers before I buy."

He lifted another weapon from the wall and went into its history. He continued the process until he'd described each one. I stood quiet, listening. It was the most I'd heard him speak in years. Possibly ever.

When he finished describing the last one, I handed back the dagger. "Cool," I said.

I hadn't realized when he was speaking earlier, but there had been a perceptible glimmer in his eyes. It vanished, replaced again with his usual, cold stare.

"Cool?" He mocked me. "That's all you have to say?"

"I think they're cool, Brian," I said, scratching my neck. "What else do you want to hear?"

"Real descriptive, Della," he said, leaning back on the bed. "No wonder you're in standard classes."

I spun around, making a dramatic exit from the bedroom. Not that Brian cared. Upsetting me was never a concern; it was his intent.

Collecting knives. I thought it was an odd hobby for a high schooler. Of course, he had a lot of time to himself now that basketball was out of the picture. Brian didn't even attempt to rejoin the team. Coach Lawson urged him to play his senior year, claiming he'd been punished enough for last year's incident. But Brian was too stubborn. He knew it would hurt the team—and Lawson—more if he rejected the offer.

Since he no longer followed a rigorous practice schedule, I couldn't understand where he was in the hours between school and dinner. He didn't have a job, and Mom never encouraged him to get one. But it was obvious to me, and eventually our parents, that Brian had something keeping him busy.

Dad asked him outright over dinner where he was going.

"Out," Brian said, taking a bite of his sandwich.

"Out where?" Dad asked, unamused.

"I go different places," Brian said. "I don't understand what the big deal is. I'm always home before curfew."

"Of course you are," Mom said, refolding her napkin and resting it on her lap. "Your dad and I would simply like to know *where* you go. That's all."

I dipped my sandwich into a bowl of tomato bisque, allowing the crust to soak in the basil-infused juices. I waited for Brian to answer. I wanted to know where he went, too.

"I'm mostly at Danny's house. Sometimes I meet the guys at the park."

"Fair enough," Mom said. She stood and carried her empty dishes into the kitchen.

Dad wasn't convinced, and I wasn't either. Other than Danny, his only friends were his former teammates. They'd visited less frequently since the alcohol incident, and I knew he couldn't spend every night with Danny.

The next night, Brian claimed he was going to Danny's house. Mom was pleased he'd volunteered the information. I decided to follow him and see if that's where he was really headed. Our birthdays were a month away. Until I turned sixteen, I couldn't drive or get a job; I had all the time in the world to be a pesky little sister.

Through the living room window, I watched him leave. I let him get several meters ahead before I snuck out the front door. It was dark, so I kept to the far side of the sidewalk; Brian walked in the middle of the empty street, occasionally skipping left to avoid the puddles leftover from the afternoon rain.

As I suspected, he walked right past Danny's house. He didn't even look at the car in the driveway or the lit bedroom window. He wasn't going to meet Danny. But where was he going? A car pulled into the cul-de-sac, prompting Brian to move closer in my direction. I stopped and bent low behind some thorny bushes, hoping he wouldn't see me.

He approached the clubhouse pool lot and sat on one of the cement parking bumps. He took out his phone. Was he waiting on someone to pick him up? Someone he didn't want Mom and Dad seeing?

A few minutes later, I heard footsteps approaching from the other side of the street. I ducked behind another bramble so that no one could see me, but I still had Brian in my view. As the person drew closer, I realized it was Amber. I crouched lower; if she spotted me, she'd offer a greeting and Brian would know I'd followed him.

Since the Jeremy Gus incident, Amber and I hadn't spent much time together. We'd been growing apart for ages, really. Amber always prioritized status. Her primary goal at school was to be popular. I didn't think we'd speak at all if it weren't for living so close.

Brian looked at Amber as she walked in his direction. He stood and slid his phone into his pocket.

"Is that you?" Amber asked. She must be talking to Brian. She would have seen him sitting under the bright streetlight.

"Who else would it be?" he asked.

I moved to my right to get a better view. Brian extended his hands to grab hers. Amber arched onto her toes for extra height and kissed him on the mouth. Not a friendly kiss you see fancy friends exchange. A real, grown-up kiss. The kind of kiss I'd never had. The kind of kiss I could have gone an entire lifetime without seeing Brian have.

"What the hell?" Without thinking, I darted into the street. Any worries I had about Brian disappeared. Amber and my brother? Kissing?

"Della, what are you doing here?" Brian looked genuinely startled, then his face turned furious.

"Are you two, like, dating or something?" I asked, my arms folded over my body.

"Della," Amber said, taking a step toward me. "We wanted to tell you—"

Brian cut her off, clearly upset. "Della, what are you doing here?"

"I followed you," I said. I wasn't worried about Brian anymore. I was angry. Brian wasn't hiding activities from my parents; he was hiding Amber from me.

"I told you we should have come clean," Amber mumbled. She gave me a look of pity, but her body language suggested triumph. In Brian, my brother, Amber had finally landed her popular catch.

I turned and made the short sprint back to our house. The front door slammed, shaking the frame and disturbing my parents' regular nightcap.

"What's wrong?" Dad asked, putting down his glass.

"Brian isn't over at Danny's house," I said, panting from both my emotions and the quick jog.

"He's not?" Mom asked from her barstool. She stood just as Brian came in the door behind me.

"Where were you?" Dad asked immediately.

"Della shouldn't be following me around the neighborhood," Brian said.

"We'll deal with that later. If you weren't at Danny's house, where were you?" Dad asked.

Brian exhaled. "I was with my girlfriend."

"Girlfriend?" Mom tried to sound shocked, but the layer of delight was too thick. She was proud of Brian. Impressed.

"Since when do you have a girlfriend?" Dad asked. His tone was calm, but it had an edge.

"It's been a few months," Brian said, looking down. "I didn't want to make a big deal about it."

"You shouldn't hide something like that from us," Mom said.

"You shouldn't hide anything from us," Dad corrected.

"I don't get it," Mom said, walking after me. "What are you upset about?"

"Tell them who your girlfriend is, Brian," I said.

"Amber." Brian looked at all of us, waiting for approval.

Dad lifted his head, as though everything made sense. Why Brian had lied. Why I was upset. I wasn't excited with Brian's first girlfriend being my former best friend. And Mom wasn't happy about it either.

"What?" she asked, the outrage in her voice returning. She walked toward Brian. "Amber from down the street?"

"Yes." Brian ran his fingers through his hair. "That's why there's no reason for you to worry where I am. We rarely leave the neighborhood."

"Honey," Mom said, flattening his hairs in place. "You could do so much better than Amber."

I felt the urge to defend Amber, despite the fact she'd ditched me as a friend and then secretly dated my brother. Mom didn't mind her as my best friend, but she clearly thought she was beneath Brian. Really, any girl probably was.

"That's not the point, Mom." I stomped upstairs and slammed my bedroom door.

That weekend, Brian agreed to help Mom at some fundraiser downtown, leaving Dad and me alone for the night. I think we were both happy. We needed the occasional absence of Mom's hysterics and Brian's moodiness.

Dad sat beside me on the sofa. "Pizza?"

"You read my mind," I said.

Mom and Brian were still running around the house when we left. We went to our favorite pizzeria. Dad even let me drive, although I wouldn't officially get my license until I passed the test next month.

Dad and I talked about our usual topics. Music and movies and politics. As we were getting ready to leave, I brought up Brian.

"Do you know Brian has a bunch of knives in his room?" I asked, closing the lid of our takeout box. "Don't you think it's weird?"

Dad sipped his drink and cleared his throat before he responded. "Lots of people are interested in weaponry."

"Out of all the hobbies he could pick up, he has a fascination with knives?"

Dad nodded again. "I think it started with some research assignment for his A.P. history class. He likes tracking weapons and learning the history behind them."

"Yeah, he told me all about the history." I folded my arms. "I just think it's creepy."

"This interest of his seems to have renewed his spark. I support him. You should, too."

Me supporting Brian. How was I supposed to maintain a good relationship with someone whose intent was to destroy me? He either mocked my looks or my intelligence or my friends. I even thought he was dating Amber to get under my skin.

"You don't see how mean he can be sometimes," I said. "It's like he's always cutting me down."

"He's an older brother." He looked at me with knowing eyes. Dad was the youngest of three boys. "That's what they do."

"It's different with him. It's… darker." I looked away. I'd given up trying to talk about Brian a long time ago. Never seemed to do any good.

"I know he can be difficult."

"It's like no one else sees it," I admitted. "How mean he can be."

"I see how he is. But I also see what he's been through, especially in the last year. Losing basketball was a big deal to him, even if he pretends it wasn't," Dad said. "But he shouldn't take his frustrations out on you. That's the hardest part of being a parent. You're always trying to balance what each child needs."

After dinner, Dad and I watched a movie at the theater. It was after ten when it ended. When we returned to the house, Brian and Mom were standing in the kitchen. They both jumped when we walked in. It looked like Mom had been crying.

"What's going on?" Dad asked.

Mom looked at me, her face full of remorse. "Honey, we can't find Pixie."

I dropped the takeout box onto the counter. "What do you mean you can't find Pixie?" I stomped up the stairs to my bedroom, then back down. "Pixie! Pixie!"

"She must have run off, honey," Mom said.

"Pixie's an inside dog!" I shouted. "She's never gotten out of the house before."

Mom looked at Dad, then me. "We were rushing around trying to get everything ready for the banquet. We must have left the back door open."

"What?" I shimmied into the coat I'd just taken off. My pulse pounded and I started to cry. "Why would you leave the door open? That never happens."

"Slow down, Della," Dad said. "Where are you going?"

"I'm going to look for her," I said.

"Honey, we've been looking for her. You don't need to go outside this upset," Mom said. "Maybe she'll turn up in the morning."

"I've been circling the neighborhood for an hour looking," Brian said.

I hadn't acknowledged him throughout the conversation, but now I did. I really saw him. That smug smile of his was about to break.

"You," I said. "You did something to her, didn't you?"

"Della, it's not like that," Mom said.

"It's exactly like that. He's done something to Pixie. She wouldn't just run away."

"What do you think I did to her?" he asked, almost like he was testing me.

"You've been dying to get rid of her since I got her. You probably killed her with one of your creepy little knives," I said.

"Oh, come on," Mom said. "You sound ridiculous."

"I know about the squirrel," I said, looking at all of them. I still didn't know exactly what happened, but I knew enough. Whatever happened had worried Dad. "He's hurt animals before."

Brian stepped closer. He was angry now. "Maybe you should spend more time looking after your dog than following me."

"This isn't on me!" I shouted. "I wasn't even freaking here!"

"Della!" Mom tried to calm me.

"Is that why you did this?" I asked Brian. "Because I outed you and your little girlfriend?"

"I didn't do anything to your stupid dog. You're just pissed your best friend would rather spend time with me than you."

"Hey!" Dad tried to interject.

"She's my best friend, but even I know she's the most desperate girl at school. Great catch, Brian," I said.

"Like I need dating advice from you," Brian said.

"She'll have nothing to do with you after I tell her you got rid of Pixie. I'm going to tell everyone at school you're nothing but a freak," I said.

Brian lunged at me. He moved quickly, like an animal acting on instinct and nothing else. He pushed me against the wall and tightened his hands around my throat. His pupils were almost entirely black.

Dad grabbed Brian's shoulders and pulled him away. For a moment, I thought Dad might hit him. I think Dad thought that, too. I'd never seen him with a red face and white knuckles. Dad adjusted his glasses and took a deep breath. Mom wailed.

"Don't ever touch your sister like that again!" Dad shouted. "Do you hear me?"

Brian pushed Dad in one swift move. Dad didn't react. I think he already regretted what he'd done, pouncing on Brian like that, even if he was defending me.

Brian stared at all three of us, taking in several replenishing breaths before speaking. He looked at Dad. "If you touch me like that again, I'll kill you," he said. He stomped up the stairs, leaving us all in silence, each one of us catching our breath.

I didn't think Brian meant his threat, and I'm sure he regretted saying it. Apart from anything else, because Dad would be dead within six months.

CHAPTER 22

Now

We need to get to the cabin soon. I don't have to google the forecast to know a storm is settling in. One of those quick, typical spring squalls, but I fear too many fallen branches will block the narrow driveway leading to our lodge. Danny and Violet shake hands before he enters the car. He sits for a moment, taking a breath before he starts the ignition.

"Do you want to tell me what happened in there?" he asks.

"I just got a little woozy. It's not a big deal." I prop my feet on the dash. "Violet shouldn't have called you."

"Yes, she should have." He starts the car and rumbles out of the near-empty parking lot. "And I should have come with you. You fainted, Della. Something must have set you off."

"I'm fine," I say, looking out the window. Tiny drops of water sprinkle the glass.

I don't want to tell Danny that Mom mentioned Brian. Bringing it up will give Brian more attention than he's worth. Even I don't know why I had the physical reaction I did. I remember feeling like I was falling, and then Violet was there, helping me off the floor. It's probably connected to my sick spell this morning.

We pull into a pharmacy parking lot. "I'm going to get you some Tylenol before we head up the mountain," Danny says. I know he's trying to shake off his worry and salvage the weekend.

"I'll go in," I say, unhooking my seat belt. "Need anything?"

Before he can protest, I'm out of the car. The chilly breeze wooshes past, and I hustle inside. I feel as though I've already ruined our weekend. I shouldn't have insisted on visiting Mom. I'm stressed enough with everything happening at Victory Hills.

I pick up some Tylenol before moving on to the vitamin aisle. I usually take a multivitamin but ran out while we were in Hilton Head. It's the only change in routine that might account for my funk. That, and the introduction of Zoey into my life, but I'm trying not to think about her.

I close my eyes and imagine it's still spring break. I remember the sun against my skin, the saltwater in my hair, Danny's hand holding mine. It's the last time I felt like life was in balance. As I exhale, I scan the plethora of pills promising to make you healthy and strong. I choose a bottle and start reading the contents. As I put it back, I realize they're prenatals.

I think back to the beach. I'd fretted over starting my period that week and was thankful when it held off. That was… three weeks ago. I rub my forehead, like I'm not doing the math right. Surely I couldn't be three weeks late? That never happens. Had I been so preoccupied I hadn't noticed? I think of how tired I've felt since our return. Nauseous. I've been stressing about Zoey and thinking about Brian. But what if there's another explanation for my symptoms? I move to the next aisle and look around a bit before making my purchases.

We've stayed at this place before. It's a small one-bedroom with a fireplace in the living room and a hot tub on the wrap-around porch. The perfect setting for a romantic weekend, and yet I feel I've already ruined that. And now I've got other worries on my mind.

I grab my luggage from the backseat and slide my pharmacy bag inside the front zipper.

"You're in a hurry," Danny says. He's still standing at the back of the car, looping grocery bags across his forearm.

"Bathroom," I say, nodding my head at the locked front door.

"Key should be under that rock by the left," Danny says. "You sure you're okay?"

"Fine," I say for the hundredth time. I skid the rock over with my foot and bend to retrieve the key. The door creaks open, and I see the familiar sight of our rented living room. The stone fireplace reaches up to the paneled ceiling which makes the room forever smell of pine. I walk down the narrow hallway leading to the bedroom. I throw my bags on the bed, immediately opening the front pocket to make sure my pharmacy bag is still inside. Of course it is. But now I feel all fidgety and forgetful, like maybe I'm making something out of nothing.

Am I supposed to just take the test now? Should I tell Danny first? No, I don't want to do that. No sense, when it could be a false alarm. I'll take the test first. I run my fingers through my hair and stare at the vaulted ceiling. The fan spins slowly above me. I don't even have to go to the bathroom yet! Maybe I am just losing my mind. It feels that way a little bit.

When I re-enter the living space, Danny stands at the counter preparing a marinade. He stops what he's doing, walks over and kisses my forehead. "Maybe you should come by the office when we get back in town. Run some bloodwork."

"I don't need all that," I say, hopping onto one of the barstools. "You know how anxious I get about visiting Mom. I just worked myself up."

He finishes seasoning the meat, then puts it back in the fridge. "Wine?"

"Maybe at dinner." I should know whether I'm pregnant or not by then. "How about tea instead?"

Danny picked up a gallon of sweet tea at the market. He grabs two glasses and fills them with ice. "You keep saying you're stressed out. How are things going at school?"

"Fine." I reach over and grab my glass of tea, immediately begin drinking.

"Are you still worried about that student? Zoey?"

I don't like hearing that name come out of Danny's mouth. The surprise of it almost makes me choke. "Oh, her. She's still a bother, but not much I can do about it."

"She hasn't caused you any more problems?"

I clench my jaw and shake my head. "I think I overreacted to the situation, really. I don't have proof she hurt her classmate." I'm not going to tell him about her other comments, or the fact I visited Ms. Peterson yesterday. Danny's already worried enough. Besides, I'm worried about me now, too. I can deal with Zoey later.

"So." Danny looks down at his drink, around the room, then at my face. He's searching for a topic. It's usually not like that between us. Words come freely. "I'll get the fire started before dinner." He leaves his glass on the counter and walks across the room.

"I'm going to freshen up," I say, slinking down the hallway. I pull the pregnancy test out of the bag, looking over my shoulder for Danny. It's not like I'm trying to be secretive. But if I take the test and it's negative, then all this fuss will have been for nothing. If I take it and it's positive, well, I still don't think I'm ready to process that. Danny and I have always said we didn't want children. Though, at times, I think it comes more from me than him.

I go into the bathroom and lock the door. By now my bladder is as tight as my nerves. I read the directions over a few times to make sure I don't mess it up, although I bought a two-pack, just in case.

I take the test, placing the stick on the bathtub ledge. I look in the mirror. My skin is a bizarre combination of pasty and pink. What I really need is rest. My mind needs rest from thinking about Zoey and Darcy, from remembering Brian. I splash my face with water, savor the immediate coolness. I need to stop worrying about other people's problems. Ms. Peterson and Pam and Mom. I'm on a weekend getaway with my husband. I deserve to enjoy myself. I brush through my hair with my fingers, making sure each strand is in place. I feel better now. Not necessarily like I can take on the world, but like I can enjoy my dinner. Victory Hills will present enough problems for me on Monday. Tonight, I want to enjoy life for what it is. I can sort out the other stuff later.

I take a deep breath, feeling much calmer and more capable than I did five minutes ago. I lift the test, expecting to see a single, negative line.

But I don't. I see two lines. That means positive. That means I'm pregnant.

I pull the instruction pamphlet out of the box and read over it again. Maybe I did mess this up. Maybe I waited too long or didn't provide an appropriate sample. There must be something, anything that would account for this test being positive. I'm a grown woman on birth control, and this can't be happening.

Just then, Danny raps against the door.

"You feel like getting in the hot tub?"

"Um, no." My voice is crackly. I hadn't realized it until I spoke, but I'm crying. "Maybe later."

"Della?" He knows something is wrong. "Open the door."

I look in the mirror at myself holding the test. I've deliberately withheld information from Danny in recent weeks, but this is too much to carry. After all, I guess it's not just my news. It's his, too. I open the door. He can see by my face something is wrong.

"Della, you're scaring me."

"Sit down for a second," I tell him.

He does. I stand in the doorway, leaning against the frame with my hands behind my back.

"I know this seems out of left field, but after my fainting spell earlier I got to thinking—"

"You said that was just nerves."

"Just hear me out. I got to thinking about everything. My behavior the past few weeks. I've not been myself. I've been tired. Emotional. I thought it was just stress at work." I look down, trying not to think about that. Not now. "It dawned on me at the pharmacy I'm about three weeks late. I picked up a test, just in case."

Danny squints and nods with every other word. "A test? You think you might be pregnant?"

I take the test from behind my back and hold it in front of me. "I don't know how this happened. Really. But it says positive."

Danny stands, taking the test from my hand. He looks at it for a few seconds, then back at me.

"My goodness, Della."

"I know. I never—"

"This is fantastic." He wraps his arms around me, lifting me off the floor. He kisses my neck. "You've acted so weird since we left your mom's. I thought you were about to break some bad news or something."

"You're happy?"

"Of course I'm happy. Especially considering the alternative. A baby... it's just great."

"But I thought we decided we didn't want children."

"Sure, that's what we said. I figured that lots of couples say that when they're young and focusing on careers. They don't always mean it unless..." He jerks his head back, like he's seeing me differently. "Unless you meant it."

I suddenly feel like our relationship has cheated him. Like I'm robbing him of what he really wants. I want to cry, or vomit, or something. I sense a physical reaction coming on, but I'm not sure what.

"Look, when I woke up this morning, I didn't expect to find this out. When I took the test ten minutes ago, I didn't expect to find this out. I need time to process."

"Right, right. I'm getting a little ahead of myself." He rubs the back of his neck, sways from side to side with the test still in his hand. His first reaction to the news was joy. Danny didn't need time to decide he wanted to be a father, and he judges me for not

being as readily taken by the challenge. "I'm going to start dinner."
He starts to hand the test back, before fidgeting and dropping it
on the bed.

A baby. *Baby*. It's a terrifying word. I've never wanted children.
Maybe that's not entirely true. I used to babysit for some of the neighborhood kids. Monitoring children for a few hours is nothing compared
to raising them. I realized that, even back then. But any desire I once
had to be a mother fizzled when I realized what Brian had become.

I never looked at motherhood the same after that. Images of
squishy limbs and big eyes were replaced with research about predisposed violence and genetic traits. Even now, as I try to envision
a combined version of myself and Danny, all I see are the negative
traits I could pass along. What does it matter if our child has my
green eyes and Danny's dark hair, if they end up with Brian's temper?

And now it's not just Brian I'm worried about. He's not a lone
monster, Zoey's entrance in my life proves that. It's a dangerous
world full of dangerous people. Can I really bring a child into this?
What if they become prey? What if they become the predator?

When I emerge from the bedroom, I can smell the hickory sweet
scent of meat. It makes me hungry, not nauseous, and I hope more
nasty symptoms don't start picking up. Danny is setting the table.
I walk up behind him and squeeze my hands around his middle.

"You hungry?" he asks.

"Starving."

He pulls me around to face him. "I'm sorry if I got too excited
in there. I wasn't meaning to put pressure on you."

"You don't have to apologize for being happy. I'm just still in
shock."

"I never expected I'd be as happy as I was. I'd got myself thinking
something bad was going on. I thought you were about to tell me
you were having an affair, or something."

I slap his shoulder before taking a seat at the table. "Seriously? What would make you think that?"

"You've just seemed so distant. Like you're holding something back. Even you said you've not been yourself. I guess I was just expecting to hear the worst."

I feel guilty. I couldn't imagine my life without Danny, but I've been keeping things from him. He doesn't know how upset this Zoey stuff has gotten me. The pregnancy might even explain why I've been so on edge. Zoey Peterson is a damaged girl, but I've yet to find proof she attacked Darcy. Maybe my hormones have me overthinking. Overfeeling.

"I love you. I wouldn't have kept this from you, but I really thought it was a fluke," I say. "I didn't expect for it to be positive, and I'm still racking my brains about whether I did it wrong."

Danny walks over and slides a steak from his platter to my plate. My mouth waters just looking at it. "Those tests are more reliable than people think. You're more likely to get a false negative. If the hormones are in your system, it's going to pick them up."

I feel a pang of disappointment. I was hoping to blame manufacturer or user error. "There's a second test in the pack. Maybe I'll take it later."

"Do it in the morning. The test is the most accurate then."

I nod my head as I cut into my steak. Red juices ink the plate as I put a bite in my mouth.

"I think this could be really great for us," Danny says. "It's not like we aren't capable. Sure, we might have to cut back on traveling and other things. But we have plenty of income. You have a great schedule."

"Danny, you know my hesitancy to have children has nothing to do with my career. Or yours."

Danny stands, walks across the room and stares out the window overlooking the porch. "You can't let him ruin this," he says. "Being his sister isn't a precursor for what our child might be. Truth be told, I could have lived the rest of my life with you the way things are. But now that there is a baby in the picture, I'm happy about what's coming next."

"Me too," I say, even if it's not totally real. I've only had a couple of hours to try and restructure more than a decade's worth of thinking. Being Brian's sister, I've felt it's my responsibility not to add more darkness to the world. But is that what this baby would represent? Darkness? Danny seems to think this baby is a beacon of light. A blessing. Maybe I deserve a happy ending.

CHAPTER 23

Now

I wake up on Monday feeling restless. The romantic weekend wasn't what it was supposed to be. We should have been staying up late and drinking wine and sleeping in. Instead of forgetting our problems, we were confronted with a whole other issue. Pregnancy. It still doesn't seem real. I've heard mothers say that before. Even after they take the tests and start gaining weight, a small part of them still can't believe it. As though someone is pulling a trick on them.

That's how I feel right now. Tricked. I hadn't asked for this. I can't ignore Danny's optimistic readiness. Even after we talked and talked about the baby, promised to make rational, mature decisions, he floated around the cabin. He couldn't hide his anticipation and excitement. I didn't know, until I showed him the test, how much he'd wanted a child. How much he'd suppressed those feelings in support of me. I'm almost jealous of his enthusiasm. All I feel is unprepared and irresponsible and scared.

By the time I arrive at school, I've pushed my thoughts about the pregnancy away. I'll deal with family issues at home, I tell myself. Here at Victory Hills, I have other problems. I'd hoped the pregnancy news might explain my behavior in recent weeks. Perhaps my concerns about Zoey were internal after all, a strange mixture of hormones and new life wreaking havoc. Hormonal or not, I can't wipe the concerned look on Ms. Peterson's face from my memory. I was surprised she was as wary of her own daughter as I was. I want to hear Pam's thoughts.

When I arrive at Pam's office, two people I've never seen before are sitting inside. She sees me standing behind the glass, walks away from her desk and opens the door a crack.

"Hey, Dell, I can't talk right now," she says.

"No worries," I say, craning my neck to get a better look at the two people in the room. One man, one woman. Both look official. Both are wearing gray.

"Come by during your planning period, okay?" She shuts the door, returns to her desk and resumes her conversation with the two official looking strangers. I can't hear what they are saying, but their constantly moving mouths indicate a lively conversation being had.

The bell rings and, one by one, the students file in. Devon and Ben and Adam and Darcy. By the end of the tardy bell, Zoey still hasn't arrived. She doesn't show up for the entirety of first block. I'm partially happy I don't have to interact with her, but I'm also suspicious. The only other time Zoey has been absent was after the knife incident.

As fourth block begins, I stand outside Pam's office door. She sees me and waves for me to enter. I take my usual seat. Danny and I decided we wouldn't announce the pregnancy yet. It feels odd sitting here, knowing I've got this transformative news, and not sharing it.

"I was just about to call you in here," she says, chomping the last bite of her lunch and throwing away the Styrofoam containers.

"I didn't mean to interrupt anything this morning."

"No, it's fine. But we've had a situation and I knew you'd want to be filled in. It involves Zoey Peterson."

My throat closes in. Was I right? Zoey was absent because she'd done something? "She wasn't here today," I stammer.

"I know. And there's a reason for that. Apparently, there was an incident at her house last night involving the mother."

"Ms. Peterson?" I recall her sour stare on the porch. "My goodness, Pam, is she okay?"

"As good as can be expected. Apparently her mother went into a drunken rage last night. She was passed out on the sofa, and when Zoey tried to wake her, her mother started beating her. Zoey called the police and is now officially in CPS custody."

I scoot toward the edge of the seat and balance my arm against Pam's desk. "Wait, you mean Ms. Peterson did something to Zoey?"

"Yes. When officers arrived last night, Ms. Peterson was barely coherent. They've charged her with domestic battery and child neglect. Zoey was transferred to a foster home last night. That's why she wasn't at school today."

"I don't understand," I say, leaning forward. "It doesn't make any sense. The woman just started beating her daughter at random. Why would she do that?"

"According to Zoey she's had a drinking problem for years. Last night, something must have set her off. I wouldn't be surprised if there have been previous incidents of abuse."

Ms. Peterson didn't strike me as abusive during our meeting. She seemed afraid of her daughter. I don't believe she's capable of harming her. All of the negative thoughts I had about Zoey have re-appeared in full force. "How do we know Zoey is being truthful?"

Pam leans back in her chair, gently swaying her weight from one side to the other. "I told you. Police arrived and could see Zoey had been attacked. The mother was wasted. They could barely get her in the car."

"But why are we immediately believing Zoey?" I ask, knowing how horrible it sounds, but feeling confident, in this particular situation, the question has merit.

Pam turns rigid. "When children come forward with abuse claims, we believe them."

"But Zoey Peterson is not a typical child!" I shout.

Pam stares, blankly. "Della, I know you've had suspicions about her. She rubs you the wrong way... I understand that. But we have no reason to think she would lie about her mother abusing her."

"I think she's lying," I say. "I've met her mother. She didn't strike me as abusive."

"When did you meet her mother?"

"I went to her house Friday afternoon. During the track meet."

"Was there a particular reason for this visit?"

"I only wanted to meet the woman. Figure out more about Zoey's background and her home life."

"But why, Della?" she asks, confusedly. "You've shared your concerns about this student with me, but why would you go out of your way to visit her home?"

"Look, Zoey has displayed, in my opinion, disturbing behavior. I still believe she wrote that essay. She had me fooled when she pulled the Bad Mom card, but that was before I knew you'd already confronted her. She was bluffing me. That whole conversation. I decided to look into her home life myself."

"What happened during the visit?" Pam asks, dryly.

"Ms. Peterson and I sat on the front porch and drank sweet tea. I was there maybe twenty minutes, but I was able to determine Tricia Peterson isn't some unstable parent. She certainly isn't abusive. If anything, she seems scared of her daughter. The reason she doesn't go to the track meets is because of Zoey. She calls her a *drunk skank!*"

"What do you mean she seems scared of Zoey?" she asks. "Did she say anything specific?"

"She said the best thing for me to do is stay out of Zoey's way," I say. "She didn't give me any particular reason, but I'm telling you, she knows there is something wrong with her daughter. And I know it, too."

"Well, Zoey is now the victim. Her mother attacked her."

"How do we *know* she attacked her? What if Zoey attacked Ms. Peterson? Organized this whole event to punish her mother or get her out of the house?"

"Della, I'm your friend." She bows her head and shakes it. "But I must tell you, I think you're reaching here. I can't just start a campaign against Zoey Peterson based on a hunch!"

"I'm just saying, how do we know she's the victim here?"

"Because Zoey is the child." She shakes her head again. "You say Ms. Peterson seemed scared of Zoey. But what else did you see? Was she sober? Can you think of any reason why Zoey would want to attack her own mother?"

I remember the ripe smell of liquor on Ms. Peterson's breath when she stumbled to stand. But I can't tell Pam that, not when she is already convinced Ms. Peterson was at fault. "She knew I had suspicions about her daughter. And instead of telling me to screw off like a normal parent would, she warned me. She knew exactly what I was talking about. She did not seem like the type of person who would attack her daughter."

"You don't know how someone acts when they drink."

I open my mouth, then stop. Pam excels at her job because of her objectivity, but now I see her opinion about Zoey's mom is personal, much like my opinion of Zoey. She knows what it's like to live with a drunk, and now that's all she sees. Zoey's situation as a representation of her pain. I don't know how Ms. Peterson reacts when she's drunk, but I know Zoey is manipulative. She found a way to use her mother's condition to her advantage.

"But it's the timing of everything," I start again slowly, calmly. "They just moved here and were left a beautiful farmhouse. Ms. Peterson wouldn't have a reason to snap now. But if she and Zoey were fighting about something else—"

"Do you know what they might have been fighting about?" Pam interrupts.

I sigh and look down. "Before I left, I told her to ask Zoey about the Spring Fling after-party."

"Della, what were you thinking?" She plops her elbows on her desk and sighs. "You can't talk to a parent about something like that."

"I was careful. I didn't mention Darcy's name or the attack or anything. I only told her to ask Zoey about the party. Which, by the way, she *did* attend."

"Teenagers lie sometimes, Della."

"Exactly," I say. We lock eyes, and I see a hint of worry on Pam's face. Concern. For me. "I don't have proof Zoey Peterson hurt her mom. Or Darcy. But I do believe she's capable of both."

"Well, if you want to hold an underage girl responsible for violent crimes, you're going to need more than a gut feeling," she says. "And you shouldn't be investigating on your own. Nothing can be done until a formal complaint is made against Zoey, and that hasn't happened yet. Considering Darcy can't remember the attack, I doubt it ever will."

"Where's Ms. Peterson? Maybe now that she's sober, she can tell police what happened."

"She hasn't said anything about Zoey harming her. She's currently sitting in jail." She clasps her hands and looks at me. "Look, as your friend and your colleague, you need to back away. Let this Zoey Peterson thing go."

"Where is she staying now?" I ask, wishing Zoey had never walked into my classroom.

"She's in CPS custody. They'll find her a temporary home."

"Will she even come here anymore?"

"Yes, they typically try to find a place within the same school district. We don't need to disrupt even more of her life."

"All right, I guess I'll have her back in class," I say, standing.

"Yes, you will." She stands, too. Placing her hands in front of her body. "But, please. There are only two weeks left before summer. Let it go."

I nod and exit Pam's office. As I walk through the hallway, I tell myself I'm not crazy. I'm more than just hormonal. Zoey Peterson is a threat, and eventually I'll make others understand that. *One... two... three.*

CHAPTER 24

Now

I can't get Ms. Peterson out of my head. I certainly wouldn't nominate her for mother of the year, but if my suspicions about Zoey are right, which I'm convinced now more than ever they are, who could blame the woman for wanting to check out mentally? She's raising a potential psychopath.

People always return to this debate: nature vs. nurture. Did horrible parenting make the kid do this monstrous thing, or was that evil inside the kid all along? I read about the topic extensively in the years after Brian's arrest, back when I was consumed by answering the question: *Why?* Why did Brian become who he became? Could something have stopped him?

I discovered the most notorious offenders typically come from chaotic homes. Some childhoods are so horrendous, it's no wonder the individual grew up to hate; he or she had spent their entire lives being hated. I imagined how that person might have adjusted if they didn't have such terrible parents and traumatic experiences. Would they have still grown up to hurt?

But that's where Brian stumps me. He's in that small percentage of people that grew up to commit heinous crimes despite having been raised in 'normal' homes. Whatever the hell normal means. My parents weren't perfect. Mom was checked out, but in a different way from Ms. Peterson. Instead of booze and cigarettes, Mom used her social life as a distraction. She was more interested in looking like the perfect parent than being one. An involved mother would have recognized there was something wrong with her son, like Ms. Peterson clearly has with Zoey. A better mother would do something about it, something neither of the women tossing around in my head did.

And Dad… he was just Dad. He saw what was inside Brian, but he didn't have enough time to do anything about it. I like to think, had he not died, he eventually would have intervened. That he wouldn't have released Brian into the world knowing he was capable of harming others. No, in my mind Brian has always had 'Nature' written all over him. He was born to be the person he became. A rougher upbringing would have only made his behavior more dangerous.

I'm still on the fence with Zoey. Is she nature or nurture? I don't know enough about her background to fully decide. Ms. Peterson didn't appear to be as functional as my parents, but she didn't strike me as abusive. She seemed afraid of Zoey, all too willing to stand out of her path. I assume that's why she's not speaking up now; Zoey can't retaliate against her if Ms. Peterson stays in a jail cell, and that poor woman was already living like a prisoner. I think of the way Zoey treated her mother, calling her a drunk skank. As I hear the words play back in my mind, it's Brian's voice I hear.

I'm also considering the differences between male and female offenders. Violent women are rare in a statistical sense, but they're not as uncommon as people think. It's no surprise Pam and others are hesitant to accept Zoey as a threat; girls don't typically hurt others the way boys do.

Most violence stems from a search for dominance, a need to exert power. That much is common ground. Often with men, there is a sexual element involved. That was the case with Brian, and most other monsters we watch on primetime cable. It's why most people assume Adam targeted Darcy. He's the angry ex-boyfriend. He can overpower her, take what he wants.

Women can be just as destructive, although their methods are usually more discreet. They often act out of need, doing what they must in order to gather the resources necessary for survival. Another common motive is revenge. I've kept returning to the comment Coach Gabe made when I had gate duty. He said some of the girls had given Zoey a hard time. Hazing her, I presume. Ms. Peterson mentioned this, too. The whole school seems enamored with the track team's improvement, but that couldn't have been the case for the girls Zoey replaced. Girls like Darcy. It would explain why the two girls seemed to be arguing at Spring Fling, and why Zoey made insensitive comments after the attack.

Zoey is also perceptive. It didn't take her long to pick up on Darcy's influence at Victory Hills. Maybe she attacked Darcy that night in hopes of retaliating, but was interrupted by the police. Once she saw the school's reaction, she realized it was in her best interest to keep Darcy on her side. Darcy became her resource. That's why she's secured their friendship and done her best to widen the target on Adam's back. The motives are becoming clearer in my mind, and yet, the proof! Proof is what I need, what everyone else needs, to truly understand what Zoey has become.

It's Tuesday afternoon and I'm sitting across from Dr. Walters.

"What's on your mind today?" she asks, peering at me through red-rimmed lenses.

There is a plethora of things I could talk about. This is, usually, my space for making sense of my feelings. I could use an outside perspective more than ever.

"I did get some news over the weekend." I look down, playing with the fringed ends of my shirt. "Turns out, I'm pregnant." This is the realest it's felt. Saying the words aloud, feeling them leave my tongue.

Dr. Walter's eyes brighten, and she lifts her head. "That's exciting. Congratulations."

"Thank you." I look down again. *Congratulations.* This is supposed to be celebratory news, isn't? It's only been three days, but happiness hasn't overridden the shock. "Danny is over the moon."

"How are you feeling?" She's picked up on something. My hesitancy, maybe. Or my worry.

"Surprised. I'm afraid, really. Considering my childhood."

Dr. Walters nods, shifting her weight to the edge of her chair. "Were you planning for this baby?"

"No." My voice quivers, feeling permission to explore my uncertainty. "That's why I'm not as excited as Danny. I was on the pill. I might have missed one or two a while back, but I don't think I did. It feels selfish to say, but I didn't ask for this."

She nods and settles into thinking position. "What specifically about having children bothers you?"

"It's not the baby, obviously. It's everything else that worries me. The world and the people in it." I think I'm talking about Brian. I want to be, but in my mind, I see Zoey.

"You don't want your child to suffer, like you did at the hands of your brother."

"I don't want my child to turn out like Brian." I feel tears sitting on my bottom lashes.

"You must know the likelihood of passing on your brother's violence is rare."

"Rare. Not impossible," I say, wiping my cheeks. "A little like conceiving while on birth control, I guess."

She laughs at this, before settling into a place of comfort. "There's always a chance a person can be bad, even if they aren't genetically predisposed. The risk is there, sure. But what if your child turns out like you?"

I close my eyes. I don't want a little miniature version of myself any more than I want one of Brian, or Danny even. I want this child to be their own person, follow their own path. I just don't want that path tarnished by Brian's actions, or by someone else who has yet to come along.

"Can I tell you something?" she asks, prompting me to open my eyes. "Lots of mothers feel this way, even the ones who don't have the experiences you have. Parenthood ushers in fears, but it also brings moments of unspeakable joy. You can't have one without the other, unfortunately. And as this child's mother, you have to decide how much of your own experience you want to impart on them."

She's right; I know it. If I'm not careful, I could color my child's future. I think of where I was in the years following Brian's arrest. I was bitter and paranoid, allowing the past to define me. I was young, too. Nobody is their fully formed self in their teens and twenties, but I'd been burdened in carrying a heavier load than anyone should. I had to grow up, but I also had to let go. I had to envision the life I wanted for myself, aside from Brian and Mom and everyone else, and fight for it. It's how I made it to where I am today, even if it feels like the façade is starting to slip.

"I'm still processing, of course. At least the pregnancy explains why I've been so out of sorts lately."

"Out of sorts?"

I'm on a roll when it comes to saying what I'm thinking, a refreshing change from all the thoughts I've kept locked inside. "On my last visit, I told you about my student. The one who was assaulted after the school dance."

"Yes, I remember," she says, crossing her legs. "How is she doing?"

"Darcy still hasn't opened up about what happened that night." I look to my left, assessing the clock on the wall for how much time is left in the session. "I think I know who was responsible for the attack."

"Tell me about this person. The one you think is responsible."

"Well, she's a new student at Victory Hills. I've had some tense encounters with her in the classroom, and I think she had reason to lash out against Darcy. Typical girl stuff." I sound foolish saying the last part. Typical girl stuff sounds so used, and it usually doesn't end with someone's leg being slashed. I consider telling her my concerns that Zoey knows about Brian, but I decide against it. "This girl has a volatile home life, and now I have reason to think she might have harmed her own mother. Problem is, I can't get anyone to believe me."

Dr. Walters sinks into thinking position. She waits several seconds, filtering her thoughts. "You don't have solid proof."

"No. It's more of a feeling. The way her behavior has changed ever since she's moved here." I can't get into all the details; there isn't enough time.

"You said you thought your pregnancy might explain your reaction to this situation."

"Well, yeah. I thought maybe I was just being hormonal and emotional." I want that to be the reason, but I don't believe it is.

"It makes sense why you would be so bothered by Darcy's attack. You don't think you did enough last time, so you're trying to right that wrong."

I know I didn't do enough. I'm well aware Darcy reminds me of someone else. "It's not just that. I want the person who hurt Darcy to be punished."

"Do you see any connections with the person who hurt Darcy?"

"Yes, totally. She reminds me of Brian in lots of ways."

"Does she remind you of yourself?"

I lean back and squint. Zoey? Like me? "Not at all."

"I'm only wondering why you're focusing on this student. You've already acknowledged you don't have proof she hurt anyone. Maybe there is something drawing you towards this girl, something besides what you label as her disturbing behavior."

"I'm not following," I say, leaning forward.

"Your pregnancy represents a new phase of your life. It's natural for you to reconsider the other phases while you're processing this one."

"I only learned I was pregnant this weekend. I've had suspicions about this student for weeks."

"Subconsciously, maybe you've known longer? You said yourself you thought the pregnancy might explain some of your paranoia."

That's because I'm desperate for something to explain these feelings, something other than I'm crazy or Zoey is a psychopath. "Her familiar behaviors frighten me because I know she's a threat, not because I think I'm like her."

"You say this student is new. She had some trouble in the beginning, but now she's making friends. She's got her whole life ahead of her. How does that relate to what you went through at her age?"

We both know the answer. I felt like I had no opportunities. Brian had taken them from me. Most teenagers spend those years chasing adventure, arms open, ready for mistakes and whatever else might come. I spent those years cradling my mother, trying to piece together the world Brian had wrecked. I couldn't trust family, friends, myself. Zoey is nothing like that. She's in control and she knows it.

Dr. Walters must know she struck a nerve. She's frozen in the listening position, waiting for me to say something profound.

"I wouldn't wish the heartache I went through after Brian on anyone," I say. Even Zoey. "I think this girl is dangerous. My past doesn't cloud my judgement."

I need that to be true. We sit in silence, both unconvinced.

CHAPTER 25

Now

By morning, I've come up with at least one plan of action, and thankfully it doesn't involve reaching out to anyone at Victory Hills. I'm going to dig into Zoey's past. Her mom insinuated she's been in trouble before. If Zoey has had issues at other schools, I should be able to access her records by contacting old schools. I need to know my fears about Zoey aren't being caused by hormones or guilt; I need validation.

On Wednesday, I take the students back to the computer lab, allowing them to revise their previous essays. Really, it's an excuse for me to keep them busy while I do research of my own. Of course, this time I take frequent strolls around the classroom, bending down and looking at computer screens to make sure everyone is staying on task. I spend extra time looking over Zoey's shoulder, making sure she's not crafting confession letters. She senses I'm watching her more closely than the others, awkwardly tensing whenever I walk by. In fact, Zoey has given me nothing but hateful looks since she walked into the lab this morning. The issue of her mother lingers between us, but neither of us has addressed it.

When I'm confident all my students are settled, I return to my computer. I log into the Victory Hills record system first, writing down the names of schools she's attended. It appears she was in the same elementary school in Kentucky until sixth grade. That was the first notable move, after which she was homeschooled for a year. She attended a middle school in Kentucky, then entered her freshman year of high school in Virginia. She attended a second Virginia high school before enrolling at Victory Hills.

I reflect upon the upheaval involved with each relocation. It's a lot of moving for a child to experience; Brian and I always stayed in the same school district. Sure, some of the moves might be attributed to Ms. Peterson's instability, but I suspect Zoey's behavior might have contributed. As Pam previously confirmed, none of the schools were located in Florida. *Lying twerp.*

Now I have a neat list with phone numbers and contact names. I set it to the side, intending to make the calls at the beginning of my planning period. Before the bell rings, I walk around to each student and tell them to place their finished essay in my hand. When Zoey hands me her paper, I notice a small scratch under her left eye. I smile.

I start dialing Zoey's former high schools first. I ask to speak with counselors, as they are typically the ones dealing with both transfers and behavioral issues.

"I'm Della Mayfair from Victory Hills High School," I say when the receptionist answers. "Could you connect me to the guidance department?"

"There is no one in guidance today," she replies.

"Maybe you can help me," I say. "I'm trying to track down information about a student who recently transferred here."

"Guidance has access to all the records," she says. "You'll have to speak with them."

"When would be the best time for me to call back?" I ask. Most secondary schools in the southeast are gearing up for graduation ceremonies. I should have known it would be a hectic time.

"I can pass along a message," she says, already bored.

I provide my name and cell phone number. I also leave Zoey's name, explaining I'm trying to help her with college admissions essays. It's not like I can say I'm calling to dig up dirt.

Frustrated by the slow start, I call the other high school on the list. That counselor doesn't provide much information. She describes Zoey as *a doll*. Her Kentucky middle school counselor has a similar take. Zoey was a star student there, just like she is at Victory Hills.

Finally, I call the first school she attended. Boone County Elementary School. It's the place where she spent the longest stretch of time before being homeschooled. A secretary answers the phone. I give her my line about college admissions essays and ask to speak with the school counselor. Unfortunately, he's unavailable.

"Sorry," says the woman on the phone. "He's doing the whole college tour mess with his daughter. She's the last of the lot to go, so he took the day to visit campuses with her."

"That's nice," I reply, thinking the secretary's talkative nature might work in my favor. "Are you familiar with the students at school?"

"About have them all memorized by heart. I've been here almost thirty years," she says, as I'd suspected given her shaky tenor.

"Well, do you think I could ask *you* some questions about this particular student?" I ask. "See, she only enrolled with us a few weeks ago. I'm trying to gain a more comprehensive understanding of her background."

"I'll help if I can. If she's looking at colleges, it's been several years since we've had her, but we're a small school. Makes it easy for kids to leave an impression. Give me a name," she says.

"Zoey Peterson."

"Peterson," she repeats. "What years did you say she was here again?"

"She left in 2015. She was in sixth grade."

"Let me think," she says. I imagine her behind the reception desk, gladly accepting the opportunity to make the afternoon round up faster with a friendly telephone chat.

"She was an only child. Dark hair. She has a single mother."

"Zoey, you say," she starts, added excitement in her voice. "Zoey Peterson."

"Yes."

"Scrawny little thing?"

"Still is, so I'm assuming."

"Yes. I do remember her," she says, but her voice is no longer peppy. "You say this is for a college application?"

"Yes."

"God bless her for making it this far," she says under her breath, but loud enough for me to hear. "I can't tell you much about that one. At least nothing you'd want in a college admissions essay."

"Well, is there anything you *can* tell me about her? Anything at all?" I ask, hoping I'm not pushing my limits.

"You're able to see she didn't choose to leave school, right?" she asks, dryly. "She was told to go."

I don't have detailed access to her records, which is the main reason I'm calling counselors to begin with. Nothing in her file says she was asked to leave.

"Do you remember why? It's not something I need to include in the essay," I assure her. "It would be off record."

"I remember her because in thirty years I've not seen another student do what she did," she says, her voice low. "We established the rule about classroom pets because of her."

"Classroom pets?"

"Yeah. It was a big mess between the school and the mother, if I remember. Probably why she doesn't have much information to give you. She was a piece of work."

"What did she do?" I ask, trying to hide my desperation for an answer.

"She killed the classroom pet. Brought a weapon from home and stabbed the poor thing."

"My goodness." This is what I need. Proof Zoey is disturbed. I'm filled with a bizarre mix of disgust and excitement. "Did she do it in front of the students?"

"No. Thank the Lord. We only caught her because we'd recently installed cameras outside along the building. If I remember correctly, she was waiting to be picked up by that mother. The poor critter curled up beside her, and she sliced it with a pocketknife."

"That's shocking," I say. "Especially considering how well-rounded she seems now." I didn't want to give up my charade. I was supposed to be helping Zoey after all, not gossiping.

"Well, I'm surprised, to tell the truth. That was one of the biggest fits we've had at the school. I wouldn't want something from so long ago to hurt her moving forward, especially if she's turned it around."

"Of course," I say. Before I get off the phone, I ask, "What kind of animal was it?"

"A cat," she answers.

CHAPTER 26

Spring 2005

I've spent most of my adult life blaming Brian for the bad things that happened. I wish there was a way I could blame Dad's death on him. But it was no one's fault. He went to sleep one night and never woke up.

The easiness of his death made it hard for all of us to grieve. I was sitting in Algebra class when I was called over the intercom. When I arrived at the office, Brian was there, too. Still, I didn't think anything of it. Someone dying was far removed from my mind; our grandparents had all died either before we were born or when we were toddlers. People in my life didn't die, let alone my father.

Mom was locked in a prison of grief back at the house. That's why Wanda, the school secretary, told us. She didn't think it was right to send us home not knowing what gruesome news awaited there.

Her words snatched all the oxygen from my body. The ground below me disappeared and I fell to my knees. I still recall that sense of falling, as though my feet would never find steady ground. For the first time, I knew what it was like to be frozen. To watch seconds tick by and not acknowledge them. To feel like I was no longer part of the world whatsoever.

Slowly, the sensations returned. First, the coarse carpet under my knees. Then I sucked in shallow, hurried breaths. Finally, I felt a hand on my back. Brian's hand. He remained standing over me, lightly touching my right shoulder blade.

"Della," he said, his voice an echoing force pulling me back to reality. "Della, are you okay?"

I'd never seen concern in his eyes before. Wanda kneeled in front of me on the floor and held my hands. Her face carried all the grief Brian's lacked. I was too young to go through this, she thought. It was the first time I'd ever received the victim look. Finally, the tears came, and I'm not sure when they stopped.

We learned later it was a brain aneurysm. Paramedics said we should be comforted by the fact he died peacefully. Our minister reiterated this sentiment, saying a serene death was his reward for living such a good life. In some ways, I agreed. Dad didn't die violently. He didn't suffer through a painful illness. But being allowed to live a little longer seemed like an equally beneficial reward. The suddenness of his death made it harder to accept.

That morning, I should have known something was off. Dad was always the first person in the kitchen, sitting upright by the breakfast bar with his coffee. I dashed through the kitchen, only pausing to grab a banana. I barely even registered his absence. I wish I had, although the paramedics assured me he was gone by that point. He'd died sometime during the night. I considered the irony, that I would feel the weight of that same absence every morning moving forward.

Brian drove me home. My Aunt Tilda greeted us at the door; Mom was already medicated and back in her bedroom. The house felt empty. It seemed larger, even. The warmth of the place was gone. I didn't realize how often music played in the house. Dad's music, whether he was strumming his guitar or playing records. It was background noise which I never appreciated until it was no longer there.

That night, I went to Brian's room. His door was cracked. I made a light knock before pushing it open. He was under his covers, writing in a notebook. He met me with those accusatory eyes.

"Hey," I said, not sure where to start.

"Hey." He looked away from me and back at his notepad.

"What are you doing?" I asked, my voice girlish and desperate. I didn't want to return to our quiet house. I'd rather talk to Brian than do that.

"I'm working on a list."

"A list of what?" I asked.

He laid the notepad flat against his legs and shifted his torso to face me. "If you must know," he said, "I'm working on a list of songs. For the funeral."

"That's nice, Brian," I said, taking a step closer into the bedroom. "Can I see?"

He held out his notebook. I sat on the edge of his bed and glanced at the list. Each one was familiar. Each one was Dad. For the first time all day, I smiled. "These are perfect."

"I know we can't play all of them," he said, taking back the paper.

"We'll see what we can do," I said. "Aunt Tilda will be here in the morning. She said she'd help us plan the funeral if Mom is, well, you know."

"Okay," he said. He was bored with me.

"Are you okay?" I knew Mom was a wreck. I was, too. As usual—even in a moment of tragic circumstance—I had no idea what Brian was thinking. He'd always been fond of Dad. Unlike Mom, he respected him. Their scuffle last fall had been uncharacteristic, but it hadn't defined their relationship in the months that followed. I was happy, for Brian's sake, they'd moved past it. I didn't want his memories of Dad to be tainted.

"I don't know," Brian answered. It was the most honest he'd ever been. He didn't know what he was feeling, if he was feeling it. He couldn't verbalize his emotions. Grief, even to me, was indescribable. But I understood my life would never be the same.

Thinking about all of this brought back tears. I started hyperventilating.

"Della," Brian said, with the same uneasiness he'd displayed in the principal's office earlier that day. He couldn't offer comfort or wise words. He wasn't Dad. No one was.

I stayed in his room for a long time that night. He watched me cry in silence, but at least I wasn't alone.

After the funeral, everyone gathered in our living room for an early dinner. We were overwhelmed with casseroles and baked goods in the days following Dad's death. Aunt Tilda organized everything on the breakfast bar so family and friends could share one last meal in honor of Dad.

Mom did her best to make conversation with everyone. She tried to be her normal, social self, but watching her was hard. She was broken. Brian and Amber sat on the staircase holding hands. I had no one to really talk to. No one to really understand me. The one person who always managed to make me feel better was gone forever.

Awhile later, I slipped out the front door without anyone noticing and started walking down the street. Outside, the sun was setting, and the streetlamps flicked on. I walked along the sidewalk, thinking about Dad and all the things I'd miss about him. His kindness. His wisdom. I thought about all the future experiences that had been robbed from me. He'd never see me graduate. He'd never meet my first boyfriend. He'd never walk me down the aisle.

I followed the circle of houses leading me back home. I hoped by the time I returned everyone would be gone and I could finally be alone. I already felt alone and feeling that way with a bunch of people in the house nearly suffocated me.

I walked past the community pool. As I passed Amber's house, a crashing sound interrupted my concentration. The sky was now completely dark. There were only patches of light streaming down from the lampposts along the sidewalk. I heard another sound, realizing it was coming from Amber's garage. The light was on, although the rest of the house appeared dark. Her parents were probably still at my house consoling Mom.

I moved closer to the garage and peered into the lower windows. Her mom's car was parked inside, and the walls were lined with shelves and boxes. I looked closer and saw a pair of legs beside the car. It was Brian. His pants were around his ankles, and the tail of his shirt fell almost to his knees. Amber was in front of him, her skirt hiked up to her waist.

Gross, I thought. I felt physically ill. I could have gone my entire life without seeing this, let alone on the worst day of my life. What was Brian thinking? Acting this way with Amber after our dad's funeral?

As I turned, I heard another sound. A painful gasp. Like someone struggling. I looked back. Brian had his hand around Amber's throat. The other hand was yanking at her hair. It didn't look like sex, or even rough sex. It looked like Brian was hurting her. My first instinct was to bang on the garage door, but before I could, Brian looked over his shoulder. He saw me.

The look on his face terrified me. I stumbled back, picking up pace down the sidewalk. The last thing I needed was Brian complaining I'd followed him again. But it wasn't just that. The whole scenario disturbed me. I was so frazzled; I didn't even notice Danny walking to his own house.

"Della," he said. "Is that you?"

"Danny," I said, dropping the hand that had been covering my mouth. I was out of breath and crying from all of it. Shock. Fear. Grief.

"Are you okay?" He stepped away from his front porch and came to meet me on the sidewalk. "What am I saying? Of course you're not okay."

"What?" I asked, my mind still picturing Brian and Amber. Oh right. Dad. "I'm still waiting for everything to sink in. I can't believe he's gone."

"I loved coming to your house over the years. He was a great man," Danny said. "He'd be so proud of you and Brian."

I blinked the image of Brian away. I looked behind me to see if he was coming. He wasn't, so maybe he hadn't seen me after all.

"Are you sure something else isn't bothering you?" Danny asked. "You seem scared."

"I just…" My mind was weary, too tired to say anything but the truth. "I just saw something really disturbing. I don't know what I should do about it."

"What's going on?"

"I just saw Brian… with Amber."

"Like, *with* Amber?" He gave me a knowing wince.

"Yes."

"Man, that's awkward." Danny looked embarrassed for me, and slightly annoyed with Brian for not being more discreet.

"It wasn't just that." The scene flashed through my mind again. "The way he was with her. He looked like he was hurting her."

"Hurting her?"

"She looked like she was in pain. He was squeezing her throat. It was the scariest thing I've ever seen."

Danny exhaled. "Okay, even thinking about that makes me cringe—"

"No, forget the sex part." I'd told Danny what I'd seen, and now all the details were pouring out of me. I couldn't hold them in a second longer. "He was attacking Amber. He's dangerous. Violent."

"Violent?" Danny put his hand on my shoulder. "Just take a breath."

"No, I need to do something about this. I need to tell Mom. Brian can't go around acting that way."

"Don't you think she's got enough on her plate right now?"

"I'm telling you, what I saw was not normal." I pressed my palms against my temples.

"Della."

"I don't know if Amber is even okay. Maybe we should go back together. Make sure he hasn't hurt her," I said, pointing down the street.

"Della."

"I've always known he was a creep, but to be doing something like that after our dad's funeral—"

"Della, will you just *stop*?" Danny shouted. His volume silenced my rant. "I know you don't particularly like Brian, but he doesn't need an annoying kid sister right now."

I stared at Danny, embarrassed I'd just unleashed the way I had. But still, I knew what I saw wasn't right. If he could only understand. "I'm not being a kid. I'm scared."

"I can only imagine what those two are up to. But it's none of our business. You don't need to make the situation more awkward by getting others involved."

"He was hurting her, Danny."

"Knowing Amber, she was probably into it. Just give the guy a break. He's grieving, too."

I started crying over all of it. Dad was gone, and he'd left me in a world where no one believed what I had to say.

"Della, I'm sorry. I don't even know what I'm saying right now. I'm only taking up for Brian because he's my best friend. I know what it's like between the two of you, but I shouldn't have lashed out like that."

He hugged me and wouldn't let go until I sank into him, my forehead resting against his bony shoulder. I knew he didn't mean to be harsh, but Danny didn't know what it was like between us. No one did.

CHAPTER 27

Now

I can't sleep. I've downloaded one of those pregnancy apps that tells you how your baby is progressing from week to week. Of course, I don't know exactly how far along I am because I still haven't had a proper ultrasound. Based on my last period, we estimate I'm between six and seven weeks. According to the app, the baby is around the size of a pea or a lentil. Strange to think something that small can make such a difference in a person. The app says expectant mothers have unpredictable sleep patterns around this stage, but I don't blame my lack of sleep on the baby. I blame Zoey.

I now know Zoey has acted violently in the past, but I have no solid proof she hurt either Ms. Peterson or Darcy. She's become skilled in hiding her violence, just like Brian. He didn't stop doing bad things, as a more adjusted person would. His acts grew more dangerous, but his ability to hide became better.

I just wish I could get someone—anyone—to see the situation from my perspective. See the real Zoey. I've already bothered Pam enough. There's nothing she can do without proof, and it's wildly unfortunate we live in a society that waits for bad things to happen before doing anything.

Suddenly, it comes to me: Marge. She's the only employee who knows more about the students' personal lives than Pam. Marge may be riding the *I love Zoey* train, but if I explained to her my suspicions in full, she might be more likely to listen. I consider this possibility some more, until I lazily drift off to sleep.

On Thursday, I rush to work in hopes of catching Marge in the teacher's lounge. Unfortunately, she's not there. By lunch, I still haven't seen her, so I send a text.

You at school today? I ask.

I skipped. Had to get ready for the Year End Bake Sale, she replies, with a cookie emoji.

Can I come over after school? I ask.

It's not unusual for me to drop by her house. It's happened in the past, although I feel I've barely seen her outside of school since spring break.

Sure. You can be a taste tester!

In Victory Hills, everything is a short drive away. Marge's neighborhood is full of homes that millennials would describe as starter homes. Little square houses with two or three bedrooms, wooden fences crossing the backyards and newly-paved sidewalks crossing the front lawns.

When I park in front of Marge's house, she's outside loading a half dozen foldable tables into the back of a truck. Marge hosts the Year End Bake Sale annually. Proceeds fund last-minute Prom expenses. Parents contribute several items, but she bakes the majority herself.

"Hey, lady," she says when she spots me walking across the street. At her feet is a large cardboard box. She bends over and starts rummaging through it.

"You have enough food to feed an army," I say, peering at a box filled with individually wrapped Rice Krispie treats.

"We've had several donations this year," she says, lifting the box and putting it inside the cab of the truck. "I'm waiting on some other parents to stop by, then I'll head to school and start setting up."

"Can I help with anything?"

"You're welcome to shop the sale," she says. "We've got cake pops and miniature pies. Tomorrow Melanie Fisher's mom is bringing apple turnovers."

"Sounds delicious."

"The bags with the yellow stickers are nut-free, the green stickers mean gluten-free and the blue stickers are dairy-free."

Marge has numerous allergies, nuts being one of them. Each year, she hosts a faculty assembly over the proper way to use an EpiPen. Bowles might get the title of principal, but it's people like Marge who keep the place functioning.

I grab a brownie in a sticker-free Ziploc bag. "How much?"

"Please," she says, waving me down. "Just eat it."

I put the brownie in my bag for later. "I'll pay you in labor. Let me help you lift these tables." The offer leaves my lips, and my hand instinctively brushes against my midsection. I don't need to be lifting anything, I remember.

"No need," Marge says. "Thankfully, I've got an extra set of hands today."

"Yeah?" As the words leave my mouth, I look at Marge's front door. Standing there, leaning against the brick, is Zoey.

"I guess I didn't tell you about my new roommate," Marge says.

"Your what?" My words trail away. I haven't stopped staring at Zoey. She sees me now, acknowledges my presence with a light wave before ducking inside.

"Marge, what is she doing here?" I ask, looking at her with frightened eyes.

"I guess you heard about what happened with her mother." She shakes her head and makes a pitiful *shoo* sound.

"Yes, but why is she here? I thought she was with CPS."

"I volunteered to let her stay with me until the end of the semester," she says.

"Marge! What are you thinking?" I bite my bottom lip, upset I've not had the chance to tell her my suspicions about Zoey sooner. It's just like Marge to help a student in need. It's what she always does. She doesn't know the potential danger Zoey presents. I soften my tone and lower my volume. "Do teachers typically take in their students in a situation like this?"

"I've fostered before, you know. Never anything long-term, and usually the children are younger. But what can I say? I like the kid. It's bad enough she came here so late in the year. I thought, if she stays with me, at least she can remain at school with a sense of normalcy."

"That's very admirable, Marge," I say, wanting her to understand I appreciate her kindness. "But there's something you should know."

Like a phantom, Zoey appears at my side holding a roll of duct tape and cutting scissors. "Happy Almost-Friday, Mrs. Mayfair."

"Zoey," I say, hesitantly. I look at her but cannot reciprocate her smile. I don't even have the spirit to fake it.

"Hold on, guys," Marge says, staring across the lawn as a car pulls up. An older man exits the vehicle holding an aluminum platter. "Looks like we have another food delivery."

She skirts across the lawn, leaving us alone. Zoey stares at me for a beat, scissors in her hands, then places them on the grass. She hauls a foldable table off the ground and into the truck bed.

"What brings you here?" she asks.

"Ms. Helton and I are friends, Zoey."

"Do you often hang out after school?" she asks, still focusing on the task in front of her.

"Sometimes," I say, irritated by her questions. Across the lawn, I see Marge is busy talking with the visitor. "I'd rather know why *you* are here?"

"You didn't hear about what happened with my mom? I thought you might know, considering how close you two are." She stops pushing the table and looks at me with those empty eyes.

"What's that mean, Zoey?" I ask, careful not to give her more information.

"She told me about your visit last week," she says. "She said you seemed like a very concerned teacher."

"I visited her, and we talked about your progress at school."

"Well, everyone at school seems to think I'm progressing just fine. Except for you. I wonder why that is?"

There are so many things I want to say to her right now. So many accusations I want to throw her way. But I can't. She probably wants me to act hysterical, react in a way that will make me seem unbelievable should anyone start listening to what I have to say.

"Your mother thinks you're adjusting, too," I say, instead. "She said you had a great time at Spring Fling. And the party."

I hold her eye contact, letting her know, as discreetly as possible, I'm onto her. I'm onto her lies, and it won't take me long to uncover more.

"Maybe I just *told* my mom I was at the party. Isn't that what teenagers do? Tell their parents they went one place, so they can really go somewhere else."

"I've not been a teenager for a while," I say. Then, whispering, "Is that what you two fought about over the weekend?"

She flinches, letting me know I'm right. Ms. Peterson did ask Zoey about the party, and the exchange which unfolded led to violence. She recovers quickly, smiling.

"I'd rather not talk about what happened." Her eyes turn from cold to pitiful. "It wasn't a good night."

"Must have been traumatic," I say. "For both of you."

I know what I'm saying is wildly inappropriate, especially considering Zoey has recently been labeled a victim of violence. But

I don't believe her. And I want her to understand my accusations, even if I can't voice them.

She lets out a quiet laugh.

"You would know about that, right?" she asks. "Overcoming trauma?" She smirks, placing a box inside the car without taking her eyes off me.

I breathe shallowly, because now I'm not the only one making allegations. *One... two... three.* I feel, for the first time in a long time, someone is looking at me not as Della Mayfair, but as Brian's sister. She knows.

"Don't stop working now," Marge says to Zoey, standing between us.

"Sorry, Ms. Helton. I was just telling Mrs. Mayfair how appreciative I am you agreed to take me in."

"Don't get all soft on me," she says, squeezing Zoey's shoulder. "And you should call me Marge. At least when we're not in chemistry class."

My entire body feels hot, and there's a thin line of sweat between my palm and the strap of my purse. *Four... five... six.* "Marge, I'm not feeling well. I'm going to head home," I say.

"You all right, Dell?" she asks. "You look pasty. Come sit on the sofa. I'll make you a drink."

"No, no. I'm fine. We'll talk tomorrow," I say, stumbling toward my car. *Seven... eight... nine.* "Thanks for the brownie."

"Be careful, Dell," she warns me, uneasy. I can tell she's concerned, but she has no way of knowing why I'm suddenly on edge. Or that I'm not the one who needs to be careful.

I get to my car, but before I open the door, I stop and turn. "Marge?" I yell across the narrow street.

"Yeah?" she hollers back.

"You don't have a cat, do you?"

"Nope," she says. "I'm allergic."

Zoey keeps her back to me as she wrestles another table. She doesn't respond to the question I ask, acts as though she didn't even hear. She has a much better poker face than I do. But I hope she did hear, and I hope she's wondering what else I know. Wondering how much of her past and present I'm starting to piece together.

"Good," I say to Marge, getting inside my car and slamming the door.

CHAPTER 28

Now

On Friday morning, I go straight to the employee lounge. As expected, Marge is inside preparing her morning coffee.

"You feel better?" she asks, stirring her cup with a spoon.

"Yeah," I say, remembering my sudden departure yesterday. I spent most of the evening on the couch with a cool rag on my head. Danny said I'm likely to feel this way the next several weeks. He thinks everything is pregnancy related. Maybe some of it is, but I think Zoey's pull is getting stronger. "I did want to talk to you about something, though."

"Shoot it, sister," she says.

"Will you come to my classroom?" I ask. I don't want to have the conversation where others might hear.

She follows me through the hallway. I unlock my door, throw my bag on the desk and offer Marge a seat.

"Everything all right?" she asks, concern in her eyes.

"I need to talk with you about Zoey Peterson," I say, rolling my computer chair toward her.

"Okay," she says, a smile on her face. "You know, I thought she was a good kid when I had her in class. You should have seen how helpful she was yesterday. I think she set up every table in the gymnasium."

"Look, the reason I came to your house yesterday is because I wanted to talk to you about Zoey. I didn't realize at the time she had moved in with you."

"Well, it was a last-minute arrangement."

"I think it's admirable you offered her a place to stay," I say, dropping my head into my hands. "But there are some things about Zoey you need to know."

"What's going on, Dell?"

"I think Zoey is disturbed." I know it sounds ridiculous, and the blank stare Marge returns doesn't make me feel any better. "I think she was the student who attacked Darcy Moore. She's displayed more threatening behavior since then. And I really don't think she should be living in your house."

"Okay." She stretches out the syllables and repositions herself in the cramped student desk. "What makes you think Zoey hurt Darcy?"

"I... I saw them at the dance," I begin, feeling already like what I say won't be enough. I clear my throat, restart with a stronger voice. "I saw them at the dance. I know she went to the after-party where Darcy was assaulted, even though she lied about attending. A week after the attack, I received an anonymous written account of what happened that night. I think Zoey wrote it."

"But why Zoey?" she asks, turning her head. "How do you know she wrote this message?"

"She was in the computer lab when it happened," I say. "None of my other students would have written something so disturbing."

"How do you know that?" she asks. "Was her class the only one in there that day? Or did you take your other classes?"

"All of my classes were in there—"

"When did you find this paper?"

"It wasn't until the end of the day—"

"So you don't know which class period it might have come from?" she asks, aggressively.

I stare at her, knowing I'm already losing the battle. "I know it was Zoey."

"Why are you so convinced?" she asks. "You're making an allegation about a student I've only had pleasant interactions with."

"That's the thing. I haven't had pleasant interactions with her. She shows me a different side. And it's not just the essay. I think she's done other things. Violent things."

"Like what?" She leans against the back of the chair, crossing her legs as best she can under the tabletop. At least she's willing to hear me out, but she wears the same expression Pam did earlier in the week. She's unconvinced.

"The week following the attack, Adam told me there were students harassing him. He even suspected someone killed his cat."

"Adam's on edge with everyone these days. I've heard his other teachers talk about it."

"I think Zoey is using that to her advantage. She's purposely pushing Adam's buttons. That's why she killed his cat." I'm afraid to tell her the next part, but I must so she can start making connections for herself. "I called Zoey's former schools. She was expelled from an elementary school for killing a cat on school grounds."

Marge raises her hand to her chin and steadies herself on the desk. She's thinking. Finally, she speaks. "How old was she?"

"She was in sixth grade."

"And none of this was on her official record?"

"The school secretary told me about it. I'm not sure why none of this is in her file." I roll my eyes and flick my hand. "Maybe she was an athlete there, too."

"Come on, Della," Marge says. "They wouldn't ignore something like that for sports."

"You're right," I say. "But for whatever reason, they didn't add it to the official file. They told her to leave and she did."

"The cat incident is… disturbing. But that was several years ago. Maybe there were things going on at the time we aren't aware of."

"Really?" Now I'm the one who sounds frustrated, leaning back and straightening my posture. "There's no excuse for it, and I don't think it's a coincidence that Adam's cat was killed, too."

"I appreciate your concern," she concedes, leaning forward. "Based on what you've told me, I will be more alert."

Her words are as empty as her face is blank. She doesn't believe me. She thinks I'm blowing this out of proportion.

"I think Zoey hurt her mom," I say, knowing it's my last hope. She thinks the Darcy attack is unlikely, and she deems the cat incident a coincidence. I can see it in her eyes. But harming another adult—her own mother—will make her see how dangerous Zoey is.

Marge, who was in the process of standing, sits down again. "What makes you think that?"

"I spoke with her mother. I don't believe she's an abusive woman. If anything, I think she's a victim."

That disbelieving stare returns to Marge's face. "When did you speak to her mother?"

"The same weekend she was attacked," I say, flailing for backup. "I told her to ask Zoey about the after-party. I think she did. And I think that's what got her hurt."

"You told the woman you think her daughter might have committed a crime against another student?"

"No. I didn't even tell her what happened at the party. I just told her to ask Zoey."

"Well, her asking resulted in Zoey being attacked," Marge says, standing and slamming her fist against the desk.

"Marge, why are you so convinced—"

"Because I believe the victim, Della," she says, her voice shaking. "I believe the child."

"I hate to even suggest something like this. But sometimes—"

"No, what you are doing is completely uncalled for. Making accusations. Tracking down her old teachers. Visiting her mother. This is a witch hunt."

I'm hunting something else entirely. Someone who is savvy and capable, and now she even has Marge wrapped around her finger. "I think the mother is the victim here. I'm not making these accusations based on one event."

She stands by my door, looking back at me. "I'm sorry, Della. You sound delusional."

I gasp-laugh, still not understanding why no one sees events from my perspective. Marge is now the second friend of mine in the past week to dismiss my allegations and label me as insane. But the only emotion larger than my sadness is my fear. My worry for her. Because she's put herself in a trap, and only I can see it.

"You might not believe me. But at least consider what I'm saying. She has a violent history. I think she's assaulted one student, harassed others. She hurt her own mother." Now standing by my classroom door, I open it to offer Marge an exit. "And now she's living in your house. Be careful."

"You can't just go around making allegations, Della," she says as she walks past me. "You're the one who should be careful."

To say I'm on edge would be an understatement. My desire to cry grows stronger when I'm alone. One of the worst feelings to have is the idea you might be crazy. It's not self-imposed. It's a marker given to you by others. And once you have it, no one ever really sees past it. *One… two… three.*

I've been here before. This exact place of trying to prove I'm not wrong, that a dangerous person is out there. No one listened to me fast enough last time, and I'm convinced the outcome will be just as catastrophic this time around. The thought of seeing Zoey in a few minutes makes me physically ill, and I feel as though I might get sick. *Four… five… six. Oh, screw it.*

With only minutes remaining before the morning bell rings, I grab my cell phone and dial the main office.

"Victory Hills High School," says Heather, our school receptionist.

"It's Della Mayfair. I don't know what's come over me, but I'm not feeling well. I've not had time to call a substitute—"

"Hey, Della," she says, cutting me off. "We can find you one, if you need."

"Would it be a problem?" I ask. I never take a day without making proper preparations first.

"Not at all. I'll announce for your classes to report to the library until someone arrives."

"Thank you," I say. "There's an emergency lesson plan in my filing cabinet."

"Get some rest." Heather is nowhere near as talkative as the secretary at Boone County Elementary School, but she's equally effective. I grab my bag and rush to the parking lot. By the time first block commences, I'm already on my way home.

CHAPTER 29

Fall 2005

The summer after Dad died was different. I still felt his absence. An almost tangible sense of loss in everything I did. There were no more musical interruptions. There were no more morning chats. Now sixteen, I was able to drive. I drove Dad's station wagon, which made me proud and sad. I worked my first job at the concessions stand at the local movie theater, scooping popcorn and drizzling butter over the kernels. Just as we settled into our new roles, everything changed again. Dad was gone, but Brian would soon be gone, too.

Brian welcomed college with open arms. He'd been a standout in Wilsonville for years, but that was getting old. He wanted to impress new people, exceed new expectations. He wasn't going far. Sterling Cove University was only two hours away. Bordering the shoreline, the campus was known for both its scenic setting and party atmosphere. Still, the college had a rigorous program. While most Wilsonville students would drop out after freshman year, the ones that did graduate entered the workforce with impressive resumés. It's why Danny was also attending SCU, hoping it would be an appropriate precursor for medical school.

On the morning he was due to leave, Mom woke up early to prepare breakfast. When I walked downstairs, Brian was already at the table. I wiped away sleep from my face with a knuckle. Mom and Brian appeared fully awake.

"I just can't believe my baby boy is going to college," Mom said, her tone fake but cheery. Her eyes danced from Brian to me. "Pancake or waffle?"

"Waffle," I said, taking my seat at the table. I knew it was an important morning when she was offering both.

"I'll take another pancake, Mom," Brian said, snapping a strip of bacon with his teeth.

"Are you nervous?" I asked him.

"Excited more than anything," he said. He was lying. I could tell. His nostrils flared, and his eyebrows arched slightly. Brian wanted to appear casual, but he had the butterflies of every other eighteen-year-old in his position.

"You're going to love it," Mom said. She took the top pancake off her stack and put it on Brian's plate. "I'm telling you, when people say college was the best time of their life, they're not lying." She took a bite of food. "Until you have kids, of course."

"Do you think you're going to miss me?" Brian asked. He didn't look at either of us directly. A person listening in would think the question was directed to Mom, but I sensed he was more interested in an answer from me.

"Of course, darling," she said. She lifted the carafe and refilled his juice. Brian smiled, then looked in my direction.

"Sure," I said, taking the last sip from my glass. It was a lie, but my response came off more convincing than Brian's denials of nervousness. "Will you miss us?"

"Sure." He didn't break eye contact. So many lies had been tossed around at this breakfast I wasn't sure what was the truth. I just knew my brother was leaving—less than a year after Dad had left for good—and my life was about to change once again.

An hour later, and they were gone. Mom followed him to campus in her car, leaving me behind. Her car was packed full of junk she'd bought for his dorm. She said we'd plan a visit sometime later in the semester.

I walked back inside the house. Dad was gone. Now Brian was gone, too. Mom was coming back. But the two of us living together would be a completely new dynamic. Like two animals at the zoo being regrouped into one cage. She'd struggled since Dad's death. I hadn't seen her cry in three months, but that worried me. I was concerned her medicine numbed her more than it should.

They'd been gone maybe ten minutes when I heard a knock at the door. I walked to the front and recognized the petite body bobbing behind the glass.

"Amber?" I asked when I opened the door.

She was facing the road, probably noting what cars were absent from the driveway. Her blonde hair was now shoulder-length. When she heard her name, she turned to look at me. Her eyes were swollen from crying.

"Hi, Dell." She tried to sound casual and calm, but her appearance ruined that. I hadn't seen her in weeks. She and Brian broke things off not long after Dad's funeral. I didn't know why, and I didn't particularly care.

"What's wrong?" I asked, stepping onto the porch.

Amber, by all accounts, wasn't one to take a breakup lying down. Whatever poor classmate had taken my place as her best friend had probably heard all about it in recent weeks. I didn't want their relationship details. I'd learned enough after Dad's funeral.

"Is Brian still here?" she asked, her eyes covered in black smudges.

"He just left for SCU," I said, leaning against the stoop.

"Damn," she said, lifting her hands to her temple and lightly pulling on her hair. She was no longer addressing me, rather reacting in front of me. She mumbled, "I really need to talk to him."

"If he had something to say, I'm sure he would have said it." I turned to go back inside.

"It's not about *him*," she yelled. "It's about what *I* have to say." She stopped talking and broke into sobs.

I took a step closer. Amber wasn't her normal, dramatic self. I couldn't spot one name brand article of clothing. I'd mistaken the darkness around her eyes as mascara. Upon further inspection, I realized her face was bare and the smudges around her eyes were circles from lack of sleep. She wasn't crying for an audience, as she'd been known to do; she was genuinely sobbing. The type of cry that made even someone like Amber appear ugly.

"What do you have to tell him?" I asked. I'd seen Amber cry over lots of things. She could conjure an almost Mom-level of hysteria, but I'd never seen her like this.

She sucked in three quick breaths and wiped her cheeks. "He's gone now. That's all that matters." She turned and walked into the street.

"Wait," I said, following her. I'd misjudged. Amber was holding back, which was something she never did. Something was wrong. "Amber, wait. Talk to me."

She stopped and whipped around. "Just stay the hell away from me," she said. "You and Brian stay away from me."

She crossed her arms and pulled her jacket tight across her torso. She marched in the direction of her house and didn't turn back.

CHAPTER 30

Now

Over the weekend, I try to forget about Victory Hills. Each time Zoey or Darcy enters my brain, I push them away. *One... two... three.* Or when I think about my tense conversation with Marge. *Four... five... six.* Instead, I focus on Danny. I focus on the baby, which according to the app hasn't grown much in size. The lungs and brain and organs are forming. The little heart is beating. I don't sense any of this activity, until a pang of nausea beckons me to the bathroom.

On Monday, I dread entering first block. I dread seeing Zoey. All I want to do is scream at her, let her know I see her for who she is. She might be able to fool her classmates and Pam and Marge. But I see her.

She's quiet when she arrives, as are all the other students. In fact, I don't think they've been this quiet since the first week of school, or maybe the week of Darcy's attack. Zoey walks to the back of the room and takes the seat closest to Darcy. Adam's former seat. When Adam arrives, he doesn't react. He finds a spot on the front row and looks forward. He clearly doesn't like that Zoey and Darcy are becoming friends. Zoey must find pleasure in disrupting two lives. Add in mine, and that makes three.

By the time fourth block arrives, I'm sitting alone in my room trying not to retch. I have a horrible headache, further provoked by my inability to eat lunch. I lean back in my seat, close my eyes and take several deep breaths. Just as I'm beginning to feel better, a shriek in the hallway distracts me.

There shouldn't be any students in the halls, and yet I hear a voice. It sounds angry. I open my door to find Adam and Darcy. Every time I've seen him since the dance, Adam has looked defeated, with slumped shoulders and swollen eyes. He looks the same now as he leans against a locker. He wipes his cheeks.

Darcy is the person who yelled, and not because she's in shock or pain. She's angry. Adam stands there barely reacting, allowing Darcy to shout through the empty hall.

"What is going on?" I ask, in my best teacher voice. "You two should be in class."

Darcy hears my voice and turns. Her cheeks are flushed and the skin around her eyes is puffy.

Another teacher, Coach Gabe, starts walking from the other end of the hallway.

"Adam?" he asks. "You okay?"

"I'm fine," he answers. He is the definition of *not fine*. And Darcy is the definition of enraged.

"Get back to class," Coach Gabe says. "Both of you."

Adam turns and slinks down the hall, but Darcy releases another cry. Coach Gabe's usually calm demeanor is useless when confronted by Darcy's raw emotion. He looks at me, his wide eyes asking for help.

"Darcy," I start quietly. "Where are you supposed to be right now?"

"M-Mrs. Lakes," she blubbers, trying without success to catch her breath.

"Why don't you come in here for a few minutes," I suggest, walking toward her. "You should calm down before returning to class."

Coach Gabe nods, silently supporting my suggestion. Sending a student back to a class this upset would only worsen the situation. "I'll let Mrs. Lakes know where you are," he says, nodding at us both.

Darcy walks inside my classroom. I follow her and shut the door.

She sits on the front row and slings her purse on the ground. She immediately leans forward, placing her head on the tabletop, and sobs. I say nothing, allowing her to cry or curse or whatever she feels she needs to do to purge the gnawing feeling inside. I don't understand her pain, but I know she has it. I've seen other people display it before.

After what feels like several minutes, her breathing stabilizes, and she lifts her head.

"I'm sorry, Mrs. Mayfair," she says, and her face sours into another frown. "I shouldn't have been yelling like that."

"Do you want to tell me what's going on?" I ask, wanting desperately to push but knowing I can't.

"It's just—" she starts, still clinging to her own body. "Adam has been really possessive. He keeps pressing me about what happened that night."

I roll closer to my desk and lean back, sinking into my own listening position. "The night of the dance?"

"I know people think Adam hurt me, but I didn't believe he was capable. Yesterday, I found out Adam sent pictures of me from that night to half his contacts. Everything was finally going back to normal. Why would he do that unless he was the one who attacked me? It's like he wants me to suffer."

I remember Pam saying people were passing around pictures of Darcy. If she were drugged, there's no telling what state she was in. Clearly not able to give consent. Adam wouldn't want to further embarrass her. Even if he's angry and hurt, I can't imagine him being vindictive like that.

"Were the pictures taken from his phone?"

"No, but people had forwarded him pictures that night. He swears he didn't send them out again." She rolls her eyes and wipes her cheeks. "He said someone took his phone out of his locker during track practice. I want to believe him, but it just doesn't make sense. Who would want to set him up like that?"

Zoey seems like the type. Being on the track team, she'd have easy access to the locker room. She's been perpetuating the idea Adam attacked Darcy since the dance. She wants to make sure someone else takes the fall for her crimes.

"Take some time to think about it," I say, hesitantly. I can't tell her my real theory. "There might be some truth to what Adam says."

"The other teachers don't ask me directly, but they hint at that night all the time. It's like they're afraid of me because they don't know what happened and they're assuming the worst. You've never acted that way." Darcy looks up, her eyes appearing empty and desperate. She wants to share her story. Perhaps she's wanted to all along but hasn't found the right person.

"You'll talk when you're ready," I say. Unlike her other teachers, I do know what happened that night. Because I've read Zoey's note.

"After the dance, Adam and I got into a fight at my house. Just the stupid stuff we always fight about. He left, and I ended up getting drunk. He keeps thinking whatever happened after he left was his fault. Maybe I wouldn't have gotten hurt if he'd stayed." She bites her lip and looks down again. "Maybe he's right."

"You don't remember much," I say. "Right?"

She takes a deep breath. "I remember drinking. A lot. I remember hanging out with different people. And once I started to feel woozy, someone walked me outside."

As she speaks, my mind remembers the words on the anonymous paper. How they detailed Darcy's purple dress and her unstable balance. I remember another person who once trusted me with their story, and my regret I didn't do enough to help. I feel my eyes water and clear my throat to gain composure.

"Do you know who was with you?" I ask.

"No," she says, almost angrily. "My next full memory was at the hospital. Mom was making a big fuss about my leg." She rolls her eyes, a teenager critical of her parent's reaction even in such an unthinkable circumstance. "Within hours, everyone in town was talking about what happened. Everyone at school. I didn't even get to come to terms with it. People were just making assumptions."

Her fists clench, and I see her anger at being excluded from her own narrative.

"People talk, Darcy," I say. "And it's unfair."

"But they don't talk *to* me," she shouts. "That's the problem. They talk *about* me. They blame me. Like, maybe if I weren't drunk, I'd be able to figure out what happened. Everybody at that party was drunk, but I was the only one who ended up getting hurt."

"I do think Adam is genuinely worried about you."

"I know. But I'm trying to move on. It's like he won't let me forget. He won't stop searching for answers. Now he's just mad because I'll open up to Devon and Zoey over him."

My throat closes in and I shut my eyes. "Zoey Peterson."

"Yeah, she's helped a lot. She'll let me talk, but she doesn't force it out of me. You know? I'm ashamed to admit it, but I wasn't even that nice to Zoey when she first got here. After this, I don't know what I'd do without her."

I take a deep breath. *One... two... three.* I want to tell this girl the truth. That the person she's painting as her savior is likely the person who attacked her. But I can't. Not without proof.

"There might be a reason you can't remember what happened that night," I say, trying to steer the conversation away from Zoey and back to the party.

"When I got to the hospital, they said there was something in my system. I've never done drugs, so I know it's nothing I took. It's something someone gave me. You'd think that would make people stop blaming me, but it doesn't."

"What happened that night was not your fault."

Her face melts, as though she's about to cry again, but she doesn't. She places her trembling hands on the desk. "Sometimes I think it is. And that's why I hate coming to school. I hate seeing Adam and talking to my parents. Because I've hurt them, too."

"Darcy, what happened that night was not your fault," I repeat, standing and walking toward her. "And if you can't remember what happened, that's not your fault either."

I take a seat next to her and feel a strong urge to hug her. I wish there was something I could do to erase her pain. But she doesn't need contact right now. She needs space. Space to talk, and someone to listen.

She looks at me with scared eyes. "I remember parts of what happened."

"What do you remember?" I ask, staring at her. If she's going to tell the truth, I hope she'll go all the way.

"I... I," she starts, her eyes darting toward the door. It's almost like she wants someone to walk in and interrupt. She wants a reason to stop talking.

"Darcy," I say. "What do you remember from that night?"

She looks back at me with full tears in her eyes. "I didn't fall," she says, her voice cracking. "I know someone was deliberately attacking me. I remember trying to fight back."

She leans forward, covering her mouth with her palms, and cries hard. I'm not sure what to say. I've been sure for weeks, but it's different hearing her say the words. It's not the first time I've watched someone break from baring their soul. Slowly, I raise my arm and rub her trembling back. She flinches but doesn't push me away. I allow her to cry, getting as much of her grief out as possible.

"Do you remember anything else that happened before the police found you?" I ask, trying to keep my voice steady.

"It's like little flashes," she says. "Which is why it's just easier to let it go. Pretend my mind is playing tricks on me. Telling people I fell made them stop asking questions, even if they didn't believe me."

"But you can't let it go, Darcy," I tell her. "You can't let it go because you know it's not a trick. You know the memories are real."

She nods, and just when I think she's about to cry again, she takes a deep breath. She holds the air for a second, before breathing it out slowly. She appears stronger.

"I remember someone walking me outside. I remember sitting in the grass. And then I was cold, like my dress was being ripped. But someone was still there with me." She takes another deep breath and stretches her fingers. "And then I remember someone on top of me. I remember someone stabbing my leg. I tried to push them away, I think. Like I said, it's all little flashes."

"It's okay, Darcy," I soothe. "If someone slipped you something, it explains your memory loss."

"I don't remember anything clearly until I was in the hospital. By then, my parents were freaking out. And my phone was blowing up with questions from people at the party. Everything was already so intense. I just wanted to get out of there."

"Your parents want what's best for you," I say, wondering if that's true.

"Are you going to tell them I remember the attack?"

"Legally, they need to know. But I think it should come from you."

"How? I've spent weeks saying I fell and don't remember anything. I can't change my story now."

"You weren't ready to tell anyone yet," I tell her. "You're not changing your story. You're telling your story for the first time."

"People won't see it that way."

"We can't control what people see. Just speak your truth," I tell her, reaching for her hand. "What you've told me today took a lot of courage."

"What do we do now?" she asks.

"I think we should go see Ms. Pam. She'll know how to handle this from here."

"But it's just pointless," she says. "I can't tell her who hurt me. I can only say I remember the attack. I have no proof."

"It doesn't matter. Now that we know a crime has been committed, people can at least start looking for someone. The police—"

"I don't want the police involved," she says, running fingers through her dark mane. "I just want all this to go away."

I take a deep breath. "I want you to do what makes you comfortable, of course. But you also have to consider other people. If the person who hurt you thinks they got away with it, they might try to hurt someone else."

For the first time, her eyes aren't filled with anger or grief. They fill with fear. She doesn't want her silence to contribute to another person's pain. "Do you think the police will believe me?"

"I believe you," I say.

She covers her face again. "Coming forward with this is going to stir up a lot of shit. My parents, Dad especially, will go mad. Adam—"

"Darcy," I interrupt her. "You can't allow other people's reactions to interfere with what you do moving forward. This is about you."

"I know I don't want someone else getting hurt."

I look at the clock. School won't be over for another half hour. That gives us time to talk with Pam. I'm proud of Darcy for admitting what happened, and I hope people will finally start looking for an assailant.

"I'll walk with you to Ms. Pam's office," I say.

"Okay." She stands shakily, knocking over her bag. Random items scatter across the floor. I help her retrieve them. A compact. Tampons. Her keys have far too many charms, ranging from a Mickey Mouse figurine to an emerald cross to a Victory Hills mascot. I retrieve the items closest to me and hand them back to her.

"Thanks," she says. Her petite body reminds me how young she is, but her face suddenly looks older. Like she's found a small fragment of peace.

Together, we leave the classroom and make the short walk to Pam's office. Before entering the guidance wing, I turn to Darcy. "I'm proud of you for doing this," I tell her.

"Thank you, Mrs. Mayfair."

I open the door, allowing Darcy to walk inside. She takes a seat in the waiting area, as students typically do. Through the glass on Pam's door, I can see she is in her office with Principal Bowles. As though they felt my presence, they look up.

I push open the already cracked door. "Excuse me, Pam," I say. "I have a student who needs to talk with you."

Pam clears her throat and pushes back her shoulders. "Who is it?" she asks.

"Darcy Moore," I say.

Pam and Bowles look at each other, then back at me. "We were actually wanting to speak with you, Della." She releases the words like she doesn't want to. Like she's being forced.

"All right." I walk inside the office and close the door, so Darcy can't hear. "What's going on?"

"What does Darcy want to speak with Pam about?" Bowles asks.

"I'd rather not say." I look down. Darcy's story will spread fast enough. Encouraging her to speak with Pam is one thing, but I'm not going to force the girl to share her story with Bowles, too. I look at Pam. "But she really needs to speak with you."

"Okay," Bowles says, walking away from Pam's desk. "Tell Darcy to come on in. Della, follow me to my office. We can talk there."

"What's this about?" I ask.

"Just come with me," Bowles says, abruptly walking past me and opening Pam's door. He marches out of the guidance office, doesn't even acknowledge Darcy sitting on the couch.

The door open, Darcy leans her head around the corner.

"Come on inside, Darcy," Pam says. Darcy obeys, choosing one of the seats in front of Pam's desk. Pam turns to me. "Thank you, Mrs. Mayfair."

"Aren't you staying?" Darcy asks.

"I need to speak with Principal Bowles about something," I say. I raise my hands. "It's completely unrelated."

I look at Pam, who is staring at me with what seems like worry in her eyes. "I'll take it from here," she says.

"Just tell Ms. Pam what you told me," I say to Darcy, before exiting the office.

CHAPTER 31

Winter 2005

Brian didn't return home that entire first semester. His reluctance to visit didn't surprise me, but it devastated Mom. She couldn't understand why he wouldn't make the two-hour trek to Wilsonville, even for the weekend. But Brian always had an excuse. He was busy joining a fraternity. He'd been selected to help tutor a freshman taking remedial English. At first, I thought his cheeriness over the phone was forced. As the weeks passed, he sounded like he was finding his place. I'd have to see him in person to know if it was an act.

According to Danny, Brian was doing all right. The two didn't see each other as often; Danny was too focused on his first-year academics. He started texting me during the second week of the semester. I'm not sure why. We didn't text when he lived in the neighborhood. He was firmly Brian's friend. But now that Danny was gone, I think I was a link back to the life he sometimes missed.

As promised, Brian returned home after he completed finals in December. It was near four o'clock when I pulled Dad's car into the driveway and saw my regular parking spot was filled by Brian's truck.

I opened the front door and stepped into a Hallmark movie. A decorated tree stood in the corner of the room. Mom had sprinkled her collection of nutcrackers throughout the living room and kitchen. She had a roast in the crockpot and was preparing cider by the stove.

Mom looked up when I walked into the kitchen. "Hey, sweetie," she said. She'd not called me *sweetie* in months. Maybe years.

"Place looks great, Mom," I said.

"Please, it's no trouble," she said, stirring. If it were no trouble, she wouldn't have spent the entire day decorating. But she couldn't cheap out when it came to Brian, especially considering this was his first visit.

"Where's Brian?"

"He ran out to see some of the neighborhood kids," she said. "He'll be back before dinner."

I wondered which neighborhood kids Brian visited, if they were sharing war stories and comparing battle scars. I thought about Amber. I'd seen her at school a few times, but never got as close as I had on the day Brian left for SCU. If she saw me, she usually turned in a different direction. She'd made it clear she wanted me to *stay the hell away*.

"Can I help with anything?" I asked Mom. She instructed me to set the table using her good china. At this point, I wondered how she would outdo herself come Christmas Day if she used all her tricks now. I remembered this would be our first Christmas without Dad, and the familiar feeling of loss consumed me.

Minutes later, the front door opened, and Brian walked inside. I'd gone four months without seeing him. He had the same thick hair combed to the side and wore a SCU hoodie. Still, he looked different. His face, still handsome, was less defined. His body seemed bigger, like he'd morphed from a scrawny high schooler into a grown adult. He saw me standing by the table and came over. He hugged me. A big bear hug that almost took my feet off the ground.

"Careful, Brian," Mom sang from the kitchen.

"I think I missed you, Della," Brian said, tightening his arms.

I wasn't used to this Brian. The same brother who used to get off on hurting me and calling me names like *skank* and *slut*. Normally all his comments came in the form of a dig, but this time he sounded genuine.

"I missed you, too." It was a lie. I couldn't miss this version of Brian because I'd never seen him before. He was all new.

We sat around the table and ate. Brian told us all about SCU. His classes were easy, and he was confident he'd aced his finals. Next semester, he said, would be even more enjoyable because he'd picked up a slew of electives. He told us about joining his fraternity and the infamous rush week, even filling us in on some of the secret group doctrine.

"I hope the hazing wasn't too rough," Mom said, putting her napkin on the table.

"Nah," Brian said. "Not for me, anyway." He assured us he was one of the most liked members of his class, which was easy to believe. Brian had the ability to charm people wherever he went. It was at home, away from the eyes of strangers, where his unflattering side arose. And yet, none of that was apparent anymore. He seemed nice. He seemed normal. He seemed like the type of older brother I wished I'd had my entire childhood, not just in the past hour.

"What about you, Della?" Brian asked. I'd purposely remained quiet as he talked, wanting to assess everything he told us. "Do you think you'll apply to SCU? You might love it there."

"I'm not sure. I still have time to decide."

"Not too much time," Mom said. "You're halfway through junior year."

"I know," I said. "But I'm retaking the ACT in the spring. If I can up my score, I might have more options."

I liked to talk about options because it made me sound older, like I had an ounce of the freedom that Brian possessed. I knew I'd end up attending the school which made the most sense financially. And SCU was a big name on that list. I didn't want to continue in Brian's shadow, but I didn't exactly have the grades or the spine to do much else.

"Well, you should think about it. It's great there," Brian said. "I'd love to give you a tour next semester. If you visit the campus, you'll fall in love."

"Now that's nice," Mom said. She walked to Brian and kissed the top of his head. "But you better not take your sister to that frat house."

"Of course not, Mom. Must keep an eye on my little sister."

They both laughed. Mom reached into the top cupboard and pulled out three mugs for cider. The two continued talking, the room filling with their jovial banter. I wanted to join them, but I was too busy trying to figure Brian out. How had this person, who seemed completely charming and rational, developed in mere months? I'd spent my entire childhood trying to relate to him. He went away for a semester and came back perfect? Brian noticed me staring at him. He didn't let on, but, as he continued his conversation with Mom, I saw his eyes dart in my direction.

"Oh rats," Mom said, looking at her watch. "I promised the committee I'd run by the community center tonight. We've got the Christmas parade this weekend," she explained to Brian.

"I'll go with you tomorrow," Brian said. He leaned back and took a sip of cider.

"Please, it will seem so lowbrow compared to all your college experiences." She kissed the top of Brian's head again. It was the one and only time I ever heard her refer to something she helped produce as lowbrow. "I'm happy you're home."

"Yeah, it's nice," he said, as if convincing himself.

"I'll be home within the hour. You want to watch a movie when I get back?" she asked. This time she addressed the question to both of us. We nodded. She grabbed her keys and left.

We sat alone at the table with our mugs in our hands. The scent of cinnamon filled the air. Neither one of us said anything. I'd been waiting for this. For the moment we were alone, and this preppy façade Brian wore would go away.

His phone vibrated on the table, interrupting the silence. He lifted it and his happy stare dropped within seconds. He turned and looked at the front door.

"What's wrong?" I asked. Something had to be, otherwise his expression wouldn't have changed so quickly.

"Nothing," he said. "I'll be back in a minute. Get me some more cider?"

He stood and walked outside. I stood, too. I refilled both our mugs from the pot. Then I walked toward the front door and looked out the distorted glass.

A red car was parked by the curb. A girl I'd never seen before was leaning against it. She was tall and slim with blonde hair that almost touched her waist. She was beautiful, the type of pretty that can only be cultivated at a place like college. None of the girls from Wilsonville had an effortless beauty like that.

I watched them. At first, they had a flirtatious exchange. Brian leaned against her car. She dropped a hand on his shoulder, and he touched the hairs falling around her face. After a few seconds, their body language turned frigid. Her arms were crossed, and she was taking a step away from him. Whatever they were talking about, she wasn't getting her way.

I opened the front door, which brought their attention to me.

"Della," Brian said. He sounded thankful I'd interrupted them.

"How's it going?" I asked, stepping outside into the night.

He turned to the girl. "This is my sister Della," he said.

She wiped any sign of frustration from her face and smiled. She waved, her pale fingers shimmying in the dark. "Hi. I'm Mila."

"We know each other from SCU," Brian explained.

"I don't live far from here," Mila said, ignoring Brian and looking at me. "About an hour away."

"Nice," I said. I looked away from her and back at Brian. "Did you want to start the movie?" It was obvious he needed an escape.

"I need to get inside," Brian said, scratching the back of his head. "Have a good break, Mila."

He walked past her and up the front steps. I could tell Mila wasn't ready for their conversation to end but felt helpless in my presence.

"Won't I see you?" Mila shouted. She cleared her throat, clearly embarrassed. "I mean, I'll be around."

"I'll give you a call," Brian said, before disappearing inside the house.

Mila turned to me. She was gorgeous, albeit clingy. "Nice meeting you," she said. Her voice was smooth and confident, the opposite of the behavior she'd just exhibited.

"Goodnight," I said, following Brian back into the house. I shut the door and locked it.

"What was that?" I asked.

"Don't worry about it," Brian said, his hand still on the back of his neck. "She's a friend from school." The word *friend* wasn't as convincing as he wanted it to be.

"A friend you don't want to see during Christmas break?" I walked back to the table and sat. I took a sip of my replenished cider.

"Exactly," he said. He followed me. "So, what movie do you want to watch?"

"What's going on with you?" I asked.

"What do you mean?"

"You just seem so… different." I didn't know how else to describe his behavioral changes.

"I think I'm just happy," Brian said. He stared at me, and a flicker of the old Brian returned. That hopeless, unexplainable stare. Then he smiled. "What's so different about me?"

"Well, you're interacting with me, for one. Inviting me to visit your campus."

"I'm just trying to be nice." He looked at me. "I get I wasn't always the nicest to you when I lived here."

My mind flashed to all the times Brian had hurt me, physically and emotionally. At least the memorable ones. It was hard to imagine *that* Brian had been expunged in a matter of months. "You were worse than not nice," I said.

"I know." Brian looked at the table, still holding the hot cider in his hands. "I think I've grown up a lot in a short amount of time."

"How?" I asked. "How does someone terrorize their little sister at every turn, attend a couple of frat parties and then change?"

"College has given me space to process things. I don't think I ever had that here. It was always so suffocating." He looked around the perfectly decorated room.

"I don't understand," I said. "You always got your way here."

"I don't know how to say it, Della. I always felt like I was looking for something. Some purpose or meaning in life. I never found it, so I took my frustrations out on you and others. I was my own worst enemy." He looked at me with honest eyes. "Whatever it is, I found it at SCU. I'm happy there, which makes me happier here."

I envied his freedom. We carry weight throughout life. It's given to us by parents and bosses and teachers. They burden us with rules and expectations. We're told it's a good thing to have all these responsibilities. All this stability. Our development would be all off-whack, otherwise. Just hearing him talk, whether he sounded pretentious or not, I knew his weight had been lifted. In a matter of weeks, Brian had given up that load. Started his own path.

"Mom was hurt when you didn't visit for Thanksgiving."

"I know." He looked down and wiped his mouth. "I was close to coming in but the thought of enduring another holiday in suburbia about made me sick. I needed more time. I'm happy to be home now."

I nodded, not quite believing.

"Listen," he continued. "I want to tell you I'm sorry. I know I was mean to you growing up. I was emotionally absent. I was just being a kid, but it probably didn't feel that way to you. It probably really hurt you."

"It did," I whispered. The closest I'd come to acknowledging that hurt was with Dad. Man, I missed him.

"I'm sorry for being an asshole," Brian said. "I know I made your life hell and I'm sorry for that, too. I'd like things to be different now."

"Thank you," I said.

I so desperately wanted to believe him, that change could be that easy. If it were, I wished he'd changed years ago. Maybe I wouldn't have wasted time feeling inadequate, living in the shadows. If he'd just shared a little bit of his light.

I feel like I'm marching toward my execution. When I opened Pam's office door and saw Principal Bowles, I didn't interrupt a friendly discussion. Something in the way Pam averted her eyes and Bowles stared in disgust made me think they were discussing me, and I was dreading finding out what it was about.

The door to Principal Bowles' office is wide open, waiting for me to come inside. He's already standing behind his desk.

"Close the door," he says.

I do, taking a seat in front of his desk. I don't say anything, waiting for him to tell me what this impromptu meeting is about.

"Pam and I wanted to speak with you together," he says, taking a seat. He hasn't looked at me since I sat down, and still doesn't. "Considering you showed up to her office with Darcy Moore, I'm guessing it'll be just the two of us."

"All right," I say, not yet knowing whether I need to defend my actions. The feeling I have isn't good.

"Marge Helton came by my office this morning. She wanted me to know what you had told her about Zoey Peterson."

Marge went to Bowles with my concerns about Zoey? I can't believe it. I was reaching out to her as a friend, and she left me in a position to be reprimanded. I clear my throat. "Yes," I start. "I did speak with her about Zoey."

"Tell me your concerns."

My skin turns hot, like I've been exposed to the elements and I'm beginning to burn. Bowles looks at me as unamused as ever.

"I think Zoey might have more issues than we are equipped to handle. I suspect she might be violent."

"Suspect," Bowles repeats. "Can you give me specific reasons why you think this?"

"Well, I'm aware of the knife incident—"

"That was a misunderstanding which took place her first week here. I handled it," he says firmly. "Go on."

"And I have reason to believe she is the person who attacked Darcy Moore. I received a note—"

"I'm aware of what you received. Pam gave me a copy of it. I thought I made it clear we would not be addressing the issue."

"With all due respect, Principal Bowles, how can we not address the issue?" I ask, trying to remain calm. "That paper detailed an attack on another student."

"A fictional account of what happened. That's what I read. Darcy Moore admitted she has no memory of what happened."

"I don't think that's true, sir," I say. "Not anymore."

He nods. "I assume Darcy is talking to Pam about that night right now, huh?"

"Yes, she is."

"Did you talk to Darcy about that night?"

"Yes, I did."

"I thought I was clear about the staff not getting involved." He looks at me with contempt. "This is an issue that should be handled by the Moores and the police, with Pam working as a liaison between them and the school."

"Yes, but Darcy told me—"

"Darcy told *you*. You didn't track down Darcy and ask her questions? The way you interrogated Adam Bryant?"

I remembered my conversation with Adam. Yes, I was the one to pull him to the side, but he wanted to tell me what was going on.

"I only spoke to him because he seemed upset. I was trying to help."

"So your conversation didn't contribute to your vendetta against Zoey Peterson?"

"I don't have a vendetta against anyone," I say. "When I see a student is upset, I get involved."

"And now you're speaking with Darcy Moore. Asking her questions about that night."

"She was screaming in the hallway—"

"What about Zoey Peterson?" he asks. "Was she upset when you confronted her?"

"I didn't confront Zoey—"

"She claims you've been rude to her since she arrived, despite the fact she gets along with all of her other teachers and has a solid academic performance in your classroom. She says you all but accused her of attacking Darcy Moore."

"I didn't accuse her," I say, my volume rising. I've never openly discussed Darcy with Zoey. I know better. "She's lying."

"Pam says you've had suspicions about Zoey Peterson for weeks now. You confronted Marge, her new guardian, on Friday."

"I did, but—"

"So, you've confided to two of your colleagues your concerns about this student. You think she hurt Darcy. You even insinuated she hurt her own mother. But Zoey is lying about a confrontation with you?"

"I spoke with Zoey, yes. It was after she had a disagreement in class with Adam," I say. "But I didn't accuse her of hurting Darcy."

"What about your conversation with Darcy? Did you mention Zoey's name?"

"No, of course I didn't. I would never lead a student in that way."

"What did Darcy say about that night?"

"You can speak with Pam. It's not my place to say."

"But it's your place to investigate the situation on your own? You've created theories and tracked down both teachers and students to try and prove them right. After I specifically instructed faculty to let the matter go."

"I think it's entirely unethical to let the matter go."

"Unethical." He pauses, staring at me. "Ms. Helton also told me you visited Zoey's mother. She told me you called her former schools."

"I was only trying to get a better idea of who she is."

"I'm going to be very clear about this," he says, standing. "Leave this matter alone. I don't want you talking to anyone else about Zoey Peterson or Darcy Moore. I don't want you looking into what happened that night."

"I'm only trying to do what's right."

He raises a hand to silence me. "Thankfully, this is our last week of school. Zoey Peterson will not be in your classroom tomorrow. That should make it much easier for you to follow orders."

"Don't you think that's a little extreme?" I ask, blinking hard.

"I think you've crossed a line, but because you've never done anything meriting disciplinary action in the past, I'm giving you the benefit of the doubt. Just as I did Zoey."

I grit my teeth at being compared to that sick little girl. Bowles might downplay Zoey's behavior by labeling her a child or a student, but being a minor didn't stop her from hurting Darcy. And it won't stop her from becoming what she's well on her way to being: a predator. I realize I'm playing into exactly what Zoey wants, which is for everyone else to think I'm the unstable one.

"All I'm trying to do is protect our students," I say, standing to leave. I begin to cry because my accusations are once again being dismissed, and I know how dangerous that can be. Last time, I was slow to act. Now I'm doing everything I can to bring Zoey's crimes to light. If only someone would listen.

"I must say, I'm upset you've allowed this student to impact your job performance. You've had students lining up in the halls waiting to enter your class. Heather told me you left work early on Friday." He sighs and shakes his head. "Be aware, these incidents will be addressed when the board reviews your application for tenure."

I close my eyes. This situation is growing, and I'm losing grip. Surely this ordeal won't cost me my job. How would that look in a town this small? A teacher losing her job because she was obsessed with a student. A rumor like that could tank Danny's practice. I've already been keeping Danny at a distance. Will he stick with me through this? If I ruin both our lives on a hunch?

I stand to leave. Principal Bowles follows me to the door. "Just so we're clear. No further contact with Zoey Peterson," he says. "She's no longer your student."

The dismissal bell rings when I enter the hallway, and suddenly I'm lost in the flood of students eager to leave. I walk past them, hoping I can make it to my classroom without being spotted by anyone I know. No such luck. When I pass Marge's classroom, she's standing at her door. I still can't believe she would rat me out to Bowles. I want to say something to her, but I don't. My watery stare says it all, and her brief look of defiance is swathed with sympathy. She is my friend, but she's always a teacher first. She thinks I'm being unfair to Zoey, and she believes her role is to defend her. Now I seem unhinged. I hope, for her sake, that's all I am.

CHAPTER 33

Spring 2006

Brian returned to SCU in January, but he wasn't his usual distant self. He called Mom more often and even started texting me. He'd tell me about the quirky events his fraternity sponsored or random happenings on campus. He started visiting every couple of weeks, which made Mom happy.

After school, I rushed home to change for my shift at the theater. I'd just hopped into a pair of black pants when my phone rang. A goofy grin covered my face when I saw the name on the screen. Danny.

"Hey, stranger," he said when I answered.

We were far from strangers at this point. We'd met over Thanksgiving and Christmas break. We continued text messaging, and now talked on the phone. It felt very grown-up to have a college boy calling me, even if it was because I was the kid sister of his best friend.

"Can you guess what I'm doing?" I asked.

"After three o'clock on a Wednesday? Let's see." He made a ticking sound over the phone with his tongue. "I'm guessing you're running late for work."

"Ding, ding, ding." I placed the call on speaker and put the phone on my bed. I stretched a T-shirt over my head and shook my hair. "I don't get paid enough to rush around like this."

"Get ready. You only think you're broke until you get to college." Danny worked most weekends as a desk clerk at the hospital. It gave him extra money and provided something he could put on a resumé. His every action was in preparation for medical school.

"When are you coming back to town?" I asked.

"Eh, not for a few weeks. My weekends are filling up fast thanks to the hospital."

"I think I'm actually heading your way next week." I bit my lip and held my breath. For whatever reason, I'd been hesitant to tell him about my plans to visit Brian over spring break. It was one thing to call me on the phone or walk with me around the old neighborhood; I wasn't sure how Danny would react to having me on his campus.

"That's great," he said. "You're going to love it here."

I sighed in relief. So I wasn't just some kid he liked to visit when he was bored back home. I don't even think Brian knew we talked as much as we did. I wasn't happy when I discovered Brian was dating Amber. *Dating*. Danny and I were just friends. In recent weeks, it felt like he was my best friend. I was happy he didn't seem ashamed about my upcoming visit.

"I can't wait," I said, picking up the phone and placing it back to my ear. "I won't be able to stay long. Mom and I are coming up next Friday. We've booked a nearby hotel, but I hope we'll spend most of our time on campus."

"Sweet. I'll check my shifts for that weekend. Maybe we could meet for lunch," he said. "I'd offer to show you around, but you have Brian for that."

"I wish Mom would just let me stay in the dorms. I've been asking her." I rolled my eyes even though he couldn't see. I opened by handbag to make sure I had the essentials: phone, wallet, tampons. Check.

"Eh, campus isn't as lively these days. Especially now that curfew has been set."

"Curfew?" I asked. College was supposed to be about freedom. I'd be damned if I left the underside of Mom's thumb only to hear words like *curfew* again.

"Yeah, you know. Because of the missing girls."

I slid behind the steering wheel of the station wagon and slammed the door, but I didn't start the engine. "Missing girls?"

"Didn't I tell you about them?"

"No," I said, curiosity creeping in.

"We've had some girls go missing. Five in total. They're just now taking it seriously. They've announced no one can walk around campus after midnight." He grunted and sighed. "Lame, really."

"That's crazy," I said, putting my bag on the seat next to me. I didn't realize I'd been holding it since I entered the car. "And all the girls are from SCU?"

"Yeah," he said. "I guess."

"When did they go missing?"

"I think the first one was in, like, the fall? More since then. No one saw a pattern until a month or so ago. Now it's all anyone on campus talks about," he said. "I'm surprised I didn't tell you."

"That's wild," I said. The drama intoxicated me. College was the real world where both good and bad things could happen. The gamble seemed exhilarating. "What do people think is going on?"

"Not sure, really. I don't follow it. I didn't know any of the girls. You know, if you want details you should ask Brian."

"Brian," I said, sticking the key into the ignition and turning to peer through the back window. "He hasn't said anything about missing girls either."

"Maybe he doesn't want to scare you. He's been really involved in spreading the word on campus," he said. "He probably has all the details."

"Really?" I said, almost laughing. Brian aimed to please, but I couldn't imagine him shouting about missing women in the quad.

"He's the person who told me about it."

"I'll have to ask him," I said. I looked at the clock on my dashboard. "Crap, I'm officially late. I better go."

"Drive safe," Danny said as I hung up the phone.

I pressed the gas and passed the car in front of me. The movie theater wasn't far, but there was always traffic after school let out. I didn't necessarily like my job, but I liked getting paid every two weeks. I wasn't going to pull the same scholarships for college that Brian did. Whether I went to SCU or somewhere smaller, I needed to start saving.

I'd been looking forward to visiting SCU, but what Danny told me cast a shadow over the upcoming trip. Girls had really gone missing? Like, vanished? I'd never known someone who'd gone missing before. During my freshman year, a girl ran away once. She was gone long enough for the school to make announcements about it. Turned out she'd snuck across state lines to be with her dad. But for someone to be sleeping in their dorm or walking on campus or, hell, rushing to their shift at the movie theater and just vanish… it unsettled me. Like most teenagers, I felt like every world event somehow had a direct impact on my life.

I also thought it was strange Brian hadn't said anything about the missing girls. If this had happened a year ago, I wouldn't have been surprised. But ever since Christmas, Brian had seemingly told us everything about his life at SCU. I knew about his stupid frat's Valentine's Day fundraiser and that the basketball team was on track to win the championship. He'd been the one to tell Danny about it. He was taking time to hand out flyers warning people about potential dangers on campus. Why wouldn't he tell us? Unless, like Danny said, he didn't want to raise alarm.

It was after eleven when I came home. Mom sat in the living room holding a glass of wine and watching Letterman.

"Hi, sweetie. Hungry?" she asked.

I slung my purse over the sofa and leaned against the back of the recliner. "Starved."

"There's some pizza in the fridge. I can heat it up for you in the oven, if you'd like."

"I got it," I said. I knew she was only being polite. She was comfortable and didn't want to get up. She didn't even move at the offer.

"Fill up and get in bed," she said. "You're working too late for a school night."

"Yeah, yeah," I said, putting the pizza on a plate and popping it in the microwave. "Are we still planning on visiting Brian next week?"

"Of course, honey," she said, taking a sip. "I think it'll be great."

"Me too," I said, looking down. "Has he said anything to you about missing girls?"

Mom twisted in the armchair and looked at me. "Missing girls? What about missing girls?"

"From SCU. There's been, like, five disappear."

"And Brian told you this?"

"No, Danny did. I was wondering if Brian mentioned it to you."

"He's not said anything to me," she said, sipping her wine. "Danny. You mean Danny Mayfair from down the street?"

"Yes," I said, regretting my slip.

"How long have you been talking to him?"

"Like, my whole life." The microwave beeped. I pulled out the plate by its edges. "We're friends, you know."

"I see." She returned her attention to the television. "I wouldn't worry about going missing, love."

"I just think it's weird Brian wouldn't mention it. Especially when he knows we're coming to visit."

"Missing can mean lots of things, at the college level especially. Girls get a bit loose and lose their way."

"You're blaming the girls for going missing?" I asked, still chewing my pizza.

"*If* they've gone missing. I'm telling you. It could be a bad breakup or homesickness. There's a whole world of reasons why a girl might walk away."

I could have kept pushing, but I decided not to. After all, the girl from my school had been a runaway. According to Danny, no one at SCU knew exactly what was going on. Maybe I was being dramatic.

I stuffed the last of the pizza in my mouth and rinsed off my plate. "Heading upstairs," I told Mom.

"Love you," she said, never taking her eyes away from the screen.

CHAPTER 34

Now

I pick up pizza on my way home from work. After I scarf down three pieces, I walk to the sofa and cover my legs with a blanket. I reach for the remote but decide against watching anything. I close my eyes. Rarely do I fall asleep so easily, especially when there are troubling things on my mind. I suppose I'm used to it now, being troubled. Dealing with another disturbing individual no longer feels as jarring as it once did. If anything, I'm most bothered by the way my co-workers now look at me. Like I'm the one with the problem. I picture Zoey's manipulative smile. Within seconds I'm asleep.

Danny says my name three times before I fully open my eyes. He's sitting on the edge of the sofa, staring at me.

"You home early?" I ask, groggily.

"Not exactly," he says. Seeing I'm awake, he stands and walks to the kitchen. "It's after seven."

I sit up and pull the blanket away from my legs. "I didn't mean to sleep so long."

"Maybe you needed it," he says, opening the pizza box, then closing it without taking a slice. He keeps his eyes low, and there's a tenseness around his mouth I'm only used to seeing after a particularly long day of work.

"Everything okay?" I ask, stretching my arms and patting the stray hair around my face.

"You tell me," he says, still standing by the breakfast bar.

"Danny, what's going on?"

He takes a deep breath before returning to the living room and sitting on the ottoman. He leans over, placing his elbows on his knees. "I received a phone call today. From Pam."

My stomach flutters as I take in a deep breath. "What about?"

"She said you've been reprimanded at work over this Zoey student. When I asked you about Zoey last week, you said the situation was resolved. You lied to me." He recoils from my touch, and I'm not sure if it's from anger or hurt. "Tell me what's going on, Dell. Tell me everything."

Danny likes order. He likes routine. We have a happy life together. Now I feel like all that is slipping away. I look down and shake my head. "I've already told you about Zoey."

"You think she might have attacked a student at a party."

"Danny, I know I'm right about this. Darcy admitted more details about her attack. She admitted she remembers someone stabbing her. And I know Zoey is the one who did it. I just know it."

"Pam said you've been questioning Zoey's former guidance counselors. She said you even visited her mother."

"I'm trying to find the proof you all so desperately need," I shout. I begin to cry, knowing I sound unhinged but trusting I'm right.

"This is impacting your job. Principal Bowles removed Zoey from your classroom. Why wouldn't you tell me all this was going on?"

"Pam had no right to call you. She's not helping." First Marge betrayed me, now Pam. I can't believe she would drag Danny into this. She must think I'm more unstable than I realized.

"She's worried about you."

"I'm not the person people should be worried about. If you could only see this kid! The way she acts. The way she manipulates people. She's just like Brian!"

I said it. The word that's more catastrophic in our household than a slew of curse words combined. Brian never left either one of us, but we've pushed him to the corners, kept him quiet all these years. Zoey brought him back.

"I'm not saying you're wrong—"

"Yes, you are. Everyone thinks I'm wrong. Just like last time. Do you know how many times I tried to tell someone how awful Brian was?" Tears come in full force, so heavy my words land in indecipherable thuds. "I tried to tell Mom. I tried to tell teachers."

Danny places a hand on my shaking shoulders. "Della, I know."

"I tried to tell you!" I shout, pushing his hand away. And there it is. The sentence I've never said. The pain I've never let him see. He didn't believe me either. It's like I'm feeling that rejection all over again.

"He was a kid," Danny whispers. "I was a kid. You have no idea how many times I've thought about our conversation after the funeral. If I'd not lashed out at you. If I'd listened. If I'd tried talking to Brian." For the first time, I notice the pain he's been keeping secret all these years, too. His anger with himself. "I'm sorry I didn't listen. How was I supposed to know my best friend was a monster? None of us knew what we were dealing with."

"I did. I knew there was something wrong then. And I know there is something wrong now."

"I believe you," he says. "But it worries me you'd hide all this from me."

"I already feel crazy when I go to school. I don't want to feel it here, too."

"I've never called you crazy. Not once. That's what hurts the most. That you'd rather lie to me than be honest."

"I didn't want to lose you."

"You could never lose me. I trust your instincts, Della. You might be right about Zoey, but this isn't your battle to fight. It can't be." He moves closer, touching my stomach. "Leave it to someone else."

"No one else sees. Am I supposed to just wait around for her to do something else? Hurt someone else?"

Danny shakes his head. He doesn't have an answer, but he's more concerned about my safety than he is Zoey's potential violence. "I know it doesn't seem fair."

"You know what happened last time because I didn't act fast enough!" I cry hard and fast, realizing all these years later I still haven't forgiven myself. "How can we live in a world that recognizes danger and does nothing to prevent it? Why do we wait for lives to be ruined? For lives to be taken?"

"Because sometimes that's all we can do." He looks at me, tears in his eyes. "And nothing that happened was your fault, Dell. It was all his."

Lacking a compelling response, I quit talking. I stand. This time when Danny reaches for me, I welcome his comfort. I lean into him, allowing him to think I'm sharing my pain with him. I am, partially. But I'm also holding back. I know part of what he says is right. There isn't much I can do about Zoey. But I also know I can't sit back and wait. Not this time.

CHAPTER 35

Spring 2006

I could barely keep my eyes open during first period. Things didn't improve after lunch. I felt tired and sluggish. Every twenty minutes or so, my mind would wander back to the missing girls. I still found it odd Brian hadn't mentioned them. It seemed like a topic he'd love to discuss. He might even exaggerate details to startle me. *I'm thinking of the old Brian*, I told myself. He'd changed. He'd grown up. But even though our relationship had altered in recent months, I couldn't shake an entire childhood's worth of bad memories

After school, I tried calling him. I thought I'd ask him about the girls directly. I didn't want to admit to hearing about them from Danny; I didn't want Brian to know his old best friend was now my new one. Brian didn't answer, so I plugged my phone into its charger and stretched out on the sofa to take a nap.

But the missing girls wouldn't leave me alone. I sat up and exhaled in frustration. I spotted our bulky desktop across the room. It belonged to Dad and no one used it now. Few class assignments required internet access, and if they did, I took advantage of the computers at school. Suddenly, it dawned on me, if I wanted information about what was happening at SCU, I didn't need to wait on Brian.

I sat in front of the computer and pressed its dusty start button. It took minutes for the ancient machine to light up. When it did, I clicked on the internet icon and typed in *Sterling Cove University*.

Standard landing pages appeared with information about academic programs and tuition scales. The picturesque campus balanced a perfect mix of green lawns and stone buildings. I imagined the fun Brian and Danny must be having there. The fun I might one day have there. Then I thought about the girls, each one being plucked from this ideal setting and plopped into oblivion.

I went back to the search window and typed in *SCU students missing*. About four links down the page, I noticed an online article from the campus newspaper, *The Dunes*:

Missing Students Calls for More SCU Security

SCU students are becoming increasingly unnerved. Five female undergrads have been reported missing since November, a disturbing trend police are calling suspicious. However, campus security encourages students to be vigilant, not scared.

"We still don't know enough about these disappearances to determine whether or not foul play is involved," says Mitch Mellencamp, head of campus security. "We do ask that students be hyperaware in coming weeks. Look out for your friends and look out for yourselves."

The campus has tightened security as a precautionary measure. The campus will be considered closed after midnight. Dormitory residents are expected to be indoors by that time. Security staff has also been increased during on-campus events. "Our priority is keeping everyone safe until we have a clear understanding of what's happening here," says Mellencamp.

For those with classmates who have gone missing, it's clear what's happened. "Someone's taken her," says Rhonda Sams. Her roommate, Veronica Albright, has been gone since early November. She was the first SCU student reported missing. "She was a dedicated student. She didn't party. She's not the type of person who would walk away without saying anything."

Others are doing whatever they can to raise awareness. "I know someone out there knows something," says Minka Meyers. "They may not realize how important their information is. But it could be instrumental in bringing my sister home." Her sister, Mila, was the third student reported missing. She cut off contact from family and friends in late January.

I stopped and reread the article. Something bothered me, but I wasn't sure what. Then I read it again. Mila. I covered my mouth and scooted my rolling chair with my feet. The girl who'd followed Brian home at Christmas was named Mila. I remembered her. It could be a coincidence—just like Brian not telling me about the girls. But what if it wasn't?

I thought of something Dad used to say: *you string two or more coincidences together, and you have a conspiracy.* Is that what was blooming in my mind? A conspiracy about Brian and these missing girls? It bothered me how normal the idea felt. I leaned over the keyboard, touching my temples with my fingers. I certainly couldn't jump to conclusions without more information. The article provided a name only: Mila. There were no pictures. I had no idea if this was the same girl who stood outside my house, and even if it was…

I started typing. I wasn't going to allow assumptions to cloud my thoughts until I had more facts. I clicked on more articles and gathered as much information as I could about each girl who'd gone missing. I pulled a blank sheet of paper out of the printer slot and started making a detailed list.

Girl 1: Victoria Albright. November. Her roommate provided a quote in the interview. Last seen walking back from the science lab at night.
Girl 2: Dana. Early December. She was scheduled to meet her mom at the mall. She never made it.

Girl 3: Mila Meyers. Late January. Lived with her sister in an off-campus apartment.
Girl 4: Becky. February. Last seen at a party with friends.
Girl 5: Melody. Last seen in March.

Looking at the calendar pinned to the wall, I realized Melody was only reported missing two weeks earlier. She'd also gone to a party and never returned.

I took a deep breath and tried to think. I compared the timeline I'd created to another, more sinister one unraveling in my mind. There was a frightening gap in December, the time Brian would have been home for holiday break. I opened the search screen and typed in the name Mila Meyers.

A handful of articles had been written specifically about her case. The second one included a picture. Staring back at me through the screen was the same beautiful girl who'd stood outside my house in the December cold. A month later, she'd vanished.

I started crying. Crying hard and fast, gulping for air. What were the chances? What were the odds? If Brian had mentioned her disappearance, I might have felt more at ease now. But he hadn't said a word. He gladly provided his fraternity's beer pong stats, but he wouldn't mention girls were going missing? He wouldn't mention that the girl I'd seen him with over Christmas break had gone missing?

From the same place where those questions arose, another alarm rang. I'd always been convinced Brian was trouble, although my mind never went this far. Was this the sibling rivalry I'd pushed down bubbling up to stir problems? Sure, Brian could be manipulative. But was he capable of a murder, let alone five?

I printed out Mila's picture, along with the photos of the other missing girls. I put them all together in a line. Some were short, others were tall, like Mila. They were all slim with blonde hair of varying lengths. They all looked like me. We could be cousins. Even sisters. I'd always read killers had a type. Was this Brian's type? Girls who looked like me? *Gah, what was I even thinking, describing my own brother as a killer?* I slammed a palm against my forehead, as though I could smack the answers into my skull.

A car door slammed outside. I rushed to get all my papers and pictures in order and stuffed them inside a spare manila folder. I shut down Dad's computer. By the time Mom walked through the front door, I was standing in the kitchen.

"There's my girl," she said, dropping her purse on the sofa. "Have you already eaten?"

"No," I said. The syllable came out shakier than I intended. I cleared my throat. "I'm not hungry."

"I was thinking Chinese," Mom said, unwrapping the scarf around her neck. With the folder in my hand, I thundered up the stairs.

CHAPTER 36

Now

Today is our last day with students. They'll be dismissed at 11:30, leaving us the afternoon to have meetings and work in our rooms. I say goodbye to my students in each block. I'm always amazed at how mature they seem by the end of the semester. They've realized they only have one more year in this place. After that, college and the world await.

I hope Adam will be all right. He nods at me as he leaves. Ben and Devon and the others do the same. Melanie pauses briefly to ask if I'd be interested in writing her a recommendation letter, so I give her my email address. Darcy exits the room and waves. I sense she wants to speak with me. I sense she feels she *should* speak to me. But she doesn't. She wants to leave what she told me about that night in the past, and I support her decision.

Zoey is noticeably not in the room.

I eat lunch alone. My co-workers are eating together in the library, a last-day-of-school tradition, but I'm in no mood to socialize. I'm counting the minutes, worse than I ever have. I can't wait to get out of this place. I enter the lonely hallway and walk to the restroom. When I return to my classroom, Marge is waiting by the door. She's holding a cup of coffee in her hands, never giving her system a break from caffeine.

"Missed you in the library," she says, with a fake positivity in her voice.

I look at her, then put my key in the lock without saying anything.

"Can I talk to you for a few minutes?" she asks. "Please."

"Sure," I say, pushing open the door and walking through. She follows me.

"I know you're mad at me," she starts, raising her free hand in defense. "And looking back on the past couple of days, I regret not talking to you again before going to Bowles."

"So, is this an apology?"

"As a friend, yes," she says, placing her coffee cup on a nearby desk. "But as a teacher, I felt you were invading Zoey's privacy by looking into her background. I still think that. I felt I owed it to her to make Principal Bowles aware of your allegations."

"Bowles said he was going to add this incident to my tenure application." I stare at her. She needs to know how much this ordeal is disrupting my life. How much Zoey is disrupting my life.

"You know that wasn't my intention." Her foot starts tapping. "I'll speak with Bowles about it."

"I'm assuming Bowles told you Zoey wasn't in my class today," I say, dryly.

"Yes, he did."

"What's Zoey say about being removed?"

"Nothing, really. She doesn't seem to pick up on the fact you dislike her."

Of course she would act like I'm not a threat. She doesn't think I am. And it makes me appear crazier if I'm the one making a big fuss.

"Zoey told Bowles I confronted her about Darcy," I say, popping a small hole in her nonchalant narrative. "That was a lie."

"She didn't say anything to me about a confrontation," she says, cocking her head to the side. "Look, let's just put this Zoey business behind us. I don't want it to hurt our friendship."

I sense her desperation to make amends, even if she still feels she acted in Zoey's best interests. "I just want you to be careful, Marge," I say, willing to let my anger with her go if it will make her more likely to listen. "I know you get along with Zoey, but she worries me."

"You know what this reminds me of?" she says, trying to sound positive. "One of those wacky photos that can be two different things. When you see Zoey, it's like you see a lamp, but I see a boot. Or you see a lady's face and I see a plant. Either way, it's harmless, right?"

"Just be careful," I say, gliding past her description of the situation.

"Again, I'm sorry if I didn't go about things the proper way. I really thought I was doing the right thing."

"Thank you."

"You going to Prom on Friday?" she asks, lightening the mood.

"My required event was Spring Fling this year," I say. "I want to get through the in-service tomorrow and officially start summer vacation."

"Can't say I blame you," Marge says, for once choosing not to guilt me for my lack of involvement. "You know I'll be there. I practically planned the thing."

"What about Zoey?" I ask. I can't resist.

"She's going, too. I'm pulling the parent card when it comes to any after-parties, though." She smiles with pride. "I'm making her clean up the place, then she'll return home with me."

"Good." If Zoey was staying at my house, she'd be locked in a cage.

"Have a good day, okay?" she says, walking closer to the door.

I watch her walk into the hallway, hoping I'm not as nuts as she thinks I am.

I head out ten minutes earlier than required. I don't want to run into anyone, especially Bowles, in the parking lot. It was bad enough I had to listen as he presented a year-end meeting in the auditorium. At least I had the buffer of the rest of the staff between us.

The lot looks empty with all the students gone. As I'm walking, a rogue soccer ball rolls past me, stopping only inches away from my car. I look in the direction from which it came and see Zoey walking over.

"Sorry, Mrs. Mayfair," she says.

There's no one behind her. I look around to see I'm alone. I wonder how long she's been waiting for me. I keep walking toward my car, but she's already standing between me and it.

She bends over and raises the ball. "I'm watching the boys' soccer practice until Ms. Helton finishes up," she says. "I might try out for the girl's team in the fall."

Another reminder Zoey has inserted herself into Marge's life. I wonder what that means for next year. I guess with her mom out of the way, there's no chance of her moving. As long as she's in CPS custody, they'll keep her in the district. Now, she leans against my car, making it impossible for me to open the door.

"Move," I say, quick and stern.

She bounces the ball in her hands, staring at me like I'm a riddle. "I hope you have a nice summer, Mrs. Mayfair," she says. "I can tell this has been a rough year."

"You've been here a month," I snap back. "You know nothing about me."

I know I shouldn't engage. I should be the bigger person and ignore her. But something about her makes that impossible for me. It's like I'm a little girl fighting with my brother all over again. Fighting with Brian.

"I might know a thing or two about you," she says, bouncing the ball. "I've always been into true crime stuff. But I'm not one of those who watches a program and forgets about it. I like to do my own research. Read old articles. Scan old photos. From the moment I saw your picture on the school website, I knew you looked familiar."

"You're a liar," I say, defiantly. We've been dancing around this topic for weeks. I can't let her think she knows. I'm reaching, desperately, for anything I can throw into Zoey's face. "You told Bowles I confronted you. We both know that's a lie."

"Huh," she says, looking down. "There are other things I could tell him, you know."

"Is that some kind of threat?"

"You ever been to Sterling Cove University?" Zoey asks. She has the pride of a card player who has just won their hand. This is what she's been waiting for. The moment to show me everything she knows.

"I—"

"Or is that where your brother likes to play around?"

I don't have the poker face needed for this game. I take in a deep breath and hold it. *One... two... three.* Everything I've feared is happening. Zoey knows about my brother. She knows about Brian.

"Zoey, I don't know what you're trying to do."

"I'm trying to be nice," she says, tossing the ball again. "It makes sense why you would be on edge when it comes to me. On edge with everyone, really. Growing up with a serial killer? It's a wonder you're able to trust anyone."

"Shut up," I say.

"I mean, it really makes sense. All the wild theories you've been running by Principal Bowles and Ms. Helton and Ms. Pam. It all comes from a place of hurt. Because of your brother. He hurt people. Did he hurt you, too?"

"Shut the fuck up." I step closer, the keys poking between my fingers like daggers. I no longer care that she's a student or a teenager. She's not respecting my role either. She never has. She's openly threatening me. Poking fun at my past started out as a game to her, but I kept pushing back. Now she's punishing me, the same way Brian punished Logan Hunt. The same way Brian punished others. Zoey is having fun with this.

"Mrs. Mayfair, that's very inappropriate language to be using. It's *distracting.*"

I look down and wipe hair away from my face. She's under my skin now. Practically set up camp and living there. I can't pretend I'm not bothered. It's all I can do not to cry.

"You don't know what you're talking about," I say. Then, unconvincingly, "*I* don't know what you're talking about."

"All right, cool." She tosses the ball again. "We don't have to talk about anything. You just stay out of my way, and I won't let slip who your brother is. I'd hate to see how something like that could change the way people look at you."

I reach for the car door and open it. Hard. The door hits Zoey's shoulder. She moves out of my way, but the intensity on her face doesn't budge. I get inside and press the lock. By the time I'm out of the parking lot, I can barely see through the tears.

CHAPTER 37

Spring 2006

I couldn't sleep. There was too much going through my mind. First, I went through all the reasons why Brian wouldn't be involved. He was my brother. A lot of people grow up with a mean older brother. It doesn't mean they're capable of murder.

Murder. My mind kept going back there, when no bodies had been found. Maybe all these girls did walk away for various reasons. Like the girl from my school who ran away. Maybe they had reasons for ignoring their families and friends, abandoning their classes. My mind didn't linger there too long because it was unlikely. Something bad had happened to these girls. What I needed to know was whether Brian was involved.

I thought of the timeline. The first two girls went missing in November and December. Brian was still on campus then. He'd avoided returning home. None of the girls went missing during the Christmas holiday. I think that detail bothered me most. The minute Brian returned to campus, girls started disappearing again. Of course, if the person responsible was tied to the school—either a student or an employee—it would make sense that they had left campus during that same time period.

Why was I thinking this way? As though my brother could be responsible for the disappearances of five college students? Brian was gifted, but could he really pull something like that off?

Mila kept flashing through my mind. Her beautiful, confused eyes out in the cold. I'd felt sorry for her that night. Thinking about her now, her whereabouts unknown, made me sick to my stomach. She almost reminded me of Amber when she showed up at the house after Brian left. I'd seen an emotional Amber almost as often as I'd seen a frantic Mom, but that day was different. There was something Amber was holding back. Every time I saw her skulking down the hallways or dodging me in the cafeteria, I could see it, but I wasn't sure what *it* was.

Now I felt I needed to know what she was so upset about. She'd dated Brian for almost a year—his most serious girlfriend by far. Did she know more about him than I did? Did she know something that could make sense of this?

After school, I walked to Amber's house. When I knocked on the front door, Karen, her mom, answered.

"Hello, Della," she said. "How've you been?"

"Fine. Can I speak with Amber?"

"Of course." Karen seemed too excited to have me visit. She'd surely picked up on our lack of interaction in the past year. "Have any plans for summer?"

"I'm working at the movie theater," I said, hoping our conversation didn't sound as awkward as it felt.

"I've been telling Amber she should get a summer job. Maybe I'll suggest she apply there."

"Sounds good," I said.

"Amber," she called up the stairs. "You have a visitor."

A few minutes later, Amber appeared at the banister. She was wearing baggy pants and a tight T-shirt. She looked at me.

"Busy," she said, and turned around.

I thought Karen might break from embarrassment. "Excuse me," she said to me, walking up the stairs. She reappeared a minute later with a welcoming smile on her face. "Come on up, Della. Amber is in her room."

Normally, I would have left. I wasn't going to beg anyone, even Amber, to see me. But I was on a mission to find out as much about Brian as I could. She was the only person who might know something about him I didn't.

I walked into Amber's room. The walls were still pink, but there were so many posters I'm not sure I would have noticed had I not visited her room a hundred times before. Amber sat on her bed with her legs folded over one another. She lazily tossed her phone from one hand to the next.

"Hey," I said. A chair by the door was filled with clothes. I made a neat stack of them on the floor and sat down.

"Why are you here?"

"We've not hung out in forever." I wanted to be polite. I could have been nicer to her when she and Brian started dating. "How are you?"

"Fine and dandy," she said, leaning against the wall and kicking her feet onto the bed. "Why are you here?"

"Have you talked to Brian lately?" I asked. Clearly she was as desperate to get to the point as I was.

Amber scoffed. "Not since he left. I told you I didn't want to talk to him ever again. To either of you, really."

I looked down. I didn't know why she was averse to Brian, even more clueless about why she was upset with me. "I wanted to ask you about the day he left," I said. "When you came by the house, you seemed upset."

"I was upset," she said. There was an urgency in her tone. "I'm still upset."

"You said you wanted to tell him something. What was it?"

"It doesn't matter now." Her shoulders wilted, and she stared at the phone in her hands.

"It seemed important."

"Yeah, well. The world's kept spinning, hasn't it? I'm just ready to move on."

"Move on from what?"

She dropped the phone and crossed her arms. "Look, the only reason you're in here is because my mom insisted. I don't want to talk with you."

"I'm here because I'm worried." I said. "About people."

"Worried about *Brian* and people?"

"Yes." Saying it out loud startled me. Perhaps I should have said it sooner. But now there was a trail of clues and I was counting on Amber to help me piece them together.

"What's going on?" Her penchant for drama temporarily reappeared.

"I don't know exactly," I said, looking down. "But I know something upset you that day. Something bigger than Brian going away to school. You two were broken up by then, but I'm not even sure why."

"Because I'm a crazy stalker," she said, twirling her finger around her temple. "At least that's what Brian tells everyone."

"What's your take?"

"I was more enthusiastic in the beginning than I needed to be." She looked away. "But I wanted out of that relationship. Not enough to break up with him myself, but I didn't like where things were heading."

"When did it go bad?"

"He told me you saw us after the funeral."

"I did." I winced. It was embarrassing, witnessing something so disturbing between my brother and my best friend.

"Well that was the first time we did it that way."

"Had sex?"

"No." She sounded harsh, then restarted with a calmer tone. "We'd had sex before. Normal sex. After the funeral, that's when he got... rougher."

"Obviously I wish I hadn't caught you guys that night. It's just weird," I said. "He looked like he was hurting you."

"He was. I thought he was just upset." She looked at me to make sure she wasn't offending me, then looked at her black nails. "But from then on, each time got rougher."

"Did you tell him he was hurting you? Tell him to stop?"

"Sometimes," she said. "I think he liked that it was hurting me."

"Amber! Are you telling me Brian raped you?"

"No! It's not like I wasn't willing. He was my boyfriend. I loved him, or whatever. But I didn't like how rough it got sometimes."

"If you told him to stop, and he didn't, that's rape."

"I try not to think about it like that," she says, her voice shaky. "I try not to think about it at all."

"So that's why you broke up?" I asked. "Because he was too... rough."

"We both knew he was dumping me before he went off to college. But we broke up before then." She paused, debating whether she should reveal the reason. The words came out with so much shame. "The last time we hooked up, he got all rough again. I told him to stop, but he wouldn't. Then he pulled down a knife."

"A knife?"

"You know the knives he kept over his bed? He pulled one down and held it to my throat."

"Did he threaten you?"

"It was more like he was trying to scare me. It worked. I totally freaked out. Afterwards, he said he was just trying to be kinky, but I knew it was worse than that. It's like he enjoyed the power he had over me. He enjoyed my fear. I knew it wouldn't be a one-time thing. That's why I broke up with him."

"You broke up with him?"

"Technically, yes. But that's not what he told people. I ignored his phone calls for a day. That's when he decided to tell half the school he dumped me. Called me all sorts of names. Told stories that weren't even true." She looked up with tears in her eyes. "I guess he wanted to ruin my reputation before I could ruin his."

"You should have told people the truth."

"Six months ago, if I'd told you Brian pulled a knife on me during sex, would you have believed me? Even if you did, would his friends? Our teachers? I just wanted him to leave for SCU so I wouldn't have to deal with him anymore."

"Did you tell your parents?"

She raised her hands and shook her head. "Way too embarrassing. Like everyone else, they assumed he'd moved on to bigger and better. They knew I was hurting, though. They signed me up with a therapist."

"Did you tell your therapist? You know, about how he was with you?"

"Bits and pieces." She looked away, and I wasn't sure I believed her. "My therapist encouraged me to confront the person who hurt me. That's why I went to your house that day. I wanted him to know even if he fooled everyone else, I knew the truth. He'd hurt me, but he hadn't destroyed me."

Amber was trying to come to terms with what Brian had done to her. She wanted closure. I respected that, but he didn't like being put in his place. "It's probably best he'd already left."

She sat up straighter. "I'm just trying to get through high school. I've already picked out some colleges up north. I'm getting the hell out of here."

I didn't know if I'd ever seen anyone transform as much as Amber. The giddy, preppy girl who'd entered high school was nothing like the despondent one leaving.

"I'm sorry Brian hurt you," I said, knowing it wouldn't be enough.

"It's not your fault," she said. "But I can't be around you without thinking of him. And I don't want to think about him anymore."

"I understand."

"So, why now? It's been almost a year since we broke up."

"I can't say."

"I tell you all that, and you just leave me hanging?"

"I know. I'm sorry. I just—I need to know if I'm right first." I didn't want to tell Amber my suspicions until I had proof, and I wasn't sure what proof would mean. Plus, if Amber already felt guilty over how she handled the situation, learning Brian's behavior had escalated might further derail her. "I'm hoping I'm wrong."

She no longer looked curious. She seemed fearful. Worried. "Like I said, being around you is hard. But I'm here if you need me."

"Thanks," I said. "It would be nice to talk again."

I left her room and rushed downstairs. I ran into the open street and gulped the humid air. I struggled to breathe. I struggled to think. Then, I started walking home.

CHAPTER 38

Now

I'm still crying when I return home. It's like Brian was this little secret I kept locked away. He's only real to me and Danny and Dr. Walters. Intermittently, Mom. But knowing someone like Zoey knows about Brian and the awful things he did brings his spirit back in full force. He might as well be in the living room with me, laughing as I cry.

I don't tell Danny about Zoey's threat. He's already worried. I don't want him to know that my psychotic student has defeated me. Danny knows I've been reprimanded at work, and I still haven't told him Bowles suggested it could cost me tenure. How would he look at me if I were to lose my job over this? Over Zoey? Until now, Brian's been a dark cloud following me from one stage of life to the next. Will he follow my unborn child's life, too? Will Brian be part of his or her legacy?

When Danny returns home, we eat and watch television, but we don't talk. With each quiet moment, I rebuild whatever walls between us I thought we'd broken down last night.

I don't want to report to school on Thursday. It doesn't matter that I'm expected to work alone in my room all day, entering final grades and making preliminary copies for next year. If there is a next year. The thought of seeing anyone makes me want to vomit.

After a few hours, I make the decision to leave. If Bowles wants to punish me for skipping out early, so be it. He certainly won't give me tenure for suffering through one last day. And that's all I'm doing. Suffering. Being in my classroom reminds me of Darcy and Zoey, how I've let this entire situation ruin my life. Just as I'm about to open my door, someone knocks. I look through the narrow glass and see Pam. She sees me, too. There's no way I can just avoid her. I open the door.

"Hey," she says. We've not talked properly since I had my conference with Bowles. I have no idea where the Darcy situation is headed. She looks at the bag around my shoulder. "Are you heading out?"

"Yeah," I say, looking down. "I think I am."

"I was coming to remind you to post your grades."

"Already did."

"Oh." She looks at the clipboard in her hand like she's not reading it right. "It must not have shown up in the system. I'm sorry."

I nod, waiting for her to move so I can walk out.

"Are you okay?" she asks.

"There's just a lot on my mind." I look around, avoiding her stare. Every time I've told someone what I think in the past week it's worked against me. And now Zoey, this person I'm convinced is deranged and dangerous, is using my greatest weakness against me.

"May I come in?" she asks. She sees something is wrong, and it's not in her nature to ignore it. "Please."

I stand back. She walks in the room and I shut the door.

"You know how crazy the last week of school can be," Pam says. She sits in the chair next to my desk and nods for me to do the same. "But I wanted to thank you for encouraging Darcy to speak with me. Admitting what happened that night is a huge step for her. And you were instrumental in helping her come to terms with it."

She's building up my confidence, but it can't distract me from the root of this problem. "Did she tell you who attacked her?"

"No. I think that's why she hesitated to come forward."

"So, nothing will be done. Even Darcy can't prove what happened to her."

"We may not know who attacked Darcy, but the fact she came forward is a huge step. At least now police can start a formal investigation. They can use her statement to find out who is responsible."

"The police are involved again?"

"I believe so," she says, rubbing her thumbs. "I can't provide too much information."

"The police can only do so much. We both know that," I say. "Besides, I know who is to blame."

Her tone changes. She takes a deep breath before continuing. "No one ever said our job is easy. It's difficult, dealing with clashing personalities and adolescent attitudes. We all have problem students."

"Zoey's more than a problem student."

"I remember this one kid I dealt with," she says. "It's like he got along with everyone in the school except me. It was all I could do to register him for classes. You can forget about trying to talk with him about behavior."

"Why didn't he like you?" I couldn't imagine anyone holding a grudge against Pam.

"I still don't know." She tilts her head upward, looking through time. "My gut says he wasn't used to black, female authority figures. Maybe we just didn't mesh."

"What happened?"

"Nothing happened." She crosses her legs and puts her hands in her lap. "He graduated and moved on. Last I heard, he was a grad student in Louisiana. Sometimes kids rub us the wrong way, but eventually even those kids grow up."

"I think that's what bothers me most," I say. "The idea Zoey will enter adulthood and still pose a threat."

"Why are you so convinced this girl is dangerous?"

"She's not a good person. I think she hurt Darcy and her mom. She's been teasing me with information this whole time. Ever since she wrote that damn essay."

"We don't know she wrote that—"

"I know she did," I shout. "And now she's threatening me."

"Threatening you?" Pam straightens her posture. "When did she threaten you?"

I'm tearing up. I shouldn't have mentioned our altercation in the parking lot. It's not a topic I can simply drop. The frustration I've been stifling since yesterday is begging to break free.

"She knows things about me," I say. "She knows things about my past. I think that's why she's given me such a hard time. It's like a game to her. And she's threatening to tell other people."

"How could Zoey Peterson know anything about you? She's only been here a month."

"I don't know. I know she's looked up stuff about her other teachers, but if she were to tell the people here about my…" My words fall away as I begin to cry. My anxieties have been building since yesterday. There's no way I can keep these feelings to myself any longer.

"Della, you are a good person," Pam says after several minutes. "Whatever you think Zoey knows about you, it can't be that bad."

"I didn't do anything," I say, defensively. "But people in my past have."

The confusion leaves Pam's face, like a mask has been ripped away. It's like she's solved a complicated equation. She smiles weakly. "Are you talking about your brother?"

"You know about Brian?" I feel like all my clothes have been stripped away and my skin is bare for the world to see.

She looks at me like she's afraid I might break. "I'm not familiar with the details, but I know your brother was convicted of violent crimes."

"How do you know about him?"

"I've known for a long time," she says. "Probably since you've been here."

"But how? How could you possibly know?"

"I don't think it's a well-kept secret. Others know, too."

I bend over and hold my head in my hands. Is she saying everyone knows about Brian? Marge and Bowles and students, too? The strong exterior I've presented at Victory Hills is a sham. People know.

"You've never mentioned him," I say, struggling to breathe. "You've never told me."

"I didn't see the point," she says. "It's not something I think about."

"Yeah, right." I lean back. As though anyone could look at me and *not* see Brian.

She moves closer and grabs my hand. I pull away, but she won't allow it. She won't allow me to retreat to my loneliness.

"Della, no one looks at you differently because of your brother. If anything, you're an inspiration. Great teacher. Happily married. When you're in the mood, you're funny. You're certainly one of the most compassionate people I've ever met." She squeezes my hand. "Your childhood doesn't change the person you are today. You know that, right?"

"But people will judge me. The students will look at me differently."

"Maybe even some of them know." This admission makes me cover my face in embarrassment. She scoots closer, puts her hand on my back. "It's not something that's talked about. I've never heard anyone mention it. Even our students wouldn't use something like that, something from so long ago that you can't even control, against you."

"Zoey has," I say, wiping tears from my cheeks. "Zoey's been toying with me this whole time. I think she's known since she moved here. Since she told me she was from Florida. Yesterday, she said if I didn't stay out of her business, she'd tell everyone."

Pam looks down. She bites her lip, like she's afraid to say more. "Her threat is an empty one. She can't use it against you. No one cares about your brother. But we all care about you."

I exhale and regain the composure I lost during my crying fit. Perhaps Pam is right. Some people already know about my past, and they don't care. They don't hold it against me. Zoey doesn't have the power she thinks she has.

"This whole time I've thought Brian was my secret to bear."

"We all have things we're ashamed about," she says, rubbing my hand. "But we can't give them more power than they're worth."

She's right. Zoey can't use my past against me.

"I must say," she says, sitting back. "I think so little about it, I didn't even make the connection. Of course Darcy's attack would have this effect on you."

I shake my head. "It's not that, Pam. I don't lose my wits every time some poor girl is attacked. I'd be in the looney bin if that was the case. I'm telling you. Something about this kid is not right."

"I will say I'm surprised she'd use your brother's past against you. That's low." She looks at me. "But I'm being honest when I say I don't believe she hurt Darcy or her mom."

I nod and look away. Getting people to trust me won't be easy. This I've known for a long time.

"I just want you to think about it rationally," she continues, not wanting to lose me. "Maybe this child does remind you of your brother. Maybe this crime is too similar. And for those reasons and a combination of others, you've created this new narrative in your head."

"I'm not creating a story."

"I'm only asking you to look at the situation objectively. I know you believe you're right. But for the sake of everyone, yourself especially, reconsider and review the facts."

"I feel—"

"Not your feelings," she stops me. "Just the facts."

I can't say I'm wrong about Zoey, but I can at least take a step back and reconsider. Chasing this gut feeling has done nothing but destroy the life I worked so hard to build. "I need to think about everything."

"Get your summer started," she says, leaning back and smiling. "Who knows if Zoey Peterson will even be here next year."

Pam wants this comment to soothe me, but if I'm right about Zoey, her marching off to green and naïve territory doesn't sit well with me. At least here, she has one person monitoring her. All I can do is hope Pam is right. That Zoey is a disturbed girl who will eventually grow up.

CHAPTER 39

Spring 2006

Brian had been violent. He'd been violent to women, in particular. I ran home from Amber's house. I wasn't sure what my next step would be. In the past when I'd gone to anyone, they'd blown me off. And I wouldn't go to the police until I had solid proof. Even then, I wasn't sure I could do that. Turn Brian in.

I opened the front door and walked into the house. Brian was sitting on the sofa watching television. I jumped back.

"Dell, you okay?" he asked, the remote still in his hand.

"What are you doing here?" There was an edge in my voice.

"I thought I'd surprise you girls this weekend," he said, looking back at the television. "I didn't mean to scare you."

The hand covering my chest felt my beating heart. I took a deep breath. "I wasn't expecting anyone," I said, as calmly as I could. "Mom home yet?"

"Nope. She doesn't know I'm here, so don't tell her. I'd like to surprise her, too."

"Okay." I walked to the staircase. "I'm going to change."

"Where were you?" he asked, still staring at the television. "Your car was here."

"I went for a walk," I said. It's not like I could admit to visiting Amber. Paranoia crept up my neck, like he would somehow know I was lying. "Trying to enjoy the weather."

I stomped upstairs and shut my bedroom door. Of all days, why did Brian have to visit now? I pulled out my phone to warn Amber.

Just a head's up. Brian is in town.

Within seconds she texted back: *Cool. Already working on a distraction.*

Coming from this new version of Amber, I didn't really know what that meant. Was she getting high? Taking off? Staying locked in her room? I didn't really care, as long as she stayed away. I needed to get to the bottom of this SCU thing. I lifted my mattress and found my research folder hadn't been disturbed. Brian had no reason to think I was onto him, and I needed to keep it that way. I moved the file to my top closet under boxes full of scarves and hats.

As expected, Mom was delighted to see Brian. She raided the cabinets in hopes she had ingredients to make spaghetti. They talked in the kitchen as she prepared the meal. I remained in the living room and listened.

Brian seemed relaxed as he stirred the sauce, then the noodles. He belly-laughed at Mom's jokes and pulled out chairs at dinnertime. In my mind, I compared the brother beside me to the type of monster who must be responsible for hurting those missing girls. Even thinking about it made me queasy. I couldn't stand to eat more than a couple of bites of pasta, pushing the soggy noodles around my plate.

"Right, Della?" Mom said, inviting me into the conversation.

"What?" I asked.

"The barbecue tomorrow night," she said. "You're coming with me?"

"Oh, yeah," I said, lifting my fork and pretending to eat. "I'm not working this weekend."

"Great. All three of us can go," she said. She smiled and sipped her wine.

"You okay, Della?" Brian asked. "You've been so quiet."

"I don't know what's wrong with me." I swiped my forehead with the back of my hand. "I'm not feeling the best."

"Drink plenty of fluids," Mom said, topping off her glass.

"You don't want to get sick before spring break. You're going to love SCU," Brian said.

I smiled, even though it hurt, and took a sip of water.

"Karen called," Mom continued. "She said you stopped by their house this afternoon. She seemed really happy about it."

I almost choked on my water, my eyes darting toward Brian.

"I didn't think you hung out with Amber anymore," he said.

"I don't. It was for some school thing," I said, looking ahead.

"Well, Karen is hoping you'll hang around more. Said Amber has been low lately," Mom said.

"Low?" Brian asked. He said it nonchalantly, but I could tell he was interested.

"I see her in the neighborhood sometimes," Mom said. "She's all, what do you call it? Emo? Wearing black, putting in absolutely no effort with her appearance. I guess she just gave up hope after you dumped her."

"Who says he dumped her?" I didn't like hearing Mom judge Amber like that. Like she was somehow less worthy now that Brian was out of her life. I immediately regretted what I'd said. In the past, it would have been registered as a flippant comment between siblings, but Brian and I hadn't bickered like that in months.

Brian noticed, could tell I had an added layer of resentment behind the remark. His eyes narrowed, then relaxed as he forced a laugh.

"Well, of course he broke up with her," Mom said. "Who is going to stay with a little rat like that when they have the entire campus at SCU to choose from?"

I almost choked on my water. I slammed the glass against the table, coughed hard.

"Dell, you all right?" Brian asked.

"I think I'm heading to bed," I said. "I'm really not feeling well. Maybe I can sleep it off."

"Night, honey," Mom said, not even protesting. I'd been a fly on the wall of their conversation. Now she could have Brian all to herself.

I locked my door before crawling into bed. I couldn't investigate with Brian in the house. We only had one computer, and there wasn't internet on my phone. All I had was the information I'd already pieced together. I retrieved the folder and emptied the contents onto my comforter.

I read the articles again, hoping I might find something to put my mind at ease. At the bottom of the most recent article was a tip line. Should I call it? And say what? *My brother goes to SCU and might have abducted those girls.* Other than Mila, there wasn't any evidence tying him to the disappearances. SCU was a small campus. Plenty of guys could have known Mila. Maybe even Danny. I decided to try my luck.

You up? I texted him.

Moments later, my phone buzzed.

No rest for the wicked, he replied. *Working late shift at the hospital. Sup?*

You know a girl named Mila Meyers?

No. Why?

She's one of the SCU girls who went missing.

I couldn't go to Danny with my suspicions. Not yet.

My phone buzzed again. *Is she the one they found?*

I fell backwards against my bed and immediately dialed his number.

"I told you I'm at work," he whispered when he answered.

"You said they found a girl?"

"Yesterday. They found a body in the woods outside campus."

"And they think it's one of the missing girls?"

"They've not identified her yet. But what are the odds it's *not* one of the girls?"

"Do they know how she died?" I asked, bracing for his answer.

"The rumor swirling around campus is she was stabbed."

I covered my mouth. I didn't want Danny to hear my heavy breathing. I didn't want him to hear the cries that were beginning to break.

"Della, I was joking about you being careful up here," he said. He thought I was some teenager scared to visit. "It's safe here. It is. Brian will watch you. And I will."

"Uh huh." I couldn't speak.

"Shoot, I got to go. Talk later," he said and hung up.

I dropped the phone and knelt on the ground. The pictures of missing girls formed a circle around me, and I tried to release my anguish as quietly as I could. I wanted to wail. I couldn't because Mom was down the hall. And Brian was in his room.

I tucked the file into the top shelf of my closet again. I climbed into bed and cried harder with a comforter over my face. I could almost hear Dad's words: *string two or three coincidences together and you get a conspiracy.* You might also get the truth.

"Feeling better, honey?" Mom asked the next morning. It was past noon when I finally came downstairs. I'd tossed and turned all night, sleeping uncomfortably for only a few hours.

"Not sure," I said, pouring orange juice into a glass. "I think I might have a stomach bug."

Somewhere between 5 a.m. and 7 a.m., I realized what I really needed was to get Brian out of the house. I couldn't access the computer, otherwise. It would be too risky. I needed to play sick. Mom and Brian would leave for the barbecue, leaving me a few hours to research. Or at least be alone. Trying to process the information I'd uncovered was agonizing. Having to put on a happy smile for Brian and Mom made it worse.

"Oh no," Mom said. She walked over and put the back of her hand against my forehead. "When did you start to feel sick?"

"Sometime yesterday," I said.

"You looked sweaty when I saw you," Brian said. He drank coffee at the table. I hadn't realized he was there. "You know, after your walk."

"Right," I said, looking at him, then Mom. "That's when I started to feel sick, I think."

"Be careful what you put in your stomach," Mom said. "Let me know if you get worse."

She walked to the table and sat beside Brian. They continued whatever conversation they were having before I arrived. Occasionally, Brian looked in my direction. I felt like he was assessing me. I finished my orange juice and went upstairs.

At five o'clock, I was still in my pajamas. Knuckles rapped the bedroom door and Mom gently pushed it open.

"How are you feeling?" she asked.

"Touch and go."

"You better stay here," she said. I noticed she was fully dressed, and her hair was curled. She'd made the decision to go without me hours ago. Normally, her easy acceptance of my absence would hurt. Tonight, it worked in my favor. "I'm sorry, sweetie."

"No, I'm sorry. I always enjoy attending your events."

"I know," she said, her face full of satisfaction. "There'll be plenty more. Feel better."

She moved in the doorway, revealing Brian behind her.

"Feel better, Dell," he said.

"Okay," I said. "Have fun."

I could hear their footsteps descending the stairs. Seconds later, the front door shut, and Mom's car engine rumbled beneath my bedroom window. I exhaled like it was the first real breath I'd taken all day. I at least had time to explore, even though I still didn't know what I might find.

I went to Dad's old computer and turned it on. As Danny said, the news was limited. I found one article which was published earlier that day. The body had been identified as Becky Whitmore, the fourth girl. Based on decomposition, it appeared she was killed around the time she was reported missing. She was found in a marshy patch of woods, about three miles away from a popular hiking trail which snaked through campus. A cause of death wasn't mentioned.

My mind pictured the knives that hung above Brian's bed. According to Amber, he'd used one of those knives to threaten her. Scare her. Assert his power. Had Amber been a trial run? A dress rehearsal?

I deleted the search history and shut down the computer. I walked upstairs and pushed open the door of Brian's room. Thankfully, it was unlocked. I looked through his belongings. As I touched each item, I took a mental picture of what it looked like before. I wanted to reposition everything exactly. Brian didn't need to know I was snooping around his room.

It all appeared ordinary. I sifted through his duffel. I lifted his mattress. I dug through his drawers. I analyzed each section of the room, searching for something strange. Something out of place.

Dad's guitar was in the corner by Brian's bed. I ran my fingers across the smooth leather case. Dad had too many guitars for a family without musicians to keep. We'd each chosen our favorite of his collection and sold the rest. Mine was hidden away in my closet. For now, it still made me sad to see it. Here was Brian's selection, on full display in his messy bedroom.

I sat on Brian's bed and lifted the case, so it rested on my thighs. I unzipped the closure to expose the honey-colored instrument. Even though I barely knew how to play, I strummed my thumb against its strings. I missed this sound. And this smell. I missed everything about Dad. How would he handle this situation if he were alive? Would he minimize my worries like I was afraid everyone else might? I didn't think so. I sensed Dad saw the darkness in Brian as clearly as I did, although neither of us suspected he was capable of murder. I still wasn't sure he was. I placed the guitar back in its case.

When I closed the lid, I felt something shift beneath my fingers. I reopened the case and saw a small zipper in the fabric lining. I ran my hand over the area and confirmed there was a small, rectangular object underneath.

I pulled back the zipper and slid my hand inside. My fingers felt something plastic. I pulled it out, realizing it was a series of cards bound together with a single rubber band. No, they weren't cards. They were driver's licenses. I slid the rubber string downward and shuffled through the deck.

They were all there. Victoria and Becky and Dana and Melody. Mila. I swallowed down the wave of nausea building inside me. My entire body started to sweat. It was like a hot, bright light poured over me, showing me what I needed to see. But I didn't want to see it. I didn't want to know I was right. I'd spent my whole life trying to get others to see Brian for what he really was. In all that time, even I didn't know what he was. And now that I did, I felt numb.

I flipped through the IDs one more time. I realized there were six, not five. I read all the names again. There was one I didn't recognize. A girl name Katie Mitchell. She was nineteen and blonde, and I'd bet my life she was a student at SCU. He'd hurt another girl and brought her ID to add to his stash. Is that why he planned a visit so soon after each abduction? He wouldn't want anything suspicious found at SCU. Our home was now a storage facility for his trophies.

I took a deep breath and bound the IDs back together. I made sure they were in the correct order. Victoria was first; Katie, this girl I knew nothing about, was last. I slid them into the bottom of the lining, closed the case and leaned the guitar against the wall, tweaking the angle.

I gave the room another check before shutting the door and running down the hall. I slung my head into the hallway toilet. I gagged and spit until there was nothing left. I'd told Mom I was sick, and now I was. Because I'd finally found what I was looking for. I'd found proof Brian was connected to the disappearances of those girls. I'd proven myself right, and it was the most awful feeling.

Another wave of sickness washed over me. I puked again. When I leaned back, Brian was standing in the open doorway.

"Damn, Della. You really are sick," he said.

I wiped the side of my mouth and put a palm over my forehead. How long had they been home? Had I been so sick I didn't even hear them come in?

"When did you get back?" I asked.

"Just now," he said.

I heard Mom's heavy steps walk behind him. "Della!" she shrieked. "My goodness, have you been doing this the whole time?"

"No," I said, sitting down on the cold tile and leaning my back against the wall. "I just started. All I need is some water and I'll be fine."

Mom felt my forehead, still damp with sweat. "Poor thing. Do you need medicine?"

"I just need rest," I said, closing my eyes. It was true. I couldn't remember the last time I had steady sleep. I didn't know if I'd ever be able to sleep through the night again.

"Get your sister some water," she told Brian.

He waited in the doorway a second longer before turning away.

CHAPTER 40

Now

It's almost noon when I wake up on Friday. I can't remember the last time I've slept so long. Danny's on call all weekend at the hospital, so I won't see him again until Monday. I think I need a few days alone. Maybe by the time he returns, I will feel better.

I roll over and unhook my cell phone from its charger. The screen lights up to reveal I have three messages from Pam.

At 10:45: *Have you heard?*

At 11:08: *Call me as soon as you can. Please.*

At 11:23: *Are you okay?*

I squint in confusion, wondering if I've forgotten some commitment. Surely not, what with school ending yesterday. The only other message I have, from Danny, reads: *Good morning, lazy. I love you.*

Sorry, love. I was resting. Hope you can do the same, I text back. Then I dial Pam's number.

"Hey," she whispers when she answers. "Give me a second."

I bite my thumbnail, waiting silently. The urgency of her messages disturbs me.

"Della, you still there?" Pam asks, this time her voice at a normal volume.

"Yes," I say. "What's going on?"

"You've not heard?"

"Heard what?" I ask, sitting upright in the bed. "Truthfully, I just woke up. You're the only person I've talked to all day."

"Oh." She sounds grief-stricken. "I forget you're not on social media and stuff."

"Tell me what's going on."

"It's Marge," she says. "There was an incident this morning at school. She had an allergic reaction and went into anaphylactic shock."

"Oh my gosh," I say, slapping a hand against my chest. "Will she be okay?"

"She had an EpiPen with her, thank goodness. That slowed the reaction. They're keeping her at the hospital for a few hours to make sure she doesn't have a second episode."

"I don't understand how this could happen. Marge is hyper-cautious when it comes to anything, especially her allergies."

"Some of the students said they were munching on leftovers from the bake sale. She must have eaten something that wasn't marked."

Again, this seemed unlikely. Marge was the one who took extra care in making sure each ingredient was displayed, to make sure this didn't happen.

"Students," I repeat. "What students? And what was she doing at the school?"

"She and the Spirit Club were decorating for tonight's Prom," she said. "After all her hard work, she won't even get to attend."

It feels like the entire room is spinning. Like the floor beneath my bed has disappeared and now I'm stumbling for foundation. Marge. Prom. I take a deep breath. Had I predicted this?

"Who all was there?" I ask.

"I told you the Spirit Club. I think some other teachers volunteered."

"Was *she* there?"

"She?" It takes her a second to realize who I'm speaking about. "Della, it's not like that."

"Was she there? Was Zoey there?"

"I think so, yes."

I take a deep breath. The last time I talked to Marge, she'd told me she wasn't allowing Zoey to go anywhere after Prom. Did Zoey resent Marge's rules? Did she poison her to get her out of the picture?

"I told you this would happen," I say, pushing the covers off my legs and rocketing off the bed.

"I really don't think that's the case here," she says, but she doesn't sound as convinced as she has in the past. There are too many coincidences. There are too many people in Zoey Peterson's way who end up hurt. "If she wanted to hurt Marge, I don't think she'd do it in a gym full of people."

Marge doesn't have a handy drinking problem like Ms. Peterson did. Regardless, Zoey found a way to incapacitate her, if only for the night, doing it in front of an audience so no one could blame her.

I clench my fists and lean over my dresser. "I'm just so frustrated. I tried telling everyone Zoey was a threat. I tried telling Marge."

"Look, I wasn't trying to rile you up," she says, no doubt revisiting our conversation from yesterday. "I called because I wanted you to know about Marge. I know you two are close."

"Yeah. Thanks, Pam."

I click off the phone.

What are the odds both her mother and Marge would be harmed only weeks apart? I'd assumed Ms. Peterson asked Zoey about the Spring Fling after-party, and that's why she'd attacked her. Living with Marge benefited Zoey. Why would she wait until now to hurt her? It must be about tonight. Prom.

I don't think Zoey has anything planned for the actual dance. It's what might happen after Prom that worries me. Like Brian, and all predators, Zoey must have figured out a routine for isolating and attacking her victims. An unsupervised party with lowered inhibitions and flowing alcohol seems like the perfect place. It worked with Darcy.

I don't know what I'm going to do about it, but I'm no longer waiting for bad things to happen. Not when I have a chance at stopping them.

CHAPTER 41

Spring 2006

My room was the only place I felt safe. With the door shut, I didn't have to hide how I felt or make excuses about not feeling well. I was sick, but in a different kind of way. I was heartsick and heartbroken and every other word that could be used to describe someone emotionally devastated. I didn't know what my next move should be. I wasn't sure if I had any moves left.

I couldn't confront Brian. He would deny involvement, anyway. But he might do something worse. He might hurt me to cover his tracks. Thus far, I was the only person connecting him to the crimes.

What if I was wrong? What if this was just my sibling brain pulling tricks? Maybe there was a logical reason why he had the IDs. I retrieved the folder from my closet and stared at the tip line phone number. Earlier, I'd convinced myself I needed proof. I'd found that, and yet I still wasn't sure what to do.

It was after midnight. I made sure my door was locked and huddled into the back of my closet. I pulled a sweatshirt over my head to muffle my words in case someone walked by my door.

I dialed the number.

"Crime Tips," said a nasal voice on the other end. I'd been expecting an automated system, not a real live person.

"Is this where you call if you have information about a crime?" I asked.

"This line is devoted to the SCU girls."

"Is it anonymous?"

"Uh huh," she said. It sounded like she was clacking her tongue. "Are you a SCU student?"

"I, um, yeah." I didn't know what to say. Wasn't sure I was ready.

"If you need counseling, I can transfer you." She sounded sympathetic. I wondered if other female students reached out for reassurance in the wake of the scandal. A scandal Brian caused. My throat closed in, and I felt like I might cry.

"Can you tell me if you've uncovered their IDs?" I asked.

"Speak up," she said. "Can't hear you."

I moved my sweater away from the receiver.

"Did you find their IDs?" I repeated. "The missing girls?"

All I could hear was clicking and breathing on the other end. "Hold a moment."

The background noise mellowed, and I heard a faint melody. They transferred my call.

"Yeah," said a voice. This time male.

"Um, I was calling about the missing girls."

"Yes," he said. "Who am I speaking with?"

"I, um. I'm Amber." It was the first female name to enter my brain.

"I'm Detective Jeffries with the Sterling Cove Police Department," he said. "Do you have information that could help us with this case?"

"I… I don't know."

"Look, Amber. Tell me what you know, and we'll go from there. You were asking about IDs. Is that right?"

"I'm sorry," I said, and hung up. The phone thumped against the carpet. I leaned forward, put my head in my hands and cried.

I'm not sure when I fell asleep. Each day I woke up feeling worse. My indecision over what to do intensified. I needed to turn Brian in. Responsible, objective people should work out his innocence or guilt. I shivered at the thought of seeing his smug, calculating face one more time.

It was near noon when I stumbled down the stairs. Mom stood at the stove making pancakes.

"Feel any better?" she asked.

"Somewhat," I said, taking a seat at the table. I looked around. The house seemed too quiet. "Where's Brian?"

"In bed," Mom said, still in her bathrobe. "I hope he doesn't stay out so late at school. He'll drop out like all the others."

"Brian went out last night?" A bolt of desperation surged through me. "Where did he go?"

"Just met up with some of the neighborhood kids."

Neighborhood kids. Who were they? Danny wasn't in town. It wasn't a holiday break, just a random weekend. Who knew if any of his old high school friends were even here?

"Did he say who he was with?" I asked.

"My goodness, Della. Why so nosy?"

Just then, I heard Brian coming down the stairs. He walked into the kitchen wearing flannel bottoms and an SCU shirt. He sat beside me at the table, smelling like soap.

"Late night, huh?" Mom looked over her shoulder at Brian. "Eat some pancakes."

Brian didn't speak much. I watched him eat. He took large, thick bites, like a person who had gone too hard last night. Like a person who needed to refuel to wake up. I wanted to ask him where he'd been, but Mom pestered him to finish eating and get ready. She was taking him to stock up on groceries before he returned to SCU. I was ready for him to be gone.

My head pounded. What little food I'd consumed over the weekend had been mostly thrown up, and my skin was grimy from all the sweat and tears. When they left, I took a shower in the hallway bathroom.

The water was hot, and the pressure was hard. Under the thundering stream, I felt momentary solace. I cried hard. I even screamed. My anguish came out so heavily I struggled to catch my breath. I couldn't distinguish my tears from the faucet's pour. I felt like I'd aged a decade in a weekend. Part of me wished I could go back to the simple unknowing of last week; another part of me resented being so naïve.

My arms were slightly red from the heat and my fingertips and feet had pruned. I turned off the water, enjoying the cool air as it hit my damp skin. I wrapped a towel around my body. When I exited the bathroom, Brian was standing in the hallway. I took a deep breath and stepped back. I wasn't expecting to see anyone, especially him.

"Brian," I said. I couldn't fake one more smile, so I just stared. "What are you doing here?"

"Mom forgot her wallet." He wiggled it in his hand.

"Oh." I looked down, hoping I could make it to my bedroom and shut the door.

Brian grabbed my arm as I passed, his fingers sinking into my flesh. "What's going on with you?" he asked. His face was impassive, as usual, but there was a tinge of confusion.

"I'm fine," I said, trying to avoid eye contact.

"No, you're not, Dell." He let go. I crossed my arms over my body. I was afraid to walk away. I didn't want to challenge him.

"I've just had a lot on my mind," I said, staring at the hallway carpet. "It's been a stressful year."

"Guys giving you trouble?" he asked. At this, I looked up. He smirked, in a frightening way.

"Yeah," I said, hoping this would be enough for him to stop pestering me. He needed a reason why I'd been acting off. I couldn't tell him I'd found out he was a serial killer. "Something like that."

Brian seemed satisfied with that answer. He leaned against the wall and rubbed the back of his neck with his hand. "High school guys are jerks," he said. "I should know. I used to be one. Once you get to college, you'll feel like you got it all figured out."

Is that how Brian felt? Like he had life all figured out. He could never be his true self here, he said. He always played a role. Was hurting these women the release he'd needed?

"You're right," I said, trying to appear unbothered.

"I knew you weren't really sick."

I cleared my throat. "I *have* been sick."

"I know you threw up," he said. "But it's not a virus. Something else is bothering you." He put his hand on my shoulder and squeezed. I thought I might faint, his grip felt so foreign and wrong. "You can't let other people get you down like this. Especially some guy who doesn't deserve you."

"Right." I shoved his hand away and walked toward my room.

"You can talk to me, you know."

"Thanks," I said. He was behind me now, so at least he couldn't see my face.

"Just tell me who the guy is," he said. "Tell him if he keeps messing with my little sister, I'll kill him."

I stopped in the doorway and looked back. He no longer leaned against the wall. He stood in the hallway with a confident and easy stance.

I didn't know what a comment like that meant coming from Brian. Everything he said had a purpose, and I now knew the seriousness of such a remark. My mind immediately went to Danny. Did he know we'd been talking, and this was his subtle way of telling me? I studied his face. I forced myself to smile. After all, most people would take his remark as a joke. It's a brother taking care of his younger sister. It's not a serial killer making a threat.

"I'm lucky to have you." My voice shook. I went into my room, shut the door and locked it. Minutes later, I looked out my window and saw Brian climb into Mom's car. She pulled out of the driveway, and they left.

*

I made a plan. I had to tell someone about Brian. Deep inside, I knew the truth. I'd always known. And our tense conversation in the hallway earlier had only hastened my urgency.

My biggest fear was that Brian would return to his room, pack up his belongings and take the IDs back with him to campus. My only concrete evidence would be gone. It was a test of fate—and patience— because if those IDs were still in the guitar case, I knew my next step.

Brian never said goodbye. I figured he'd deemed our earlier conversation in the hallway enough. I was afraid he'd return, and I'd be caught snooping. I decided I wouldn't enter his room until he confirmed he was back on campus.

Mom leaned over a counter reading a cookbook.

"There you are," she said when I entered the kitchen. "I've been worried about you. How are you feeling?"

"Better," I said. I took a seat at the breakfast bar.

"I've decided to make you some soup," Mom said. "You need something easy on your stomach."

"Sounds great," I said. I didn't want to eat or force a conversation, but I needed to know when Brian returned to SCU. Also, I wanted to enjoy this night with Mom. *Enjoy* wasn't the word, but I wanted to try. If I was right about Brian, this would be the last night I'd see Mom carelessly flitting about the kitchen. Because in many ways, what I was about to reveal would be worse than a death.

As we finished eating, Mom's phone buzzed. "Oh good," Mom said, staring at the screen. "Brian made it back to campus."

"Good," I said, taking a sip of water.

As I was heading upstairs, the doorbell rang. I paused, not expecting a visitor so late. Mom opened the front door.

"Hello, Karen," she said.

I came down the steps, hoping to get a better look at Amber's mom.

"Sorry to bother you," Karen said, her arms folded over her body. She looked over Mom's shoulder to me. "Della, have you heard from Amber?"

"Not since Friday," I said.

"I'm probably overreacting, but I'm worried," she said. "When I went to her room this morning, she wasn't there. I thought she just took off somewhere, but it's been hours and she's not responding to my texts."

"Does she usually do this sort of thing?" Mom asked.

"She has more lately," Karen said, turning again to me. "I thought maybe the two of you were becoming friends again. Maybe you might know where she is."

"I'm sorry. No," I said, feeling a wave of panic rise. "I'll try giving her a call."

"I'd appreciate that," her mother said, looking back at Mom.

"They're just kids," Mom said in a conciliatory tone. "Here, let me walk you home."

Mom grabbed her coat and hurried outside, leaving me alone on the steps. I pulled out my phone and dialed Amber's number. It rang twice before going to voicemail, like she was out of service. My skin felt prickly. It was strange Amber would take off the same weekend Brian visited. Maybe she just wanted to leave the neighborhood until she knew he was gone, but everything was too coincidental. I thought about what Mom said this morning, about Brian being gone all night. Something didn't feel right. I swallowed down my fears and focused on what I could control.

I went upstairs. A part of me wished he'd taken the IDs back to campus. If that were the case, I wouldn't have to go forward. I could just bury my thoughts and label them as just that: thoughts. No proof. But I knew if I did that, girls would continue to go missing. He'd keep hurting people.

And that's why when I reached into the guitar case lining and pulled out the bundle of IDs, I knew what I had to do.

CHAPTER 42

Now

My phone rings and I answer. It's Danny. "How's it going?" he asks.

"Fine," I say, biting off the end of a chocolate bar. "How's work been?"

"Ah, exhausting." He sighs into the phone. I can hear the tiredness in his voice. I pity him, but I need to remain focused. "What are you doing?"

"A bit of this and that," I say, pulling the lever of the driver's side chair and leaning back.

"You know the drill," he says. "I won't be home until Monday. You think you can stay out of trouble until then?" he asks. I think it's only partially a joke.

"I'll try my best. Love you."

"Love you, too," he says. The call ends.

I blast the air conditioning. Outside my car, the air is thick and muggy. I feel sorry for all the teenagers with styled hair. It's bound to frizz with weather like this. Prom has been underway for more than an hour, but there are a few late additions. I watch each person enter, either hooking elbows with their dates or holding their friends' hands. As predicted, all the dresses are longer and some are puffier. This is their biggest night of the year. Some of them have been planning it for months. Tonight, I'm worried about what Zoey has planned.

Now, it's ten o'clock, which means the dance is officially over. Many people have already left, but I'm waiting on one in particular:

Zoey. Finally, I see her. She's standing outside the auditorium doors holding a phone to her ear. Her dress reminds me eerily of Darcy's Spring Fling ensemble; there's the same silky fabric and slit, but this version is floor-length and black. A silver car slowly makes its way to the front of the pick-up line. Zoey, who is still talking into the phone, bends down and looks through the window. A second later, she opens the door and enters the passenger side of the vehicle. I start my engine and follow the silver car into the street.

Three cars separate me from Zoey, but the single lane street makes it unlikely I'll lose track of her. After about ten minutes, the direction we're headed starts to seem familiar. As we move further away from concrete buildings and sidewalks, I realize we are drawing closer to Zoey's house. It would be the perfect place for a party, or worse. No one is living there, and with Marge out of the way, there is no one to stop her from doing what she pleases on the property.

The silver car leads the way, coursing down the narrow gravel path. The cars in front of me follow, as do the few behind me. I keep driving straight, not wanting anyone to spot me. I slow my speed, trying to count each vehicle. Five, six, seven. Zoey must be hosting the party, controlling the night's events. Had this been her goal all along? Usurp Darcy's position as Queen Bee?

I pull to the side of the road, killing the engine. There's plenty of room for anyone to pass, and if someone spotted my car from this point, they'd probably assume I ran into trouble. I see the lights from Zoey's house in the distance.

Darcy's party was broken up by police. Even though the night is barely underway, I know this is my best option for keeping everyone safe. I don't even have to mention Zoey. All I need to do is make a noise complaint. The likelihood of them finding underage drinkers when they arrive is high. It will cancel whatever events Zoey has planned. I dial 911, provide the address and say loud music is blaring from the property. I'm sure police are on the lookout for rowdy teenagers.

Thirty minutes pass, and the police still haven't arrived. At least a dozen other cars have, carrying who knows how many boozy youths. I know I should let the police handle Zoey. Like Danny says, I should be thinking about the baby. I can't be putting myself—and him or her—in dangerous positions. But what if Zoey is already up to something? What if she hurts someone before police arrive? If I can just get my eyes on her, I can protect someone else from getting hurt.

Wet grass tickles my ankles as I exit the vehicle. Under my feet, the ground feels spongey from all the mud. I'm about a half-mile away from Zoey's house at this point, and there are no longer streetlights lining the road. No one will be able to see me as I approach. I pull up the zipper of my coat and start walking.

Five minutes later, I'm close enough to throw a rock at Zoey's mailbox. I take a deep breath. It's foolish for me to be here, not to mention wholly unprofessional. But how many people has Zoey hurt since she's moved here? Darcy. Ms. Peterson. Marge. In the past, I waited too long to express my concerns, which only led to more bloodshed. I'm not going to wait this time.

I scan my surroundings. I can't very well walk down the same gravel driveway everyone else is using. In the backyard stands a small gardening shed. I sprint across the yard, hoping no one sees me, and crouch behind it. From here, I can look into the house through a series of windows. There must be over twenty people inside, and that's only counting the ones I can see. Most are standing around the kitchen holding solo cups. I worry they'll move the party to the backyard, which would reveal my whereabouts. Instead, it seems like most people are staying indoors or huddling under the covered front porch. I suppose I have the weather to thank for that.

The back door opens, and two people walk outside. I scoot further behind the shed, obstructing my view so that all I can see are feet. They're walking towards the side of the house.

Shrill laughter pierces the dense air. The voice is girlish and unsteady.

"Be quiet," says another female voice.

Is it Zoey's voice? I think so. Then again, I'm not sure. I want it to be her. I want to catch her doing something bad so I can finally proclaim I am right. Deliver the precious proof.

"No one can hear us," the girl's voice replies. They're walking to the side of the house.

"Let's keep it that way." This time I'm certain the voice is Zoey's.

I listen as feet pat against the wet grass and debris from fallen branches. Then there's silence again. I'm certain no one went back inside. Someone is in the dark with me, but I can no longer see or hear them.

Who is out here? I think of Darcy, how the police found her outdoors on a night not unlike this. Does she have any idea Zoey, the new girl posing as her friend, is the one who hurt her? Has Zoey lured another girl outside with the intent to hurt her? Do more than cut her leg?

I take a deep breath. I tighten my fists inside my pockets and skate to the side of the house. As I get closer, the sounds of breathing and movement become louder. Finally, I see something. No, someone. Two someones. In the darkness, I can't decipher faces. I pull out my phone and turn on the light.

"What the hell?" says a voice. I know that voice. It's Devon, and she's with Zoey. She raises a hand to block my light, not recognizing me. They've both changed out of their formal attire. I smell marijuana and realize the girls must be hiding their stash from the people inside. And yet Devon looks out of it. She isn't just high. She's disoriented. Has Zoey drugged her, too? Lured her out here with the promise of pot, so she can get her alone?

Zoey steps forward. Unlike Devon, she recognizes me. I lower my phone and run. I dart past the shed and sprint toward the road. My feet crunch atop gravel as I run down the driveway. I move further away from voices and music. As I reach the fields, I hear footsteps behind me. Someone else running. It must be Zoey.

I pick up speed, looking back to try and identify who is chasing me. It's too dark, but I can clearly see the shadowy silhouette of someone behind me on the road. I look forward, raise my arms and pump harder in the direction of my car. I stay focused, making deliberate strides. Whoever is running behind me is fast. I can hear their steps moving closer. I look back again, can see the person has made considerable gains in my direction. I still can't see a face; it's too dark. Behind them, I see faint flashes of blue and red. Police? Did they decide to break up the party after all? Whoever is chasing me doesn't take notice. They're still running.

The moon bounces off my windshield, bringing the outline of my car into view. It's nearby. I can't quite touch it. But within a minute, I will. I look back one more time. The shadow is still chasing me, and I see the police vehicles have stopped at the entrance of Zoey's driveway. Maybe the person following me will see and turn around.

As I face forward, my foot slips on something slick and I fall. My shoulder breaks my landing, and I howl in pain. Whoever is behind me now has a considerable advantage. I listen as their footsteps pound closer. Stop right by my body. I feel a sharp pain on my head.

CHAPTER 43

Spring 2006

I waited for Mom to come downstairs. I'd been dreading our conversation.

"Della," she said, her voice weighed down with anger more than surprise. "Shouldn't you be at the theater by now?"

"I need to tell you something," I told her. I'd spent all night preparing, and yet I still wasn't ready. She'd find out eventually, but she deserved to hear it from me.

"Oh no." Mom collapsed in a chair and leaned over the table. "You're pregnant, aren't you?"

"What?" I was temporarily distracted by the absurdity of the question. There was no way I could be pregnant. I was still a virgin. I felt immediately guilty. Never in my life had I so badly wanted to be pregnant. Or arrested. Or suspended. Because anything—any tragic circumstance a parent could imagine—would be easier to digest than what I was about to tell her. "No, Mom. I'm not pregnant."

"Thank God," Mom said, letting out a deep breath. "Well, it better be important if it's worth skipping work."

I looked down and immediately started crying. I'd worn a brave face all weekend, and I just couldn't anymore. I knew how destroyed Mom would be when I told her what I had to say. Here she was going through a laundry list of my possible failures, all the while clueless about the horrible truth.

"Della," Mom said, shaking the back of my chair. My sudden burst of emotion scared her. "Are you worked up over this Amber mess? Honey, I'm sure it's nothing. She might already be back."

But I knew Amber wasn't back. I'd stayed up half the night calling her, receiving no reply. This morning, while Mom was soaking up the last of her sleeping pills, I walked across the street and asked Karen if Amber had returned. She hadn't. She hadn't responded to any texts or calls. She was gone. Just like the others.

My entire childhood, I tried to get others to see the darkness within Brian. It didn't work. That was my only comfort when it came to the SCU girls; I couldn't have done anything more to save them.

With Amber, it was different. Brian had hurt her before—hurt her more than she was even willing to admit—but that's not why he killed her. For whatever reason, she got in his way. She became a roadblock in his path, and I put her there. He knew I'd talked to her, and that what she told me wouldn't have been good. Even then, I'm sure he didn't think I was on to his crimes at SCU. To him, I was dumb Della. He never imagined I'd be the person to out him. Still, Amber remained his only living victim. He needed to snuff out the one person who stood witness to his violence.

All I wanted to do was call Brian and ask him what he did to her. However, I'd been told to wait. So that's what I did. Wait for a response. Wait for Mom to wake up.

"She's not coming back," I said.

"What do you mean she's not coming back? Did you talk to her?"

I took a deep breath. "She's not coming back because Brian hurt her."

"Brian? What are you talking about?"

"You said he was out most of Saturday night. By Sunday morning, Amber was gone."

"That's a coincidence, honey. It doesn't mean anything."

I rocked in my seat, trying to regain the breath I'd lost crying. "I have to tell you something. It's about the missing girls at SCU."

Her posture turned stiff. She almost seemed frozen. "I asked Brian about that," she said. "He said he didn't know anything about it."

I shook my head and blinked away tears. Brian was still playing different roles, pretending not to know about his own horrors.

"I thought it was weird he didn't tell me," I started, before sharing the rest. I tried to connect each piece directly, cutting through dramatics. I explained how Danny said Brian had volunteered to pass out pamphlets about the missing girls, proving he must know something. I told her about my timeline; Brian was on campus when each girl went missing. I told her I'd seen Brian arguing with Mila over Christmas break. I told her about my conversation with Amber. That Becky's stabbed body had been found this weekend.

"And then I found these in Brian's room," I said. I slid over the Ziploc bag that contained the bundle of IDs. We didn't need to add more DNA for the forensics team to sort out.

Mom had never been this quiet. She didn't argue with anything I said. She wanted me to finish. She still didn't speak when she picked up the bag, but I could see tears in her eyes.

"What are these?" she asked, her voice shaky and weak.

"The IDs of all the girls who've been reported missing." I bit my lip, trying to remain strong. "I think he's been storing them here. That's why he's been coming home."

"Are you accusing Brian of hurting these girls?"

I'd expected this. Brian was her golden boy. I'd always been afraid of Brian, and yet even I'd struggled to believe he was capable. I'd wanted to be wrong. But I knew I wasn't.

"Yes, Mom." I knew it was important to eliminate any wriggle room. "I think he hurt them. Why else would he have their IDs hidden in his room?"

"There could be tons of reasons," Mom said, dropping the bag on the table. She didn't even take the time to look through and see each name. Each face. "Maybe they belong to someone else. Maybe he knew these girls."

"I think it goes beyond that."

"It doesn't mean he hurt them," Mom said, her arms crossed. "Maybe he was helping them. Almost all of them are still gone."

"The one who was found had been murdered."

"Listen to what you're saying, Della," she said. Now she was angry. "You're accusing your brother of murdering a girl."

"I know." I looked down, wishing more than ever Dad was here to help. "You know Brian has had issues—"

"Don't give me that bullshit." Mom pushed her chair away from the table but remained seated. "You two have had this rivalry for years. But this? This is a whole new low, Della."

"I'm not making this up." I knew she saw the proof. She was pretending not to see.

"What type of sister is quick to believe such horrible things about her brother?"

"I've been wrestling with this for days."

"And now you think he's hurt Amber? Our neighbor. Your friend."

"Amber knew things about Brian. Things he wouldn't want her sharing with anyone."

"That doesn't mean he'd hurt her! You've been conducting this silly investigation. Why don't you just talk to him? He's your brother." She stood and walked into the kitchen. She rummaged through the junk bowl. "Where is my phone?"

"You can't call him, Mom. It's too late."

She turned around, her pupils dilated and wild. "You took my phone?"

"Yes."

She marched over to where the landline charged, but I'd moved it, too. She let out a hurried breath, like she was being chased. "What do you plan on doing, Della?"

"I plan on doing the right thing."

She ran over to the table, but I'd already grabbed the Ziploc bag and was holding it tight in my hands. Mom panicked.

"We have to talk to Brian," she said. "I know he wouldn't be involved in something like this."

I'd considered all weekend what I would say to Brian. Did I owe it to him, as his sister, to give him a warning? But that would just play into his manipulations. It would provide him time to create excuses, concoct a convincing version of events.

Watching Mom's reaction hurt, but nothing compared to the pain those girls must have gone through. The pain six other families were currently experiencing. Seven, including Amber's family. They were still searching. We had answers. Those families deserved to know what happened to their loved ones, even if it hurt us.

"The police will talk to him," I told her.

She slammed her fists against the table. "Do you know how ridiculous you sound? Like a spoiled child! How will you feel when the police look into this and discover Brian wasn't involved?"

"I'll be relieved." I started crying again. "I hope I'm wrong about this."

"Let's talk this out," Mom said. She pulled her chair closer to mine and sat. She leaned on her elbows, her hands reaching in my direction. Pleading. "Let's go over the timeline again. There must be an explanation. Something that doesn't line up."

Before I had a chance to respond, the doorbell rang. Mom looked toward the front. "Who is that?"

"The police," I whispered. I lowered my head.

"No, Della," she said. "You can't."

But I already had. After I'd returned from Amber's house, I'd called the tip line. This time, I asked to speak with Detective Jeffries by name. I told him my name, my real name, and that I thought my brother might be connected to the missing women at SCU. I told him I'd found the IDs in his bedroom. After we hung up, I went downstairs, hid the phones and waited for Mom to wake up.

I walked to the front door and opened it.

"Are you Della Mayfair?" an officer asked. Several other officers stood behind him, waiting to tear apart our home and our lives.

"Yes." I stepped back.

Mom wailed in the background. As the officers approached her, she started screaming. "She's a liar. That little bitch doesn't know what she's talking about."

The officers tried to calm her, which only made her rage more. I felt scared. I knew Mom's reaction would be bad. I didn't want her to get in trouble. Or hurt. Eventually they took her into another room, but I could still hear her broken screams.

"Della," the officer said, trying to distract me from Mom's outburst. "This is very important. Have either of you contacted your brother today?"

I shook my head.

"Are you sure?" he asked again.

"I just now told her what I found," I said. I handed him the Ziploc bag and sat down.

For a split second, the officer's stern expression cracked. I was a teenage girl doing the unthinkable. I was accusing my brother of a horrendous crime. My mother was having a nervous breakdown on the other side of the wall. I saw the sorrow in his eyes as clearly as he saw the fear in mine.

"You're doing the right thing, Della," he said. "It's going to be okay."

I didn't feel okay about it. Not for a long time. That lonely pain consumed my life for what felt like years. It lasted longer than anything else. The arrest was quick, as was the sentencing. The press dubbed Brian the *Sterling Cove Stabber*. I didn't think the press would ever drop Brian's story, but eventually even the articles subsided. I left school and cut ties with everyone, even

Danny. Mom and I took her maiden name and left Wilsonville for northern Florida. But the pain followed us. I didn't know if it would ever go away.

I used to make myself sick thinking about different alternatives. If Brian never knew I'd visited Amber that weekend. If I'd only told Detective Jefferies about my suspicions the first time I called the tip line. If I'd only acted sooner. If I'd only done more... Amber would still be here.

Brian's crimes were notorious. People remembered the college freshman who managed to kill six female students in under six months. They often forgot about the ex-girlfriend in his hometown who also lost her life. I never forgot. Amber was my cross to bear. Amber was my fault. On the nights I blamed myself most, I repeated the responding officer's words to myself:

I did the right thing. I did the right thing. I did the right thing.

CHAPTER 44

Now

As I creep closer to consciousness, I hear Danny. He's in conversation with another man about my condition. I pull at the tight sheets covering my legs. When Danny sees me, he immediately ends his discussion and comes closer.

"Della," he spits, before adopting his calm bedside manner. "Della, are you awake?"

"What happened?" I ask, as the throbbing in my head returns.

I recall my most recent memory. I was running along the fields. I fell, and something cracked against my skull.

"I'll speak with her," Danny says to the other man, a doctor. I'm not sure the tactic would have worked with any husband, but the man shows Danny some professional courtesy by quietly exiting the room. He closes the door on his way out. Danny turns to me. "You had a nasty fall. An ambulance brought you in."

"A fall?" I ask. I remember slipping. Had I hit my head on the pavement hard enough to knock me out? I didn't think so. I recalled being hit a second time by something else. The specifics are rushing in so quickly, nothing quite makes sense. The most important detail comes into focus, the fear making me hold my breath. "The baby. Danny, is the baby—"

"The baby is fine."

He squeezes my hand, signaling it's okay to breathe. It's okay to feel. I begin crying immediately. I'm consumed with my own foolishness and regret. What if I'd been more injured? What if I'd lost the baby due to my own stubbornness? I didn't realize how devastated I'd be until this moment.

Danny gives me a few minutes to regain my composure. He's relieved I'm all right—that we're all right—but underneath that relief is anger. I jeopardized more than just myself, and he's going to make sure I know it.

"The police were responding to a noise complaint when they found you beside your car," he said. "Can you tell me what you were doing at some high school party?"

"I called the police," I say, leaning my head against the pillow. "I was only there because I wanted to prevent something bad from happening."

"Something bad?"

"You know what happened at the last party," I say, staring at him. "And this party was held at Zoey's house. I had to make sure no one was in danger."

"Here we go again," he says, pulling away.

"Please, don't be angry."

"I am angry! What were you thinking? You could have been hurt. You could have lost the baby."

His words cut like a knife, because he's right. I should have waited. I should have protected my own child instead of chasing down Zoey. "I only left my vehicle because I wanted to make sure everyone was safe."

"You were the only person in danger, Della. You're lucky the police found you."

"But the party—"

"Nothing happened at the party. They found some underage drinkers and called their parents. The most eventful incident was them finding you bleeding from the head."

"I don't think I just fell," I said. "I think I was hit with something."

This could be my opportunity to implicate Zoey. I could say I remember her hitting me. Finally, she'd suffer the consequences of something. But I don't want to provide a statement Zoey can refute.

Danny stands and walks to the front of the bed. He places his palm on my head as I lean forward. I feel his fingers as they stroke my scalp. I wince when he comes close to the bandage. The throbbing in my head is nothing compared to the anxiety building in my chest.

"I know I didn't just fall, Danny."

"Do you have any idea how foolish that was? Especially considering your concerns about Zoey. The last thing you need to do is track her down by yourself."

"Someone has to do something."

"Just hear me out. Please." He leans over the bed and looks into my eyes. "I believe you think Zoey is dangerous. Based on everything you told me, I think she's dangerous. I only want you to consider the other side of things. Just for a second. This other student was attacked, much like the girls Brian hurt. Much like Amber. Maybe all the similarities are pulling you back to that lonely place you were in fourteen years ago. Maybe you're projecting all of this onto Zoey. Even if you're right, is it worth the toll it's taking on you? On us?"

I think back to what Dr. Walters said in our last session. It's not a far stretch from what Danny is saying now. I haven't been myself, and maybe that's what I've really been searching for in all of this. Proof I'm still the woman who can trust her gut, hoping it will make a difference this time. I was too late for Amber. We were all too late for Brian. Whether I like it or not, the past is still very much a part of me. It courses through me, bumping and fluttering.

"I was only trying to do what I thought was right." I lay my head against the pillow, feeling the tears roll down my cheeks. "I didn't want to lose Darcy the way I lost Amber. I want things to be different this time."

He sighs and stares out the window. "The last thing I want is an argument, but you have to promise you'll let the police handle Zoey from here on out. I need you present, okay? I need you here."

Suddenly I do feel foolish. All I'd found was two teenagers smoking a joint, and I can't explain much else after that. I look at Danny, who is studying my face. He needs me. I see that now.

"I'll let it go," I say, one hand rubbing my blanketed midsection. "I promise."

Monday marks the first full week of summer break. Somehow, the sun seems brighter and the house is quieter. I need quiet. I need time to think. Danny has returned to his practice. His absence allows me space to process everything that's happened.

I'm at least trying to take on a different perspective. Zoey pushed my buttons when she mentioned Florida. The knife incident, for obvious reasons, reminded me of Brian again. Maybe she typed the letter, and then again, maybe she didn't. Maybe her mother really did lash out at her, and Marge really did eat the wrong brownie. All these coincidences, but no evidence. I certainly didn't find proof of violence at the party.

Maybe the pregnancy is heightening my emotions and causing me to feel more passionately about things than I normally would. I feel the need to protect people and prove I'm right, because those were two things I couldn't do at a crucial point in my life. Zoey Peterson can no longer be my problem. As callous as it feels, neither can Darcy. I need to focus on myself. Focus on my baby and moving forward.

For the first time in weeks, I feel peace. There's still a lot to hash out, particularly with Danny and the baby, but I have time for that. Hell, I have all summer. Everything else can wait, even the Europe trip I never got around to planning.

I sit on the couch and prepare to start summer break with a midday nap. My phone rings. I don't recognize the number.

"Hello?"

"Hi. This is Bridgette Cooper from Virginia Valley High School. I'm responding to a message I received about a former student," she says. "Is this Della Mayfair?"

"Yes, it's me." Even when I decide to strip Zoey from my world, she finds a way back in. "I was helping Zoey Peterson with her college admissions essays."

I decide to stop talking. I've already dug a hole with Bowles. If he knew I was still discussing Zoey with former counselors, that hole would plunge deeper.

"Yes, Zoey Peterson. I remember her." I can hear she's smiling as she speaks. "How's she doing at Victory Hills?"

"Fine," I say, not wanting to say too much. "Summer vacation actually starts today."

"Oh, I hate to bother you." I hear movement on the other end of the line. "We've still got two weeks left. We were hit with a heavy snow this winter."

"I appreciate you following up with me, but I won't be revisiting her file until I return in the fall."

"I completely understand. I won't keep you. I just hope she's doing all right. She was such a sweet kid."

I bite my lip. "She's adjusted just fine."

"We were sad when she left so suddenly. But selfishly, I'm happy she left when she did. Our school has had a difficult year, and it's not getting any easier."

"Yeah?"

"It's been traumatic for our students. Zoey really stepped up. I thought it would make for an empowering piece in her admissions essays, but if you've already put away the file—"

"Traumatic how?" I cut her off, my interest in the conversation renewed. "I could always make a note and revisit it later."

"That's why it's taken me so long to get back to you." As she speaks, I imagine a Virginia version of Pam, scrambling around the school trying to sort everyone's schedules and problems.

"You said Zoey helped. In what way?"

She breathes heavily. "This fall, we had a student go missing. A sophomore. I hate to say it, but it's not uncommon around here to have runaways. Our district isn't as upscale as Victory Hills." She laughs. "Anyway, Zoey was very close to her. She was one of several people who volunteered to be a peer counselor for students having a difficult time dealing with the disappearance."

"Sounds just like her," I say, hoping she won't sense the sarcasm.

"Anyway, a part of me is glad she wasn't here when the news broke. She'd probably be seeking counseling herself."

"What happened?" I ask. "Did you find her?"

"They found her body two weeks ago," she says. "She'd been out there a long time. Looks like she'd been stabbed…"

I drop the phone. I get off the couch, stumble to the living room desk and open my laptop. I hurriedly type in the words *Virginia Valley High School*. That's all I'll need to find out the rest of the story.

Every article is about her. The girl. Abigail Morrison, 15. Her body was found in a rock quarry, a local hangout for rowdy teens. She had died from multiple lacerations to her body; the fatal wound was inflicted on her right thigh.

I scream in horror. It's just like last time. The crime is different, and the names are different. But I was right. I didn't want to be, even though it validates everything I've felt these past several weeks. I'd been trying so hard to stop Zoey from doing something horrible. I didn't realize I was already too late.

After what feels like forever, I stop crying. I click through a few more articles, trying to grasp the situation. I flick through a gallery of photos featuring Abigail Morrison. Over a decade ago, when I was in this same situation, scrolling through pictures, there weren't many. Each victim had two or three photos available, all provided by family members when they still believed there was hope.

There must be close to a hundred photos of Abigail Morrison. It's the culture these days. Taking selfies and posting to social media as often as possible. My students snap their own image multiple times a day, sending the pics to friends or uploading for others to see. They never imagine the pictures with the goofy facial expressions and vibrant eye shadow might one day be posted on a website announcing they've gone missing. Or worse, that their body has been found.

Abigail Morrison didn't know that. And yet here she is with her haunting green eyes and vibrant red hair. It's curly in most photos, but in some it's straight. She looks happy, happiest when in a photo with friends. That's probably all she wanted: people to like her, to connect with someone. Unfortunately, that someone ended up being Zoey, and her beautiful smile was ripped from this world.

I look closer at one picture. She's wearing a formal dress; it could even be her high school's take on Spring Fling. The same event where Darcy Moore was attacked. Had the police interrupted Zoey that night? Is that why Darcy didn't end up like Abigail?

I look closer at the picture. Abigail is wearing a green dress that seems to radiate against her pale skin. Her red curls are pinned high on top of her head, and she's picked the perfect shade of lip color to complement her look. Around her neck I see something… familiar. Something I know I've seen before. I click through more of the pictures, making sure this isn't just a one-off, my mind playing tricks on me. It's not. I stand, grab my keys and run to my car. I think I've finally found the evidence I need.

CHAPTER 45

Now

I knock on the curved door guarding the Moore residence. There's no telling who might answer. It's only the first day of summer, and while Darcy was likely the only person at Victory Hills more eager for a break than I was, I have no way of knowing her plans.

I sigh in relief when she opens the door.

"Mrs. Mayfair?" she asks, her head cocked to the side. I'm sure she's not used to receiving visits from her teachers, apart from Pam. "What are you doing here?"

"I'm sorry to show up like this. I really need to ask you something." I offer a smile. Darcy isn't wearing any makeup, but her face is red. "Darcy, are you okay?"

"Come inside." We walk through the foyer into the living room. My house is considered upscale, but this place could qualify as a McMansion. The foyer floor is marble, and the living room carpet feels thick under my feet. There's a large fireplace in the room, one that seems to be double-sided, so it can be enjoyed from the outside as well. Above the fireplace are two large portraits: her older brother in his college football uniform and Darcy wearing a formal dress. She sits in a cushioned armchair, which almost seems to swallow her small frame.

"I figured you came by because you heard the news," she says, pointing toward the sofa, and I sit. So much news has been passed around in the past week, I'm not sure what I've missed. "They've taken in Adam for questioning."

"Adam? Why him? What evidence do they have?"

"I'm not really sure. Now that the police are involved again, they're trying to find the person responsible. Everyone seems to think he hurt me." She starts crying. "I really didn't think it was him."

"Darcy, if they're questioning him that means they're trying to get more information. It doesn't mean he's the one who hurt you."

They're making assumptions based on rumors and Zoey hacking into Adam's phone. They don't have real proof yet. Not like what I might be able to provide.

Darcy clears her throat. "I'm actually happy you're here. I wanted to thank you again for speaking with me. You were the first person I was able to confide in." She smiles softly. "Ever since I told you, I've felt the hugest weight lifted. Like I really can get through this."

"I'm proud of you, Darcy. It takes guts to do what you did," I say. "I hope Pam is helping you find the proper resources."

"She is. I think even my parents are getting on board. I thought they'd blame me, but they've been more supportive than I would have thought."

"I'm happy to hear that." I'm torn, because while I'm proud of the young woman sitting in front of me, I'm still mourning the girl a state away who never received the chance to get better. And I'm worried Adam will be blamed for something he didn't do. "I need to ask you for a favor now. It might seem odd."

"Just tell me what you need, Mrs. Mayfair," Darcy says, uncrossing her legs.

"I'm wondering if I can see your keys."

"My keys?"

"Yes. I know it sounds strange."

She walks out of the room and returns carrying her purse. She digs into the bottom of her bag and pulls out her keys. She hands them to me.

As I noticed last week, there's at least two charms for every key on the ring. And one is a diamond and emerald encrusted cross.

The same cross I saw around Abigail Morrison's neck in at least a dozen photos. I rub my thumb across the jewels.

"Darcy, where did you get this?"

She tilts her head. "Zoey gave it to me."

I sigh and my eyes fill with tears. Darcy notices, and she seems uncomfortable at my sudden display of emotion.

"I know it sounds odd, but I need to take it," I say to her.

"What do you want with my cross?"

"I can't say right now. But I need to give this to someone. It's very important. I'll explain more when I can."

She looks down and fidgets. "It has a lot of sentimental value. Zoey gave it to me after my attack, right around the time we became friends. You know, I was real nasty to her when she first got here. Since then, she's been one of the most supportive people. I don't know what I'd do without her."

"Are you talking about me in there?" asks a voice from behind. I turn in horror to see Zoey walking into the living room. My heart pounds as she moves closer, looking at me with a terrifying blank stare.

I cling tighter to the keys and look at Darcy. "What's she doing here?"

"She's living with us for the next few weeks," Darcy says.

"I didn't have anywhere else to go," Zoey says, sitting on the armrest of Darcy's chair. "First there was the incident with my mother. Then Ms. Helton. I thought I was going back into the system until Darcy's folks offered to take me in."

"Obviously we have plenty of space," Darcy says, twirling her finger. "She's staying in my brother's room."

"Are your parents here, Darcy?" I ask, trying to hide the fear in my voice.

"No, they're working," she says.

"Looks like it's just us," Zoey says. She knows I'm not asking to be polite. She senses my anxiety. "Say, why are you here Mrs. Mayfair?"

Before I can answer, Darcy speaks. "She wants my keys for some reason."

"Keys?" Zoey looks at me.

"She seems to like the cross you gave me," she says.

"The cross?" she asks, looking in my direction, staring at my hands. Her wide eyes offer the first sign of real emotion I've ever seen on her face. Worry.

"Darcy," I say slowly. "We need to leave. Now."

But she doesn't move. She sits there, her knee against Zoey's body. "Leave?" she repeats.

"Come over here to me," I tell her.

Darcy looks at me, then Zoey. "What's so special about the cross?"

"Yes, Mrs. Mayfair," Zoey says. She stands and takes a step closer. "What's so special about the cross?"

"I think you know," I say, staring at her.

Darcy stands, looking back and forth between us. "Will someone tell me what is going on?"

I look at Zoey, whose eyes almost appear black. Her fists are clenched as she breathes steadily. Darcy seems scared, but she's not sure which one of us is the threat.

"You stupid bitch," Zoey says, walking toward me.

"Zoey," Darcy yelps, mortified Zoey would dare speak to a teacher that way.

"Darcy, run," I yell, moving so that the sofa separates me from Zoey. She comes closer, although she's not yet chasing me down. She doesn't have to. She knows she has the advantage.

"What is wrong with you two?" Darcy shouts, walking backward toward the patio door.

"Darcy, this pendant is from a necklace belonging to a girl named Abigail Morrison—" I start.

"Shut up," Zoey says, hate spewing.

"This girl went to Zoey's old high school. Her body was found two weeks ago," I say.

"Shut *up*," Zoey shouts.

"What is she talking about?" Darcy cries.

"Both of you. Shut the hell up!" Zoey screams.

"Abigail was murdered," I tell Darcy, hoping she'll listen and put the pieces together. Hoping she won't think I'm paranoid and delusional like everyone else. The entire time I speak to her, I never take my eyes off Zoey. "This cross belonged to her, and now Zoey has given it to you."

"Shut the hell up," Zoey shouts again, this time lunging toward me. She pushes me against the wall and tightens her hands around my throat. I struggle to breathe, amazed by the strength coming out of her.

Darcy walks up behind her and pulls on Zoey's shirt. "Zoey, stop," she cries. "What are you doing?"

Zoey pushes her with enough force to make Darcy land on the ground. I raise my knee and aim for Zoey's torso. I wiggle away and stumble to Darcy.

"Stand up. We need to go," I say.

I pull Darcy to her feet and try to walk past, but Zoey grabs my shoulder. She pushes me onto the couch. She climbs on top of me, trying to press down on my chest. Darcy rushes over, pounding at Zoey's back.

"It's harder when they fight back," I grunt. "Did Abigail fight?"

"You don't know what you're talking about," Zoey shouts. But I do. I know exactly what I'm talking about, and that knowledge is what has transformed Zoey from calm to rabid. She wanted to toy with me. She never imagined I'd be smart enough to piece everything together.

"You wanted me to know, didn't you?" I ask, blocking her body with my knees. "It's why you wrote the essay about Darcy in the first place."

Zoey pulls back her hand and slaps me. I keep resisting and pushing her away. Darcy grabs Zoey's shoulders and pulls her off the sofa. She falls backward, her body thudding when it hits the floor.

"What is she talking about?" Darcy yells at her.

"She's crazy, Darcy." Zoey's voice sounds disturbingly rational, as though someone flicked a switch. "She's on the verge of getting fired. She has this weird obsession with me, and now she's trying to attack me. She's filling your head and everyone else's with lies. I don't even know an Abigail!"

"No," Darcy says, standing over her. "What is she talking about when it comes to me? What essay?"

Zoey's mouth opens, but she doesn't speak. She catches her breath. "I don't know. I told you. She's freaking crazy."

"The person who attacked you wrote about it, then turned the paper into me," I tell her, trying to catch my breath. "I know it was Zoey."

"She doesn't know shit," Zoey yells.

Darcy looks at me. Then she turns to Zoey. "Did you attack me that night?"

"Darcy, no. Of course I didn't—"

"Tell me the truth!" she shouts. Her eyes dance around Zoey's face, as though she's finally piecing it all together. I don't know what she remembers, but it's something. She knows.

Zoey senses she's losing. She yanks at Darcy's leg, pulling her to the ground. Zoey lands on top of her, but this time Darcy fights back. Like a cat who has been thrown in water. She claws at her, making use of every bit of rage she's kept inside for the past month.

Zoey finally retreats, exiting the living room and running into the backyard. Darcy helps me stand.

"Let's get out of here," Darcy says.

I follow her to the front door but stop. "Do you have your keys?"

"No," she says, pausing. "Let's just leave."

"Run," I tell her, turning and sprinting toward the backyard.

I walk outside and see no one. The space is huge, with a large pool in the center. There's no sign of Zoey, but there's also nowhere she could have gone. The fence would be too high for her to jump, and there isn't enough traction for anyone to climb it. I know she must be back here. I circle the parameter of the pool, passing the stone fireplace and looking around the columns connecting the back awning to the ground. She's nowhere. I spot a shed in the far corner and am walking toward it when I see movement in my peripheral vision. Zoey grabs me from behind.

"Stop, Zoey," I yell. "You've done enough."

"Why couldn't you just leave me alone?" she shouts. "Why couldn't you have listened to everyone?"

She returns her hands to my neck and squeezes. She grips tighter and tighter, until I've lost the strength to fight back. Then I see Zoey's face turn, and a spray of blood exits her mouth and lands on my chest. It's enough to make her move away from me. She slides off, raising herself on her knees. As she moves, I see Darcy standing behind her, clutching a fire poker in her hands. Darcy whacks her again, and Zoey's limp body falls into the pool.

For several seconds, I remain seated. I stare at Zoey face down in the water. I look at Darcy. She's dropped the poker, her eyes focused on the pool.

"Go inside and call 911," I tell her.

I catch my breath and stand, moving toward the water. Darcy grabs my arm.

"No," she says. "Don't."

"She's knocked out," I say, pushing past her. "If we don't do something, she'll drown."

"If you save her, what will she do next?" Darcy looks at me, rage lighting her eyes. She's not asking about now. She's asking what Zoey will do in the forever of years to come. Who will she hurt? Who else will suffer? My body fills with both shame and understanding.

"Go inside," I say.

Darcy obeys, leaving me alone to choose Zoey's fate. I descend the steps leading into the water. My clothes soak from my ribcage down. Zoey's body is near me. So close I can touch her. Flip her over. I could hoist her onto the ledge and give her a chance.

Instead, I do what everyone has told me to do all along.

I do nothing.

CHAPTER 46

2014

Brian will never leave prison. He avoided a death sentence because he agreed to disclose the locations of the other missing women, including Amber. Her body was found in a patch of woods near our house. Why he went after her remains a mystery. Did he figure out I'd been asking questions about him? Had she decided to confront him after our conversation, and he lashed out by taking her life? I don't think I'll ever know what brought them together that weekend, but I know if I'd acted on my suspicions sooner, she'd still be alive.

I often imagined what life might have been like with a different Brian, or no brother at all. Sometimes I imagined Amber's life, too. I liked to think she would have left Wilsonville. I don't know what she would have done, who she would have been, but she would have existed, and that is enough.

I also think he pleaded guilty to save Mom from further scandal. Everyone I've talked to since then—the therapists and counselors—have all told me Brian is incapable of thinking about anyone other than himself. He's devoid of feelings and compassion. I still don't know if that's true. His narcissism would have pushed him to proclaim his innocence for years, despite the piles of evidence they eventually collected. And yet he confessed for Mom. To spare her a trial.

We do things for the people we love. That's why I visited Brian for as long as I did. I would have been happy never seeing him again. The conversation we had in the hallway that day could have easily been our last. But out of respect for Mom, I continued to go. At least for the first few years. I never said much. I usually waited for Mom to have her conversation and only agreed to speak with Brian after she pestered me.

Eventually I stopped. All those knowledgeable people—the therapists and counselors—said it was for the best. Keeping Brian in my life would only continue my pain. I believed them on that one. I've never regretted not seeing him, and he finally took the hint and stopped sending letters.

On my last visit, I had recently graduated college. I was older than his victims ever were. I was engaged to Danny and had only come because Mom threw a fit. She wouldn't leave until I agreed to talk with him, so I begrudgingly followed the officers down the narrow hallway. I sat in front of Plexiglas and saw Brian on the other side. He'd shaved his head and bulked his shoulders, but he still had a handsome face. I wondered what he might have become if he'd committed his mind to anything other than evil.

He lifted the phone, and, out of habit, I did the same.

"Mom doing all right?" he asked.

"Fine," I said, looking away. "As good as can be expected."

Seeing his face, hearing his voice, brought back all the memories. The cruelty and the cunning. Dad. Brian held the power to resurrect my ghosts.

"And you?" he asked, looking at the ring on my finger.

I quickly slid my hand under the table. "Damn it," I said. "She said she wasn't going to tell you."

"You know Mom likes to share good news." He smiled, wanting me to show some kindness in return. All it did was make me cringe. "I always saw a spark between you two."

"I don't want to hear what you saw in us," I said, slapping my palm against the tabletop.

Brian looked down. "You deserve to be happy, Della."

"You're damn right I do." I took a deep breath. I refused to cry in front of him. It was the one thing I'd promised myself.

He waited, looking at me. "You know, I don't blame you for putting me in here."

"You shouldn't," I said. "You should blame yourself."

"I do," he said, straightening. "I'm in here because of what I've done. I know that. I just want to make sure you know, too."

"Why wouldn't I know that, Brian?"

"Well, I'm on the inside. You're the one living in the world. Dealing with the whispers and Mom's hysterics. There must be a part of you that thinks you caused this by turning me in."

"Don't play games with me," I said, poking my finger at the glass. This was what Brian did. He wormed his way into my mind. Tried to pull out my deepest thoughts. "I know I did the right thing. You wouldn't have stopped killing otherwise. If turning you in hurt Mom, so be it. I had to do something."

"I just wanted you to hear me say it," he said. "I see what coming here does to you. You don't have to do it for her. Or me."

"I just don't understand why, Brian." My lip quivered, and I blinked hard in an attempt not to cry. "Even after all these years, I don't understand why you did what you did."

"I don't either—"

"No, there has to be a reason," I said. "Maybe you need to dumb it down for me to understand, but you have to have a reason. You have to tell me."

"I just..." He clenched his jaw, and I saw his eyes watering. "I've always had this darkness inside me. As messed up as it sounds, it only lifts when... I do what I did."

"That's sick," I said, leaning back in the chair and taking him in. His jumpsuit and his smile lines and his stupid shaved head.

"You know, when we were kids you always talked about how I was smarter. You had to work for stuff. Figure it out on your own.

I didn't try to be smart, but you didn't try to be good." He smiled at me, a genuine, even jealous, smile. "You just were."

Maybe people are wired differently. Maybe there's something within each of us that makes us who we are, and there truly isn't any reason behind it. The whole world knew Brian was a monster now. That same monster had moments of light only I remembered. The day he saved me from Jeremy Gus. The night he let me cry after Dad died.

"Are you trying now?" I asked. "To be good?"

He nodded but didn't say anything. I stood to leave, and I could see the loneliness consume him. He would return to his empty cell with its rules and restrictions. I might carry the weight of Brian, but at least I could carry that weight into a world of my choosing.

"You're right, Della," he said, before I left. "I wouldn't have stopped."

That was the last time I saw him.

EPILOGUE

Fall 2020

I'm not going back to Victory Hills High School, at least not this year. The baby will be here in December. It's a convenient excuse. Those halls house memories I'm not ready to face.

Darcy isn't returning either. Her parents enrolled her in an online learning program for her senior year; I offered to help her with any English assignments. We keep in touch through text. No one thinks I'm crazy anymore, but she's the only person who really understands what happened that day.

"So, Evergreen Mist or Cobalt Tide?" Danny lifts two paint swatches, waiting on an answer. We've debated for weeks which color we should paint the walls of our guest room, which is now being repurposed as a nursery.

"Try both," I say, sitting in the wooden rocker. It's the only furniture in the room. We've bought loads more but won't arrange it until the painting is complete.

"Okay. Get going," Danny says from his seated position on the floor. He looks up and smiles.

"I think I'll be all right." I plant my heels and rock back.

"You will," he says. "But the baby doesn't need to be around fumes."

"You're putting swatches on the wall. There's not enough paint to bother him." I rub my stomach, which seems to have doubled in size this past week. "Besides, *he's* a fighter." This baby has already withstood a hit to my head and the fight with Zoey.

Zoey. She never walked out of the pool that day. Sometimes I can still see her floating in the water, her black hair branching outward. She was close. I only needed to take a few steps to touch her, and yet I didn't. I let her stay. I let her drown.

It was what Darcy wanted. In the moment, she was fueled by learning that Zoey had attacked her. That Zoey manipulated her in the weeks following Spring Fling. Darcy made a rash decision with a teenaged mind. I was the one who could have stopped it. I was the one who could have saved her.

Police were suspicious at first. However, it didn't take much digging for them to piece together what had happened. Darcy and I gave them our account. We confirmed she attacked both of us. Then I told them everything else I'd uncovered. For once, someone took what I had to say about Zoey seriously and investigated.

They eventually strung together a parade of evidence. As I'd suspected, the emerald cross on Darcy's keychain belonged to Abigail Morrison. She'd been known to wear the necklace almost daily, and her mother was always disturbed that it wasn't recovered with the body. After that, they found more proof: DNA and cell phone data pinging Zoey's location around the time Abigail went missing.

They found journals, too. The essay she wrote wasn't her first account of what happened with Darcy. She liked to relive her attacks through writing, providing details only she could know. Within days, police stopped asking questions about what happened at the pool. Ms. Peterson was released, eventually leaving Victory Hills and her own collection of secrets behind.

And yet, my questions still linger. Did I do the right thing? Should I have given Zoey a chance? Had Zoey been my child, would I have wanted someone to save her? I think of Brian, and his sad, hypnotic eyes behind the glass on the last day I visited him. His final words. *I wouldn't have stopped.* I don't think Zoey would have stopped either. I cling to that.

"What do you think?" Danny asks. I blink and look ahead. In my mind, I was back in that day, wading in the water. I forget I'm different now. That I'm thirty pounds heavier and sitting in my future child's room. My future son's room.

"I really like it," I say, swallowing down the urge to cry.

"Which one?"

"Either."

Truthfully, I'm happier now than I ever thought I would be. I didn't realize how much I'd been longing for a new adventure. I'd associated having children with continuing the past. Some days, I still worry. As Dr. Walters once said, there's always a chance a person could be bad. My child will be no different, but I choose to hope for the best. I choose to see the good.

"I agree," Danny says. He balances the brush against the paint can and crawls toward me. He leans against the chair's curved legs and rests his head on my lap. "It's going to be a beautiful nursery."

I lean over to kiss the top of his head when I feel a tight tug in my middle. I flinch.

"You all right?" Danny asks.

I smile. "Fine," I say. "I think the baby's moving."

Danny puts his hand on the center of my stomach. I shift to the left and wait for the little one to nudge again.

"Kicks will get stronger toward the end," he says.

"I think that's my favorite part. You really feel him moving in there. It makes it real."

"I'm around pregnant women all the time, but it's different now that I'm having one of my own. It's got to be weird for you, right?"

"I'm getting used to it."

"What does it feel like?"

I lean back and look at the ceiling. I rub my belly, waiting to see if he will move again. I close my eyes. Try to envisage his face. Try to envisage his future.

Then I say, "It's like a flutter."

A LETTER FROM MIRANDA

Dear Reader,

Thank you for taking the time to read *What I Know*. If you liked it and want information about upcoming releases, do sign up with the following link. Your email address will never be shared and you can unsubscribe at any time.

www.bookouture.com/miranda-smith

Most story ideas have been building in my mind for months, even years. The idea for this book developed very quickly. I was intrigued by the concept of someone growing up alongside a disturbed sibling and being resilient enough to overcome that trauma. I wondered, how would a person with such a background react when confronted by another dangerous individual? Della's story was formed, and it was an emotional and exciting story to tell. I hope you enjoyed it.

If you'd like to further discuss the novel, I'd love to connect! You can find me on Instagram, Facebook or my website. If you enjoyed *What I Know*, I would be thrilled for you to leave a review on either Amazon or Goodreads. It only takes a few minutes and does wonders in helping readers discover my books for the first time.

Thank you again for your support!

Sincerely,
Miranda Smith

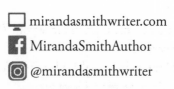

mirandasmithwriter.com

MirandaSmithAuthor

@mirandasmithwriter

ACKNOWLEDGEMENTS

Most importantly, I would like to thank my readers, especially those who reached this page after reading *Some Days Are Dark*. I very much enjoy writing these novels, and your readership makes that possible. Thank you.

I'd also like to thank all the bloggers and reviewers for promoting my books. The best way to sell a book is through word of mouth. Nothing makes me happier than reading an uplifting review. I appreciate your support.

Thomas Sheridan's *Puzzling People: The Labyrinth of the Psychopath* was a great resource in writing this book. It's an insightful, common sense explanation of why people do the things they do. Check it out!

I'd like to thank my editor, Ruth Tross. Thank you for continuing to champion my writing. I've very much enjoyed working with you on these books. Your brilliant Zoey suggestion made this book even scarier.

Huge thanks to everyone at Bookouture, especially Kim, Noelle, Sarah, Leodora and Alex. Thank you to my copyeditor, Jane Eastgate, and proofreader, Natasha Hodgson. There are so many people involved with each stage of the publishing process. Each person makes the final product better.

Thank you to my family for all your support, positivity and promotion in the past year, especially Whitney, Jennifer, Allison, Seth, Tyler and Carol. As the oldest of four girls, it was really fun to imagine life with a sadistic brother. As always, thanks and love to Mom and Dad.

Harrison, Lucy and Christopher: I love you. Thanks for reminding me of what matters.

Chris, you told me to pursue this idea. Thanks for your encouragement during this crazy year. I love you.

Made in the USA
Las Vegas, NV
22 October 2021

32845949R00187